Burning thought he saw fighting in and around the stronghold, but that hardly mattered since there was no going that way. He prayed Ghost had made it safely back to the SWATHship. Either the GammaLAW mission could be salvaged or the whole business would come to nothing. Making his way south remained the most sensible plan ...

Scanning the milling masses, his eye had been drawn to some barrow-coolies struggling with a two-wheeled cart. By the light of torches, he saw that a tarp had been partially dragged off the cargo, exposing a trussed up body. There was no mistaking the hood pulled down over the prisoner's head. Given the glitter of its circuitry, the gleam and configuration of its neuralwares, it could only be the Cybercaul his sister had plucked from Rhodes's bedchambers.

"Ghost!" he shouted. "Ghost!"

THE BROKEN COUNTRY

Book Three of GammaLAW

BRIAN DALEY

ISBN 978-0-9971040-8-0

In memory of my father, Charles Joseph Daley,
and of meteor watching on warm August nights

ACKNOWLEDGMENTS

The author wishes to express his heartfelt thanks to the following people, who aided and abetted him over the many years: Officer Michael Kueberth and Cpl. Garland Nixon of the Maryland DNR Police Hovercraft *Hunter,* Dr. Yoji Kondo of Goddard Space Flight Center, Greenbelt, MD; Calvin Gongwer of Innerspace Corp., Covina, CA; Ray Williamson, formerly of the Office of Technology Assessment; Professor Conrad Neuman, Oceanographic Department of the University of South Carolina; Drs. Frank Manheim and Allyn Vine of the Woods Hole Oceanographic Institute; Masaaki Hirayama, for the crash course in Korean history; skipper Richard J. Severinghaus and men of the USS *Annapolis;* the boys and girls of *sensei* Tom Fox's "American Rock and Roll Karate," for massive intrusions of reality; physicist Dr. Charles Melton and the late Dr. Al Giardini of the University of Georgia; Drs. John Camerson and Eric Seifter, for both their concern and their efforts on my behalf; and to Lucia Robson, Owen Lock, and Jim Luceno for their love and support.

Some features of the LAW 'chetterguns are drawn from the research and recommendations of Lt. Col. Morris J. Herbert, formerly Assistant Professor of Ballistics and Associate Professor, Department of Ordnance, U.S. Military Academy, West Point.

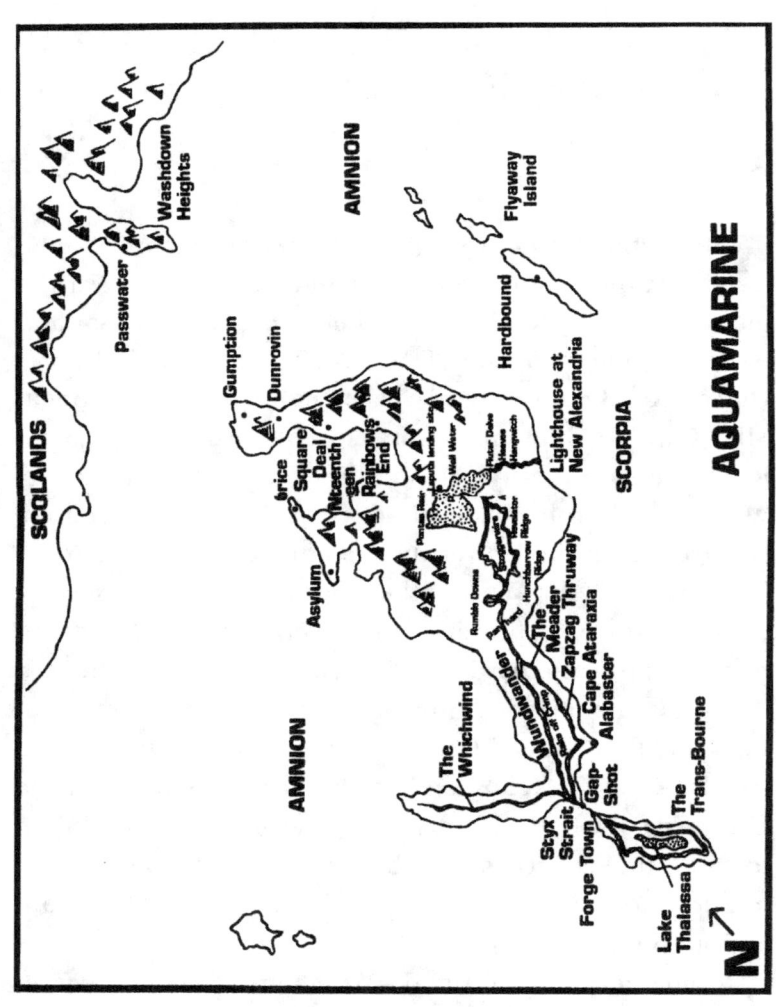

CHAPTER ONE

Wall Water burned while Captain Chaz Quant looked on from the bridge of the *GammaLAW*, safe for the moment—or at least out of range of Aquam catapults and steam cannon. In the wake of the sinking of the indigs' teamboat they were lying low, but suicide troops or vengeful kinfolk could put a quick end to the momentary calm. Quant wasn't allowing himself to dwell on the teamboat except as it bore on the present situation, though he already dreaded the dream or pensive moment that would conjure memories of the drowning of those poor devils in the slave tiers. *The GammaLAW* had eased up to a second survival beacon since the teamboat sinking—an ejection chair from one of the downed VTOLs with part of its occupant still in it.

In the middle distance, skimming the dark surface of Lake Ea and outlined by running lights, the hovercraft *Northwind* was closing on Quant's ship. The safe return of the shore party members from the Grandee Rhodes's stronghold was both gratifying and irritating. The returning Exts would constitute a major increase in the *GammaLAW*'s meager assets, and the *Northwind* would enhance search and rescue capability by an order of magnitude.

The irritation, of course, was Dextra Haven. From the *Northwind* she had sent word that she would be heading for the bridge after a quick stop at the signals center—for

Quant's bridge—despite his near-order that she lay to the Commissioner's Information Center or to her quarters.

When the hovercraft had come alongside its mother vessel, casualties had been transferred to medical and the waiting Glorianna Theiss. The dead were moved, as well, for bagging and deposit in a stores locker that would have to serve as a morgue. The deck watch reported damage to the *Northwind's* plenum skirt, but the hover was pronounced seaworthy nevertheless. That Kurt Elide had manned the controls struck Quant as yet another violation of the laws of the universe.

He was tempted to use the damaged skirt as a rationale for keeping the hovercraft close by the ship for the time being. Having himself been adrift in a survival suit in dangerous waters, he could sympathize with anyone who might be bobbing in the water, awaiting pickup. But that didn't alter the fact that he needed all the firepower he could get or that he would soon have to give thought to mounting an amphibious op to rescue friendlies trapped on the shore. There was also the matter of the Oceanic. If Aquamarine's marine overseer had hard-deleted *Terrible Swift Sword*, it might be in a mood to cleanse the planet of humankind once and for all.

Quant knew, however, that he would ultimately dispatch the *Northwind* on search and rescue. To do otherwise would send a disastrous message to the patchwork, greatly understrength ship's company. He had to show all hands that the SWATHship wasn't a frightened, helpless giant and that she certainly wouldn't abandon her own. With radio-telephone frequencies still jammed as a result of the *Sword's* annihilation—or the inscrutable work of the Oceanic—one of the *GammaLAW's* precious microwave amplification units would have to be installed to ensure commo.

"Commissioner on the bridge," the sentry of the watch announced suddenly.

Quant became aware of a flurry of activity. Forgoing the courtesy of asking his indulgence, Dextra Haven had climbed the portside wing ladder and was even then stepping into the captain's holy of holies.

She wore a pair of field pants and what was left of her embroidered bodice. The bodice dangled scraps of ruching and ruffles, and her swooping-bird hairdo was in disarray, yet she somehow managed to project dignity. Haven's hermaphroditic lieutenant was a step behind, looking soldierly in a wearwithal jumpsuit, LAW emergency vest, and helmet. Tonii was still wearing the flechette pistol 'e had fired only moments earlier at incoming antiship missiles launched by AlphaLAW Commissioner Starkweather's now-destroyed *Jotan* weapons platform. Lod, Haven's liaison with the Exts, was hanging back on the wing of the bridge.

Quant let his displeasure show in his tone. "Madame Haven, you *will* please lay below with these—" He cut his gaze to Tonii "—*individuals*. I've no time to brief you or—"

"The mountain has come to Mohammet, Captain. I know you can't leave the bridge, but we have to confer—immediately, if you'd be so kind."

It wasn't a request; she had him over a barrel of military discipline and they both knew it. The GammaLAW mission couldn't withstand a further breakdown in the chain of command. Even so, Quant was about to argue the point until he saw a Manipulant looming at the top of the port bridge wing ladder, an unreadable look on its hardened bunker of a face. "What the hell is that thing doing here?" he barked, all reserve gone.

Haven blew out her breath. "We saved him—after he saved us. I suppose he's grown attached."

"*He?*" Quant said contemptuously. "Be serious."

Haven swung to the diminutive Lod. "Take Scowl-Jowl below." When he hesitated, she added, "I didn't say to delegate it. See to it yourself."

Lod managed to look both sulky and wary as he motioned the Manipulant to precede him down the ladder. At the same time phone talkers began to vie for Quant's attention, citing status reports and assessments of light damage to the *GammaLAW* as a consequence of her missile-evasion plow through Lake Ea's aquaculture clutter.

Haven waited out the talkers, gradually comprehending that the conversation was over as far as Quant was concerned. "Captain, be reasonable," she said at last.

Quant was busy checking surface radar plots. The equipment had been seriously glitched by EMP from the exploded *Terrible Swift Sword*. "Madame, this is hardly the time."

"Would you oblige me to make it a direct order?"

Tonii, unblinking, watched Quant over 'er mistress's shoulder. The undeniable comeliness of the gynander's face only increased Quant's loathing.

"Very well, madame," he said, straightening. "My sea cabin, if you please."

He gave the conn over to Lieutenant Gairaszhek and led Haven out the starboard wing of the bridge, around and into the spartan compartment that served as his working and sleeping space while under way. She left Tonii behind in the pilot house. Quant closed the cabin door and stood by the bunk, leaving it for Haven to take the one chair, but she ignored it. Glancing around, she remarked, "Not the love hotel decor Hallowed Hall preferred, is it?"

The reference to the ship's former commander worked a change in Quant. Getting a grip on his temper with the firmness of long practice, he removed his helmet and set it on the bunk. "I would respectfully ask you to be brief."

Haven ran a hand through her curls. "I take it we're in agreement about the destruction of the *Sword*? I mean, that the Oceanic was responsible, not the Roke."

Quant's initial assumption was that the aliens had destroyed the starship; after all, one of their vessels had engaged the *Sword* shortly after its arrival in the Eyewash system. There had been no follow-up attack by the Roke, and all the evidence suggested that the Oceanic had wiped out the *Sword* by launching a storm of electrical energy up along the tether the ship had dropped into the Amnion, as Aquamarine's single sea was known.

"Madame, what compelled Captain Nerbu to choose that moment to embark on a fishing expedition?"

Haven snorted. "It was Starkweather's idea. On the end of the tether was Raoul Zinsser's sampling device."

"Pitfall?" Quant said in genuine surprise.

"Starkweather apparently cracked Pitfall's operating codes. No, Captain, I don't think Zinsser had any complicity in it. As to the timing, Buck was hoping to prove to Rhodes and the other grandees that he could dominate the Oceanic. He promised them that he'd dump Pitfall's dredgings in the middle of the Panhard desert."

Quant was shaking his head in angry disbelief. "Do Rhodes and the others understand what happened?"

"They understand that the *Sword* is gone. They suspect that we deliberately antagonized the Oceanic in the hope that it would lay waste to what passes for civilization here."

"In advance of a 'legal annexation' by the forces of Periapt," Quant said knowingly.

"Exactly."

"And Zinsser—how did he react to this?"

Haven managed to make her lush lips a thin line. "I wish I could tell you, but we couldn't locate him. Or Burning, Ghost, and Mason."

"Captured or killed?"

Haven shook her head. "We'll know that if and when Rhodes or some other grandee issues hostage demands. There's more at work here than even Rhodes realizes. The person who touched off the firefight in Wall Water wasn't one of Rhodes's praetorians or Starkweather's Manipulants. It was a follower of Mason's son, Purifyre."

Quant was perplexed. A votary of the Creed of Human Enlightenment, Purifyre was a man of peace, or so the members of the GammaLAW mission had been led to believe.

"I'm as puzzled as anyone," Haven said, as if reading his thoughts. "But I know one thing: We need the cooperation of the Aquam if we're going to deal with the Oceanic."

Quant shot her a look. "It seems to me that we have more pressing concerns than rapprochement with the Oceanic. To begin with, madame, this ship must be made secure from attack. Once the Aquam realize that we have no way off their world, they'll try every means to take the *GammaLAW* by force."

Haven nodded, though distractedly. "I concur, Captain. But I'm more convinced than ever that the Oceanic can provide a resolution to the Roke Conflict. In light of what it did tonight, it's no wonder that the Roke have steered wide of Aquamarine for who knows how many millennia." She looked at him. "There's a secret here, Captain, just waiting to be discovered. In the shape we're in, discovering it is our best means of survival."

Quant confused her by moving into her personal space. But instead of offering an encouraging embrace or some more intimate exchange, he said, "I hope you'll understand when I ask you to lay below to the CIC or your quarters and let me get back to keeping us afloat."

Haven gazed at him poker-faced, quoting Plain Ned Ward's words regarding a sea captain. " *'For 'tis impudence for any to approach him within the length of a boat hook.'* Plain Ned tacked a grin on to it. Of course I'll do as you ask—for the time being."

Chapter Two

With Haven cast from the bridge, Quant could devote his full attention to conning the ship and putting right the wrongs that had been done her and to preparing the ship's company—and himself—for what was to come.

There were precious few virtues the Navy or Quant prized more highly than forehandedness; but despite the forehandedness he'd devoted to the mission thus far, events beyond his power or purview had flung his ship, unready and damaged and only marginally capable of protecting herself, into a planetful of harm's way.

He thought again of the Old Earth quote, *grande nao, gran cuidado*, "great ship, great anxiety." The inevitable crisis had come with a vengeance. It was what he had dreaded but also what he'd been born for. Where forehandedness failed, sheer resoluteness would take up the slack.

He took stock.

The ship would have to stay at general quarters until daylight at the very least. The Aquam had tried one suicide run at him with a wallowing, slave-driven millship and might again. Then, too, there were the Shadow-rat ninjas of the grandees; if they were as adept at frogman stunts as they were at stealth, they could pose a worse threat than a flat-out surface attack.

With the *GammaLAW*'s actuator-disc propellers cleared of debris, Quant had begun to move her into deeper, more open water—not that even expansive Lake Ea could ever feel anything but shallow and claustrophobic to a salt sailor. He had no idea how Grandee Rhodes's steam-powered cannon worked or what its true range and caliber were, but he was not inclined to find out by playing target.

Among lesser concerns, insulating the hull sheath emerged as a priority. To inhibit growth of organic buildup, refitting had included the application of an electroconductive doping to the three hulls' outermost layer. Tests had turned up nothing in the Ean aquatic ecology that presented any threat to integrity, but Quant felt uneasy about the system's down status. Incomplete electrical insulation bothered him, too, but neither problem was likely to be remedied anytime soon.

Food for people stuck at their stations was more easily addressed, at least in the short term. Palletloads of army-style ration pack meals had been brought aboard for distribution during extended periods at full alert. Quant had nixed the idea of installing an automated food-mover system simply to avoid unnecessary systemry penetrations of watertight bulkheads and decks.

Through Row-Row Roiyarbeaux, his principal phone talker, Quant dispatched additional sounding and security patrols to look for signs of internal damage, malfunction, and leaks. Then Quant himself got the Exts' General Delecado on the line. To augment naval lookouts, Daddy D had assigned Exts with vision enhancers to walk all three hulls bow to stern, watching for divers or other signs of clandestine assault.

"Got reaction teams mustered in the chain locker, the midships boat station port side, and at aircraft elevator one," the old soldier updated Quant.

"Very good, General. Who'd you tap for acting XO?" The Battalion of Exts' executive officer, Big 'Un Boudreau, had been vaporized along with two-thirds of the unit when the *Sword* had gone Bigtimer.

"Zone." Delecado advanced the name unhappily but firmly. "Allgrave Burning may say different when he gets back aboard, Skipper, but in the meantime Zone fits the socket pretty good, especially for the kind of fuckup fest we've got on our hands."

Zone had a reputation for violence and sexual excess, but he was a topflight field officer. "Your call, General," Quant told him. "What's your manning and arms status?"

"With the effectives back from the shore party, one hundred eight fit for duty and five in sick bay—but three of those can fight if we need 'em. Lethality component's mostly battle rifles and sidearms, one each per troop. Five spare boomers on hand and half a dozen 'ballers."

Boomers were shoulder-fired weapons that used 20-mm caseless ammunition; 'ballers were over-under sidearms that fired both .50-caliber hardball and sonic energy pulses from an accoustor the Exts referred to as a 'wailer.

"After what we used up on the AS missiles and the teamboat, we're at a hair less than basic issue ammo levels," Daddy D continued. "Say, two hundred rounds per person, plus some RPGs for the rifle launchers."

"That's all the ammunition you have?"

"I screamed my nuts off for more, but LOGCOM kept finding reasons for not shuttling it down. It's almost like Starkweather and Nerbu knew what was coming." He paused to interject a rueful laugh. "Anyway, I've ordered all weps locked on semiautomatic to husband what's left. Not that we're given to firing on full rock and roll, you understand."

"Hand grenades?" Quant asked, figuring they would do as makeshift depth charges.

"Basic issue, two apiece. Plus some flashbangs and shocks."

"Heavy weapons?"

"Just the fireball mortar and the two crew-served sonics. My troops from the shore party tell me 'wailers weren't stopping Aquam who were wearing gel-padded armor."

"Perhaps we won't need them to."

Quant hoped that the locals had been sufficiently awed by the firepower of the ship's aft-mounted coilgun, which had taken out the teamboat. If so, he'd be spared the onus of another show of force. With coilgun shells in short supply, he couldn't afford much in the way of warning shots in any case, and God help the Aquam if he had to fire for effect.

A line of fire in the night sky drew Quant's eye. Delecado said, "D'you catch that—in the west? There's another."

"I saw," Quant answered soberly. "*Terrible Swift Sword*— big pieces."

"Maybe my follow-on baggage'll land on the flight deck," Daddy D speculated. "Or the LOGCOM commander's head; that'd be nice, too."

Quant thought that was carrying gallows humor too far. On the other hand, he hadn't weathered the attritions and atrocities of the war the Exts had waged against LAW on Concordance, their homeworld.

"General, there's something else," he said after a moment. "I was told that your people set demolition charges aboard the hydrofoil *Edge* before it was abandoned on the beach. But *Edge* didn't blow as far as we can tell. Could the charges have malfed or been incorrectly set?"

"I'd bet against it, same as I'd put long money against the Aquam decoding the disarms. My surmise is that one or more shore parties got there after *Northwind* shoved off, then pulled the charges' teeth, hoping to use *Edge's* commo, life raft, whatever."

"The Allgrave? His sister?"

"No telling. But more likely them than Zinsser or Mason."

Still running priorities, Quant tried to decide who he most needed among Burning, Dr. Zinsser, and Claude Mason. Ghost wasn't really in the running. The Discards, her pack of wild-child Exts, would simply have to do without her leadership. Then he thrust the thought aside, fearing it only invited bad news.

Delecado agreed to have contingency proposals roughed out for a crisis-management session later that morning. Quant was about to sign off when the general added, "I'm assembling a team for aircav rescue, for when we get a fix on the MIAs."

"We don't have any air assets left," Quant thought to point out. "Not even flyable reemos."

"Well, that's not exactly right, Skipper. See, I brought along something special from Concordance: a packaged Hellhog helo we used at Anvil Tor."

The news brightened Quant's night momentarily, and he smiled into the headset microphone. "Keep me updated, please."

Ringing off, he wondered what might be in store if the Allgrave didn't return. Even more than Daddy D, Emmett Orman—Burning—had been the main compliance and diplomacy buffer between the GammaLAW mission leadership and its Ext janissaries. Given current discontinuities and absent Burning, the Exts—hard-tempered, often testy paroled POWs all—could present problems, especially with Zone in the XO slot.

Still, Quant would've piped Satan aboard with twenty-one guns and two dozen sideboys if it had held promise of keeping his ship safe. He set aside his concerns about Zone as well, refusing to let forehandedness lure him into borrowing trouble. He was already carrying far too much ballast of that sort.

With the last of the immediate details cleared away, Quant moved to the port wing of the bridge—a quieter place now that all flight ops had been suspended—and beckoned Gairaszhek over. The gangly, overgrown lieutenant whom Haven called "Mr. Jurassic" had lost some of his boyish exuberance since leaving Periapt, and even more in the hours following the *Sword*'s supernova. Gairaszhek followed Quant's example in removing his headset to huddle confidentially.

"Eddie, I'm putting another rock on your sledge. When you're relieved here, I want you to turn to and review our readiness for antibiowarfare. Life support, countermeasures, decontam, the washdown system—everything. Do it yourself and keep it to yourself. Nobody has need to know except me, got it?"

The lieutenant shuffled his size 18EEE shoes. Quant knew he wanted to know more, might even consider it his duty to ask, but he only said, "Yes, sir."

The SWATHship's main line of biowar defense lay in sealing her up and maintaining positive internal pressure with filtered air. The remote servo and autodeck antipersonnel hardware were as gone as the *Sword*. Assuming that the seals hadn't been compromised, buttoning up would invite Aquam with runny noses to board her unopposed and wreak havoc at will. Quant doubted that the Aquam had access to biowarfare agents, but there was no telling what the Oceanic might decide to spew into the planet's atmosphere.

Thanks to their battlesuits, the Exts could function in a biowar environment for weeks at a stretch, but the ship was otherwise woefully unprepared. Since she wouldn't remain seaworthy for long without trained sailors on deck, that meant putting naval personnel in Ext getups. Added to that, the ship's internal climate gear was mostly off-line—forced air being the only method of cooling the majority of her internal spaces—and the dry season heat made a lot of her almost unbearable by day.

Gairaszhek had lingered with an afterthought. "I can tell you this right now, sir. Doctor Theiss was shooting complaints back to orbit from the time she hit the med clinic. She hasn't even got thirty percent of her basic TO&E. She was yelling for everything from sterilizers to longevity equipment."

Quant didn't let his startlement show. "She'll be giving me those particulars later. Carry on, Mr. Gairaszhek."

The only one on the bridge permitted to sit, Quant sank into the swivel-mounted chair in the starboard corner of the wheelhouse, working through the realization the lieutenant had triggered with the mention of longev.

The military didn't unpocket for life-extension treatment for any but its most senior chair warmers. In any case, no service personnel on the GammaLAW mission, Quant included, required any significant level of ongoing therapy—save one. Only Dextra Haven, the former Hierarch, was old enough, wealthy enough, and important enough to be dependent on the equipment and supplies that had vanished along with the starship. She looked and comported herself so much like a wise, self-assured, pleasingly filled-out thirty-year-old that one tended to forget she was nearly two and a half times that in subjective years alone. Lacking a longev facility, however, she was about to provide a graphic reminder that the wages of mortality eventually came due in full, to everybody.

And she knows it, Quant thought. But she'd given no sign, had said nothing about it while fencing with Quant in his sea cabin. She'd worked her billet by concentrating on her mission's overriding dilemma.

Quant could tip his cap to that, even if her days were now numbered. He suspected that no amount of forehand-edness could prepare him for how Dextra Haven's demise would effect a marooned GammaLAW mission and where it would leave Chaz Quant in terms of opening contact with the Oceanic.

CHAPTER THREE

Wedged into the WHOAsuit he and Souljourner had appropriated from the hydrofoil *Edge*, Burning maneuvered along the 'foil's partly submerged, canted deck into deeper water. Only *zanshin* kept him from losing balance when something hit him from behind like a wrecking ball, striking a note from the suit like the tolling of noon by the great Bastion Orman clock on Concordance.

The Water Hardshell, One Atmosphere exo did a belly flop that almost sent his face into the padded chin control panel. Souljourner's weight landed on him despite her efforts to brace herself. His holstered 'baller bone bruised his ilium, but it was nothing he couldn't tolerate in Flowstate. He registered a weighty splash nearby, and through the suit's half-awash dome he saw a war hammer settling in the soupy shallows. A lucky throw from some Aquam onshore had found him.

He remembered his orientation sessions well enough to go into a forward pike, a modified push-up position that brought the suit to a horizontal attitude, allowing him to regain control. Then he used his momentum to stroke and pedal-foot forward.

"You all right?" he asked Souljourner. The hurled *martel-de-fer* must have hit the armored hump in which Aquamarine's only female Descrier was scrunched.

"A rude blow to a part of me that's well padded—" she said with the faint lisp her prognathism gave her. "My head. No matter."

His chuckle caught in his throat as he shifted and took a measured leg push sideways off the 'foil's sunken bow. His boots barely churned the lake bottom. He thrashed, returning the suit to vertical, while Souljourner wriggled and muscled herself back into the humpspace. Whatever else she was, she was no whiner.

Turning toward open water, Burning hit the powered exo's thrusters, and the little turbulator water jets propelled them ahead in upright attitude at three knots. Retractable control surfaces deployed on the hull for added maneuverability. He steered around an anchored punt, taking on water ballast and depth. Wavelets closed around the dome like silty champagne, and the WHOAsuit sank beneath water as murky as Lucifer's id.

Arms raised close to his chest and feet dangling slightly behind him, he steered out beyond Wall Water's combination breakwater and defensive perimeter before increasing thrust to five knots. The depth finder showed the lake bottom dropping away sharply.

Lake Ean oddities floated by: moogles, like great nests of eyeballs, and slug-lugs, which resembled undulating protoplasmic torpedoes. Disinterested, they nevertheless set him thinking about what else might be out there. In the pitch blackness he recalled briefings about the Nixies, powerful wraiths that allegedly dragged their victims into the muck.

He brought up conventional and sidescan sonar, a blue-green laser imager, and ground-penetrating radar. Then he switched off all but the sonar because of what the devices demanded from the suit's half-charged power reserves.

17

His compass and inertial tracker were of minimal use because he had only the vaguest idea where the *GammaLAW* was. His plan was to move a good distance from shore, then surface and get a fix on the SWATHship either by commo or by eyeball. If necessary, he would make use of the suit's lights, signal beacon, and emergency flares.

Souljourner was kneading his trapezius muscles distractedly, watching what she could over his shoulder. She didn't squirm around unduly, though her contortion had to be uncomfortable. Her breath was odd but pleasant, like an Aquam spice.

"We're clear now," he told her. "I'll call for extraction as soon as we surface." He tried to sound casually confident, as Daddy D or Quant would under the same circumstances. "We'll probably be on the flight deck in half an hour."

Her thumbs worked the ridges of his muscles mercilessly, but it felt wonderful. With his cock squeezed up against the front of the suit, he became aware of a certain erotic stirring.

"What will happen to me when we reach the ship?" she asked quietly.

"Everything'll be optimal plus. You're one of us now." Which in effect she was, having been gifted to Dextra Haven by the Grandee Rhodes himself.

He had hoped to run submerged for at least five minutes, but the gloomy impenetrability of the water, Souljourner's disquieting question, and his sudden need to dispel the urge he was feeling toward her made him revise the plan. He blew ballast with pressurized air, and the WHOAsuit broached the surface.

"We'll try the commo first," he was saying as miniature chop broke around the peak of the dome. "Maybe I can spot *Gamma*—"

18

He stopped as fire flared and flickered nearby. The streaming dome mask blurred it at first, and then he saw that he'd surfaced in the middle of a cluster of boats and rafts mounting cressets, rushlights, and lanterns. The suit's audio pickup was switched off, but he could see figures pointing at him, waving torches.

A sling-gun pellet ricocheted off the dome's harder-than-steel ceramic glass. Burning whipped his head around to see where it had come from, bumping his nose on Souljourner's cheek. The suit was bobbing, but he made out a man reloading an enormous sling-gun and gesticulating to his comrades. Two more Aquam in aquafarmer reed sampan hats had set up one of the heavy bolt throwers that rested, harquebuslike, atop a linstock.

Another missile rang off the WHOA, and smoke rose past the dome as paint began dissolving. *Acid*, Burning understood calmly, probably loaded in a glass tube. He doubted it could harm the exo, but it reinforced his decision to crash-dive like a lead-assed anchor.

Opening the ballast pods, he threw his weight to the left, tilting the suit that way as it went down. The second harquebus round missed, passing in a blur but trailing a braided line.

"They're trying to harpoon us!" he said because he couldn't stop himself.

He considered shooting a flare at the aquafarmers, but water was already closing over the dome. Iridescent lines zipped down into the darkness—pilehead rounds fired in the hope that they would penetrate the WHOA as they did Aquam armor. He adjusted suit attitude, descending two meters, five, ten. If the Aquam were still firing, nothing was reaching that depth.

Intending to run silent and deep for a long time, he returned to his former heading. The dome was quiet except for the sound of the life support, the systems tones, and his and Souljourner's breathing. Sonar said the Aquam boats were milling around without changing position.

All at once, however, acoustic sensors and the conduction of the WHOAsuit hull picked up a deep vibration, as if someone was playing woofer notes through a submerged transducer. As the notes became a rondo, cycling faster and faster, Burning recalled the pipe organ contraptions he had glimpsed on some of the aquaculture rafts during the hovercraft ride to Wall Water hours earlier.

A signal? he wondered. He increased sonar range until he detected the lake's western shoreline and the immense return two kilometers to starboard that was the ancient dam. More troubling was a ghostly paint he was getting forward; similar bogeys showed up to either side, and then the bottom beneath his feet began to stir.

The first paint was closing, although the laser imager showed nothing. His brows knotted; he was no image-interp expert and had little experience with sonar. "It's not fish," he told Souljourner. Whatever it was kept coming. He glanced out the dome into water as black as tar.

Souljourner leaned forward to see, her cheek pressed to his temple. He hit the suit lights. Lensatically concentrated mercury-vapor spotlights cut through the silty gloom as if through smoke. Souljourner made a strangled sound.

"Nixies!" she gasped, jerking her head back.

Burning heard her head clunk the dorsal humphull. He began plying the controls to reverse thrust, and eventually the exo came to a weighty, unwilling stop. *Nixies*. Why had he even questioned their existence after what Aquamarine had already revealed about itself—the Oceanic, medieval grandees, muscle cars, steam-powered cannon. Not only were the Nixies real, *the Aquam knew how to summon them*, or at least how to agitate them.

The question now was, How many of the horror stories about them were true?

All tales conceded that the Nixies inhabited the bottom ooze, had little intercourse with humans, and played an indispensable role in the ecology of the lake. Viewed in a book or holo, the creature closing on the WHOA would probably have struck Burning as more peculiar than menacing. But seeing it spread like a phantom nebula to envelope the suit, huge as the high-holiday flag at Bastion Orman, sickly white as frozen flesh, showing gaps and then fusing whole again like a vampire cloud—that was a different bag of beans.

Nevertheless, the Skills already had him reacting with Flowstate proficiency. He drew his feet up close to kick, then brought up the exo's arms, waldo hands poised like cutlery displays. Souljourner grunted a bit as the WHOA rolled, the shift pressing him back, squashing her against the rear of the suit. The hard-on he'd had moments earlier withered and was gone.

He reversed the suit's thrusters as the rippling sheet came at them like cirrus ectoplasm. He couldn't imagine how something so gauzy could so effortlessly overcome the resistance of the lake water. Where the Nixie's rufflings met or chance convolutions came together, it extruded spiral-arm extremities that swirled and searched, then were reabsorbed by a main mass the size of a motor-stable door.

Animal, monster, or specter, it was approaching with an air of definite purpose. "More terrible than the tales," Souljourner breathed. "The Nixie's touch is death itself."

"If it can kill intermetallic-compound armor, let it," Burning answered equitably.

The Nixie was big but as fragile-looking as a single ply of used nosewipe. Since retreating carried risks, Burning elected to simply swipe and wad it aside. He had no desire to damage or kill, but if pressed he'd rip it with the waldos or torch it with a flare.

He reached to brush a flounce of it that twirled at him like the hem of a flamenco dancer's skirt, and blue sparks crackled across the WHOA's neck ring and leapt off bare metal in the interior. A surge of current crackled through the suit, penetrating spots where the Aquam acid had eaten through the rig's non-conducting sheath.

Systemry spat and sizzled while Souljourner shouted, "Damn it to *brine!*"

Burning saw stars and grimaced from the center of his *ki.* He felt hair stand upright all over his body as the voltage belted him, coursing with effervescent pain. One or two more jolts would likely disable the suit or stop the hearts of its occupants.

Skills training allowed him to discard the distraction and maintain focus. He reversed the thrusters hard, and the WHOAsuit wobbled backward at two knots, then three. The Nixie billowed in pursuit, though it appeared unhurried, making him wonder if it was recharging.

At three point five knots, the thrusters maxxed and the Nixie overtook them. Burning used his weight and limbs to flip over, scissor-kicking clumsily. Again Souljourner crouched astride his back, spitting out one of his red braids. In that attitude and with the thrusters realigned, he gained another two knots, but the suit's cams were burned out. Rearview mirrors spotted around the dome showed him nothing but darkness and the glare of his own lights.

With so little mass the Nixie hadn't seemed capable of producing such devastating voltage. Nor could Burning figure out how the wispy pseudopod completed a circuit. For all he knew, the things communicated electrically, but he had no way of improvising a repellent signal or field. Sound had provoked the attack, but the exo lacked acoustics capability.

"Yonder!" Souljourner said suddenly, motioning to the right. "Another!"

The second Nixie drifted in on a convergent course. Burning drew in the suit's arms and legs, streamlining as much as possible in an effort to squeeze past. He angled left, away from the shallows and into the deeper water at the foot of the dam. He made sure he wasn't descending, fearing that the ooze below was alive with the creatures. Purposely or not, the pair of pursuers were boxing him toward the dam.

He tried to dope out a way he and Souljourner could survive a double jolt in the event he was forced to turn and rip through the Nixies, assuming that was even possible. The extreme option would be to surface and try to shoot his way aboard a raft or boat, but that idea smacked of suicide.

He heard and felt Souljourner hyperventilating as she lay on him. "You all right?"

"Catching my breath ... "

Oxygen was falling, carbon dioxide climbing; the temp was up, and both of them were sweating buckets. The suit circulated air through CO_2 scrubbers and purified it with a metal hydroxide compound, adding supplemental oxygen and breathable nitrogen. But two people strained the system, and it was possible that the Nixie bolt had caused a malfunction.

He chinned a switch, and O_2 from the emergency bottle blew in, lifting the indicator momentarily. It was crucial that they break contact with the creatures and find a safe place to surface.

Souljourner was peering over his head. "A third one!"

Burning changed headings again, hoping for a clear path between the Nixies. In seconds, however, more of the living veils loomed to starboard. He maxxed the thrusters, but the Nixies continued to gain.

"They're nearly upon us," Souljourner said. "Perhaps the Holy Rollers were wrong about us, after all!"

Burning wondered exactly what her recently lost divination dice had said but didn't ask. The first lake wraith was looming hard astern. If he couldn't blow it up, he had to at least impede it.

With Flowstate certainty he angled one arm behind him and triggered the envelopment specimen-collection system. A glob of epoxy, intended to trap small marine life for retrieval and study, was extruded by a nozzle telescoped from the waldo, right into the path of the billowing Nixie. As the creature slowed to enclose or perhaps taste it, the suit's lead widened, but that was the last of the epoxy and the dam's curtain wasn't far off.

Burning launched a blinking marker buoy that shot upward without enticing the creatures. He then released a cloud of luminescent marker dye, but that didn't interest them, either. He wished he could jettison the main power pack as a decoy, but the suit wasn't built for that. Finally, he thumbed the control that extended the waldos' saw blades. Time to give the Nixies the tensile strength test, he decided.

"Wait," Souljourner enjoined him, craned around to look where he couldn't. "They're falling behind."

The WHOAsuit's true speed indicator said it was making *decreased* headway despite the jets' laboring at full choke. When the hardbody was buffeted by unseen currents, he understood. "The dam! We're in the flow from the lower outlets."

The chaos at the stronghold notwithstanding, reservoir water was being vented to keep Ean aquaculture supplied. The Nixies, he guessed, found the strong currents unpleasant to buck. Even so, he caught the flutter of translucent white off to his left.

"Brace yourself," he warned.

Souljourner did that, with what felt like a proprietary grip on his shoulders. "The Holy Rollers knew!"

The laser imager, aimed horizontally, showed him a big circular gap in the curtain of the dam—one of half a dozen—just large enough to accommodate the WHOAsuit. Burning pushed thruster power into the red, fighting toward it in the middle of its fairway, the invisible river getting more and more violent. He gulped air in short, shallow breaths. Realizing that the CO_2 was up again, he vented the last of the reserve oxygen.

The suit's water jets sounded as if they were about to fly apart, but he managed to hook the left waldo gripper on the lip of the outlet, then the right. The lights revealed a circular conduit a meter and a half in diameter crusted thick with softshelled Aquam mollusks, a horizontal forest contorted by the vent's current.

Three overgrown, equidistant tracks ran the length of the conduit—purchase, he supposed, for robotic cleaning machinery back before the Cyberplagues. Power was low, but the exo still had some strength left. He picked the bottom track and locked one gripper on a slot, hauled hard, and got the other gripper to the next. He was on his stomach with Souljourner doing her best to keep her weight off him.

He cut the failing turbojets to conserve power and drew himself to the next handhold and to the one after that, concentrating on little victories of ten, twenty centimeters at a time. The water's fury was constant. Each new hold broke loose crud buildup and living organisms that the current ripped away into Ea. He didn't let himself dwell on how long the conduit was—how wide the base of the dam was.

Souljourner's breathing was as labored as his own. Sensing the ebbing of his coordination and strength, she gasped hoarsely: "You're weakening."

"We'll get there." He was having trouble forcing his arm to the next hold.

He heard a papery rustling, and a moment later Souljourner was holding a pinch of aromatic stuff under his face. "This is Apex," she wheezed. "For some it dispels the headaches that come with the ability to descry quakes and the moods of the Oceanic. Take some under your tongue."

He wouldn't ordinarily have sampled an unknown Aquam liniment but the stuff smelled right to him and he had little to lose. Licking her cupped palm held little sensual thrill; he was too far gone for that. The granular Apex left nothing more than a warm wake down his throat until he suddenly found the world coming into sharper definition.

The WHOAsuit's energy levels had dropped, but he moved its arms anyway, rising into a clarity and numinous purity of total effort. Each moment dilated wide, yet there was no lag in the passage of time. The feat of dragging himself up-current became a work of art, occupying his whole field of attention like a hypnotic trance. That heightened Flowstate should come from some local pharmaceutical contradicted everything the Exts knew about the Skills.

But even the strongest Flowstate didn't make an Ext superhuman or infallible. A handhold gave way. The material of the track crumbled, and the ferocious current pried him loose in a split second, flushing the WHOAsuit back down the outflow, straight for the plunge pool and the waiting Nixies.

CHAPTER FOUR

All this general quarters lather was what Lod's sainted mother would've called a whole lot of shaking and no martini. The calamities that had come crashing down around the GammaLAW mission weren't going to be set right by dogging hatches, manning guns, and buckling up flotation vests. The leadership should be working out an initiative to put a stop to the bloodshed between indig and Visitant before it escalated—just the sort of closed-door strategy session where Lod would shine, as he had in the early stages of the Concordance War, except that Dextra Haven had given him an errand more suitable to a junior flunky.

Or maybe a wild animal tamer, he reflected, sneaking another nervous glance over his shoulder at the creature dogging his heels, taking one step for every three of his. It had to bend at the waist and turn sideways to pass through the lower, narrower hatches. Lod had no idea how to tell it to yield the right-of-way to others in the passageways, but that turned out not to matter since everyone stepped aside for Scowl-Jowl.

Lod was used to being noticed for his small size; indeed, he invited attention with impeccable tailoring and a polished elan. But that wasn't why he was drawing stares even in the midst of a Condition IV alert. With a seven-foot-plus-tall

Manipulant tagging after him like a tame bogeyman in a combat coverall, Lod doubted that many of the people he passed even registered his presence.

He wished he could foist the chaperoning job on the first likely mark he saw, but Haven had ordered him to escort the lone survivor of Starkweather's Special Troops contingent belowdecks in person. Worse, he had no idea where he could stash the engeneered giant, and he couldn't ask it for suggestions since, like all of its kind, Scowl-Jowl spoke only its own secret battle-*gullah*. Its name was known only because one of the AlphaLAWs at Wall Water had used it during the madness of Starkweather's exit.

Lod heard the Manipulant making ruminative sizzling noises like frying fat meat and couldn't help inhaling its wet clay smell. The smell, too, brought back to him his time as a collaborator with Commissioner Renquald and the other LAW and First Lands overlords on Concordance. Lod had seen a Manip the size of a shower stall—slightly smaller than Scowl-Jowl—overpower a First Lands sergeant driven synaptshit by three days of internecine combat at Santeria Corners. The human was a bruiser, but the Special Troop had wrung the man's neck as if he were a dodoid pullet headed for the dinner pot.

Manipulants had every reason to hate Exts implacably. There hadn't been two more unrelenting enemies in the Broken Country War, and while the Legal Annexation of Worlds forces had eventually triumphed, it was the Manip unit that had been withdrawn from combat after suffering unsustainable losses.

Lod could feel Scowl-Jowl's hot breath on him and thought he could sense the creature's thick talons opening and closing in anticipation. Light conversation—Lod's forte—wasn't very promising under the circumstances, but it was all he had.

"We'll get you squared away, no worries. Did I mention that I became quite chummy with some of your brood on Concordance? Used to loan them money until payday, no interest. What outfit were you with, by the way?"

He felt Scowl-Jowl looming close over him like a snow ridge about to come crashing down, and the sensation triggered his essential Ext core under the diligently cultivated unctuousness and disdain for violence. Accustomed to being outweighed and outnumbered, Lod was too contemptuous of bullies to go down without a fight. His hand went to the grip of his sidearm.

"That's close enough, Grendel! I—" He blinked at Scowl-Jowl, taken aback. The creature had turned to show the cryptic unit insignia on its shoulder patch.

Chitinously inhuman, its face was reinforced by wishbone-shaped ridging that bracketed the mouth and by heavy brow and cheek bulges. Its teeth belonged on a multi-blade survival tool. Even so, there was what appeared to be hardworking intellect behind the deep-set nacre eyes.

Lod shook his head. "My apologies, Major Gargoyle, but I can't read that worm trail." The Manip held its dogtag out to him. "Mm-mm, that, either."

Scowl-Jowl's effort drove two things home, nevertheless. The first was that the creature was obviously brighter and more adaptable than most of its kind, a fact borne out by the initiative it had demonstrated at Wall Water. The second was that, marooned and isolated as the GammaLAW survivors were, they were still humans on a human-populated planet, whereas Scowl-Jowl was little more than a time-limited monstrosity, not unlike the Anathemite infants the Aquam readily put to death.

Unable to make itself understood, the Special Trooper made a rumbling noise that, deep as it was, held a note of keening despair. Lod was at a loss for something to say; he certainly wasn't going to pat it on the shoulder.

"Now, now, bear up," he began, when a voice interrupted him.

"Doing some peer counseling there, little man?" The question came in an instantly recognizable jeering drawl.

Zone was in better, more malevolent spirits now that the killing had started. He was the Exts' most able fighter, though he'd probably have ended up institutionalized or executed in any peacetime society. He was in full combat gear, his demon-face breather hanging open on his helmet and his 20-mm boomer at high port arms. Flanking him were Kino, Strop, and Wetbar, his subordinates and stooges, as well as members of his sexual ménage—his several.

Lod showed half-lidded unconcern. "Not at all, Colonel. Just confiding the name of my tailor to our new—recruit? Shipmate?"

"Freak?" Kino grinned, unslinging a boomer almost as big as she was.

So much meanness in such a petite, adorable-looking woman, Lod thought. The battle rifle bores looked as big as trench mortar tubes. He knew he didn't have a prayer in perdition of drawing his 'baller fast enough to do any good, and Scowl-Jowl's bloopgun had been left aboard the *Northwind*. Lod doubted, in any case, that the creature appreciated the peril that suddenly faced it.

"Fellow survivor," Lod told Kino. "Team player in getting Rhodes's funicular under way, remember? I'm seeing it to a holding place. Commissioner Haven's order."

"*De*commissioned Haven," Wetbar sniggered, alluding to the showdown on the beach between Haven and Zone during which Zone had made it clear that he answered to no one but himself. Like his guru, Wetbar was rangy and intense, but his aura of menace registered many roentgens lower than did Zone's.

"We'll finish securing it for you," Zone said. "You go on back and hide behind Commissioner Spreadlegs' skirts some more."

Boomer safeties clicked off. Zone and his severalmates were deadly serious.

A man of fine sensibilities among rugged, flinty people, Lod hadn't survived and thrived without learning the better part of valor. He stepped aside before Scowl-Jowl could sort out what was going down and snatch him up as a shield, consoling himself with the belief that Burning would have it out with Zone one day soon.

Watching Lod comply, Zone threw in, "Move out on the double, midgetman."

Something that felt like napalm catching fire raised hackles all across Lod's neck and shoulders, and warmth radiated off his face. Ignoring the many prudent arguments against it, he planted himself squarely in front of the Manipulant. "There isn't even sex or money involved," he remarked.

Zone's underlings were suddenly studying Lod as if he were more of an aberration than Scowl-Jowl, though Zone himself showed only malign pleasure.

"Too bad your asshole buddy Frankenstein went bugscat with that big chopper knife," he sneered, "and *you* got in the way when we had to mow it down."

They were all raising their boomers. Lod considered saying that they wouldn't get away with it, but even he didn't believe that. In the expectant silence that blossomed in the passageway, everyone heard the ping of the hand grenade pin on the deck.

The Manipulant stick grenade was much bigger than anything the Exts used, suggesting a checker-grooved piston out of a huge old interbust engine. With the pin pulled, Scowl-Jowl's grip on the spoon was the only thing keeping the outsize ordnance from taking all of them off the rollcall, battlesuits or no.

Lod stepped aside again, thinking, Why shield Zone from the blast? "I don't think it's in the mood to be shot, Colonel," he confided to Zone.

His severalmates' savor of the moment was gone, but Zone, never at a loss, gave Lod an inimical mouth-only smile. "Too bad you haven't got a grenade," he said, swinging the boomer's muzzle to bear on him.

Lod's own brand of refined Flowstate kept him above tawdry panic as he waited to see how the business would play itself out. Then Scowl-Jowl took a hand, gargling something and brandishing the huge potato masher like a Jovian thunderbolt. Three talon fingers were off the spoon; the thumb and the fourth clasped it only lightly.

Disingenuously, Lod widened his eyes at Zone. "Dear me! That certainly seems to have stolen the pea from your whistle."

Zone held his fire but widened the hungry-zombie grin. "This is *ripe*! You're already jumpin' 'n' humpin' that Aggregate freak Piper, and now you've got another for a baby-sitter. Some Ext!"

When he slung his piece, the others followed suit relievedly. "No big issue, Lod. But you just might want to have Crunch-face here whack off Private Grenade the rest of the way. It'd be quicker than what I'll have for you one of these days."

Zone turned and led his set away. Flowstate, survival, and victory sang in Lod's veins. He bent to retrieve the pull-ring safety pin and offered it to Scowl-Jowl, who was watching him inscrutably. Reinserting the pin, the Manip clipped the grenade onto its belt.

"What's *really* ripe," Lod continued chattily, "is that that patho gave me an idea." His fingers beckoned to Scowl-Jowl. "Come along; there's someone I want you to meet. Oh, and spread the tips on that grenade pin to make sure it stays put, would you, like a good sport."

Scowl-Jowl obliged him, falling in behind Lod once more.

"I've always thought it behooves us to keep in mind the fact that our weapons were manufactured by the lowest bidder," Lod said. "What're your views on the subject?"

"The truth, Dex? Very well. It's not going to be a happy ending."

For all her ice-queen aplomb, the mission's surgeon general, Glorianna Theiss, knew how to lay one right between the eyes of anyone who pressed her too sharply. But journalism and politics, marriage, family, and love affairs had all taught Dextra how not to let them see her sweat.

"Doctor Theiss, did I *ask* you for a happy ending? I know the destruction of the rejuve equipment and supplies aboard *Terrible Swift Sword* means that my number's up. Just give me the log-line prognosis so we can both get back to work."

Glorianna's understaffed and underequipped surgery had received wounded from the *Northwind*. Her preoccupation with the patients made her indifferent to getting the better of a skirmish with Dextra. "There'll be a sudden onrush of accelerated catabolism. I can't say when, but soon."

The two were standing in a small consultation area to one side of the sick bay's central receiving and triage area. Dextra could see it had penetrated to staff and patients alike that the obliterated *Sword* had taken with it a large portion of the wonders of Periapt medical care. Dextra wasn't the only one in for bad health news. Of those present, only the Exts seemed un-fazed by the abrupt stacking of odds against them; they had expected it—and worse.

"You'll age perhaps twenty somatic years in the course of a few weeks," Glorianna speculated. "In time that will plateau. Using what courses of treatment I *do* have aboard, I can stabilize you for a while. But ongoing and irreversible deterioration will resume within, oh, a month or two in spite of the suppressants. There are few precedents for your situation, but complete reversion to your subjective age should take not more than one baseline-year."

Dextra absorbed it. "What I need to know is, How long will I be effective?" The expression that flickered over Glorianna's face had Dextra thinking of a coiffed Brunhilde about to pass sentence, but the reply wasn't what she expected.

"Depends on what you hope to effect. Your physician's advice is to cease thinking like a slab of politico-media cheese-tart." Glorianna indicated the bulkhead with a toss of her majestic blond mane. "Out across Aquamarine, squalid human zoo though it is, people older than you are effective—in whatever ways they've found. Forget about life on your terms and start figuring out how to make the best of what time you have remaining. That's my Rx, Commissioner."

Dextra nodded and moved for the door; there was still work to do. As she emerged, more casualties appeared at the surgery. Glorianna's staff and the Ext medics were coping as best they could. There would be no limb replacement, no burn and scar regeneration, no tidy and precise pain alleviation by neuroblock probe. The sight made abundantly clear just how far the GammaLAW mission had fallen after one blow.

And if we have amputees, will we be giving them wooden legs and iron hooks? Dextra wondered. *MeoTheos!*

Daddy D had ducked in to check up on his wounded Exts, battlesuits having protected most of them from the slings and arrows wielded by Grandee Rhodes's Militerrors and houseguards. The general sometimes put Dextra in mind of a mass of tanned leather that had been flung out sopping wet to dry on a scarecrow-shaped frame, but she counted her blessings that he was there, especially after her disastrous face-off with Zone. Still, the sight of Delecado reminded her that if Burning wasn't back aboard soon, the Exts might present some distinct problems.

"Any signals from shore?" Dextra asked.

Delecado shook his head. "Our best bet's to go and look for 'em. There's a possibility that one of 'em made it down to the beach after *Northwind* left." At Dextra's show of interest, the general added, "Somebody zeroed the destruct charges on the *Edge*."

Dextra took heart at the news. "It would have to be Burning or Ghost, wouldn't it?"

"That's just what I told the skipper. Which means either of them could be lying low in the vicinity of Wall Water. What about Mason? Where'd you see him last?"

Dextra thought for a moment. "He was with his son, Purifyre. I feel certain that Purifyre and his followers got Mason out of the stronghold alive."

"As an ally or in captivity?"

Dextra compressed her lips and shook her head.

"And Dr. Zinsser?"

She kept shaking her head. "For a time we were all together in Rhodes's bedchambers. I didn't see him afterwards." She paused briefly. "General, I realize how important Burning is to our cause, but I want you to make Zinsser a priority. If anyone is going to discover some means of communicating with the Oceanic, it's him. Are we clear on this?"

"We'll do what we can, ma'am. I only wish we had a little something to go on. Assuming for the moment he didn't get himself blown to pieces aboard Starkweather's *Jotan*, where would a man like Zinsser conceal himself? I mean, he didn't exactly strike me as the heroic type."

Dextra nodded in agreement. "I don't know why, General, but I've got a feeling that if we locate Ghost, we'll find Zinsser."

CHAPTER FIVE

Over the edge...
Raoul Zinsser had gone over the edge of the Wall Water footbridge into the abyss and black infinity. He repented his decision to leap; he had rued it even as he had yielded to it on impulse. He knew there was still, stagnant water down below—but how deep? It was the broiling-hot Big Sere season on that part of Aquamarine, but to him the midnight air felt icy.

Above him Wall Water was crawling with various factions of Aquam out for blood; below him, somewhere in the dark, the Ext soldier-woman Ghost preceded him in free fall. The Manipulant incendiary grenade she had tossed onto the footbridge threw no light into the void. Opposing phalanxes of indig warriors had been closing in on the two of them from opposite ends of the span connecting the stronghold to the heights opposite. Ghost, low on handgun ammo and always ardent for risk, had accepted his plan and taken the plunge with a dark elation Zinsser hadn't even pretended to muster.

But elation wasn't required. The choice was between the yawning gulf and the cutlasses, halberds, and sling-guns of the low-tech troops, and Wall Water was splattered with gory proof of what those could do.

The oceanographer fell, hugging his arms to his chest. As outriggers they'd have destabilized him, and a tumble just now would likely be the death of him. For stability he and Ghost had packed several kilos of sand-gravel amalgam into their socks, tying them so tightly to their ankles that circulation was cut off. A clean, feetfirst entry was the only way, as Zinsser had known from a dare he'd been synaptshit enough to accept but smart enough to survive in his long-gone undergrad days.

He still wasn't clear on how or why the get-acquainted fête at the Aquam stronghold had turned into a bloodbath. The worst sight of the evening had been the bright flash below the horizon that had been the starship *Terrible Swift Sword* blown all to skyfire in low orbit.

The catastrophe had hit him with the force of a seizure, owing in part to the fact that no human act had destroyed the *Sword*, or any assault from humanity's alien enemy. Another agency was responsible, and its attack had stemmed in some measure from Zinsser's own actions—or inaction.

He began filling his lungs against prolonged submersion, because he knew he'd be going deep. His ears popped with the abrupt change in altitude. He tucked his chin to his chest and drew his shoulders up around his ears.

SAT imagery had indicated that Wall Water aquaculturalists raised special delicacies year-round in the dam tailwater toward which he was falling. If he or Ghost hit a seine kraal pontoon or a work floater, it wouldn't be much different from striking solid ground.

He was still musing on that when he impacted.

At that velocity the diverted reservoir water couldn't get out of his way fast enough. As he was shoved deep into blackness with a cocoon of bubbles all around him, his knees were rammed toward his ribs, but by luck he'd come down at a slight lie-back attitude, so they didn't cave in his chest. The shock to his spine was like being ass-slammed onto a titanium launching. All in an instant he was jolted irresistibly out of his tuck, but he had avoided dislocating his shoulders or putting out his eyes with his own thumbs.

Zinsser didn't recall closing his eyes, much less opening them, but he suddenly found himself gazing at faint luminescence. He felt eerily lucid, reflecting that if there were any predators in the sluiceway, they would have been frightened away by his concussive splash. The water felt warm. The weights on his feet were still pulling him down, however, so he began to grope for the knot at his right ankle.

The length of cord cut from Ghost's aiguilette came undone like a ribbon from around an elegant gift box. His nails scraped flesh from his leg as he peeled away the sock. Then the left knot refused to untie.

Zinsser fumbled at it calmly. It was inverted somehow, or perhaps he'd tied it wrong. He reached for the skin-diving knife he'd tucked into his cummerbund as a de rigueur ceremonial weapon for the Grand Attendance at Wall Water, only to find it vanished, sheath and all. He kicked in an effort to bring the knot closer; then it dawned on him that his left foot was moving with little impediment. The weight of sand and gravel amalgam was gone, and he was already rising.

The sock had apparently burst on impact.

Zinsser's strongest diving days were behind him, and his lungs told him that they were losing patience. He let out a trickle of air to relieve the pressure and kicked for the surface, following the phosphorescent foam his plunge had whipped up. Breaking the surface, he peered anxiously to all sides even as he whooped deeply for air.

The din and firelight of the stronghold were far above him. From the howls, roars, and banging of metal, it was clear that Fanswell's Fanatics and the Wall Water houseguards were having at each other on the footbridge. The nearly stagnant tailwater was vilely organic but nectar to him now that he'd cheated death. He searched urgently for Ghost, fearing that she was injured.

A pebble chunked into the water not far from his head, and he heard a low whistle. To one side, the sheer rock of the stronghold rose straight out of the channel; to the other, a narrow bank lay at the foot of the heights. From the bank came the low whistle once more.

"Over here, Doctor," Ghost called softly.

He breaststroked toward her, hearing minimal splashing as she waded onto the bank. "There's something big in the water," she warned him. "Shag ass, Doctor—delta V!" At the same time something brushed muscularly along his right hip, bowing him as if he were a cello.

With his feet still bleeding from their traverse of the cliff face above Wall Water, he was self-chumming bait. Still, he didn't panic but scissor-kicked in a blur, surging forward with temporarily redoubled strength.

His fingers clawed the bottom in the shallows as his elbow glanced off a submerged branch. Ghost was there to lend a hand, and moments later they were standing on a beach of coarse gravel, barefoot and muddy to the knees.

Both were unharmed except for minor damage. The dress uniform knee boots Ghost had slung from her belt were gone. "The keepers broke, and I lost them," she explained. "No time to diddle around looking for them. The Aquam're hunting us—or will be soon."

Wonder of wonders, Zinsser's formal dancing slippers had somehow stayed fastened inside his shirt. Gallantry demanded that he offer them to her, but why should he, he asked himself, when she was so parsimonious with any gesture of gratitude? Then, too, from the look he'd gotten at her maltreated feet—grunt feet, feet of a prison camp survivor—she was accustomed to going without. Easing the slippers over his lacerated toes and raw-meat soles, he waited for her to acknowledge his inspiration and daring in proposing the leap that had saved them, but she didn't.

She was as curt and distant as she'd been from the start—with the single exception of their interrupted sexual interlude on Periapt. He reminded himself sourly that her perversity knew no limits. She was probably *waiting* for him to intimate that he'd saved her life so that she could rub his face in the fact that she'd saved his on at least three occasions now. Rather more, depending on how one chose to tabulate events at Wall Water.

"We'll make for the lakeside," she said. "Try for line-of-sight contact with the *GammaLAW* by plugphone." He heard the safety on her pistol click as she brusquely turned her back on him to move out. "Stay behind me." It was not a suggestion but an order.

He felt his self-restraint, never abundant, going up in smoke. He was Raoul Zinsser, winner of the Lyceum science medal, the GammaLAW mission's best hope of communicating with the Oceanic, whereas Ghost was nothing but a paroled war wog from a defeated planet who'd been sentenced to serve LAW under arms, a minor Ext peeress driven half-feral, half-preter-human by the atrocities of POW and concentration camps.

He had never resented a woman worse or needed one so excruciatingly, and his conquests were legion.

A commotion erupted farther down the watercourse, in the direction in which it emptied into Ea. The glimmer of lanterns and torches appeared at ground level, Aquam numbered in the dozens, their armor, weapons, and gear clanking. It was unlikely that they were looking for Zinsser and Ghost, but that didn't change the fact that the soldiers were beating the bushes and blocking the way to the lake. With the *Sword* atomized, no Aquam were likely to be merciful to offworlders that night.

"We'll push inland, circle east," Ghost revised. "Break our trail. Then bushwhack back to the beach, signal for extraction."

There were far too many indigs for the ten rounds she had left in her 'baller. The Ext-issue sidearm had a sonics acoustor mounted under the barrel, but sound weps had already proved ineffective against Aquam in padded armor. The thought of being gutted like a fish by an Aquam pole-arm made Zinsser forget all about rebuking her. They moved across an open aquaculture work area, where he bumbled into a stack of traps and bumped his hip on a sorting table.

Ghost scanned the wood line with her pistol scope in IR mode. "There's a footpath leading uphill."

Moving on, she squatted to retrieve something she'd spotted: a couple of decayed and perhaps infested rags from the water-farming operation. But she knotted them around her feet without hesitation.

"Barefoot escape and evasion is no fun at all, Doctor," she told him with gallows amusement.

Zinsser understood that she was speaking from experience. He trailed her between overhanging fronds and branches while grasses and undergrowth brushed their legs. The strange odors of the Aquam plant life smelled like exotic medicines. Flying things swarmed around them: bite-mites, bloodflits, teardrinker midges, and earborers. The need for speed and quiet kept Zinsser's swatting and slapping to a minimum. Ghost didn't seem to notice the pests' existence.

There were rustlings and skitters in the branches overhead and *ool?-ool?-ool?* sounds from a multitude of small voice boxes. Wetness sprinkled Zinsser. He thought a freak rain had broken the dry spell until he got a whiff of himself.

"Sonuva*bitch!*"

"Mum up, Doctor," Ghost told him in an undertone. "Tree imps. Can't hurt you."

Perhaps not, he told himself, but the little fiends could keep pissing at him. After a bit they started a haphazard bombardment of feces, twigs, and rotten fruit, making Zinsser feel the imps had taken up where the fates had left off.

A hundred meters up the winding footpath they struck a more open stretch, and the tree imps broke off their sport. That far out of the chasm, moonlight showed Zinsser that they'd intersected a cart or sledge track. He almost turned his ankle in a deep rut, bumping into Ghost's back as she halted without warning. As she turned, the smaller of Aquamarine's two moons, Sangre, highlighted the dark patterns of the death scars etched into her face. Having administered them to her beautiful face in a long-unpracticed Ext ritual, she considered herself dead, freed of the life she'd known as Fiona Orman. As a result she had, so far as Zinsser could tell, no fear whatsoever of physical danger or oblivion.

She put her had over his mouth to keep him quiet; someone was coming up the trail from the direction of the tail water outlet where they'd spied the Aquam troops. It didn't take Ext Skills training or a nightfighter's ears to tell that it was someone thoroughly winded, bulky, and not given to stealth.

Ghost chambered a round, clicked off the safety, and aimed the weapon in a two-handed grip. "Stop where you are," she said coolly and low in passable Aquam-dialect Terranglish. "Move and I'll kill you."

CHAPTER SIX

Wrenched from the outflow conduit's service track, Burning struggled to ward the WHOAsuit from impacting against the walls. What with failing power and air supply, repeating the long climb was out of the question, and so he went with a high-risk contingency plan.

Souljourner was grunting and muttering incoherently. He bridged against her to spare her what battering he could as the exo was washed along like a toy soldier in the torrent of a fire hose. If his body continued to gobble its stores of oxygen as hers had, he'd be in the same shape before long. But for the moment the Descrier's Apex was helping to keep him highly focused.

The hull gonged with the overlapping notes of impact; one of the mercury-vapor lamps shattered. The clear dome hit once, again, and a third time, but the ceramic glass held. Burning's Hussar Plaits protected his head from the bashings it took against the dome rim.

At last the sides of the vent were gone, and their speed diminished a sliver as they were whirled through the dam's plunge pool. When he managed to arrest the violent tumble, the suit's remaining lamp showed him more Nixies than before—a curtainy hemisphere of them, closing in. He thumbed the emergency hydroturbojets into active mode, and the ram pump-fed jets blasted them into motion. Deploying auxiliary control surfaces, he described a snapping arc just short of the lead Nixie's swirling tendril, then rocketed back into the outflow vent like a bat reentering hell.

The chemical reaction in the hydroturbojets sent the heat gauges spiking, and the turbines sounded as if they were trying to tear loose of the exo's back. But he went full throttle nevertheless, shooting into the outflow vent at twenty-five knots and climbing. With the suit's arms hugged close, he steered with a thumb ministick and a thumb-forefinger pistol grip. The infested sides of the conduit flashed by in a blur as the suit's speed climbed to thirty knots, then forty, the opposing current notwithstanding. A telltale signal warned that the jets' liquid lithium was almost depleted, as was their air supply. Souljourner lay heavy and silent on him, dead or dying.

When the left jet sputtered for a split second, Burning corrected it infinitesimally; then the same thing happened to the right. As the turbo's thrust diminished, he prepared himself to reach out, grab hold, and fight on. Suddenly, however, the conduit walls disappeared, and they were jetting through the still darkness of the Pontos Reservoir. The final moments of thrust had put them beyond the suction of the outflow vent. But something massive filled the sonar: an intake tower for diverting water to Rhodes's stronghold, the Optimant dam's former water-testing station.

Burning veered sharply, but what began as a bank ended as a drift as the hydroturbos died. The remaining lamp dimmed, so he shut it off to keep from drawing Aquam eyes. The WHOA lacked sufficient compressed air to blow all the ballast water, but he groggily realized that he could drop any buckled-on hard ballast. When he did, the exo began to rise, unpowered, for the surface.

Souljourner was still slumped against him. Mercifully, there was no need for decompression. Even so, the world was rapidly fading to black. Burning waited punch-drunkenly with one hand on the dome control and the other holding his pistol for the waters to part and the lake to admit it was beaten.

No sooner did the suit surge to the surface than he cracked the dome seal and muscled it back. The night air felt wintry and oxygen-enriched after the body-heated and much-rebreathed atmosphere of the exo; filling his lungs was like rebirth itself. The unprecedented Flowstate brought on by the Apex concoction had subsided, but being able to draw breath was sheer ecstasy.

A crackly frond from a drifting algeol raft brushed the open dome, and he pushed it away quietly. His most immediate concern—that there'd be a flatboat of Aquam ready to pour flaming oil down the open collar ring—went unrealized.

They had surfaced a few dozen meters offshore. Burning saw a modest hamlet, poorly lit. A glance at it through his 'baller's IR scope revealed aquaculture tackle everywhere but no sign of inhabitants. Faint chirps and birrings issued from the place, but they were largely overwhelmed by the rumble of high explosives from the far side of the dam.

Souljourner stirred the moment the fresh air hit her. Eager for as much of it as she could get, she pushed at him. He forced himself to hunch down and lean aside, warning, "Don't capsize us."

She partly unlimbered from her place in the dorsal bulge and propped herself on his shoulders to suck in the sweet atmo. Her skirts fell from where they had been bunched around her sternum to drape his right shoulder, her knee crushing his epaulet. He sculled cautiously with the suit's hands and soon felt its feet touch bottom in a clod-hopperish toe-dance.

"Can you walk us to the strand?" she panted.

"Not in this steel stroller. Besides, we can't have it falling into indig—uh, enemy hands."

Burning had no idea where the hamlet's loyalties lay—with Rhodes, with other grandees, or with the pom-pom-wearing raiders who had attacked him and Souljourner in Wall Water's PeelHouse. The Aquam were technologically regressed but not stupid; given a few clues and some free thinking, someone was liable to figure out where they had gone.

"Does the reservoir harbor Nixies as well?" he asked after a moment.

"I think not. All tales have them in Ea."

He stood on the suit's crotch saddle and dragged himself up to view the dam crest road. Sangre was casting a soft salmon light on the press, struggle, and stymied milling of thousands of people. In flight from the fighting at Wall Water, everyone was attempting to cross the dam from the north side to the south. Even without vision enhancers he could see there would be no returning to the stronghold by way of the crest road. He supposed it would be possible to make his way to the lakeside from the south end of the dam.

Both onshore and on some of the floating aquaculture equipment were the faint lamps commoners often made do with—translucent fish-gut bags containing blue-green bio-phosphorescent algae, looking a bit like softly glowing balloon figures. By their light, as well as that spilled from cressets on the dam, Burning saw a nearby floater moored to a pontoon, tied in turn to a dock of undressed wham-boo, a red carpet to dry land. The suit had just enough juice to tweak the propfans. The exo wove ponderously among glassy filaments of twistgrass, floating purse seine maw-maw hatcheries, and submerged casks of fingerfin roe.

Burning couldn't resist whispering, "What's the deal with that pep powder you gave me?"

Her faint lisp in his ear tickled. "Apex is a Descrier secret, although it doesn't turn them as dauntless as it does you. I myself find it unpleasant, but, um, I procured some from the praepostor of Pyx before I took leave. Want more?"

"No, thanks," he said quickly. That might be pushing his luck too far. "But don't lose it."

He bumped the suit against the floater and grabbed hold. Souljourner happily jumped ship, squirming past him while he got a grip on a coarse line of snort-heather hemp that was attached to a piling. She stepped on his head as she crossed over, but he didn't care. She was agile despite her mass. She lay low and quiet on the floater, rolfing her leg muscles with her thumbs and keeping watch.

The WHOA had to be disposed of. He tied off the line on its hoisting hardpoint, then stripped to his cod-cup, which required close-quarters gymnastics. He passed clothes, boots, and—after a brief hesitation—his pistol to her. Untying the WHOA and backing it off a few meters, he sat on the collar ring and opened the water-ballast tanks manually.

He rocked the exo, and it surrendered woodenly, shipping water through the open collar, first a little, then, with a rush, enough to drag it under. It sank silently beneath him as he breaststroked away, Ka-Bar knife in his teeth and watchful for hungry lake dwellers. Someone would find the suit eventually, but that was a problem for later.

Souljourner stared openly as he dressed. Serving in a mixed-gender military had gotten him past much of his body shyness, but he was glad she couldn't see how furiously he was blushing. She'd taken a lantern from one of the boats but was shrouding it.

Burning tried his plugphone, but all freqs were still howling with static. Drawing his sidearm, he led Souljourner toward the discord of the dam crest roadway, the floater and dock creaking under their weight. Along the water's edge were work huts, storage lean-tos, and such, all as movable as the pontoon catwalks. The hamlet proper was a hundred meters up the slope, above what was likely the high-water mark during the Big Drench monsoons.

The gun's scope showed Burning that the place consisted of three sizable black glass domes—Optimant artifacts—surrounded by trapezoidal cottages of brick and tile clustered behind fences of wooden fretwork. Family compounds, they looked to be locked up tight, as were the glass domes themselves. The night was punctuated by chirpings, fluting caterwauls, and other eerie sound effects uttered by caged and penned watchpets, but no one came forth to investigate.

"Don't they care that someone's out here?" Burning whispered.

"With Visitants hurling skyfire and Militerror fighting Killmonger?" she said. "With the world run riot and mobs afoot? Floaters and traps are easy to replace. Canny farmers will sit behind locked gates with their crossbows and tridents handy until order returns."

He grunted. "My kind of people."

Shortly, they found a hard-packed little barrow track that led uphill. Walking it, they heard reverbs and stridulations in the undergrowth from sources even his IR scope couldn't always pick out. The racket that sounded like metal files grating together were bronze boo-hoos, Souljourner told him.

"We need disguises," he remarked as they ascended the rise and the uproar on the road grew louder.

Souljourner made a mocking hum. "Redtails, every Ean is engaged in battle or scared for his life. The highways teem with the fleeing. Who'd pause to ogle us? And who outside Wall Water knows what a Visitant Ext and a jinxed Descrier look like?"

"Are you jinxed?" he asked.

She was slow answering. "*I* think not. The only bad luck I've had is with people who believe I'm bad luck. Rolande, back at Pyx, said it's all a lot of taradiddle and whigamaleerie."

"Exactly what I was gonna say."

She clicked her tongue and gave his shoulder a pat, relieved that he didn't subscribe to the superstition of a disaster-bringing female Descrier. Feeling her touch and recalling her pubis pressed to his back in the WHOAsuit, Burning supposed it was just as well his codcup was clammy and cold. No time for fantasies just now.

The barrow track swung up over a hillock that over-looked a rugged, rutted excuse for a connector road and the dam crest highway itself, illuminated by the glow of occasional palanquin lamps and rush lights.

Hordes of Aquam—foreigners, itinerants, those with no safe ground to call their own—didn't share the hamlet inhabitants' willingness to sit tight behind locked gates. Traffic had overflowed the connector and margins, and it was clear that no one had ever heard of keeping to the right. People and livestock milled, shoved, and struggled violently. One look told Burning that there would be tramplings and death. But Souljourner was right about the needlessness of disguises. What few soldiers and paramilitaries he saw—none in trappings he recognized—were intent on making themselves scarce rather than exerting authority. It was all they could do not to be bodily swept away.

The stretch from the dam south to the muscle car parking mounds showed cataclysmic damage from the Cyberplagues two hundred years earlier. The few remaining fragments of hardtop were buckled, tilted, and decaying, and the dirt and gravel connector rambled over and around the broken terrain. Neither Rhodes nor anyone else had gotten around to improving the route, and so the cumbersome, underpowered muscle cars were obliged to halt some eleven kilometers from the dam itself.

Barrow-coolies, palanquin bearers, and porters moved people and freight between the mounds and points north, including Wall Water and the landing ground of the Flying Pavilions. Mission intel indicated that Rhodes preferred it that way as a means of keeping any mobile invasion force away from his stronghold.

Burning took his bearings. Soldiers had tried to seal off the dam crest road, but the sheer weight of people and other traffic had brushed them aside. He thought he saw fighting in and around the stronghold, but that hardly mattered since there was no going that way. He prayed Ghost had made it safely back to the SWATHship. Either the GammaLAW mission could be salvaged or the whole business would come to nothing. All he and the Exts could do for the present was stay alive and serve out their parole. In retrospect, surrendering to LAW may have been a mistake. And after tonight, if the Exts wanted to choose a new Allgrave, he would accept it.

A smokey haze hung over Lake Ea, obscuring the *GammaLAW*. Even so, making his way south remained the most sensible plan. Taking on native camouflage wouldn't present a problem, since every other wayfarer was veiled, helmeted, or shielded from view in sedan chairs.

Souljourner pointed southwest. "I came this route from Pyx. An hour along the connector meets a byway that will take us to the lakeshore pike."

"Yeah, but how long before Rhodes's soldiers start beating the bushes for Visitant stragglers from the Grand Attendance?"

Souljourner returned a forelock toss that on Scorpia was a shrug. "All is uncertainty and danger. There's proof—those people making ready to travel far and fast if need be. See them don their shoes?"

Aquam of all types stopped at the side of the road or twisted around where they were stuck in traffic to pull on footgear. Buskins or sandals went on feet that looked accustomed to going bare; clumsy wooden sabots or worn-out straw slippers were exchanged for boots and other stout wear by those who had it. The average Aquam was poor beyond most Periapts' or Exts' comprehension, and good walkware was nothing to waste on day-to-day use. Back before the Concordance War Burning wouldn't have understood what Souljourner was getting at. But now the mere act of donning footware said volumes about people's apprehensions.

Scanning the milling masses, he suddenly felt his distance from events evaporate. "*JeZeus!*"

His eye had been drawn to some barrow-coolies struggling with a two-wheeled cart. By the light of torches he saw that a tarp had been partially dragged off the cargo, exposing a trussed-up body. The face was turned away from him but there was no mistaking the hood pulled down over the prisoner's head. Given the glitter of its circuitry and the gleam and configuration of its neuralwares, it could only be the cybercaul his sister had plucked from Rhodes's bedchambers.

"Ghost!" he shouted. "Ghost!"

CHAPTER SEVEN

Zone's cruel mention of freaks had given Lod his temporary solution for the all too substantial problem of what
to do with Scowl-Jowl. Reaching the Science Side of the
ship—the starboard trimaran hull—Lod led the Manipulant
to the Aggregate's new and makeshift Habitat, the group's
nest-commune-lab spaces.

The habitat looked less like a working-berthing complex than an organiform art installation cross-pollinated
with an array of cyberinterface gym machines. While most
GammaLAW belowdecks spaces were stifling hot even in
darkness, the Aggregate's domain was comfortably cool
thanks to a thermocouple water chiller unit they'd cobbled
together.

Piper came to stand before the Special Trooper. A shaven
headed gamine with enormous, wounded eyes flecked with
apricot hues, she seemed even smaller and younger standing
before the devil-faced Goliath in the bloodstained combat
coverall. She had a scattering of freckles across an upturned
nose, and her lips always struck Lod as incongruously full
for her waifish face. She looked slight and underfed even in
her baggy everywear onepiece.

"Why do you bring this one here?"

Piper didn't say it with quite the same slow, deliberate
emphasis most constituents used speaking to Alones—their

word for unaugmented humans deaf to the rich forms and dimensions of the group's all-senses Othertalk. Brought together on Periapt as hero and heroine of the Lyceum Ball, Piper and Lod had reached a heightened level of communication all their own.

"Your former mentor conceived and managed the early phases of the Manipulant project," Lod explained. "You know Sarz's design theories and technical secrets better than anyone."

Piper winced when he said the name. Some of the dozen other constituents, silent as usual, showed agitated kine-sign microgestures. Piper had killed Byron Sarz—both her mentor and lover—during the insanity at the ball to stop him from murdering a total stranger named Lod as well as nearly all the members of Periapt's Hierarchate. Ironically, it was Sarz's death that had resulted in Piper's elevation. As his handmaiden and the only other constituent competent to deal with Alones, she had been thrust into the role of nexus—leader and orchestrator of the group mind that was the Aggregate.

She moved a step closer to the Manip. "It's wounded."

"Yes, not that that's slowed him any. He's called Scowl-Jowl. Sick bay's sending over a medic as soon as they can free one up, but I thought you could do something in the meantime."

Piper moved closer to the Manipulant, who'd begun making low, gurgling, somehow imploring sounds. Lod saw her nostrils flare and quiver as she moved in, trying to scentse what Scowl-Jowl was attempting to convey, to understand by olefaction, as constituents did one another. It was the Aggregate's faculty for Othertalk that Dextra Haven hoped one day to employ in communicating with Aquamarine's Oceanic.

Piper made low, guttering sounds of her own. Then, all at once, Scowl-Jowl snatched her close, her shoulders and upper arms disappearing under clawed hands as big as seat cushions, her bare feet hanging a half meter above the deck. Lod held his place, but only because he had a clear shot at the Manipulant from that angle, just in case.

Here, in the habitat, Lod was the freak or, rather, the handicapped one, insensate to a rich medium of nonverbal, not conventionally visual interplay all around him. An Alone, just like the rest of the human race.

Normally timid around anyone who wasn't an Aggregate member, the other constituents looked untroubled by the presence of the engeneered soldier. Scowl-Jowl was handling Piper tenderly—reverently, Lod might have said. Its nose flaps mantled wide as it sniffed at her mouth and armpits; it raised her effortlessly to snuffle at the crotch of her everywear.

Lod cleared his throat uncomfortably. "Here, here, now..."

"Lod, hush," Piper ordered.

She made another bottomed-out sump pump noise that prompted Scowl-Jowl to lower her. Even before her feet touched the deck, she was conveying instructions to her fellow constituents with Saytalk, kinesign, and more. The conventional speech of the Aggregate, Saytalk was so condensed and accelerated by elisions, aphereses, and surd words that it was lost on Alones.

Doogun, Wire, and the rest jumped to their tasks, some turning to their odd systemry and others breaking out containers and vacpacks of Aggregate-style food concentrate. They spoke incomprehensible bursts of cyber-argot to chemical assemblers and programmed a sound synthesizer to make the habitat resound with nearly subsonic biorhythm pulses, to which Scowl-Jowl nodded in time.

As Piper gently eased herself out of Scowl-Jowl's grip, Lod caught new, alien aromas being compiled and breathed into the workspace by Aggregate apparatus. Scowl-Jowl inhaled mightily, eyes closed in what approximated bliss.

Miri and Kape had dumped liters of food concentrate into a mixing bowl—a glop that resembled pulpy porridge or high-fibre papier-mâché. Piper hand scooped the stuff into her mouth until her cheeks bulged, worked it around, then spit it back into the bowl. Miri pitched in on the masticating and spitting while Kape worked the expectorated food into the mass with a large ladle. Other constituents bustled by to dab or squirt additives into the congealing mess.

Bolus rations, Lod told himself, the dietary staple of the Special Troops. He shuddered to think what a Manipulant mess hall might be like.

When Piper flicked a brief bodybraille message on the back of Kape's neck with her fingertips, he filled a smaller bowl with the intermixed virgin and pre-chewed food concentrate. Then Piper offered it to Scowl-Jowl like an attending vestal.

Lod expected the creature to fall to like a ravenous ogre, but Scowl-Jowl accepted the bowl with stiff dignity. He slurped down a mere taste and restrained himself from upending the bowl, although his huge body trembled with reaction and craving. By what Lod took for an act of will, the Manip set the serving bowl aside. Then he swept out his enormous chopper knife—a cross between a butcher's axe and a martial arts meat cleaver—and raised it high.

Lod gulped, having once seen a battlesuited Ext cut most of the way in two by a single blow from one of the giant *moplahs*. The constituents' Alltalk wasn't apprehensive, however, and so he did his best to stay staunch. Piper was standing stock-still in expectation.

Having shown the blade to all present, Scowl-Jowl dropped to one knee before Piper and placed the chopper on the deck with a clang like a fallen manhole cover, its haft toward her. As he reached for her right foot, Piper leaned on his shoulder to allow him to press a ritual kiss on her instep.

She received the obeisance as solemnly as a queen. When Scowl-Jowl had set her foot back down, she drew the creature to his feet. Both hands were needed to lift the *moplah* and return it to him. At her urging he sat, and when she pressed the serving bowl into his claws, he dug in, gulping greedily. Miri and Kape were already filling another bowl.

Lod let go of his pistol. Well, polish my wagstaff and call me Smiley, he told himself. Scowl-Jowl had found himself a home aboard the *GammaLAW.* Unexpected, too, was that fact that Lod could actually envy a monstrous, engeneered war 'ware.

When the medic showed up at the habitat, Piper made Scowl-Jowl lie still and endure treatment. The Manipulant's wounds turned out not to be life-threatening, though he was nearing the end of his limited life span. The medic had also brought Scowl-Jowl's bloopgun and bandoliers of ammunition, which Kape and Doogun unobtrusively piled in a metal equipment locker.

Lod joined Piper to one side while the corpsman worked. "I should be getting back to Commissioner Haven," he told her.

Piper's enormous eyes searched his. "It was ... terrible at Wall Water?"

"Worse. It was needless, wasteful, and bestial. Violence always is." He refused to burden her with mention of the face-off with Zone in the passageway, even though she was bound to grasp from his Othertalk that he was withholding something.

Piper caressed his hand and watched his face, reading his untutored scentspeech, bodybraille, and kinesign. "Lod, don't leave yet."

Her existence was defined by Alltalk rhythms, inner harmonies, and dissonances. He knew enough about that wider perceptual world to appreciate that she needed to bring their sync closer, or she would feel pain from it.

The area surrounding the habitat's compartments was in refit disorder. Constituents were bunking right there in the work spaces, so there was no private snuggery to which they could retire. Lod took a flier, opening the communicating door to the next compartment aft and leaving it to her to follow. Luck wasn't with him, however, in that he entered a onetime stores locker no bigger than a clothes closet with another door giving access to the passageway. For whatever reason, the locker had timeworn, slightly raised flooring that gave out tortured squeaks and creaks with even the slightest movement. Piper followed him in, anyway, latching the door to the habitat behind her.

"No good," he whispered. "No room to stretch out. If we move around, your comrades will hear the deck squealing." *JeZeus Chisto*, he thought, the fish would probably hear it downriver at the New Alexandria lighthouse!

She contradicted him with a look he'd learned to recognize and respond to. "We don't need to do either."

They shifted as minimally as they could to bring his shoulders up against the bulkhead. Then she opened his dress uniform, and he, her baggy every wear onepiece. A few deck creaks and the clunk of his pistol belt hung from a convenient spigot were all the noise they let slip, aside from their own panting.

After months of flirtation he was avid for her. He knew she was giving off very different aroma messages now, even if he was only scentsing them on a subconscious level. She was adjusting her pheromones and smart secretions to him, cultivating erotic control and ceding him the same over her without any Alone qualms about free will or morality. Utterly unlike the glamour-painted, spike-heeled sex Valkyries he was usually drawn to, Piper was imprinting herself on him with the alien demeanor of a nexus, though what she would receive from him in return, he couldn't guess. Perhaps his Aloneness was a partially blank canvas for her, a cool medium for her self-definition. Or maybe she was an oddity even among the constituents, craving to grow and make contact beyond the confines of the Aggregate.

Whichever, he understood that she was about to ruin him for other women and, he surmised, willingly ruin herself for constituent lovers. One small comfort: They were safe from unwanted conception. Lod had undergone the mission's standard contraceptive regimen. The constituents had them waived because of their acute sensitivity to physiological change.

Piper lifted one foot out of the everywear, and he clasped her to him in a standing embrace. Partially nude, their bodies showed hints of arrested adolescence. They were a good match in height, as well. She stood with her right arch on the instep of his right foot; each wrapped their left leg around the other. She ran her small fingers through his sandy hair, and he caressed her sleek pate.

They inhaled, tasted, and stroked each other; probed with tongues; and drew deep, intimate breaths. Piper angled her head and jaw to his to achieve a sliding taste-buds-to-taste-buds interface that aroused her even more, communing with his senses there, too, calibrating herself to him.

Surely she could read his hidden emotions in the composition of his sweat, his preoccupations, in the kinesign of his face. When, long afterward, he considered it in the abstract, it disturbed him that she'd penetrated his defenses so effortlessly. But united with her, it was impossible to be abstract about it.

With his help and only halfhearted objection from the flooring, she went on tiptoe to sheath him in herself. Slickened and feverish, she clenched almost prohibitively tightly, making it a challenge for him, knowing how the drama of it would incite him. And when he was inside her, her arms around his neck and his under hers to bear her up, she wrung ragged breaths and stifled moans from him.

Clinging to him, Piper gripped and expressed him with rolling, varying contractions, while Lod forgot about everything else that had ever happened to him or ever might and merely soared. Anticipating his climax, she increased her pace and force to join him. The sensations were so forcibly ecstatic that she had to cover his mouth to keep him from crying aloud. They shivered and shuddered, bit their own lower lips and one another's shoulders, but kept their ardent passion silent.

God help me, was the thought that sneaked in at the edges of his transcendent bliss. I'm petrified; I'm undone. I've fallen in love with her!

But so happy, damn me.

"How long till daylight?" Kurt Elide heard somebody ask. "What time is it, anyway?"

"Zero gooner hundred," a disgruntled voice with an Ext accent retorted. "You supply a crock, we'll drink to it."

That sounded good to Kurt. He doubted, though, that there was much of the Aquam brain solvent aboard the *GammaLAW*. Now that indig had slain Visitant, and Visitant indig, supplies of both LAW-issue grog and bootlegged local stuff were likely to be hoarded with a vengeance.

Not that an intoxicants shortage was high on Kurt's list of apprehensions. Aside from the fact that he could take the stuff or leave it, the GammaLAW mission had been pitched into a crisis worse than any he'd faced in his eighteen baseline-years. He couldn't even get a real grip on it. A former civil service transport pool driver, the only child of well-off if somewhat detached parents, he'd enlisted on impulse, after meeting Captain Chaz Quant.

Somebody bumped into him where he was sitting, exhausted, with his back against the bulkhead. A combat boot kicked his foot hard. "Keep your big flatbeds out of the damn way, crewie," the Ext who'd spoken warned, gruff and threatening in the way that had earned them all the sobriquet Growlers. Kurt struggled wearily to move, but the Ext's voice suddenly took on a less hard-ass note.

"You were the one took the blowboat's controls, right? Got us outta that shoot-up on the beach. Nice play. As you were, kid."

The Ext was helping another Concordancer whose dress uniform was bloodied at the left side. The wound couldn't have been too serious, however, since both men had tarried by the hovercraft *Northwind* instead of reporting to sick bay. Ordinarily, with the ship at general quarters surface action, there would have been a battle dressing station nearby for more timely aid, but with the *GammaLAW* so shorthanded, medical resources were being concentrated in the ship's surgery.

Comradely words from a Growler left him gaping, but Kurt struggled to his feet once the Exts were past. With everything gone to shit in a centrifuge, his days as Dextra Haven's assistant were probably behind him. Now he was supposed to report to some watch, quarter and station he couldn't even recall.

A half dozen steps down the passageway he heard the stagy voice of Lazlo-Lazlo calling him. "Kurt! I've been searching high and low for you. Have you lost your senses?"

Kurt swung around to confront Lazlo's mad-poet face and the camera that had come to seem like a biosynergic adjunct of it. An avant-garde artist, he held that fiction and drama had been eclipsed by the vicarious reality of electronic reportage and actuality media. He'd signed on for the mission intending to make its story his magnum opus, though Dextra Haven, woefully underfunded, had approved him only because his participation had opened the door for a sizable arts grant under an obscure funding title.

Once under way, however, Lazlo had discovered that no one was in the least interested in abetting his bid for immortality, though that hadn't kept him from settling, for his own eccentric reasons, on Kurt as the personification of the GammaLAW experience.

"Lazlo, turn that fucking camera off."

"I heard there was utter mass murder ashore. I *knew* I should've insisted on going!" Lazlo-Lazlo was circling him, trying different cam angles. He was a pale, sleepy-looking young man with a scraggly goatee, many finger rings, and a penchant for Regency clothing.

"I don't have time for this synaptshit stuff, Lazlo."

"Don't be absurd. Without my footage the mission might as well end here and now. I must have you while it's all still fresh in your mind. So start at the beginning; omit no detail or nuance!"

"Lazlo, we're at battle stations! Even you're supposed to be…somewhere."

"Bosh." Lazlo paused in his camming to record as little as possible of himself. His documentaries were said to be antiseptically free of Lazlo except in that his presence hovered above and around them invisibly, like God's.

"Some officious sprocket tooth ordered me to report to some other sprocket tooth," he was saying. "I ignored her, of course. What would you have me do, Kurt, ignore all these wonderful scenes playing out to every side? It's glorious, it's *figmental!*"

" 'Glorious'? God knows how many we've lost, we're marooned about as far from Periapt as we could get, our lives 're on the line—"

"Stop being infantile! My genius and this admittedly sticky run of luck are going to give us everlasting celebrity!"

"You viewfinder-blinded jerkpud! Take off that cam and open your eyes! *You're in the picture now!*"

Kurt reached for the headset, but Lazlo resisted with surprising energy. Words were fast devolving into grunts and curses when somebody yelled, "Neutral corners! Break it up!"

Ungentle hands pulled them apart. Kurt swung around to confront a large bosun's mate damage controlman from Engineering and Hull Group, backed up by enlisted ratings of various ranks.

"You two meatslappers need exercise," the big bo snarled, "I'm just the guy you want." He checked Kurt's newly issued insignia. "Deck Division, huh?"

"Yes, but they're going to slot me into Aviation Group—or were, anyway." Kurt had been planning to hack for flying officer training once the mission was up and running.

"As of now you're in my repair party," the bo declared, then turned to Lazlo-Lazlo. "What's your story, Scarlet Pimpernel?"

The documentarian drew himself up. "Out of my way, you dullskull. I'm a civilian, part of the commissioner's Arts and Education Advisory board."

"All I care is you're a warm body," the bo countered, "which means you're just another workwog like the rest of us. Captain's orders."

Lazlo stiffened. "This is enslavement—"

The bo plucked him off his feet by the lapels. "You give me any lip, and I'll chuck that fancy cam out a porthole."

The documentarian's expression told Kurt that he didn't care much for being on the far side of the lens.

CHAPTER EIGHT

"Ghost!" Burning called again. "Ghost!"

There was no reaction from the bound figure in the barrow, though the same couldn't be said for the eight seminaked coolies who had been hauling and pushing the two-wheeled cart. The biggest of the coolies, a burly lug in a ragged poncho and a veil that showed only his eyes, heard Burning's calls, pointed to him, and yelled something to his comrades.

Like most of their ilk, they wore rakish turbans and face paint in bizarre individualized designs—a poor man's version of the elaborate vizards and masks better-off Aquam sported. The coolies' faces were also streaked by sweat and coated with road dust, but Burning sensed something familiar about them, especially their apparent boss with his jagged crimson slashes, black eyebands, and white border.

"Pur—*Purifyre?*" Burning shouted. A Purifyre startlingly transformed from Human Enlightenment *rishi.*

Recognizing Burning, Claude Mason's indig son barked orders to his men. While half of them stayed at their fore-and-aft collars, the others began to grope in the barrows. One came up with a sling-gun, another with a brush hook–like weapon.

Burning already had his pistol out, but he was too far away to drop anyone with the 'wailer, and risking a hardball shot was out of the question with the uncertain light and the barrow with the bound captive jerking back and forth. Even with the IR scope, a round might catch Ghost, not to mention some passerby.

"Let's go!" he shouted to Souljourner. He cast himself down the hillock's sheer face in long, plunging side steps, leaving the Descrier to follow as best she could.

The lead barrow surged forward, some poor sod getting knocked down and run over by one of its wheels, then one of the wheels of a second barrow. Burning considered firing into the air to scatter the throngs but feared inciting a stampede that would block his path or unify everyone in an assault aimed at him.

Uncaring, he bulled into ranks of people milling at the roadside. A woman in a kimonolike robe, carrying a live rock-eel in a cage, swung at him with a gnarled wooden crook. A tinker in a tall, pink conical leather hat, bent under a sack the size of a bag chair, tried to bite him as Burning spun the man while passing by. He absorbed their blows, kicks, and curses without wasting an instant on retaliation.

Alien faces, attire, and smells whirled by him in a flash-card blur of Aquam. Other barrows hemmed him in, as did bunched-up families, clutching beggars, and overburdened porters. When he came up against a coffle of pack thralls trailing a six-bearer palanquin filled with a household's worth of curvilinear furniture, chests, and bedding, he let go a .50-caliber round into the dark sky. The report shook the ground as orange-white flame gushed from the porting and barrel mouth.

In the general frenzy to get clear of him, people were trampled and bowled over. The thralls—their collars roped together—wrenched one another in conflicting directions as their whip-bearing bullyraggers took to their heels. The coffle started to fall. Burning leapt over the line and saw, by the flicker of rushlights and butrywood knots, a barrow he recognized. It was the second of Purifyre's pair, laden with cargo boxes.

The commotion around him made it impossible to guard himself on all sides, even in Flowstate. A swipe of movement to his left brought him pivoting in that direction in time to see the veiled coolie complete a throwing motion, a knife already leaving his hand. At the same time, he felt a robust yank at his arm from behind.

Pulled off balance by Souljourner among the jostling and zoolike din of upset wayfarers, Burning watched the dark blade whicker past him and *bok* into the side of a beautifully carved mollywood harpshatina two pack thralls had dropped, stirring faint notes from the instrument's metal strings.

He flicked his 'baller's selector from .50-caliber to sonics and laid a sustained sound chain straight into the coolie, who collapsed bonelessly. Purifyre popped up to lower his man onto the second barrow, exercising remarkable strength for a guy his size. In the process the veil and turban were pulled away, revealing the face of Essa, Purifyre's female sidekick.

Braced against Souljourner, Burning regained his balance with *zanshin* dexterity. He brought the gun's 'wailer up for another shot, only to find that a palanquin and team of four had blundered into his line of fire. He was figuring his best route to the barrow-coolies when he realized that Souljourner, snarling between locked teeth, was trying to fend off a man who had seized her by the hair.

Her would-be assailant was an armed and armored fighter but not a soldier, Burning concluded, probably a guard employed by the people who owned the neck-roped thralls. He was a solid middleweight in muscled breastplate and culottes, holding a two-handed shortsword in his free hand. Souljourner was thudding his panoplied ribs with her left while fumbling at her waistband with her right. Again the hired guard shook her by the hair.

"Thief! Berserker! You'll pay for our losses!"

Burning had no clear shot, so he swung the 'bailer straight down on the man's sallet. The sallet made a ringing metallic thud like the report of Rhodes's steam cannon, and the man went cross-eyed. Letting go of Souljourner's hair, he rubber-legged back to topple onto a travois being hauled by a journeyman astrologer and his apprentice. The helm was strong, though—Optimant alloy, perhaps—and the 'wailer was worse for the acquaintance. The sidearm's housing was staved in, and busted components dropped from it.

What a fucktastrophy, Burning thought while he steadied Souljourner. "You hurt?"

She shook her head.

He had his mouth open to thank her for yanking him out of harm's way when his eye fell on the knife Essa had thrown. It was Ghost's soot-black, ripsaw-hilted heirloom dagger.

"They've got my sister," he rasped to Souljourner, launching himself once more. "Stay with me!"

"I'm fated to," she snorted, rising to the challenge.

The palanquin and team of four that had blocked Burning's second 'wailer shot was lost behind even more jumbled traffic. Several rickshaws were jammed around a gold-and-purple enameled four-seater sedan chair carrying a well-fed merchant family. Mixed in were vendors swinging iron-ferruled sticks at anyone who came too close. Teamsters to the rear were pushing and heaving a high-sided wain loaded with bolts of precious cloth and sloshing kegs, while hemming the gridlock in front was a clan of vizard sellers with their wares displayed on poles three meters high.

Burning wrenched his way through, drawing angry shouts, and evaded blows, kicks, and flung dung. When he arrived at where he'd last seen Purifyre's lead barrow, it was gone. Trying to scramble up over a grain sledge, he almost got himself quilled with sling-gun darts. People were ready to kill rather than be trampled. More wayfarers surged in around him, cutting off his view.

With an effort he made his way to the eastern shoulder of the road, thinking that he could move faster through the woods than Purifyre's barrows could through the crowd. Open fields were only meters away, but walling them off was some of the thickest undergrowth he'd ever seen. He was working up the resolve to begin thrashing his way through when Souljourner overtook him, tugging him away from long-thorned lianas, leaves that shone with greasy iridescence, and prickly scrub, all interlaced and looking tenacious.

"Are you ignorant to shinglewort and festerweed? Farmers plant them to protect the fields. Those spikes give one the creeping black sarcoma."

"So that's why nobody's boondocking it," Burning said.

"Cut over to the other shoulder," she advised. "It's somewhat thinned out there."

"I keep getting blocked," he told her as he did. "It's like people are deliberately running interference."

"Some may be," Souljourner told him somberly. "You've heard tales of the Embedded Way? No? Old Descriers say they are many who conspire to help Human Enlightenment in diverse ways. Let us circumvent any impedance they've arranged."

Burning complied. Having spent years in a retirement home for human earthquake detectors, Souljourner was the one with Aquam road savvy. After the way she'd come through the night, especially at the Peelhouse, he felt he could trust her—within reason. And, of course, her Holy Rollers had decreed that she was fated to travel with him.

They made better time on the western shoulder of the connector. Pushing forward with him, she panted, "Did you spy other Visitant prisoners in addition to your sister?"

"Not in the barrow."

She gave the tap of the forehead that meant *No, think again.* "In the second cart were boxes designed to contain Human Enlightenment's sacred ark and coffer. But anyone or anything could be inside."

It made sense. "Shit fire and save on ammo," Burning muttered.

For all he knew Dextra Haven was inside one of the boxes, sleeping off a conk on the coiffure. Or maybe Purifyre's group had made off with a warhead from Starkweather's *Jotan*. But those things didn't matter. He wasn't about to turn back, in any case, not until he had rescued Ghost.

Triggering up on the unidentified newcomer in the darkness of the hillside trail, Ghost hadn't used her IR scope for fear its dim light would make her a better target. Zinsser didn't doubt she'd drawn an accurate bead by sound.

As soon as the other squawked, "Spare me! I'm a harmless man sworn to peace and rationality!" they both knew who he was. Zinsser could almost feel the misty lisp coming from the man as he added, "Who's that purring her ruthlessness at a well-respected Sense-maker? Mistress Ghost, or am I wrong?"

"Spume!" Zinsser whispered. How he'd made it safely out of Wall Water was anyone's guess, especially given how his physical refurbishing at the hands of Glorianna Theiss hadn't won him many friends among the stronghold's court-iers. "Will this road take us down to the lake?"

"Ho, the good pedagogue Zinsser, sir! You'd get to the lake too quick for your liking, dragged by your dead heels by soldiery the grandees have set after me. They think that I'm enslaved by your offworld vitality treatments and that I connived in the bloodletting and sneak attacks tonight. Hence, with your permission, I've far to go in whatever direction will have me."

The old gasbag had been in bad enough odor at Wall Water when the GammaLAW mission had arrived: past his prime, vastly overweight, and sottish. His confidence and self-respect had been broken by the abuse and ridi-cule of his new principal, the Grandee Rhodes, the son of Spume's former liege. That he was acquainted with Claude Mason from the days of the *Scepter* survey mission put him further out of favor among the Aquam. A blowhard and a debaucher he was, but a collaborator in the violence? The idea was too asinine for words. It was the white-pom-pommed interlopers who'd thrown the whole stronghold into chaos, a force seemingly exterior to the Ean grandees' power struggles.

"Don't the grandees realize that those pom-pom raiders were responsible?" Zinsser started to say, when Ghost cut him off.

"He can tell us while we lam ass." Her civil tone owed to the liking she'd taken to the Sense-maker when he was aboard the *GammaLAW*. "Time to trot, Spume."

"I concur," Spume replied, wheezing and chugging as he took the lead and set a surprisingly strong pace. They followed him up a series of sharp switchbacks. When he turned back to talk to them, his voice was frequently lost in the huge, hardened leather shell of his ceremonial collar.

"—various sets of homicidals abroad. Those behind me bear rock-eels with which to sniff after quarry and enough sling-guns and cutlery to 'whelm even *you*, m'lady Scarmask."

"Sweet sanity," Zinsser hissed to himself.

"I thought the grandees were going at each other?" Ghost said in a field whisper.

Spume answered at like volume. "They realized in due course that they'd been had by the white-pom-pom raiders Dr. Zinsser made mention of and by DevOceanites who were sighted on the Wall Water grounds. As well as by, they believe, you offworld Visitants." He waited for the remark to sink in. "The Grandee Rhodes commanded his troops to capture or kill those DevOcean demonstrators who were out here earlier in the evening. He's in such an unbalanced mood, I shouldn't wonder if he decides to decrease local population pressure in general."

Zinsser had begun perspiring from the climb and the Big Sere midnight heat. The Sense-maker's news made him sweat harder and shiver at the same time. "So the grandees have agreed to form a united front?"

Old Spume made a juicy, flatulent sound. "They're a pack of conceited snollygosters, but they know it's the end of them if they don't. Your great ship is well armed, and their only chance against Madame Haven is to band together, at least for now—lo!"

Ghost and Zinsser had seen it, too: dim flickers of flame through the trees. They caught the acrid smell of smoke as Ghost swept the area with her 'baller scope. "The DevOceanites' rally site," she reported. "And now their burial ground."

As they eased closer, Zinsser saw what she meant. The hillside clearing was deserted except for three lifeless bodies wearing robes. The wooden post with its infinity symbol that the DevOceanites had burned to demonstrate their zeal had fallen and was all but consumed.

"I don't see their prophet Marrowbone here," Spume panted. "If he's canny, he'll flee all the way home to Passwater."

Zinsser knew that the sect's beliefs bordered on heresy in the minds of most Aquam. The DevOceanites held that true believers, reaching a state of grace, would one day enter the planet's single endless sea to become one with the Oceanic—a place, an entity, and a fate all regarded more or less as hell by other Aquam. Orientation briefings and materials had not mentioned friction serious enough to spark a pogrom, however.

Several trails converged in the clearing. The Sense-maker squinted hard in the moonlight. "That way leads back to the footspan where I saw houseguards battling Fanswell's Fanatics and from which you jumped, I take it. Right, so, we want this other one."

Zinsser could hear soldiers down below, working their way up the switchback. Peering down, he saw torches and long poles with cages at the end—the rock-eels, sniffing for spoor.

"What's your plan?" Ghost asked Spume as nonchalantly as if inquiring how his scalp follicle regen was holding up.

"A wise fish hides in the shoal," Spume answered. "It's over the hills for me, to the crowds at the landing ground of the Flying Pavilions."

"What about the other direction? Crossing the dam crest road?"

Spume pulled a long, overfleshed face. "It's now so packed with people that I saw some fall off, hit and skid, hit and skid all the way down the face of the dam. Getting across is out of the question for any who didn't start earlier. No, it's a nice ramble among the Laputa crowds for me."

"Invisibility's where you find it," Ghost pronounced.

Zinsser knew that dissent was useless. Out there in the aroused and murderous Aquam night he had no purchase on her. So on they went, topping the hilltop north of the stronghold that reared nearly as high as Wall Water's upper ramparts. Zinsser, like the other two, caught the stench and heard the wails long before they left the wood line.

An impromptu campground-market had been pitched there, a waiting place for the thousands of pilgrims and petitioners who had hoped to plead before the grandees or speak to the Visitants. Now it looked and smelled like a war zone. "One fiery lance from Commissioner Starkweather's air ship struck here," Spume explained.

"Close air-support missile," Ghost concluded. "Off target or no one would've survived." The *Jotan* aerospace shuttle had retaliated massively, pointlessly, against the stronghold and the countryside, but Starkweather had paid for it. Something had sent his flying fortress pranging and burning into Lake Ea.

Except for mourners wailing over the dead, the acres of camp were abandoned. Tents and shelters had been left where they stood, many riddled by shrapnel or split to ribbons by the blast. The smell of high explosives stung and rankled Zinsser's nostrils. Deserted cooking fires had burned out, some scattered by what must have been people stampeding right through them. From that vantage point they could see the dam crest road packed with humanity. Thousands more were crushing one another at the northern end to funnel onto it.

Spume struck a declamatory pose. "As you see, my astuteness is still strong." In the open and the moonlight they could see his tall, painted amphitheater of a collar and the robes that had been restored to their glory onboard the *GammaLAW*. They were as out of place on the bluff as Periapt formal wear.

Ghost had been trying her plugphone again, but all freqs were jammed. Worse, the SWATHship was nowhere in sight, and there was some kind of fog or cloud bank on Lake Ea. No picket ships could be seen, no CAPflights or recon helos, not even a surveillance reemo. "Spume's right," Ghost decided. "It'll have to be the Laputa landing grounds for now."

Zinsser curbed himself from looking at the twisted corpses, the bits of human anatomy scattered here and there. They came to a trio of children wailing over a sprawled body that might be a mother or father. It was difficult to tell since the corpse wore layered robes and had no head. Ghost surprised Zinsser by asking Spume, "D'you have any scudos? No? Any hard clink on you, Doctor?"

"Hardly. Nor is this the time for acts of charity."

Having lent her carbon-black combat knife to Claude Mason, she drew her backup knife—a short, flat one—and sliced free a gold cuff button. She shoved the button into the palm of the biggest child and wrapped the girl's fingers around it. "This is real," Ghost told her. "So they don't tip off the Militerrors about us," she explained to Zinsser and Spume.

Then she went to the corpse's other end and pulled the well-worn, dirty wooden klomps off it. With dirt-encrusted, long-nailed toes showing, the cadaver's sex was still impossible to call. Ghost tugged off the rag wrappings that had been holed and shredded on the climb up the hill, though she hadn't made a sound about it. Zinsser could see that she had a good eye: the wooden shoes were a fair fit on her, if a bit wide.

A sound like a lovelorn behemoth cut the night. Old Spume cocked an ear back the way they'd come. "Hist! An aeoliophone—Rhodes's Militerrors, signaling. Time to take heel, Mistress Ghost."

Ghost urged the kids toward the wood line to the west. "Soldiers. Go hide." They did, stumbling in shock.

"Ahem," Old Spume ventured. He plainly didn't want to move on without them. "Let us away. Let us, as the redoubtable Exts put it, 'deal a vee'. Just what *is* a 'vee,' by the by?"

CHAPTER NINE

"Signal officer reports no success defeating current jamming interference," Seaman Astarte Thu told Quant. "Our frequency agility does not avail. Signals inquires whether the captain wishes to deploy the aerostat."

Quant had given it a good deal of thought. Trailing a communications balloon from the fantail would increase the ship's range far beyond its present limits, even though that would mean little with all RATEL pushes jammed. Sig center could bounce microwaves off the 'stat's repeater, but the four missing shore party members' plugphones wouldn't likely be monitoring for them. In any case, no one had any idea which way to aim the transmissions.

Quant went onwire with the signals officer personally. "Signals, bridge. Do you have a positive fix on the jamming source?"

"Negative, Captain. We're getting lateral and bounce from everywhere. Analysis would indicate multiple emitters spotted all over this part of the hemisphere, principally in the Amnion. Beam strength in the gigawatt-plus range."

"Emitters how big?"

"By rough estimate, ranging in size from thirty to two hundred square kilometers, sir."

The answer staggered Quant, but he calmly told signals to keep him informed. If he had doubted just how powerful the Oceanic was, he knew now. Though how a superorganism of living plasm could whip up emitters of that size, much less power them, he couldn't begin to fathom. Much more important but even more unknowable was why. Perhaps the Oceanic thought it was rebuking the offworlders in a language they could understand.

Quant mentally reconsidered priorities. Raoul Zinsser might indeed be a far more crucial MIA than Burning or Mason, but it didn't alter Quant's decision about the aerostat. On top of other disadvantages, the towed 'stat might hamper maneuvering and crew effectiveness at action stations. Besides, it was the only gasbag the ship had, and he didn't want to risk it until he knew how hostile an environment Lake Ea had become.

"Hold the aerostat for now," he instructed signals. "Have you got the ARAAs unlimbered?"

"Yes, sir. Constant probe beam working." The voice from belowdecks was rueful. "It's become a very burst-rich environment up there."

The adaptive retrodirective antenna arrays were another backup system, designed for long-range communication via meteor burst—transmissions bounced off streamers of ionized gas painted briefly across the upper atmosphere by vaporizing space debris. Signals was grave and the incidence of wakes was high, because much of what had been *Terrible Swift Sword* was filtering down to be consumed on a funeral pyre of thermospheric air. Again, the MIAs' plugphones would be a long shot on the ARAAs, but the commo watch had to be tried.

Quant left the circuit and swung to his helmsman. "Bring her onto course three-one-niner."

"Coming to course three-one-niner, aye," the helmsman acknowledged. "Checking course three-one-seven magnetic. Maintaining turns for six knots."

It would be shallower water—closer to the lake's eastern shore—but Quant had decided to hazard it, hoping to see flares, strobes, or other visual signals from some of his lost aircraft and picket-boat people. The impact of Starkweather's *Jotan* munitions had been so terrible, Quant believed in his heart that most or all crewmembers had been killed instantly.

Earlier on Aquam rafts and floaters had been spotted by the dam, accompanied by highly anomalous acoustical signatures and signs of electrical activity. At the time Quant had been too busy looking for survivors, but now he wanted to know more. The floaters had withdrawn for the most part, but as the *GammaLAW* stood in closer to shore, detectors picked up the sonic output once more, originating from several sources close to the lakeside.

"Sounds like somebody doing sea-monster birdcalls underwater," a tech summed it up.

Quant thought of the mysterious pipe-organ contrivances that had been observed on some of the bigger aquaculture flat-boats. Before he could call for analysis, readings of underwater electrical activity leaped, quavered, and spiked again. Active sonar reported shadowy contacts against the bottom scatter, then lost them, then reported inconclusive ones. Tracking computers were getting dizzy designating and separating individual plots.

"Don't hand me 'inconclusive,' Chief," Quant told the sonar CPO softly but cuttingly. He moved out onto the abbreviated port wing of the bridge to scan the water and shoreline. Lieutenant Gairaszhek, Row-Row, and Astarte Thu moved after him, staying alert but out of his way.

"Large, multiple returns but not solid," the sonar chief updated.

When Quant summoned a feed of the imagery on his own visor, he saw that that was exactly the case. "Size?"

"In constant flux, Captain. Estimate up to one hundred meters square. Some movement against prevailing currents."

Quant recalled something from background briefings. "Biologicals?"

"Possibly, Captain."

Quant, who had had a hundred thousand things eating up his time and attention ever since he'd agreed to come to Aquamarine, regretted not having had just enough more of both to press for solid information regarding the half-mythical creatures rumored to live in the Ean bottom mud—the so-called Nixies. Those organisms had such eccentric and obscure life cycles that no substantive data about them had been gathered by the *Scepter* survey team. He got on the hardwire to engineering. "How many ROVers do we have operational?"

"Two, sir. A Mark X and a Travis civilian model from Science Side."

"Get the X ready for a swim."

Row-Row had had word from sonar: more plots were appearing with every passing moment. "The closest returns are at twenty fathoms and rising," he told Quant. "More ghost returns converging, directly beneath us."

"Sound 'collision,'" Quant ordered the quartermaster of the watch without taking his eyes from the water and furious that LOGCOM foot-dragging had deprived the ship of any way to strike at the creatures preemptively.

"Electrical field activity up," Astarte Thu chimed in. "Mean readings of forty volts across plots' surfaces."

Because seconds counted, Quant went on the PA personally. "HazCon warning, HazCon warning. All hands stand clear of electrical gear and conductive surfaces."

As he was repeating it, a fierce sibilance over the hardwire and howls from the flight deck mixed with the spattering and crackling of electrical arcing. Blue sparks snapped from the rail to Seaman Astarte Thu's poised hand, sounding like a string of miniature firecrackers.

As she was flung backward with a cry, Quant's visor went dark before his eyes.

"Is that Purifyre's barrow?"

Burning swept his pistol's scope to where Souljourner was pointing, down the dirt meanders of the beach spur track that ran from several lakeshore villages to the connector road. The connector was still packed with people but was less panic-tossed than it had been back by the dam.

"No. It's a rickshaw with a broken wheel."

"Then they must have gone on to the muscle car parking mounds on Jitterland Heights," Souljourner told him.

"How far?" he barked.

"Pushing hard, we can arrive by dawn."

Burning had asked himself over and over if he shouldn't get back to the ship and mount an airamphib operation that could carpet beat Scorpia up one side and down the other until Ghost was found. Given what the *Jotan* had done to the sky, however, there might be nothing to spare for a search-and-liberate op. And what if the so-called Embedded Way allowed Purifyre's group to simply vanish into the woodwork? With luck, the commo jamming would subside and he'd be able to call in enough mobile firepower to make all Scorpia roll over.

Without warning, Souljourner grabbed his epaulet. "Listen. Hear that?"

He cupped his ears. It came from the north, a martial-music ruckus raised by several different kinds of Aquam instruments. "Ululiphaunts?"

"And tubular gongs, aeoliphones, and ocarettes. You don't understand? Musics of the diverse grandeean elites, warning people on the road to clear the way. Burning, whatever happened at Wall Water, the grandees have banded together! Or at a minimum their best troops have— Militerrors and Diehards, Fanswell's Fanatics and the rest."

"They'll be making better time than us," Burning mulled, "even if they have to toss people into the shingle-wort to do it. You up for moving faster?"

Thumbing the rubbed-black drawstring pouch around her throat, she gave him the slow sideways head tic to signal *yes.* "For you I am."

She was rubbing it for luck, that much he understood, reinforcing the juju of her treasured Optimant dice, the lost Holy Rollers. He didn't understand how he'd gotten so involved with someone in a single night—and an Aquam nube, at that—how he'd gotten involved with a woman again at all after what Romola had put him through at the bitter-sweet conclusion of the Broken Country War. Souljourner seemed to think him some kind of hero. He wondered how she'd deal with the disillusionments she had coming if and when they made it back to the *GammaLAW.*

"I don't think we missed Ghost or those false barrow-coolies," Souljourner remarked as they set out at a rapid pace. "Our haste notwithstanding."

"You're right; she's ahead somewhere," Burning answered, elbowing two pharmaceuticants out of the way.

"But you're certain you saw her earlier?"

"Positive. Well, I didn't actually see her, but I saw the cyber-caul—the Optimant info-hood she was wearing at

Wall Water. There can't be two of those on the road tonight. Besides, the knife that Essa threw was Ghost's knife. It was bequeathed to her by our mother."

Burning had been so intent on saving his sister that he'd put the knife completely out of his mind. It was one of the few keepsakes the Ormans, orphaned young, had from either of their parents. Turning back for it was out of the question, yet he cast a despairing glance the way they had come.

It was just then that Souljourner handed him the knife, hilt first. "I assumed you'd want it, so I plucked it from the harpshatina."

Burning beamed at her. "You are *staunch*." He slipped the custom blade into his pistol belt.

"You're welcome, Redtails," she said, smiling back at him.

They pressed on through pilgrims, peasants, backpack peddlers, walking wounded, and soldiers of fortune. Soon a widening of the rough and rutted connector road eased the crush. The way was still hemmed in by farmers' defensive hedgerows of shinglewort, canker thorns, and festerweed, but Burning and Souljourner wove in and out among the jams of people like hounds casting for the spoor of Purifyre's band.

Souljourner had mentioned that growing up a virtual prisoner in the Descriers' retirement cloister at Pyx, she hadn't gotten to run long distances; her exercise had come in the form of constant labor and dashing around the grounds and ramparts. But Burning wouldn't have known that from the way she kept up with him. Maybe it was just youth, he told himself, or—the thought pained him— youthful passion.

Throughout the long and chaotic night, he hadn't had a chance to tell Souljourner that they could never be more than platonic allies. Should he take her as his mistress, the damage his misuse of rank would do to Ext morale and discipline would be nothing compared to the grief he would get from Daddy D, Captain Quant, and the rest. Dextra Haven especially would ream him out from asshole to appetite.

Even so, he was glad he hadn't gotten around to explaining the facts to the Descrier. In fact, after the kiss they had shared in the Peelhouse and the feel of her against his back in the WHOAsuit, he wasn't at all sure that he would ever get around to spilling the truth.

CHAPTER TEN

Mason's awakening from unconsciousness was eerily peaceful, uniquely so after the anguish that had built in anticipation of meeting the son he had abandoned on Aquamarine twenty years earlier, and inexplicably so in the aftermath of the violence in Wall Water, whose exact nature he couldn't recollect.

He grasped that his unnatural sleep had to do with lethe, because he knew the stuff from his time on-planet and could smell it all over himself just then. Limited use was as free of after-effects as it was with some of the better Periapt tranks. No skull-expanding headache, no disorientation or nausea; his mouth didn't even taste particularly bad. There *was*, however, a vile, smoky smell he recognized as an Aquam campfire fed by flat hand-patted rings of dried dung. The dung rings crackled as they burned; wooden utensils and ceramic cooking pots rattled and clicked.

He heard instruments playing both near and away to all sides. Closest were a trio of zils, sonitar, and tambouriif. And there was dancing going on to onlookers' approval. Mason listened tranquilly to shouts, laughter, hawking and spitting, handclaps, and stamping feet. He caught, in the distance, a drunken woman passionately declaiming a heroic ballad.

Memories of being carefully choked unconscious by Purifyre flashed before his mind's eye. The boy hadn't realized that it was Yatt's will, not Mason's, that kept him bleeding data from the computer in Rhodes's bedchambers long after Purifyre had ordered him to stop. Mason didn't blame his son for a bit of it and suspected that he himself would have done likewise.

As for Yatt, the self-created antiviral AI that had been downloaded into Mason's brain back on Periapt, he could feel nothing. Perhaps the choking or the lethe had quieted the program.

Mason vaguely recalled what he had thought to be a dream, in which Burning Orman was calling out Ghost's name. Mason had been unable to answer because, at least in the dream, he was still wearing the cybercaul Ghost had found but Mason had worn and used to access the computer. Whether or not it had been a dream, no caul blindfolded him now.

He opened his eyes to campfirelit smoke eddying over him. He was unbound and laid out on haphazardly spread tarps and tatters; a gritty woven mat had been placed over him against night air that wasn't all that cold. He was draped in a thin, soiled duster that covered his LAW formalwear, and his flechette-firing 'chettergun was no longer in its holster.

Firelight flickered shadows on the smoke, and he turned his head to see a number of barrow-coolies, recognizing them by their sweat, body-grease, and face-paint odors and familiar squatting postures. They wore only cheap, fanciful turbans and loinwraps, some of the latter unfurled as thin midthigh kilts. They were smoking resin pellets in unfired clay pipes and wax-wort leaf in spliffs. They gambled at bones, flip scudo, and dice while they watched the dancers, and they passed among themselves skins and pails of cheap hooch. Their food was a bit of bean and millet gruel and unleavened flatcakes with a smear of sweetgum.

The dancers were a coolie and two women—whores, gooner sellers, fortune-tellers, or maybe all those and more. They hopped and writhed to the music and mimed comically exaggerated seduction, rebuff, sex acts, and orgasm. The women, wearing threadbare shifts and colorful shawls, looked middle-aged by Periapt standards, but Mason knew they probably hadn't hit twenty-five baseline-years. They presented their breasts, made kissing and fellatory mourthings, and lifted their shifts to crunch bare pelvises and roll their clefts at the barrow-coolie.

Younger, small, muscled like an economy-model Olympian, he made the dance buffoonish and erotic at the same time. The audience howled and convulsed as he rolled his glutes, pumped at the women's crotches with his, and arched his tongue. The spectators urged him on by name—Go-lightly—and his dancing partners crooned to him, stroking their inner thighs.

Go-lightly walked on his hands, pantomiming upside-down carnal acts. He completed a handspring with his erection protruding from the top of his loinwrap. The crowd screamed with delight when one of the women draped a flower garland over it. As Go-lightly danced around his circle of onlookers, Mason realized that the coolie satyr was Purifyre.

More men and women jumped up to join in the prurient japes. As the onlookers' attention shifted, Purifyre stopped bobbing the garland hung round his hard-on and bumped and ground his way out of the limelight. Then, satisfied that no one was watching him, he rearranged his loinwrap, tossed the garland aside indifferently, and retreated to where Mason lay on the tarps, watching.

The boy wasn't just disguised as a coolie, Mason saw; he *was* one, complete with a greasepaint mask of dramatic scarlet zigzags, black eyeband, and white face border. His waist-length mane of auburn hair was done up now in a dusty barrowman's queue decked with beads, baubles, fetishes, and other decorations. His feet were road-beaten with hornlike nails that grew over the fronts of his toes to ragged or pointed ends, and his shoulders were calloused by the rub of the barrow collar. His body tattoos of Aquam-style robotic dragons, wanton women, and lucky symbols were genuine, but his face looked different: cheeks filled out by what Mason took for some kind of dental appliance, chin made less prominent by a phoney patch of beard, jug ears held flat against his head. Only his eyes—eyes the color of Aquamarine—were as intense as ever.

Even so, Mason could see through all of it to the frankly ugly face beneath, a face much like the one he himself had worn before Periapt cosmeds had turned it eerily handsome. Purifyre, though, had grown up on a primitive world where that kind of remake was inconceivable.

"Are you recovered?" he asked, dropping into a squat next to his father.

"Mostly."

"I regret that I was obliged to choke you out, but you left me no choice. I warned you to cease downloading data from the awakened Beforetimer machine."

Mason thought back to Rhodes's bedchambers and the towering bust of Altheo Smicker that concealed an Optimant computer. Yatt, in conjunction with the cybercaul, had been responsible for bringing the machine on-line after hundreds of years of dormancy. Mason thought hard about the download, recalling flashes of data—the names and locations of other Optimant AIs and some compelling evidence that the Cyberplagues had had their beginning on Aquamarine.

"You did what you had to," Mason said finally, opting to keep Yatt and the revelatory data out of the equation for the time being. "Where are we? And what's the meaning of all this?"

"We are in the Feckwash—just below the Jitterland Heights parking mounds."

A steel triangle sounded up on the Heights. The music stopped, and Aquam of all estates began breaking camp. Mason saw then that a number of the coolies had been Purifyre's votaries at Wall Water or had been among the raiders who had sported white pom-pom armbands. Like authentic barrowmen, they tucked sparkwheels, dice, and half-smoked spliffs into folds in their turbans.

"Eyewash is entering," Purifyre explained. "The muscle cars are loading. We're going south, to the Trans-Bourne. There are things there that I need to show you."

"Across the Styx Strait bridge?" Mason said, having viewed the span from orbit aboard the vanished *Sword*. "Did you build it?"

"I helped build it."

"What's waiting for us in the Trans-Bourne? Why all this mystery?"

"You'll know soon enough. Now, up you go."

Mason wasn't surprised that the boy could haul him to his feet with such ease. Free of the symbolic gloves of a Human Enlightenment *rishi*, Purifyre's hands were as rough and toughened as any peasant's.

Purifyre's followers were making sure the burdens lashed to the second barrow were fast. "Your Science Side modules," he confessed.

Mason had a brief image of Old Spume aboard the *GammaLAW,* and of the Sense-maker's suggestion to Dextra Haven that she bring examples of Periapt "teknics" to the Grand Attendance, if for no other reason than to awe Purifyre and the Ean grandees.

"Was that what tonight's violence was all about?" he asked. "If so, you didn't need to steal the modules. I told you there were other ways to get what you want."

Purifyre said nothing. He merely fell in alongside Mason and the barrow-coolies as they began wending up a Feckwash gully for the parking mounds.

The flat-topped mound of Jitterland Heights had come alive hours before dawn. The parking mounds teemed with workers, and triangular irons rang to the churning of metal strikers.

Breasting a rise with his son alongside him, Mason stopped in his tracks. He knew changes had been ushered in on the high roads of Aquamarine by the flexor-powered wagons, but this was his first close look. Skippers were haggling with prospective passengers and shippers, while crews and hummockers got the big wooden wains ready to unchock. It would have been madness to drive the ancient and unlit Optimant autobahns in darkness, but most muscle cars set forth in the pre-dawn to avoid wasting even a moment of daylight.

JeZeus! Hippo Nolan would get a belly laugh out of this, Mason told himself. Killed along with the rest of the *Scepter* team while in LAW detention on Periapt, Hippo was the engineer who had tinkered together Aquamarine's first muscle car to amuse himself during the survey mission. Powered by semi-alive bundles of freshwater mollusk muscle from the Trans-Bourne and galvani stones from the Scourlands, the cars operated on essentially the same principle that worked and fired the indigs' sling-guns. The prototype had inadvertently been left behind and intact that disastrous night when *Scepter* crew, under Mason's interim leadership, had departed the planet in fear and haste, the night Eisley Boon, Mason's best friend, had died in the Amnion. The night Mason had abandoned his Aquam wife, Incandessa, and their unborn child, now called Purifyre and Go-lightly and who knew what other names.

On the walk out of the Feckwash Purifyre had intimated that Go-lightly wasn't his only alter ego. Demonstrably, the boy was a revolutionary or a terrorist. He had masterminded a raid on Wall Water that had netted two GammaLAW bio-science field modules and, evidently as a crime of opportunity, Mason. Even more unexpectedly, events had yielded Purifyre a Pre-Cyberplague caul.

To Mason it was less than two years since Purifyre's birth owing to time dilation on the return voyage to Periapt and the one back to Aquamarine. But Purifyre was nearly eighteen baseline-years old. Exactly what he'd become in that time—much of it spent wandering the length and breadth of Aquamarine—Mason had yet to learn. He had resolved to be patient about Purifyre's motives in traveling to the Trans-Bourne, an island off the tip of Scorpia's southwestern claw. Since the night *Scepter* had raised ship, his conscience had racked him about abandoning Incandessa and their child, and when finally he had met the boy, the scales had fallen from his eyes. Mason understood that his life henceforth lay in being father to his son. Gladly, he relinquished everything from his old existence, including his unflagging allegiance to LAW.

Well, almost everything, in any event. As he topped the Heights, a huge face formed before his mind's eye and words drummed silently in his skull.

"*What's become of your promise to us, Mason? Our bargain, your debt?*" The face was hairless, amber, and full as a moon. Modeled on the laughing Buddha, it served Yatt as a facade. "*We agreed to return you to Aquamarine, and we have. You agreed to help us locate Endgame—the resolution to the Cyberplagues— and instead you abandon the GammaLAW mission.*"

The impact of the AI's *uberpresence* made Mason reel. Quick and strong, Purifyre caught him by the arm and kept him balanced, though he stood only chin-high to his father. Mason knew better than to answer Yatt aloud; he formed the words in his mind. *I had no choice. It was more your fault than mine—your insistence on draining data from the Optimant machine.* Yatt had also been responsible for bringing down Starkweather's *Jotan* fortress, Mason recalled, by activating and directing a long-dormant dish array atop one of Wall Water's tallest keeps.

Yatt conceded the point by his silence.

"Are you faint?" Purifyre asked, demonstrating more a leader's concern than a son's worry.

"I have to catch my breath," Mason lied. He feared what the boy or any other Aquam would do should they learn that his neurowares were harboring an artificial entity abstract. No other living soul knew his secret.

"Rest a moment," Purifyre was saying, though his followers were grimacing in impatience. The brawny, horse-faced old woman called Essa, who shadowed Purifyre like a guardian ogress, snorted loudly. Mason knew she detested him, and he was beginning to nurture a like sentiment toward her.

Yatt took advantage of the lull. "*You may have been taken by force, but you are awake and unbound now. Plot an escape while you still have time.*"

Mason studied the ground in front of him, sending, *I'm not leaving my son. Force me if you think you can.* Yatt could be a considerable affliction if he chose to be, but he wasn't some possessing demon out of a horror story.

Mason, we told you that we would never compel or harm you in that way. You know that we need you.

Back on Periapt, the actual Yatt wasn't so much an AI as a Cyberplagues counterforce—an evolved form of the antiviral programs and highest defense strategies of the TechPlex, the planet's compu-commo infrastructure, a cyberantibiotic that had attained self-awareness and self-directed evolution. As far as Mason knew, he was the only human being aware of Yatt's existence.

The grail that drove Yatt was an end to all strains and vestiges of Cyberplagues, which Yatt believed could be found in the ruins of the civilization built by the Optimants, Old Earth refugees who had colonized Aquamarine centuries earlier. Rather than clash wills with the AI again, therefore, Mason parried.

If endgame resides on Aquamarine, it does so in some Optimant artifact, not back aboard the GammaLAW. By remaining with my son I'll have opportunities to search for additional artifacts. Besides, my son has the cybercaul, which might be the key to this whole business.

The laughing Buddha turned baleful in a way Mason had never seen on any statue. *We have already considered that, and we calculate it less likely than the chances of success if you simply take possession of the cybercaul and return to the ship. We must, of course, accede to your decision. But be advised that we are incapable of relenting. Bear in mind your obligation to act in our interests or we will be forced to find some way to circumvent our reliance on you.*

"If he's too feeble to walk," Essa was growling to Purifyre, "wrap him back up in the tarp and I'll drag him."

Mason stirred himself, and the phantom Buddha faded. "No need. Which muscle car are we taking?"

Purifyre pointed. "The eight-wheeler atop that parking mound."

Mason appraised it. "A beauty. It'll be a relief to travel sitting down for a change. What's it called?"

Essa let out a jeering laugh. "*Shattertail.*"

CHAPTER ELEVEN

Taking their cue from Old Spume, Ghost and Zinsser tried to blend in with the tossed medley of Aquam headed toward the Flying Pavilion landing ground north of Wall Water. Given the number of terrified, shell-shocked, and displaced oddities, Zinsser doubted that he would stand out even in his bedraggled Periapt tropical formalwear. Nor would Ghost, with her facial scars and bib-fronted dress uniform.

Patricians masked in costly vizards rode palanquin chairs alongside barrow-coolies in garish facepaint. Travelers in chastity veils were shoulder to shoulder with pilgrim penitents whose faces were rubbed with ashes. Hired bodyguards marched in visored helmets. Wandering entertainers flaunted their stage makeup.

Aside from the fact that the newly formed trio had few alternatives, the landing ground had the added advantage of being a truce place. By a generations-old compact with the Insiders—the inbred and closeted clans who ruled the Laputas from within—people were free to buy, sell, seek passage, and conduct other affairs there without fear of vendetta, persecution, or military conflict. Spume thought it likely that such compacts would keep the grandeean troops from harrying the place for himself and Visitants.

Dream Castle, the currently grounded Flying Pavilion, was the airship whose liftoff Rhodes's guests had been scheduled to witness as a climax to the Grand Attendance. Seeing the superannuated Laputa up close, Ghost was transfixed. An ornate alloy and ceramic glass minipalace executed in tech-baroque, it would have made an arresting sight on any planet. Artificial illumination from portholes, windows, and skylights in its sealed hull cut through the darkness, the campfire and brazier haze, and the incense and forge charcoal smoke that fogged the landing ground.

The bottom third of the former Optimant pleasure barge, where passengers and cargo were carried, was girdled by a retrofitted outerworks of roughly dressed and caulked timbers. The Insiders suffered no ground dwellers within their hull proper owing to fear of piracy as well as contempt for Aquam humanity at large.

Below Zinsser's line of vision the base of the Laputa was a huge inverted bowl that shielded them against the fusion-powered propulsion section. The bowl rested on the floor of a quarrylike pit twelve meters deeper than the embarkation stage itself. A single gangway lit by cressets, torches, and lanterns connected the outerworks to the stage.

Most of those fleeing Wall Water had left the trail where it debouched into the open hectares of landing ground. There was no point in the refugees approaching *Dream Castle*, since few had anything like the money for passage or much worth selling. Those doing business around the Laputa would only drive the unfortunates away, in any case. The outlying fields had the air of the crudest kind of field hospital or disaster relief effort.

The trio kept moving for the thicker crowds around the Flying Pavilion, passing under a giant yussawood arch carved with totemic figures. As they worked closer, Zinsser spied butchers and meat sellers displaying their wares on racks and spits. While the grandees had been careful to keep such sights away from the Attendance, it was plain most Aquam still considered human flesh as edible as any other. The sight of a fillet cut from a child's carcass made the oceanographer turn away, swallowing bile. His desire to return to the relative sanity of the *GammaLAW* skyrocketed.

Showing no missile launchers or gun turrets, *Dream Castle* didn't look big enough to accommodate much of a defensive force, and in that it was locked eternally on a circuitous course, the Laputa was all but useless as a bomber.

"How do the Insiders make the truce stick," Ghost asked Old Spume, "or keep grandeean soldiers or wildmen on some atoll from storming their ivory tower when it's on the ground?"

Old Spume huffed. "Tales vary, but everyone agrees that the Insiders have their ways. Hijacking has been attempted elsewhere and failed. And not even the most rapacious grandee cares to lose the great profits Laputa traffic brings."

Ghost was examining the Laputa through her upraised pistol scope when Zinsser ahemmed. "I should like a closer glance, too." She gave him a weighing look, but instead of handing over the 'baller, she flicked two quick-releases and gave him just the scope. Big as a half-liter beer can, it had its own integral power supply.

Working the controls the way he'd seen her do it, Zinsser zoomed in on the balconies and windows high up the hull, where figures were silhouetted against the interior lights.

Like Ghost and Spume, he turned when he heard a martial din of aeoliphones, fanfaronatos, and tambourines. Aquam men at arms had appeared, rousting people out of the way with music and whips. They were forming skirmish lines as they made a slow sweep down toward the Laputa.

Rhodes's Militerrors were side by side with Fabia Lordlady's Unconquerables, the Grandee Paralipsio's Killmongers, and the Autocrat Haleso's Apocalyptics. Several men carried poles with openwork cages attached.

"*Briny!*" Spume quavered. "You Visitants smell so alien the praetorians won't *need* rock-eels to single you out!" Easing away, Spume stopped when Ghost waggled the 'baller in his direction.

"If you bolt, I'll turn what brain cells you have left into curdled flan. Can we escape across the landing pit?"

Zinsser saw that she meant the blackened open ground that spread out from the base of the Laputa. "It's a sheer wall on the far side," he assessed stridently. 'They'll stick us like pincushions if we try more rock climbing. Besides, there could be residual radiation from centuries of blast."

The three of them gauged the density of the herd around the embarkation stage. "How many will be staying behind when *Dream Castle* lifts off?" Zinsser asked Spume.

"Almost all."

It made sense. The Laputas were the only connection among the planet's scattered discrete landmasses; the Insiders could charge the maximum the market would allow. Passage would be truly a seller's market, with profits to be made on trading ventures correspondingly steep.

Most people at the landing ground, then, had come to ship cargo or receive it, hear whatever news there might be, barter among the crowds that gathered, and meet travelers or see them off. Virtually all would be leaving when the *Dream Castle* took flight—a sizable horde to hide in.

Spume pointed toward the embarkation stage. "See there! Those religious zealots of DevOcean! They're boarding even now!" In his excitement he sprinkled the air.

Zinsser recognized the sea-green robes. "You'd think those revelationist flatheads would all be slain or scattered," he reflected, watching them file aboard the wooden outerworks.

The Laputa emitted a synthesized deep toning. "Five minutes and the gangway goes up," Spume explained. "Two minutes after, *Dream Castle* rises. Anyone close by is charbroiled."

Scepter's survey reports had made it clear that there was no way to alter the countdown. The Laputas had been following their various preset routes around and around Aquamarine for more than two hundred years. Even the Insiders were powerless to change the PreCyberplague programming.

People were starting to move away from ground zero. Zinsser handed the scope back to Ghost, but rather than remounting it, she simply fastened it to a pistol belt pouch. The scope was harder to replace than to remove, and she didn't have the time to fiddle with it.

The Killmongers and Apocalyptics with the rock-eel cages were sorting through the crowds. Trying to slip through the tightening cordon by blending with the throng didn't look promising. Additional reinforcements had arrived to seal off the entire landing ground area. Phalanxes of sling-gunners were arrayed to shoot mass hedgehogs of quarrels, making any break across the open terrain of the pit a suicide run.

Zinsser was contemplating the safest way to surrender when he caught the look in Ghost's eye as she checked the magazine of .50s and slipped it back into the handgun. She offered him the hilt of her backup knife.

"We won't stand a chance," he suggested.

Lush processional music was suddenly issuing from the Laputa. Zinsser looked up to see people in rich fabrics, elaborate casques, and intricate lappet headdresses gazing down from an upper balcony. The *Dream Castle* Insiders were veiled, cowled, or vizarded, still an enigma.

"We'll board instead!" Spume babbled, terrified of being in the cross fire of another battle. "*Dream Castle* stops at Hangwitch, a four-day march downriver. We can return to Ea in one day by muscle car, assuming your *GammaLAW* hasn't sailed downriver to Hangwitch by then. Of course, I'm currently somewhat embarrassed for funds."

Reholstering the sidearm, Ghost used her knife to slice two gold buttons from the long cuffs of her uniform, leaving another two apiece to hold them closed. "Will this be enough?"

The Sense-maker was all smiles. "*Briny*, I should think so!" A stridulating sound had risen above the din of the crowd. "The rock-eels have your scent! This way!" He forced his bulk through the throng like a one-hundred-thirty-kilo icebreaker, making for the gangway.

In the other direction, a flying wedge of Diehards and Killmongers were trying to break through by laying about them with whips and meteor hammers—morningstarlike weapons whose short metal cables ended in wicked, sharp-flanged weights. Others came behind, using halberds, sling-gun butts, and cutlass hilts. There was isolated resistance, but most of the refugees fell back so frantically that many were trampled.

Some loud, gravelly command voice shouted, "Look to seize the DevOceanites as well!"

The gangway was a jam-up of a dozen passengers boarding, paying the purser, complaining, or inquiring. The entrance to the outerworks resembled a medieval lumber and iron version of an air lock, watched over by a mate and two bruisers in saffron robes who carried basket-hilted cudgels. Spume's forward progress was arrested by a man almost his size and a lot younger.

"Wait your turn if you wouldn't have me cast you into the blast pit!"

"Come down from there!" an officer of the Diehards yelled, waving his swagger stick at Spume, Zinsser, and Ghost. She'd drawn her sidearm again, but along her side, where it was partially concealed by her body.

Zinsser approved her restraint. "Maybe the crew will turn them away."

Brassy notes from a resonato sounded up above. All heads turned to where a man stepped into view on the top of the outerworks. He wore a somber djellaba of black and green with intricate pleats and pin darts and a long-billed cap with a red cockade over his right ear.

"The supercargo," Spume said. "The Insiders would never emerge so."

The supercargo pointed to the troops with his baton of bronze, horn, and dark maoriwood. "Lay back!" His tone said he was used to being obeyed. "Either put down your arms or go back beyond the wooden arch and the truce boundary. I won't warn you again."

The Diehard officer in the lead looked undecided, but some praetorian with an itchy trigger finger objected to being backed down. A blunt, nonlethal sling-gun round hit the supercargo square in the chest and rebounded.

Before the crowd or soldiers could react, a subsonic vibration was propagated from the hull of the Laputa itself. Immediately it had all Zinsser's organs quivering like jelly. As it gained force, it turned into a solid wall of oscillating air. Spume had stopped pushing at those ahead of him. Zinsser felt as if a set of inner eyelids in his head were beginning to close.

Ghost's head was lolling. She began bringing up the 'baller, but her hand and arm went limp, along with the rest of her body. The big handgun fell, bounced off the gang-way, and disappeared down into the black-blasted landing pit. Zinsser made a grab for Ghost but never reached her. He seemed to be falling through a dark void again, toward the stagnant aquaculture canal below Wall Water—never reaching it, just falling and falling.

CHAPTER TWELVE

Like the Oceanic from which they'd diverged—and by which they had been cast out as bad plasm—the Nixies of Lake Ea had phenomenal powers of bioelectrical generation and delivery.

The ones unseasonably stirred up against the *GammaLAW* by Aquam using the underwater sound devices called syrinxes were potent with replenished electrolytics and newgrown electrocyte cells. In their frenzy they were capable of delivering hundreds or even thousands of kilowatts in brief bursts, and when they linked up for a concerted attack, their output was astonishing. The fact that their discharges were AC made them even more dangerous.

The Ean grandees of twenty years earlier had kept the capabilities of the Nixies close to their collective chest, and so the drastically diminished *Scepter* survey team, stretched thin to begin with, had never gotten more than a hint of the syrinxes' power to incite the creatures. In all the contingency planning for confrontation with the Aquam, no one on the GammaLAW staff had even conceived of such an attack.

The SWATHship would have been immune to the creatures but for Logistical Command's coercive foot-dragging. The delay in reinsulating the trimaran's hulls had been yet another way to let Dextra Haven know that Starkweather expected compliancy. The LOGs were just so much vapor and debris now, but the damage they'd done lived on.

Capricious and unpredictable, the underwater lightning bolts found their way into the *GammaLAW* via labyrinthine routes of connection and least resistance.

The first Kurt Elide knew of the onset was a flash of blue light amid the deck illumination, attended by a crack like a snapping drumstick. He spun left just in time to see one of his fellow damage repair party members—an air controller—fall back stiff as a door.

Kurt's party had been working to free up a standoff firefighting dumbot that had gotten jarred clean off the flight deck when the ship, pursued by two Heron missiles launched by the *Jotan*, had plowed through a slew of submerged and floating aquaculture apparatus. The dumbot had dropped onto a big air exchange intake and filtration unit, getting itself well and truly fouled. If the mishap had a fortunate side, it was that the dumbot had missed striking the mount of the Close-in Weapons System's 30mm, just now the only functioning heavy weapon aboard.

At close quarters and with so many systems off-line, getting the dumbot clear of impediments had been a job for small cutters and torches, unpowered pinchbars, and muscle-tearing manual labor. The work was exacting and dangerous, the urgency great. Stirred-up Big Sere dust choked Kurt despite the rag around his mouth, and spilled fire suppression chemicals had him light-headed and often on the verge of puking. When a heavy-lift crane on the flight deck had at last hoisted the dumbot free, he felt an unqualified elation of human victory over inert metal.

The *GammaLAW*'s defensive posture was improved, too. The only surviving picket boat, the hovercraft *Northwind*—which Kurt had piloted back from Wall Water—was being lowered back onto the lake with a replacement crew, its plenum skirt repaired. Captain Quant's response options and available firepower were thus greatly increased. The great SWATHship's survival would unquestionably determine Kurt Elide's peace of mind, and just now Quant was the key to that survivability.

As the air controller bounced on the deck, more electrical arcs spattered among sections of exposed metal, and sparks rained where materials of differing potentials met. From areas across the weather decks, screams and angry yells went up against the sounds of short explosions. Fire and damage alarms began to blare, making it hard to think.

Something in the fallen air controller's mouth was smoking, and for a second Kurt thought that the man's tongue was charbroiled; then he recalled that the controller had been about to chew a ration sausage before the electrical bolt struck. The sausage had burned black right there in the guy's mess hole.

Lazlo-Lazlo, Kurt's current work mate, leapt back with a screech as sparks danced under his shoes where the deck non-skid had been peeled away by the crashing dumbot. The mission documentarian was terrified but only a bit singed. Kurt was about to tell him to stay back, when an impact like a crashball tackle hit him. It was the bosun's mate from Hull and Engineering Group who had press-ganged the two of them into work duty in the first place. At the same time, Kurt became aware of metal reaved and crumpling and laboring servos shrieking.

Kurt never found out if it was mechanical failure, electroshock to the operator, or some combination, but the hoist had shifted and toppled, sending the standoff firefighting dumbot crashing back down into the air handler. Whatever was juicing the ship let her have it again.

Miniature tangletrails of high voltage danced among the stove-in wreckage and whipping hoist cable.

The bosun's mate plucked Kurt upright as the others in the repair party gawked at the shambles. "Wake up and turn to! We gotta save the gun!"

Arcs and sparks were also coruscating along the multibarrel gun. Kurt knew there were live rounds in the CIWS's chute ammunition delivery system as well as in the turret's helical feed mechanism. Fail-safes should already have retracted the chute and made fast the blastproof cover plates over the magazine elevator, but it was possible that the current had malfed the mechanisms. An explosion would rip into the ship's vitals.

"Step lively!" The bosun's mate had grabbed a manportable fire extinguisher and was now shoving it into Lazlo's gut. "We'll have to retract the feed and close the blastplates manually!" He motioned Kurt to a power cutter. "Shake a leg!"

The only rational course was to take cover. But it was the irrational that had made Kurt enlist in the GammaLAW mission to begin with, so he followed the bo's directives.

Together with two other sailors and a reluctant Lazlo-Lazlo, who was being dragged by his shirred lapel, Kurt swarmed up around the automated saltshaker-shaped gun turret that was the CIWS. The electrical surges had subsided for the moment. Still, he couldn't figure out the turret cowling latches.

Pinchbar in hand, the bo hip-bumped him aside, yanked the releases, and heaved armor-plate panels wide. Kurt saw by the rounds' color-coding that the helical feed and chute systems were loaded with electrically primed, armor-piercing incendiaries. If enough current reached them...

One of the sailors tried the magazine elevator's manual operating gear. "It's not budging."

"Stand away," the bo warned, shifting his pinchbar. "It's about to."

The capture claws that held the chute to the helical feed were seized up and wouldn't ungrip even in answer to their worm-gear, so the bo set to work on them with the two-centimeter-thick metal bar. An enlisted rating grabbed Lazlo's extinguisher and began wetting down the rounds in the chute, since malfunctions and power outages had bled all pressure from the ship's firefighting hoses. Other party members were crouched to see if the blastproof plates would still move into place.

"You two!" The mate designated Kurt and Lazlo with pokes of his chin while he pried at the capture claws. "Drag that patch up here."

The patch was nothing but a square of metal, but it was better than nothing for sealing off the magazine elevator. As Kurt grabbed his side of the plate, another surge hit the ship. Current frolicked along the fallen dumbot, and burning motes hissed, falling from the air handler.

An explosion—a big one—roared in the distance.

A signal flare that had somehow gotten loose and been ignited back toward the fantail went whooshing over their heads like a red comet to ricochet off the surface-search radar dish and carom away in the direction of the Science Side hull.

"Lazlo!" Kurt could see it in his eyes: the guy was about to break and run. "There's no place to go! Bear a hand while there's still time!"

"Yeah—time for *dying*," Lazlo remarked as he approached.

Kurt almost grinned. "Hey, you're in the picture now, remember?"

"See? Told you it'd be empty," Roust said.

With Nixies jazzing *GammaLAW* from all sides, the Commissioner's Coordinating Center was as vacant as promised, but it earned Roust no praise from Zone. Zone was as sparing with approval as he was openhanded with punishment.

"It's only half-wired-up, but it's got what we need," Wetbar observed. "Haven doesn't use it. They were talking about making it the backup CIC."

The compartment had originally been the command post for any higher brass in residence aboard the SWATHship. At the aft end was a small Science Side liaison booth, also unmanned. Refurbishing the place as a situation room for the commissioner had been put on hold owing to competing priorities and Haven's preference for either the CIC or Battle Two for alerts or crises.

"Data management and displays all on-line," Strop declared, checking status lights and menus. Removing her helmet, she shook out mounds of curly auburn hair, much of it braided tight and thin into the Hussar Plaits the Exts favored for tradition and a modicum of protection in edged-weapon combat. Like most in Zone's several, she had a reckless, even self-destructive need to push limits, but she knew how to stroke-job systemry and hack.

"Now what?" Strop squirmed a little in anticipation of new sport. "Phreak the CIC?"

Zone turned up his sleeve and removed the whatty he had been issued before the Grand Attendance—one that he had put to good use in Rhodes's bedchambers. "Stuff in here's from an Optimant comp." He added the various connectors, the brute memory unit, and other archeo-hacking 'wares he had used. "I bled it some. Find and display. Decrypt, interpret, all that."

Strop took the hacking tackle smiling with anticipation, her tongue tucked in one corner of her mouth. She wasn't the most talented data diver aboard, wasn't even the best among the Exts, but she was one Zone could count on to keep silent even in contravention of her oath to the battalion.

The CCC systemry had been designed to accept the whatty adapters and connectors. With the air of a gifted child doing an educational puzzle, Strop mated the brute memory unit to the central display console. It took several reassurances to convince the console that it was all right to go off-line from the rest of the ship's computational ecology. The con job having flown, however, data lit the main holo display and various side fields and screens like stained-glass panoramas in a cathedral of information.

The formats and data paths were different, but Zone saw it was indeed the material that had been spilling out of the reactivated PreCyberplague supercomp. It had been a strictly serendipitous find; he'd actually been out to find and kill Burning at the time.

Zone didn't know who or what had raised the armored housing that had concealed the comp—a housing cast in the form of a bust of Atheo Smicker, the original master of Wall Water—nor was he sure if anyone else had done the same kind of bit chipping he had done. He was satisfied, though, that nobody would do so again, since he'd packed the machine with Oblitex-7 detonator cord and had heard the resultant explosion a few minutes later.

The data being displayed in the CCC didn't parse very far. The steady march and flash of information confirmed his earlier guess that the machine had been stuck in some kind of loop.

"Somebody was digging," Strop muttered, slowing and altering the frantic cycle. "Somebody *good*, spoofing into a system like that one."

Zone considered who that might be. Zinsser? Mason? Strop slowed down and froze various displays:

AbomiNation	DoomsData	Firegod	EarthMover
PathoLogic	Apocalyst	CorruptScion	HorrOrgasm

They were the names of the most infamous of the computer viruses that had ravaged all human-colonized worlds two hundred years earlier, archdemons among the Cyberplagues. There were broad details on their design and capabilities but none, curiously, on the bloody swath they had cut across human space. Zone caught other names in passing.

Hyapatia	Akashic Record	EndGame
PathoLogic	Passwater	New Alexandria

Those weren't viruses so far as Zone or his severalmates knew, but the four of them were hardly experts. When Roust reached for a hardwire phone to query the ship's central data banks, Zone casually backhanded him one on the ear, so fast that even Flowstate didn't let him dodge. A stocky man whose battered face looked like he used it to go through locked doors, Roust would have gone for anybody else's throat, but he simply accepted the clout, rubbing his ear.

"Security lid on this," Zone drawled. All his instincts told him there was untold power to be had from these lost Optimant marvels, and he wanted it all. With the GammaLAW mission thrown into utter disarray, his time was coming.

He pointed to the Endgame designation and its apparently corresponding location, the Optimant lighthouse at New Alexandria. "It's southeast of here, at the mouth of the fucking river that drains this lake. We'll start there, find out more about it on the quiet. Pump drinks 'n' sexchat into some civic affairs piecework or an intel—"

"New Alexandria is indeed where the payoff is, Colonel," a voice concurred over a compartment speaker.

Everyone but Zone froze. A light came on in the darkened Science Side booth, and Wix Uniday revealed his presence.

"Security compromise," Wetbar commented softly, clicking his boomer's selector switch from safety to semi-auto. Zone gave him an unobtrusive hand signal to wait; the AlphaLAW rep was coming into the CCC proper, not running away.

Uniday had come aboard as the late-Commissioner Starkweather's liaison man with Haven, but he had a look and a way about him that were leagues different from LAW's typical kissass go-betweens. Close to Zone's height, he was built more like a decathlete, and something in his gaze said that he liked and knew how to fight. With his touseled blond hair and raffishly handsome face, Uniday had the carriage and exquisite tailoring of Periapt gentry, yet there seemed a hint of first-strike ruthlessness behind the facade. Rumor had it that he had served LAW in the Political Security Bureau, an agency noted for making things happen no matter what the odds. There was no point asking Uniday how or when he came to suspect that Zone had stumbled onto something important in Wall Water, since stealth was PolSec's stock in trade.

"What do you know about New Alexandria?" Zone asked.

Wix Uniday sat one ass cheek on the corner of a console. "Not much, to tell the truth. But I do know a bit about Endgame." He was still wearing his dress uniform and a LAW 'chettergun, but he crossed his arms on his chest, ignoring his weapon and theirs. "Endgame is something the Plagues experts mostly believe to be a myth. I do, too, but now I'm beginning to wonder."

"What's it do?" Strop blurted, then caught herself, fearing Zone would cuff her one. But he ignored her, reserving his eerie, unblinking gaze for Uniday.

"Allegedly, it's a panacea for the Cyberplagues," Uniday said. "Creators' fail-safe, backdoor override—call it what you will. Whoever controls Endgame could supposedly erase every vestige of the viruses as well as immunize new machines against reinfection."

Uniday paused briefly, then added, "There might be a dozen or a hundred other dormant Optimant IDentities, brAIns, and technologies intact on Aquamarine. But Endgame's the key and the control. And if the data you found are genuine—" He nodded toward a map of Scorpia. "—then Endgame's just a float downstream."

Zone slid his right hand back along his load-bearing harness, not to his pistol but near the belt-mounted carrier in which his edged entrenching tool hung. "Why tell me?" he asked.

"Because Haven knows nothing about it. And with the *Sword* gone, she and Quant will certainly try to sit out the Big Sere up here, figuring Lake Ea will remain their safest bunker. The food supply's good, and they'll eventually be able to jerry-build new boat and aircraft assets. I know, because I've read the contingency plan files."

Uniday's easy smile faded. "But I, for one, don't care much about bootstrapping the Aquam to prosperity. And

Haven's kidding herself if she thinks she'll get the Oceanic to open a dialogue with her. No, the real power's downriver, Colonel—for people who understand power, that is. People like you and me, perhaps."

In one Flowstate fast sequence, Zone had his e-tool out and, with a flourish, had flicked a blond curl from Uniday's forehead. It was customized to his hand with ergonomic alterations of the grip and carbon-vapor-deposition edges on its cutting surfaces, and Zone preferred it to a knife or hatchet. He brought it onto a new course straight for Uniday's crotch, but the liaison man just watched. At the last instant the eeter turned just enough so that its bush-knife feature cleaved the corner of the console between Uniday's leg instead of his spermworks.

"Does that mean we have an understanding?" Uniday asked in a thanks-for-passing-the-salt tone.

Zone wet his lips. "What's my guarantee you'll keep your mouth shut?"

"You have the data fragments, Colonel," Uniday reminded him, "and the boomers, and the kamikaze gunsels. My money, in fact, is on your commanding the Exts in short order. Assuming, of course, you look to contingencies."

Zone levered his eeter free of the console with just the strength of his wrist. "Such as?"

Wix Uniday slid to his feet. "The signal center's short-handed. You'll want to think about loaning them someone who could, say, stand watch on the meteor-burst commo antennas—the ARAAs. The Oceanic is apparently respon-sible for the RATEL jamming we're experiencing, but let's assume for the moment that Allgrave Burning is still alive. He might try bounce-beaming a transmission to the ARAA rig. If one of your own is working the poz, Burning's contact could be dealt with as you see fit. Could even be kept out of the logs completely."

Zone allowed an appreciative nod. "What else? What other contingencies?"

Uniday touched his chin. "You may want to give thought to getting this ship downriver." He turned to go. "I'll be talking to you."

Zone slid the e-tool back into its belt carrier. "Keep those mastermind ideas coming, Wix. We'll end up running this boat, this planet, and plenty more. Have ourselves a real blowout."

Uniday raked a leering look across Zone's underlings, who glowered back homicidally or gave him seductive straight eye, according to their inclination. "Oh yes, *a fête noir* that'll go down in history."

Zone waited until Uniday was out of earshot. "Watch him," he told his severalmates. "Dog him."

"What's *fête noire?*" Roust asked.

"A play on words," Strop volunteered, staring after Uniday contemplatively. "A dark festival."

"Once we find out the deal he's running, what?" Wetbar inquired.

Zone took pleasure in saying it. "We'll have ourselves a high old *fête noire.*"

CHAPTER THIRTEEN

At ground level, the Jitterland Heights seemed to be a blend of wainwright's yard, medieval fair, and squatter camp. But to Burning the muscle cars chocked atop their parking mounds seemed like a place of primeval worship. The cars came in all sizes and conditions, from rattletrap four-wheelers resembling dugout canoes to twelve-wheeled merchantmen sporting baroque woodwork, green and gold paint, and big bench windows in stern castles. Prayer flags, from the splendid to the shoddy, rustled on the Big Sere breeze, their inscriptions meant to be carried to the gods by wind and weather.

Bundles of mollusk muscle, sheathed in preservative membrane sacs and sustained by biofluid concoctions, drove the big drays via crude treadle mechanisms. The cars' mass and relatively low power made it difficult for them to get under way, and so the mounds had cropped up in one form or another along Scorpia's remaining Optimant roads and bits of similarly negotiable terrain. Once the muscle cars got moving, they seldom stopped or turned aside.

Veering among the mounds with Souljourner keeping pace, Burning saw crews and carfitters laboring over, under, around, and within the wagons. Rutted and moguled access roads networked the Heights like maglev tracks in a switching yard. The Grand Attendance had had its aberrant moments, but the workaday alienness of the parking mounds brought it home to Burning that he was on a planet not his own. He and Souljourner hurried on nonetheless, glancing every which way for signs of Purifyre, both of them acutely aware that grandeean troops were moving in at the foot of the hill.

Food vendors had woks and braziers sizzling, hawkers cried their wares, and car crews saw to last-minute preparations. Souljourner told him a large tepee was a pawnbroker's kiosk, while a small yurt held a midwife-abortionist's practice. The man heating glass cups with a little torch and applying them to a recumbent man's back—exerting suction as the air in the globes cooled—was drawing boils. Tattooists tap-tapped needles, scribes sat at writing trays, and phrenologists read the past and the future in cranial bumps.

"This must seem a barbarous place to you," Souljourner ventured, in a smaller voice than he was used to hearing from her.

Her despairing tone stopped him from agreeing in spades. "Mmm, in some ways it's like home—the Broken Country, I mean. On Concordance." He nodded his head to where people were doing call-and-response songs, drumming, dancing in lines. "Exts engage in similar activities to cultivate the Skills. If you think this place is rough, try being cooped up in troop berthing spaces with a battalion of Exts for a few months."

"Gladly, if you were there," she blurted, then avoided his eyes.

There was a brisk trade in mandseng and other antimutagens—or at least what were palmed off as those prophylactics. Aquamarine's natural environment caused high numbers of birth defects, and newborns afflicted with them, called Anathemites, were terminated at once. Healthy children meant the survival of bloodlines, families, entire clans. The desperate commonly bought mandseng even when they couldn't afford food. Souljourner said fraud was rife because demand was always high.

Faith healers, mountebanks, wandering shamans, and witches promised protection against Anathemite births, as well. Hope pounces eternal, Burning thought. Those in the Anathemite-prevention racket traveled light and kept an eye peeled for dissatisfied customers.

"Purifyre will want to hit the road as soon as he can," Burning predicted. "We're looking for cars getting ready to release their grabs and push off." He heard the martial music of grandeean troops quick marching through the Feckwash, below the Heights. "Clock's running for us, too." He would have walked up a nearby mound for a look around, but she caught his arm.

"Never ascend a mound unless you're part of a car's company or have business with such. The hummockers get highly peeved at people who make more work for them by treading down their slopes." Hummockers were the workers, usually families sharecropping under a liege or landowner, who operated one or more mounds. They collected parking fees and kept the slopes well dressed in addition to lending a hand when cars parked or pushed off.

To give the torchlit Heights a visual sweep, Souljourner clambered up on an empty barrel where a game of dominos had just broken up. Turning, Burning saw three men of indeterminate age coming their way. Grimy and seedy-looking, one held a tarboosh hat in both palms. Recalling the several cut purses he had had to lay out with the butt of his pistol on the connector road, Burning stepped away from the barrel to confront them.

"What do you want?" he asked defiantly.

One smiled, showing a gap where his front teeth had been knocked out or purposely extracted. "How outlandish you talk! See, new fella, we're good pious boys who've got us a deceased sere wren."

The one with the tarboosh tilted it to show Burning the body of a pretty little flying creature, more like an immense moth than an avian. A harmless thing that abounded at that time of year, the sere wren looked as if it had been killed with a stick. "So we'll thank you for an iron scudo," the spokesman finished with a big smirk, "to help pay for the funeral, of course."

Skills readiness had Burning on the balls of his feet, just in case. "A shakedown?"

"Don't know your migrant word for it," the one with the tarboosh added. "We're just poor wren boys starving for some wake-up eatsies. What's one sorry iron scudo to the likes of you, with them fine boots and your handsome getup and gold buttons?"

If Burning had had so much as a plastic slug, he would have forked it over to avoid creating a scene. That his looks and accent had made the wren boys mistake him for a rube traveler from some remote corner of Aquamarine—wandering abroad as so many were doing these days—gave him an idea. He put on a thick dialect. "Not to touch me, otherhow I shall kicking you!" He jerked a toe at them to clarify.

The wren guttersnipes were predatorially amused. "That's hard-hearted of you," the third one said, and started to sidle around to the left. Burning got ready to go for his knife, hoping to warn them off without having to use the 'baller.

The leader stopped his chum and showed a gap-toothed grin. "Maybe he'll feel sorry if we touch him up later." They sauntered into the crowd with a few backward looks, chortling and elbowing each other.

"If you'd given so much as a mud shekel, a dozen more like them would've been here in no time," Souljourner commented from atop the barrel. "Perform a cesarean on your purse if they could." She surveyed the mounds again and pointed. "I see one old heap of sticks just yonder that's going soon. A fine great carrack wagon off by the out ramp that's finished loading."

"Let's try the closest." Opening his holster's thumb break as he walked, Burning kept one hand on the pistol grip.

Souljourner hadn't exaggerated the condition of the nearby car. It was a battered old six-wheeler with haphazardly patched body panels and peeling paint. The metal bands of its tall wooden mud-cutter wheels were corroded, and its elliptical spring suspension sagged defeatedly. Eight meters long and two and a half in beam, the crate featured counterbalancing drag staves, a raised steering station toward the bow, and long grabs—brake levers—set over the four-wheeled rear. While neither barrows nor any of Purifyre's band was in evidence, Burning kept his hand on the gun butt.

The car's apparent skipper was a sour-looking, smallish guy with a repertoire of nervous tics and frowns who was arguing with a teenager amidships. The man wore a loincloth, a ratty scarlet turban, and a loose shirt that had once been brilliantly floral. But before Souljourner could hail him, the carman came under an outpouring of wheezing, gravelly verbal abuse from an enormous woman who looked like a sumo in a fright wig and blinding paisley mumu. Her gums were stained black from a lifetime's slackwort chewing, and her teeth were discolored and decaying.

"Boner, *dear husband*, you flatheaded, ass-eating sisterfucker! You said our passengers would be here by now!"

Boner seemed less intimidated by than resigned to her tirade. "True, Manna."

"Bad enough that Turnswain's taken aboard all the best Trans-Bourne cargo. Does he have to beat us there by a half day as well? Quit drifting around out here like a fart in a toga and go find those fares!"

"I was just about to, Manna," Boner said, leaving.

Manna spit a jet of maroon-black slackwort juice over the rail that barely missed Burning. Shifting her chaw, she squinted down at him, setting fists big as rib roasts on her pillowy hips. "What're you overfed lumpkins gaping at? Speak your piece."

While Burning was debating just what tone to take, Souljourner asked, "How soon do you shove off?" She used a regional accent unlike the carefully pronounced north Scorpian Terranglish she had been speaking. "Some barrowmen told us they're headed for the 'Bourne on a fine car, and since we, too, must depart at the earliest—"

"Barrow-coolies?" Manna slapped the rail, making the hull planks tremble. "What coolie has money for car fare, you daffy young jism swigger? If you want to ride aboard *Racknuts*, show me the glint of your money. Elsewise, all you'll get is tire ruts across that plump bum of yours!"

Souljourner took it in stride. "Forgive me, good woman. Then they must have been speaking of some *other* fine car."

Manna pointed to the eight-wheeled carrack Souljourner had spied making ready near the exit ramp. "Then stop pestering me with your face as ugly as a blind wainwright's thumb and go query the crew of *Shattertail*!"

Burning dragged at Souljourner's arm and began to race toward *Shattertail*'s mound. The Skills helped him dodge a group of men who were approaching Manna's mound with empty blivet skins. "Halloo, Manna!" they called. "Sell us a bit of your Analeptic Fix before you loose grabs and push off!"

"Not you, cheap bastards! You married jaundiced wives because their skin reminds you of gold!"

Burning had no time to wonder about Analeptic Fix. The sound of the grandeean troops was getting louder. He calculated that it would take the praetorians ten minutes to work their way across the Jitterland Heights, and by that time the sky would be light enough for *Shattertail* to unchock.

He was wrong on both counts. His first rude awakening came when he saw flames flare aboard the eight-wheeler. The carrack had been rigged with outsize lamps and lanterns, especially at the bow.

"*Shattertail* launches in darkness!" Souljourner gasped, running along beside him.

Burning poured on all speed, leaping over spread trading blankets and bursting between clusters of people, but failed to arrive in time. *Shattertail's* chocks were pulled away, and hum-mockers helped push it off. The banging of the muscle car's treadles came to him clearly as it gathered speed, hitting level ground and trundling for the exit ramp, stern lamps swaying and joggling.

Fast losing distance, Burning was considering trying a shortcut around the Heights when, streaming toward the vacated mound, there came Killmongers, Diehards, and other grandeean elites, led by horned and plumed officers. A captain of Rhodes's Militerrors waved his cutlass at the departing muscle car, shouting, "Purifyre!"

The sight of the three wren boys conferring with the officers was even worse news. Shadow-rats, Burning realized, secret agents in the employ of Grandee Rhodes, like the one who had suicided on the main deck of the *GammaLAW* three days earlier. Already retreating, he caught Souljourner and drew her with him. He started to lead her back toward the Feckwash, only to halt when he saw search parties combing the gullies with torches. "Have mercy."

Souljourner understood the situation. It was time to face the fact that they couldn't do any more for Ghost on Jitterland Heights. "Hoo! Whither us, Redtails?"

Burning glanced around him. "Is there a way cross-country?"

"Possibly—for farmboys who know secret gaps in the shinglewort and canker thorns. But not for us and not with daylight coming on. How about taking passage south, far enough to dodge the soldiers? We could work our way back north by lakeshore routes and might even catch *Shattertail* before we leave the Beforetimer roads."

He gave it thought. "Think we could find a muscle car called *Plushbottom* or *Downyglide*?"

After a brief survey Souljourner turned toward Manna's parking mound. "No. *Racknuts* it is or none for perhaps hours to come."

Manna stood on the deck of her clunker. The group of carmen were departing, having apparently haggled for blivet skinbags of Manna's Analeptic Fix. "An *elixir vitae* that nourishes the treadle muscles," Souljourner had explained. "There are many secret recipes. Analeptic Fix must be a good one."

The six-wheeler's other crew members were squaring the car away, with one gangly kid sweeping up with a maoriwood broom. The Fix transaction appeared to have put Manna in a comparatively good mood. Spying Burning and Souljourner she cackled moistly, the great mumu'd body gel rippling.

"Left behind, eh, you crotch floggers? Fah, *Shattertail's* rolling in darkness. It'll come to grief before it's gone a league. Show me the size of your purse and you may yet get to the Trans-Bourne."

Each parking mound had a built-up berm so that cargo could be carried or rolled straight aboard on a gangplank, but *Racknuts*'s gangplank had already been shipped. Before he followed Souljourner up the boarding ladder, Burning used his Ka-Bar to slice off a cuff button cast in the shape of the Battalion of Exts unit crest. When he held it out topside, Souljourner made a strangled sound.

"That's for first class fare for two to the *end* of the Trans-Bourne!" she said hastily. "With a prorated refund if we disembark earlier. And you owe us change now, of course: two silver scudos each—"

Manna pulled her lower eyelid down with a middle finger to indicate the salt water of tears and hooted, "Go to!" which was, on Aquamarine, to say, Go to the ocean—*Go to hell.*

She inspected the cuff button with great affection, however. "Deck passage as far as the Styx Strait is all this will buy you. And no changes or refunds here, Mistress Merry-Merkin. Find seats and stay out of our way. We push off as soon as our other cargo and fares arrive and we have a hint of dawnlight."

Shy a limb, Manna was balanced on a carved peg leg with a leather cap on the bottom. The prosthetic was a startling piece of work, a panorama of life on the muscle car routes done in deep *repoussé*. She didn't appear to need a crutch but thudded around with all her mass wobbling inside the mumu—sway-bump, sway-bump.

"The rest of you, hop to or I'll denounce you to the monitors for the Anathemites you are!"

She paused at the call of her name. A gaunt carman in a loincloth, black leather cloche, and many-pocketed vest leaned against the rail. "Manna, just heard! Troops and customs flunkies coming to search *Racknuts*!"

She stumped back over to kiss his leatherbound pate and say, "Bless you, Dilly." Then she thrust him squawking off her vehicle and turned to her crew. "Spin, Yake: stand ready to pull chocks! Missy and Pelta, get your skinny slots below and make ready to wet the pullers! Boner, light the lamps!"

The adolescent boys, Spin and Yake bore some resemblance to Manna's husband. The two prepubescent girls, Missy and Pelta, bore enough of a resemblance to Manna for Burning to conclude that *Racknuts* was a family business. Spin, the taller boy, sang out, "Ready here, Manna!"

She gave her head a twitch of acknowledgment, but she was seething. "Search *Racknuts*, is it? Fah! Steal my Analeptic Fix and wring the recipe out of me's more on the mark! That'll be a dry day in the Amnion! Spin, Yake—raise the drag staves, my clever boys!"

Her sons leapt to retract the hinged poles that had been lowered fore and aft to help keep the wagon parked. "Boner, my studly pilot," Manna sang out in her rasping command voice, "take the helm!"

The small, rusty lamps at the bow made Burning wish urgently for sunrise. He led Souljourner aft to find places amid the kegs, bales, and wicker hampers. Burning's need to know what he'd gotten himself into made him stoop to investigate a hatch farther astern. The space reeked with odors that made his eyes water; a sewage leak in a slaughterhouse during a heatwave might come close.

Missy and Pelta were down there, huddled between two vertical rows of what looked like elongated blood sausages or malformed constrictors flensed of skin and sheathed in translucent membrane. The muscle sacs' upper ends were connected to the hull frames, the lower ends to two long treadles that ran lengthwise through the stern third of the car. Spaced between the encased muscles were stout cables of natural rubber that helped opposing muscles provide reciprocating force to the treadles.

Missy, the smaller of the two, held cords attached to nozzles in blivet skins mounted on the overhead—a gravity-feed system for Analeptic Fix. Pelta grasped a handgrip squeezer in either small, dirty paw. The devices were connected to the ranks of contractile bundles by cables that looked like antique salvage. The girls had made an effort to brighten their surroundings with withered bouquets of flowers tucked into gaps between frame timbers and hull planks: a faceless straw doll to one side, a torn rag one to the other.

"Wet the pullers!" Manna cawed.

Missy tugged carefully on the nozzle cords. Thin, pinkish liquid seeped down through the sheathed muscles, making them tremble. Pelta squeezed one piezoelectric handset and then the other, and the ranks of muscles to either side flexed with each squeeze of the galvani stones.

The treadles banged, spinning a mollywood driveshaft bound by steel rings and wrapped as tight as a wound armature with fibrous line. The shaft ended in bevel gears that weren't yet engaged.

Manna was bellowing, "Pull chocks! Release the grabs! Girls, kick in the gears! *Push*, back there, all you worthless, wang-choking hummockers!"

Missy and Pelta kicked a spring-loaded release, and the treadle shaft's bevel gear swung to engage its mate on a shaft running down to the six-wheeler's hind axle. Pelta began squeezing the handsets, alternating rhythmically, and *Racknuts* banged forward with a jaw-snapping jolt.

Souljourner grabbed Burning's pistol belt to keep him from sliding into the preposterous engine room.

The muscle car shot forward a half pace at a time. Tough as the native mollywood was, Burning wondered how often drive shafts splintered, treadles split, or wooden gear teeth went flying. With a flash of insight he knew how Manna had lost her leg.

Racknuts gathered speed as it rolled down the mound. Souljourner yanked his arm. "Burning! Up!" The rest was drowned out by Manna's bellow.

"Stand by to repel boarders!"

CHAPTER FOURTEEN

When she came to after a few seconds of unconsciousness, Ghost was being lugged by the armpits and knee backs toward the adzed-beam and wrought-iron boarding lock of the Laputa *Dream Castle*. She experienced none of the sense of failure or despair that would have eaten up Fiona Orman, her Concordance incarnation; she clung to a subdued Flowstate that kept her lucid despite her body's sluggishness. The sonics that had poured from the grounded Flying Pavilion's hull had briefly kayoed everybody on or near the ramp, including the grandeean troops. She was being carried by Laputa crewmen.

The acoustic weapons the Optimants had installed in their air palaces were different from the 'wailers the Exts used. Battering-ram concussion was the signature of a system using very high-power, low-frequency sound to shove plasma impact waves into its targets—something even armor wouldn't buffer. Whereas 'wailers had been ineffective on some Aquam warriors at Wall Water, the Flying Pavilion's defenses had put the wood to all and sundry.

Ghost now understood why the pavilions weren't molested by sabre-wielding Darwinian capitalists or stone-ax-wielding egalitarians while grounded. Offhand, though, she could think of a half dozen ways to defeat the acoustic defense even with the grandees' primitive siege warfare

127

capabilities—especially since the Laputas landed and lifted off from an unalterable rota of sites on an unfaltering schedule. That only suggested that the Insiders had additional gimmicks to protect their sweet setup. It was no wonder the truce between them and the land-dwelling Aquam had stood valid for two hundred years.

The saffron-uniformed men who'd piled out of *Dream Castle* had either been watching the drama at the gangway or were being commanded by somebody who had. They had gathered up only the fallen who'd made it to the gangway and were waiting to board, ignoring the praetorians laid low at the foot of the ramp and the bystanders who had been dropped out to a distance of thirty meters.

It took four of them to get Old Spume off the gangplank, two apiece for Zinsser and Ghost. Scorpian Aquam generally hewed to at least a passable personal hygiene even in the water-scarce Big Sere season, but the saffrons were an unwashed and fetid-smelling lot.

Ghost remained limp as a dead snake, eyes open although she was unable to shift her gaze much, let alone move her head. Beyond the affected area some of the troops and a few civilians were watching uncertainly. With liftoff imminent, most people were beating a hasty retreat. With the Laputa in an irrevocable countdown, the snatching up of fallen items on the gangplank was slapdash. Ghost's 'baller lay somewhere down in the blackened landing pit, and no crewman knew or cared. Fiona might have agonized over that, as well.

The vessel's supercargo was at the hatchway, gesturing with his baton and barking orders while the gangplank was being raised by a windlass in the wooden outworks. He raised his megaphone to the men still on their feet.

"Come bear your comrades away or see them burned. *Dream Castle* raises in two minutes, regardless." The alloy dome of the lower hull was making faint shuddering, clunking noises, like heavy ports opening.

Ghost had a brief glimpse of the boarding lock as her bearers hauled her along at a clumsy gallop. There were worn and scraped deck and hull planks and the feet of saffron-liveried crew; then she was in a more spacious place where voices drowned each other out with commands, acknowledgments, warnings, frantic questions, and colorful invective.

Something brushed her right shoulder with noticeable force as she was deposited on the deck, not ungently. Prelaunch tremors made the air quiver; then the deck surged against her back, and *Dream Castle* lifted off, rocking a bit on ascent. The vibration was no surprise; the surprise was that the huge Optimant craft was still airworthy after two baseline centuries of continuous operation.

The fusion-pumped laser pulsejets had been operating that way since PreCyberplague days, heating precise pockets of air under the armored dome to 30,000 degrees K, exploding the very molecules, propelling and maintaining the Laputa aloft with closely spaced blast waves. The Beforetimers' blind faith in their technology had, like their elitism, set them up for oblivion, but some of their work demanded respect. This apparently wasn't going to be the inevitable moment of their catastrophic failure.

Her scarred cheek on the gritty deck, Ghost recognized Old Spume by the absurd wing-chair collar of his robe. Lying nearby, he had a large purple splotch painted on his right shoulder. *Dream Castle* rumbled against her back, ascending, as she worked on her next course of action. She had been exerting her willpower to regain control of her body without result. It came as a surprise, then, when she found her head cradled and Zinsser bent over her, looking like he had just come off an all-night narcosio bender.

Individual reactions to a dose of sonics varied greatly, and the oceanographer was evidently one of those who shook off a jangling quickly, though a violent quiver of the Laputa made him struggle to remain upright. His movements were spasmodic, but he controlled them well enough to begin patting her cheeks gently with his other hand.

A flash of saffron cloth indicated a crewman's presence. A horn container was uncapped under her nose, and she smelled a searing ammoniac compound that made her blink rapidly. A quick paroxysm ran through her. She arched, then slumped as she resumed control over her body—even if that control was accompanied by shakes and tremors. She pushed Zinsser's hands away without anger or resentment; she simply didn't need him patting her. She saw that, like Spume, he had a purple splotch daubed on his right shoulder. That she did as well explained the touch she had felt earlier. The other gangway victims were similarly marked.

Zinsser scowled at her pressing him off, then dragged himself to Old Spume. She felt weak and vile, but at least the Optimant sonics hadn't stimulated a vomiting reflex or loosened bowel control the way a 'wailer sometimes did. Ghost made herself sit up and survey her surroundings.

She was in a junction of passageways just beyond the main hatch—the *Dream Castle*'s quarterdeck of sorts. A smooth alloy bulkhead inboard was dark with soot and dust. Around her were walls of sawn and stained lumber well along in years and showing generations of furtive graffiti and carvings. The deck planks were only moderately cruddy; she guessed the crew members had to keep decent footing under themselves. The smells were evocative of unwashed bodies, broken plumbing, sickrooms, and live-stock pens, sufficiently evocative of the prisoner camps to put Ghost lethally on guard. She cycled an atman breath and put her thoughts through a quick cognitive pliometric to bring her Flowstate back into sync.

The boarding area was walled in and fitted with heavy interior doors, a design that smacked of security and crowd control. Lighting came from grids screwed into the wooden overhead, some completely burned out and doubtless irre-placeable and all of them showing darkened sections. Rank-smelling saffron-clad crewmen were rushing about, and a few other gangway casualties were lying unconscious or coming around with the same twitching and flopping she'd experienced. Not much else to see.

Some of the saffrons carried basket-hilted cudgels, but they were all acting relieved, joking overloudly and forcing laughter, replaying events to each other to cover their fright and vent tension. From what Ghost gathered, the troops at the landing ground *had* rushed in to pull their soniced bud-dies out of the wash of the superheated pulsejets.

"Everybody get moving, clear the boarding lock," one of the cudgel wielders ordered. "Common passengers belong in the steve spaces. You with the purple markers—the purser'll be around to collect your fares directly."

Ghost and Zinsser helped Spume to his feet. Zinsser groaned. "Common passengers—sounds like 'bilge class.'"

Ghost suspected bilge class would be luxury compared to common passenger status but didn't bother to share the thought.

Sky swabbies herded the revivees out the boarding lock and into a curving passageway that featured pit-sawn plank-ing for overhead, deck, and outer bulkhead. The composite hull of the Laputa proper served as an inner bulkhead. The outerworks, Ghost understood, were like a shack encircling a mountain peak.

The latecomers made their way up a spiral ladderwell, with Zinsser helping Spume along. Ghost had little patience with hard luck cases, but the Sense-maker *was* useful to the effort of getting back to the *GammaLAW*. Then, too, he had kept his mouth shut when he had seen her filch the cyber-caul in Rhodes's bedchambers. She gripped the old man's unpainted shoulder and led the way, tugging him up step by step.

The treadles of the *Shattertail* tapped a steady tattoo, driving the eight-wheeler south along the RambleRove, toward the Trans-Bourne. The cadence put Mason in mind of some Old Earth man-o'-war's drummer boy sounding "beat to quarters" in the Age of Sail. Purifyre and his confederates had seemed more irritated than dismayed that the praetorians had somehow trailed them to the mounds, but the contingency plan had worked. The pumpwagon's risky flight in darkness had left the Ean troops behind.

Night was just beginning to yield; the coming day already hinted at a classic Big Sere ordeal by fire. Mason was clutching a lacquered rail in the prow, braced to ride out the sways and bounces. Gazing out on the onetime Optimant motorway, now quickened with human activity, he marveled that so much enterprise could be generated by a mere toy Hippo Nolan had cobbled for his own self-amusement—a few galvani stones, some freshwater bivalve tissue, a bit of mucking with nutrient solutions along with blocks of *Scepter* computer time that weren't needed because in the wake of the catastrophe at the Styx Strait, the survey team had been reduced to carrying out an abbreviated version of its original mission. A novelty puttered up in one person's spare time had, in a generation changed the land-scape of an entire world.

Mason recalled that it had been Eisley Boon who had lent help and encouragement to Hippo's flexi-flivver hobby—about the closest the dour Boon had ever come to frivolity. Mason could only wonder how Boon, who was now nothing but anonymous molecules dispersed in the great Amnion, would have reacted to what he and Hippo had wrought.

The RambleRove coursed with predawn traffic—pedes-trians, sedan chairs, barrow-coolies, and the rest, stoic work-ing stiffs abroad in darkness by the flicker of mollywood knots, dim phosphorescent algeol lamps, and rushlights or through sheer familiarity with the route.

Wayside villages were long since awake and astir to make the most of Eyewash's light. The RambleRove's sides and shoulders were crowded with those who had decided to keep moving south, away from the carnage at Wall Water and perhaps in fear of the midnight sunburst that had been the destruction of *Terrible Swift Sword*. On the road's fair-way the eight-wheeler had right-of-way by prerogative of weight, speed, and invulnerability to collision with lesser traffic. The GammaLAW mission had of course planned to upgrade and expand the PrePlague highway system as part of its infrastructure building, but muscle cars hadn't been part of the concept, and indig-controlled mass transport *definitely* hadn't.

Aquamarine had no large domesticable animals suit-able for draft or saddle work excepting the Scourland Ferals' bounders, and those malicious two-legged jumping jacks quickly sickened and died anywhere else on the planet. With only human motive power available, the Aquam's ability to distribute goods had been severely curtailed on Scorpia as elsewhere. Mass production and economies of scale had languished for lack of access to markets until some mysterious protoindustrialists down in the Trans-Bourne had changed everything with dyes and muscle cars.

It occurred to Mason that his son might be working for a syndicate or a cabal of robber barons, though upon reflection, it scarcely mattered. Mason was aligned with the charismatic, tough, idealistic Purifyre, like it or not. The boy gave every indication of having accepted his father's acceptance at full face value. But one question kept buzzing Mason's brain: How had Hippo's prototype gotten all the way south across the Styx Strait in the first place? The last Mason had seen of Hippo's prototype, it had been lying at the foot of the Optimant lighthouse at New Alexandria on Scorpia's southern coast. He had kicked the thing there himself that final night onworld.

Mason glanced to the lamplit bow, where his son and the boy's confederates were conferring with *Shattertail*'s master and chief pilot, Turnswain, a small, sunburned man from the Trans-Bourne, gaunt as a starveling, who cut a striking figure in a fuzzy sarong died orange with blue zebra stripes. The conspirators were still in their coolie waistwraps, turbans, and greasepaint facial decorations.

What were meant to appear as the ark and coffer of the Human Enlightenment faith were lashed down belowdecks, disguised as common freight and better guarded than Mason himself. Just why Purifyre had stolen the GammaLAW Science Siders' DNA and micro/biolab field units had yet to be explained.

Purifyre, too, was still in character as a barrowman—disturbingly so, Mason thought. He squatted with coolie-muscled haunches brushing the deck, sharing a flax spliff. When his turn came, he toked it peon fashion, held upright between the middle and ring fingers of a loosely clenched fist, taking carburetor hits from the mouthpiece formed by his thumb and forefinger. Mason was spared the need to nag his son about smoking when a grabsman sang out a sighting. Everyone swung to look back at what could only be another muscle car rolling down from the distant parking mounds in darkness, leaving a fireball meteor trail of wind-whipped flame, whirling sparks, and popping embers.

The amazed obscenities from Purifyre, Turnswain, and the rest had less to do with its suicidal careen over unlit roads than with the fact that the wagon was exiting the parking mounds by way of the entrance ramp. Somebody with eyes like an intel-SAT said he thought it was *Racknuts*, a name that meant nothing to Mason.

Purifyre came out of his squat, flicking the spliff roach over the side and tossing back his long barrowman's queue. "A fighting car?"

Turnswain tapped his forehead, signifying *uh uh, think again.* "A coffin on wheels, a benjo cart—although its master, Manna, mixes a potent *elixir vitae*—her Analeptic Fix. Too potent, if you ask me. But her pullers are long overdue for replacement. No worries. We'll pull away."

"She's already slowing," Essa remarked.

That Purifyre's graying, fierce-eyed bodyguard passed for a barrowman in a tattered poncho and yashmak veil hadn't surprised Mason much; nor had the discovery that her front teeth had been chipped and filed into frightening points. And Essa was right: The car was fast losing ground, its meteoric wake dwindling to something more like the fire flecks of a far-off sparkwheel. As everyone watched, the fiery brand went dark, lost to sight as *Shattertail* dipped into a low spot in the road.

Purifyre turned to the others, handling himself with nonchalant road legs. He stretched, making the tattoos of yin and yang, robotic dragons, and wanton women move. His coolie face-paint was getting dry and caked. Mason lurched and staggered forward, arriving just in time to hear his son say, "We'll make that pause at the Wiseacres, just in case. Put yourselves in readiness." Purifyre thumped Essa's shoulder and indicated Mason. "And see to him."

Essa gave Mason a meat-ripper grin that was 100 percent congeniality-free.

CHAPTER FIFTEEN

Up on the CIWS mount the bosun's mate had one ammo chute capture claw free and was getting the other. "What's keeping that patch?" he yelled.

Moving like a sleepwalker to Kurt's exhortations, Lazlo-Lazlo took the other side of the heavy metal square; then the two of them wrestled it up to the weapon mount. Kurt was painfully aware that the falling dumbot had scraped away insulating nonskid, leaving exposed metal under their shoes.

The bo got the second capture claw pried open. Like a conjuring trick, the chute feed system disengaged from the Gatling and vanished below, but the blastproof plates refused to deploy, leaving a virtual touch hole by which fire or explosion could set off the magazine. Not everything down there required electrical priming.

Kurt and Lazlo got a corner of the patch up on the gun mount catwalk. Being the closest, Kurt squirmed up to help the bosun's mate manhandle it over the gaping magazine elevator shaft. The other two enlisted ratings were on their bellies grappling with the multibarrel's helical feed, trying to unload the ten rounds of armor-piercing/incendiary still lined up there.

The bo heaved, and Kurt strained so hard that his vision began to blur. The patch finally swung, clanking into place over the magazine shaft with a ringing finality. The two enlisteds had broken open the helical feed and brought out the first of the unlinked 30-mm rounds.

"Form a relay line," the bo said, urging Kurt back down to where Lazlo stood, petrified. "We'll drop the rounds overboard."

Kurt silently concurred; irreplaceable as the 30s were, better safe than sorry. He was about to jump down the meter or so when the biggest surge of all hit the ship.

Lazlo rose into the air and flew backward as if being reeled in on invisible cable, his hands and forearms contorted against his chest as if malformed. His hair stood out on all sides; his jaw was clamped shut but off-kilter. One of his shoes had been blown off and was arcing away from him like a spent, streaming booster. His eyes held a horrible round wonderment.

At the same time Kurt heard electrical popping and bursting behind him. The surge had found the helical feed. Then he was suddenly airborne, propelled by the bosun's mate, who was scrabbling to leap for safety. Kurt flailed to spare himself, but one foot touched exposed metal close to where Lazlo had been zapped.

He felt as if he'd been whacked with a huge square of armor plate. His innards, rather than his skin, seemed to be on fire. He saw a white light but heard nothing, not even the detonations in the turret behind him as the 30s in the feed were detonated. Though Kurt knew nothing about it, the bo and the two enlisted ratings were killed instantly, and the CIWS breech mechanism was blown wide open.

The next thing he did know, he was being awakened by a sharp pain in his right earlobe. He was prepared to find himself in the afterlife but instead saw a smoke-blackened, drawn, and anxious face under a navy battle helmet. Tonii was kneeling by him and digging 'ers thumbnail into his earlobe to bring him around. In the aftereffects of electrocution he didn't feel his usual unease around the genblender.

"Kurt, can you hear me?"

"Yeah—the gun!" Everything sounded muffled, including his own voice. "Got to unload it!"

"Easy, Kurt." Tonii kept him still with steely engeneered strength. The gynander's sloe, jade-green eyes peered into his, searching for signs of concussion or other injury. "The danger's past, but you took quite a hit."

He realized that other people were moving around nearby, and he began recalling fragments of what had happened. He coughed from the stench of scorched hair and skin, spilled fire-fighting chemicals, and burned 30-mm propellant and explosive charges. He turned his head and saw a detail shaking out a body bag over an unmoving form. One of the corpse's shoes had been lost, and the nail of the man's right big toe had been blown off by the lightning. Kurt recognized the urine-stained trousers.

"Lazlo!"

"You can't help him anymore, Kurt," Tonii said, though she helped him into a sitting position anyway. The stink of seared meat made Kurt want to retch. Lazlo's hair had puffed out around his head like a nimbus; his face was strangely askew.

"Contractions fractured his jaw," one of the body detail said when he noticed Kurt staring. "Two places, looks like." He bent to seal the bag.

"Wait."

Kurt had spotted a dark shape against Lazlo's burn-stained poet's blouse. It was the scene-framing reticle Lazlo had used to gaze at life, its nickel finish turned black by current. Kurt fingered it uncertainly, with an impulse to have it as a keepsake but a dread of pilfering the dead.

"Take your buddy's medallion, kid," the body detail sailor prompted. "Won't be any personal effects shipped home from *this* cruise anytime soon."

Tonii went to remove the reticle's lanyard from Lazlo's neck, but Kurt stopped 'erm. Lazlo-Lazlo had used the device to put himself outside the picture, outside the GammaLAW mission. Maybe that ultimately was what had caused him to be struck down. With the stink of his own singed hair in his nostrils, Kurt had no wish to tempt fate, the joss of GammaLAW.

"I don't want it on me," he said.

As Tonii tucked the reticle back, Kurt saw with tremulous clarity that being in the picture was the only hope of survival any of them had now. Being in the mission, without reservation.

"All hands, jettison headsets!" Quant shouted to his bridge watch. He had torn off his own and thrown it aside, blue sparks having popped in its visor when the first power overload hit.

The second electrical surge had been even stronger; watch members were already standing clear of all bare metal. Shock-wilted Astarte Thu had been carried off the bridge, and a runner stood ready to take her place as the telephone talker. Quant motioned him not to.

"Belay that. Bosun's mate of the watch, get all hands off hardwire sets before half our complement are brain-fried."

Keeler used a polymer plotting table compass to push the PA button; the system was still working thanks to emergency power. The bridge and weather decks were lit with the same reduced wattage, like a fort under siege and short of fuel. Tight-cast and hardwire commo had both been knocked out.

Quant crossed to the acoustic speaking tubes, pulled the stopper from one, and blew hard to sound the whistle in the stopper at the far end. The engineering officer who answered had a note of disbelief in his voice; aside from occasional drills, the speaking tubes had always seemed to be just so much archaic decor. Designed for maximum sonic conduction and passive amplification, they were far superior to preelectric brass pipes in Old Earth vessels, but they still smacked of coal-fired boilers and gunboat diplomacy.

"Engineering, bridge." The force of Quant's voice rattled the tube. "I need turns on the actuators and my helm back."

Sounding as if he would rather have been in the water with the Nixies, the engineer explained why that wasn't to be, at least for a while longer. Damage from the power surges and unfinished refit work had left nothing in the way of backup. Emergency manual steering might be on-line in an hour; engine power, perhaps less.

Quant's retort was cut off by another zap from the Nixies. He jumped back from the speaking tube even though it showed no arcing. Other components and instrumentation did, however, with more spurts and crackling and an odor of smoldering insulation.

"Bosun's mate of the watch, pass the word. All non-critical systemry is to be taken off-line."

While Keeler put the word out over the PA, Quant ordered inertial tracking started, matched against the sonar and ROVer charting they had of the lake bottom. He then turned to Gai-raszhek. "Eddie, try to get me back the bow cam feed. I need to know what those devil rags are doing. Helmsman, what's your bearing?"

It wasn't good. As little freeboard as she had for a flight-decked vessel, the *GammaLAW* had sides that still presented a lot of surface to act as a sail. The prevailing wind, as well as the currents in that part of the lake, had her drifting slowly side-on in the direction of Wall Water, the vengeful Aquam, and Grandee Rhodes's steam cannon.

Quant dispatched a runner to get all available RIBs ready for deployment. The rigid inflatable boats lacked the brute power to tow the SWATHship clear, but they could slow her drift into harm's way—provided that they could be put into the water without being pan-fried by the Nixies. Quant's first notion was to use the ship's measure IV ice-breaking system, but with the mains off-line, the system was useless. His next thought was to use Ext hand grenades.

He had given the runner only half his message when another wave of voltage rocked the ship, followed by a tremendous concussion from aft. A streak of orange incandescence shot forward, clearing the pilot house by mere centimeters. Quant realized it was a CIWS tracer round.

The report Gairaszhek brought back from a quick visual wasn't catastrophic, but it was bad enough to make Quant want to punch the bulkhead. The Gatling was history; his ship had no long reach left.

Daddy D was spotted by the Ext marksman position in the main hull bow, where Quant could speak to him over a handheld bullhorn. "I need grenades in the water off the Science Side bow, General—concussion-type if you have them. Throw them well clear with five-second fuse settings."

Delecado didn't have a bullhorn, but he did have a tactical handlight with concentrator lens. Gairaszhek read the general's longs and shorts aloud: "F, R, A, G, S."

Quant snorted. Then fragmentation grenades it would be. Their underwater shock waves might be something the gauzy water wraiths would respect. He raised the bullhorn again. "Understood. We need them ASAP, General."

Daddy D loped off with two more Exts, carrying all the grenades from the bow detail and obviously planning to commandeer whatever others he could on the way.

Quant grabbed a night-vision binocular and moved to the port side. As he had feared, wind and lake currents had pushed the SWATHship clear of an intervening point of land, putting Wall Water in line of sight two thousand meters away and ever so slowly closing. He was about to order the signal bridge to instruct one of the RIBs to stand away from the ship when another wickedly sudden ball of flame and brightness mushroomed up close to port, partially blocked by the flight deck.

The *GammaLAW* jerked under Quant's feet. Smoke wreathed the explosion as scraps of the inflatable and its crew were lofted on various arcs, stippling Lake Ea with debris. Crew members on the flight deck, unfreezing, made ready to throw flotation devices and life rafts to any survivors, but Quant knew in his pith and his most dispassionate reason that barring miracles, there wouldn't be any.

CHAPTER SIXTEEN

The 'cess has hit the circulators, Burning mused as the *Racknuts* sped across the Heights, bottoming out in ruts and hurtling off moguls of the feeder road. But it wasn't only the rush of grandeean troops that jarred him. As if shaking off a dream, he realized just how far his pursuit of Purifyre was about to draw him from the *GammaLAW and* his bounden duty to the Exts.

Clinging to Burning's pistol belt, Souljourner helped haul him up from where he'd been studying *Racknuts's* flesh-and-wood treadle engine. His last view of Pelta and Missy found them pale with fright but sticking to their job, staunch as Exts.

He hitched himself back prone on the deck, leaving his pistol holstered. Courtesy of the three wren boy Shadow-rats, the praetorians had probably surmised that he was an offworlder, but it would only make matters worse to confirm his identity with a hasty gunshot. If she learned that the troops were after Burning rather than her precious Analeptic Fix formula, Manna would probably toss out the anchor and feed him to the soldiers.

The Jitterland Heights were in a loud hurly-burly as the six-wheeler gained speed with each chassis-shaking pump of its treadles. Burning glanced around to get his bearings by the flare of the car's torch and rushlight lamps.

Assorted praetorians were blowing and banging on Aquam instruments. Officers, noncoms, and enlisteds hollered orders, threats, and curses. They had been caught off guard by Manna's abrupt pulling of the chocks but were racing to try to board the car or at least halt it with an improvised barricade. The parking mounds' denizens were variously fleeing for safety, yanking goods and dependents out of the way, cheering Manna, screaming for the troops to draw blood, and placing bets on the action.

Burning got to his feet, pulling Souljourner to hers. Spin and Yake were now at the rear grabs. Boner was forward at the steering wheel, which looked for all the world like an ancient sailing vessel's wheel. Manna was helping her husband by throwing her vast bulk into it, keeping her balance handily despite her ivory peg leg.

Since *Racknuts*'s scheduled passengers weren't aboard, the mumued harridan belabored her only supernumeraries. "Step lively, you useless suckholes! Let none arrest us!"

Burning motioned Souljourner to stay down and moved forward, where he clung to one of four tall, hinged, sparlike poles that were lashed upright on either rail. A squad of the Autocrat Haleso's Apocalyptics were reversing field to the left, trying to match velocities with *Racknuts* but failing to gain ground. To the right a dozen Killmongers of the Dominor Paralipsio had come swarming around a bawdy tent with halberds and other polearms raised to use as boarding hooks and grapnels. Two files of Militerrors had been forming up to block the way, but with the muscle car careening straight for them, they broke ranks, scattering, save for a fugleman who disappeared under the bow and became one more jolt of the suspension.

A sling-gun quarrel bounced off the upright wooden spar a few centimeters from Burning's head, and he scrunched down and called to Souljourner to take cover. She half crouched by a woven reed hamper but stubbornly stayed where she was, thumbing her neck pouch so fast, he thought it might start smoking. More missiles were zinging past Manna and Boner, who were still bent to the medieval rack-and-pinion wheel. The car skidded sideways a bit— nothing graceful enough to be called a turn—and most of the ragged sling-gun volley went wide. Burning clung to the spar for balance, and Souljourner grabbed freight lashings. It became clear why the deck cargo was so well tied down.

One longish, blunt-nosed quarrel came straight for Manna—either through sheer luck or because one of the harquebusiers knew how to lead a target—but it glanced off the heavy wicker basket lid she was holding and didn't budge her. Spin and Yake had taken up half-cylinder shields of leather on wooden frames, bulky but small enough to allow the boys to continue to work the grabs levers. A ball-headed bolt from a light slinger glanced off Yake's shield and rebounded upward, wobbling and spent, to arc out over the port rail.

Burning had the distinct impression *Racknuts*'s crew had done this sort of thing before. They showed no concern about making themselves fugitives; they had the freedom of the Optimant high roads while the Ean grandees' writ was limited.

Manna and Boner cut a course for the exit ramp, with Spin and Yake skillfully helping with deft applications of the grabs. In spite of the lever arrangement, it was obvious that the twitch-mobile wasn't built for quick braking. Moreover, Burning reckoned, a panic stop would break gear teeth or snap the treadle driveshaft like a pretzel stick.

As *Racknuts* was slamming and wallowing along the dirt track, he spied activity on other cars. Troops on and around them were gesticulating, shaking fists, and squaring off with the crews. They're commandeering chase cars, it came to him. Not for the pursuit of *Racknuts*, however, which had only just made its break, but apparently for *Shattertail*.

Burning kept himself from picturing how Ghost might be faring in Purifyre's hands, let alone the idea of her falling into the hands of Grandee Rhodes. He was scanning for men at arms within boarding distance when he heard Manna's caterwaul, "Roadblock!" A barge of a car had been lowered from its mound, despite two missing wheels, to bar the way to the exit ramp.

"Turn haw! Turn haw!" It was car jargon for "left." Manna had called it to Spin and Yake; to Burning and Souljourner she added, "Man the outriggers! Counterweight us!"

Souljourner staggered upright to the left rail, grabbing the other of the hinged poles, the mate to the one Burning was hanging on to. She slipped a retaining loop off a hook on its side.

"Do likewise or we'll heel over!"

He had noticed *Racknuts* was partially cut under—built so that the front wheels could angle beneath the body—meaning it could hang a sharp turn in a pinch. The six-wheeler was coming hard left, and so, as in small boat sailing, it needed occupants to shift their weight to the inside of the turn to keep centrifugal force from flipping it. Taking his cue from Souljourner, Burning freed the other outrigger, which featured handgrips and foot loops, and swung out twenty-five degrees from the vertical.

Manna was coaching Spin and Yake on the grabs and calling commands back to Pelta, who was standing with her head out the treadle-engine compartment hatch. The muscle car began to slow just where the feeder track merged with another track at a wide spot in the maze of rutted arteries.

"'Ware all," Manna called out. "Coming haw!" She and Boner turned the weighted steering wheel hand over hand over hand, and *Racknuts* heeled, the left rail rising and the rear wheels on that side of the bogey leaving the ground.

"Now or never!" Souljourner cried. She leaned out over the side, clinging to the outrigger, one foot in a loop bound to it and one on the rail.

Never would be nice, Burning thought, but he aped her anyway. The muscle car seemed to be taking the turn in slow motion. Aquam scattered, military trumpetry sounded, timber groaned, and metal creaked, threatening to splinter. Lanterns swung and banged on their mounts, kindling a dizzying light show. The outriggers came closer to the vertical. As Souljourner leaned into hers, the springy wood bowed and gave her another ten degrees of tilt. Burning did the same.

The deck kept canting. Unsecured items skidded down to the right and lashed freight shifted ominously. Burning was deciding which way to jump when Souljourner gave a series of wild yips and swung herself up onto the outrigger with one foot hooked over it, her weight bowing it radically.

Flowstate didn't keep Burning from thinking, Damned if I won't, and copying her. His boot toe couldn't find the foot loop, so he wrapped his legs around the pole. It arced in a way that said breaking point. They slowed the rise of the deck, but his pole bent even more perilously. It was on the verge of snapping when Manna and Boner began to bring the front wheels back amidships, both of them braced against the tilt of the car.

Racknuts slewed onto a straight course, its left-side rims slamming into contact with the ground. Bottoming out the elliptical springs, the car's hull crunched against its undercarriage, and some of the leather thoroughbraces snapped with a sound like cracking bullwhips. Still clinging to the outriggers, Burning and Souljourner scrabble-walked madly up the side of the car and over the rail, almost shaken loose as the six-wheeler did an ungainly fishtail onto an even keel. It had lost speed, but the power of the treadles bucked it forward again in head-snapping surges. Burning continued to wonder how Missy's hands didn't cramp up solid, squeezing those galvani-stone grippers.

He and Souljourner got back to the deck, she slightly more adroitly. Her prominent-jawed face that had looked so plain among the vamps of Wall Water was joyous, vivacious in the pell-mell light splashes.

"Hoo, Redtails! Haven't done that since I was a girl!"

Manna left Boner to steer and hobbled forward to hammer a bronze bell secured to the bow. "Make way, you phlegmatic butt-snufflers, you wang-strangling zombies!"

The crew's frenzied efforts made sense when Souljourner cried, "We're going the wrong way!"

Burning saw immediately that they were departing the Heights via the one-way entrance ramp and that *Racknuts*'s night flight was defying the most basic rules of the road. Shrieks and curses sounded out in the dark, along with the trip-hammer clangs of other cars' bells.

A ten-wheeler built like a Conestoga loomed in front of *Racknuts*. Boner's steering and Yake and Spin's genius with the grabs levers let *Racknuts* veer off the track just enough to avoid a head-on, only to send the car careening through a wain-wright's works. Timber-shaping frames and barrels of gum sealant went flying, jacks were bashed aside, and a hoist toppled. Boner skirted the forge by centimeters. A hawser, stretched taut, just cleared the bow, ripping out both

Racknuts's lamp masts and nearly clotheslining Manna, who ducked at the last second.

With the lamps gone, the track was almost impossible to discern; just as appallingly, those in the way had no warning light to alert them. Manna stopped pounding the bell long enough to yell to Burning, "Get up here and make a warning light, you craven whistle-dick!"

With Ghost's fate wedded to *Racknuts*'s for now, he sprang to obey, motioning for Souljourner to stay where she was. Manna was still bell ringing and yelling. Only Boner's thorough knowledge of the mounds prevented them from piling up. One lamp had vanished, and the other was shattered, though a little guttering wick was flickering in the very bow.

Burning had begun looking for something to use as a torch when pandemonium in the road ahead made him look up. Someone else was making warning noises, but there was no way to pinpoint the direction.

"Burning! Heads up!" Souljourner cried. Still clinging to a freight lashing, she tossed something that skittered against his foot—the broom Spin had been using to sweep down the deck earlier. Burning grabbed it, spun it like a drum major with a baton, and took a light from the spilled wick. It was a splint broom carved from a single young log of maoriwood; its bottom was cropped into thin slats, and its upper length was shaved into splints that had been bent down and bound in place, leaving only a handle—not a long-burning torch but more effective than straw. The Seredry slivers caught fire quickly, and Burning held it up. The broom took on a rippling, multicolored crown of flame.

He braced himself in the bow like a figurehead, holding the blazing firebrand high, while the wind sent sparks and cinders slipstreaming in his wake. It didn't do much to illuminate the way, but it did signal danger. A large lumber sledge was dragged and heaved off the arterial, just far enough for Boner to squeak *Racknuts* around it.

The blazing broom's sparks scorched Burning's skin and charred his hair. Streaming flames lit his face and Hussar Plaits, his uniform, and the gold buttons on his bib-front blouse. If the grandeean troops had any description of him there would be no shortage of witnesses to confirm that he had passed that way.

The muscle car left the mounds behind and came to a gentle, curving downslope to the south. Boner slowed to take it.

"Never gone it in this direction before," Spin whooped.

Souljourner had fetched a stern lamp, and Manna was rigging it on the bow. The broom splints having burned away to stumps, Burning was about to chuck it over the side when Manna scolded him. "Desist, Redtails, you arse-berry! Put that good maoriwood aside for rebinding! Wasteful codthwacker!"

"Yeah, so you can jam it up your bottom line," he muttered under his breath.

CHAPTER SEVENTEEN

Essa blocked Mason's way when he would've followed Purifyre belowdecks. She held out a hand as calloused as an oarsman's. Like the other ersatz barrow-coolies, she stank of liniment, gooner and slackwort, sweat and grease-paint. "Take off your clothes," she ordered, showing a filed-toothed smile worthy of a giant old rock-eel.

"Eh? See here, *my son* knows he can trust me, Essa."

"Don't call me by that name! We're not at Wall Water any longer! Ballyhoot, I am!"

"It suits you," Mason said, nodding. "Do I get a new name, as well?"

She searched his face to determine if he was mocking her and couldn't tell for sure. "Just see that you address me proper or there'll be trouble." She reached into a wicker pannier and medicine-balled a bundle of Aquam clothing at his gut. "Go forward somewhere and change!"

The attire was second- or thirdhand. Had he been less curious about the purpose of their mission, he might have objected to the sweatstains, the stink, and the likelihood that it harbored vermin. The pantaloons were what Periapts referred to as Siams but were known on Aquamarine as side-loaders: wrap-tie waist, commodious legs with outer seams slit to midthigh, and hem ends knotted above the calves. With the Siams came husk-rope sandals and, worrisomely, a car rider's stomacher of four-ply diffodar hide with bone slat reinforcements. He welcomed the lightweight mantelet, however, for protection against a sun that would be merciless by midmorning.

There was also a cheap maizeshuck-*mâché* vizard sculpted in the form of a vampire-like ghoul of Aquam folklore, but Mason set it aside, wanting his son to see his face. That the ensemble didn't include a turban cloth was fine with him, since he had never been much of a hand at wrapping the Scorpian headgear-carryalls.

The only thing he was wearing from his previous life was his codcup. He transferred his plugphone, whatty, and other belongings to a drawstring pouch that tied to the stomacher. He no longer had to worry about his flechette pistol, cummerbund holster, spare ammunition cassettes, or propellant cartridges because Purifyre had taken those, along with the cybercaul.

Gently fingering his throat, Mason found neither tissue damage nor residual soreness from Purifyre's choking him out at Wall Water. Mason was a duffer when it came to hand-to-hand, but he knew that it took an expert to work the blood choke so cleanly.

And Yatt was quiet. Mason assumed that the AI realized that it was in its own interest to remain so, especially on *Shattertail*, where Purifyre's followers might infer that Mason was possessed. The Aquam had their own PostPlague taboos about cyberinterface, and even Mason's relationship to Purifyre might not offer protection from a drastic, possibly lethal exorcism.

In the time it had taken to switch clothes, the RambleRove had carried the eight-wheeler back up onto higher ground. Eyewash's first chlorine-yellow beams were streaking the clouds. Only Turnswain and the rest of the *Shattertail* crew were on deck. Before Mason could inquire after his son, a cry went up from one of the grabsmen. "Car-ho! Coming south from the Jitterlands. And another—no, two!"

Shattertail was cresting a rise from which momentum could be easily regained, so Turnswain told his engineer to disengage the bevel gears and his grabsmen to put their shoulders to the levers. Instead of setting chocks, the master pilot retrieved a handmade spyglass of flaking leather, tarnished brass, and scratched lenses that might have been two hundred years old.

"Two greatwagons and a gig," Tumswain said. "*Rut-Rider, Rattlebones*, and *Bunbanger*. Rails crowded with Militerrors, Infrangibies, Diehards, and kindred grandeean torque dorks." The three muscle cars were coming fast.

"Chasing *Racknuts*, maybe?" someone asked.

"Manna may think so, but no. So it's onward to Wiseacres. Make ready to pump treadles! Prepare to let go of the grabs!"

Turnswain got the car moving at a speed that was guaranteed to deplete the flexors at a prodigal rate, but Purifyre's coconspirators had more pressing worries than eventual re-muscling costs. Mason found himself a place among the sparse deck cargo where those afoot couldn't spot him as the wagon topped hills and raced through valleys.

The Big Sere day was already simmering. Mason spied a sheaf of dunefeather fronds, worked one free, and began folding it into an improvised Aquam-style sunhat. Incandessa, his late wife, had taught him the trick; he delighted to find the technique coming back to him so easily. Peel back strips of petiole rib and knot them up a hand's length from the lobate tip to give a good concavity, then use a thorny stipule from the stem to pin the tip up and hold the shape.

"A dead giveaway, Father," Purifyre's voice came over his shoulder. "You are dressed as a man from the Trans-Bourne, but your sunhat's typical of New Alexandria. Not to mention that you'll lose it straightaway on a moving car."

Mason looked over his shoulder. "It hadn't occurred to—*MeoDeos!*" The sight of his son's latest transformation nearly stopped Mason's heart.

On the outerworks of *Dream Castle*'s upper level individuals and groups of embarking common passengers were trying to negotiate an allotment of deck space with those already aboard. The carpentry of the place suggested the interior or a wooden ship, a post-and-beam house, or an Aquam muscle car, yet nowhere did the framing actually penetrate or tie to the Laputa's hull proper.

With Spume under his own power now, Zinsser jerked a thumb back at the passageway. "Mm! How'd *he* get here?"

As Ghost caught sight of the man, her eyes widened, deforming her scars and giving her a distinctly predatory look. She steered her companions behind a partition, then angled around just enough to see down the passageway.

Zinsser followed suit.

"Testamentor," Old Spume exclaimed softly, misting a little. "One of Purifyre's closest votaries. But he's dressed as a Dev-Oceanite! This is a complication even I cannot explain—whoops."

Off balance, the Sense-maker slipped, bearing Ghost and Zinsser into clear view. Testamentor's glance was drawn by the sound and movement. He froze in surprise at seeing two Visitants and the grandeean adviser. Breaking off his conversation with one of the Laputa's saffron-robed guards, he ducked through a stout three-batten wooden door.

"Clumsy fucking gutbarrel!" Zinsser hissed.

Spume ignored him. "Lo, Testamentor—disciple to a wandering mendicant *rishi*—accommodates himself in the luxury of a stateroom. That's a beggar's bowl I'd share. Nor was he glad to see us. Come, let's find a place to take our ease. I'm all undone."

Ghost had to agree; she hadn't slept since the previous morning. They moved in the opposite direction from Testamentor, sizing up the dimly lit, clamorous, and noisome steve spaces.

Dream Castle had been rising constantly if somewhat tipsily since liftoff, maintaining attitude with turbofan thrusters powered by the ancient fusion plant, though not as well as it must have in its prime. People were reacting visibly to the drop in air pressure. Ghost and Zinsser relieved the pressure in their heads by blowing hard with mouths clamped shut and noses pinched closed. The crew and many passengers knew the technique, but Ghost had to coach Spume.

"I thought you knew your way around these birdcages?" Zinsser asked him.

"Formerly," he said. "But not in recent years, I admit."

Cold winds were already whistling through the outer bulkheads, and a few loose planks of the outerworks were rattling. The steve spaces had only thin slots of unglazed window to allow light in. Some heat seeped up from the supremely thermal reflective bowl, inside which the pulse-jet explosions were contained, but none of it penetrated beyond the lower deck in which the crew was quartered. Air currents and the movement of the Laputa against its scratch-mounted superstructure made the outerworks creak and groan.

Still slightly damp from the plunge into the tailwater, Ghost and Zinsser began to shiver; the wooden klamp shoes Ghost had found in the blasted campsite were like ice carvings. With water a precious commodity, it was no wonder the saffrons stank, she realized. Even whores' baths would be expensive and an invitation to cold, flu, or worse.

Braziers, hibachis, and traveler's stoves were forbidden for want of ventilation and the danger of fire. Common passengers wrapped themselves in blankets, shawls, capes, and coats. Groups huddled for warmth, and some people even erected small windbreaks and lean-tos. The shuddering of the outer-works was punctuated by wracking coughs, feuds over deck space, squalling children, bickering, and vomiting. Most of the nauseated ones ignored the reeking buckets chained to every fourth upright and spewed where they were, hitting themselves and their neighbors. Few made it to a window, but the windows were so small that they were useless in any case. Those obliged to wait in line were worse off than if they'd stayed put.

"I've been around fish guts most of my life, and I've never smelled anything like this place," Zinsser observed. To Ghost he added, "Your lips are blue."

"I'm only cold from the skull out," she said absently. "Means nothing." She asked Spume, "How long is the run to Hangwitch?"

It wouldn't be fast, she knew. The Laputas had been designed to move with stately leisure, since the Optimants had had other means of transport for haste. The ability to build one in the first place, as well as mount lavish skyborne revels, was proof of highest TechNoble status. PrePlague records showed that the longest continuous party on record had lasted just under three baseline-years.

"A few hours; a mere flit," the Sense-maker assured her. "By noonday we'll be on the Agora, with tall tankards of their renowned fungo in hand."

Cudgel-wielding crewmen were moving through the steves to ensure that no one was using fire. Gamblers had gotten out cards, Holy Rollers, knuckle wheels, and so forth. Smokers lit up flax spliffs, pipes of resin pellets, and pinrolled whackweed cigarettes. People dug out flasks of gooner, pyro, hoppie, and crank for a few dawn bracers against the cold. A woman put a chaw of slackwort between her gums and lip, then loosened her bodywraps enough to suckle her infant. Hawkers and vendors circulated, as well, charging ruinous prices to a captive market.

The Flying Pavilion wallowed, making the outerworks complain as if they might rip loose from the hull. "The safest spot would be below, with the crew," Zinsser concluded. "They must have some means of relocating everyone to inside the hull in a pinch."

"None," Spume answered with beetling certainty. "The crew are no more welcome in the precincts of the Insiders than are the likes of us. But be of good cheer; we won't need to trust to the outerworks' integrity for long."

They followed the curve of the hull, picking their way among common passengers. Their outfits drew glances, but people tended to look away when Ghost returned the stares. She wondered how so many people had managed to pay for passage.

There were buckets of sand for use against fire, but the steve spaces' only stab at creature comfort were the latrine sheds built every ninety degrees into the outer bulkhead. That amounted to only three jakes, since the fourth side was located inside the stateroom accommodations. The sound of skirling winds coming from the lavs suggested that they were simple holes in the deck. Ghost speculated on what the people living along *Dream Castle*'s route thought of its waste disposal engineering.

She went to one of the slot windows, hoping to get her bearings. The Laputa was at perhaps 2,500 meters by then; the sky was just lightening, and she found herself looking back at Lake Ea, Wall Water, the dam, and a black splotch that might have been the landing ground. There was no sign of the *GammaLAW* on that part of the lake she could see. She had no idea just how high the Laputa would rise but assumed it wouldn't be inordinately far—not if the passengers in the unpressurized outer-works were expected to survive the trip.

Dawn raked Scorpia, rouging the hills and treetops. The sight was so ethereally beautiful that for a moment she forgot the stench of the outerworks deck and her separation from the Exts and her brood of Discards. In the POW camps—as Fiona—she had come to accept that any chance instant of transcendent beauty had to be seized, embraced, venerated in defiance of the agonies of life to invest survival and its atrocities with meaning.

Zinsser crowded up next to her. "Reminds me of an Old Earth proverb." He was worn out, barely aware he was talking or to whom. " 'The morning is wiser than the evening.' I don't think I quite understood it until this moment. And now I own the copyright."

She almost liked him for that one.

CHAPTER EIGHTEEN

The honorable Wix Uniday started only momentarily when the metal-rending detonation of the CIWS Gatling came beating the air and sent splinters of steel and alloy, bits of gun mount, and spitballs of human tissue rattling against *GammaLAW*'s main superstructure. He was trying the Mark VI headset when one of the RIBs went fireball. Since the bloody disaster didn't immediately affect or imperil him, he ignored it and concentrated on utilizing the headset's integral transmitter to pierce the horrendous jamming.

"This is Wix Uniday hailing His Excellency, Grandee Rhodes. If you can hear this transmission, Your Magnificence, please answer or acknowledge by waving a bright light source on the upper battlements of Wall Water."

Uniday had brought a battery-powered light signal unit to the starboard bow rail of the Science Side hull, unlikely as it was that the Aquam would heed or respond to a Visitant spotlight, strobe, or laser signal. Shielded from observation from the bridge by a cluster of research-related deck enclosures while the vessel slid stern-on into view of the Aquam stronghold, he also had a good line of sight on the place.

Reaching the grandee by light or RATEL signal was a long shot, but any possibility was worth the effort. With his previous designs on power and advancement in ruins, he had to gain leverage in the reshuffling planetary situation before others beat him to it. Acting as peacemaker between Haven's side and the Aquam would be an ideal start. Thanks to Starkweather, he had already gotten to know Rhodes, which was why he had the Mark VI headset in the first place—a counterpart to the one the AlphaLAW commissioner had given the grandee.

"This is the honorable Wix Uniday hailing. I urgently need to establish contact with Grandee Rhodes—"

He broke off as another wave of high voltage struck arcs and sparks in various places on the trimaran's hulls. While he understood that Nixies weren't far from where he stood, the spot he had chosen was one of the better-insulated areas aboard.

The jamming, however, was unremitting. If the headset didn't avail soon, he would have no choice but to align himself with other venues of influence. Zone and the Endgame business certainly filled the bill, but Zone would be a hazardous implement to wield, and Uniday preferred something more manageable, as a fallback. He hadn't exaggerated when he'd pumped Zone up about Endgame, but he had no intention of sharing the incalculable potential of recovered Optimant technology with a patho Ext.

For that matter, Uniday doubted that he himself would simply hand PrePlague technology over to LAW PolSec or to any other upper echelon even if one miraculously appeared on the scene. Not when Endgame and what it entailed were the kind of touchstone to predominance he had been seeking all his life.

He toed the light unit nearer. A sign from Rhodes was looking less and less hopeful, but the headset merited at least one more go. "Grandee Rhodes, Grandee Rhodes, please respond. This is—"

"—a friggin' traitor in our midst."

Uniday turned to the drowsily amused yet minatory voice behind him. Zone was accompanied by Roust and Wetbar. Uniday supposed that Strop, the petite kewpie with the sometimes crazed gleam in her eye, had been infiltrated into the signal center on ARAAs watch per his suggestion to Zone.

The Ext colonel gave no sign of being grateful for advice, however. It seemed early in the game for Zone to be turning on an ally of such prospective value as Wix Uniday, but Zone's demeanor put him at heightened alert.

"More like an irreplaceable asset," Uniday returned with a poker grin. "But if Haven or Quant gets wind of this get-together, we'll lose a substantial advantage of secrecy." He glanced around casually for witnesses.

"Too busy jumping through their own assholes," Zone contradicted. "So let's see you prove this irreplaceable asset crap. You're right: Haven and Quant are already updating feasibility studies on staying on Ea clear through to the Big Drench and maybe beyond. But I can't figure a way of prodding them into going downriver to New Alexandria and that lighthouse."

"Given up so soon, Colonel?"

"No games, Wix."

Uniday gave Zone an indulgent smile, letting a moment's silence mark how the Ext needed him and not vice-versa. "It's not a matter of *prodding* them downriver. Not, in any case, if downriver is the most natural way to go if they can't remain here. The solution is to remove the desirability of Lake Ea, and the key to that is obvious."

"Not to me, it isn't," Zone conceded, in spite of himself.

"The dam," Uniday said.

"Blow the dam?" Wetbar asked after a moment, his usually dull eyes lit with a fey anticipation.

Uniday made a sour face. "Spoken like a classic thug. Blowing the dam would destroy food production and wipe out dozens of communities between here and the Amnion. We need Scorpia and the rest of Aquam society intact insofar as we can get it. Remember, they'll all be working for us one day soon."

"So what, if not blow the dam?" Zone pressed.

Uniday cut his eyes to him. "All we need to do is sabotage the lower outflow gates. With the lakewater levels dropping fast and shallows hemming him in, you'll see Quant standing downstream whether Haven likes it or not."

Contemplatively, Roust plucked his lower lip out between thumb and forefinger and let it snap back. "Yeah, but Quant and Haven'll execute anyone they think screwed up the dam."

"Any *LAW*," Uniday amended. Instead of finishing, he glanced to Zone.

"So we make it look like the Aquam did it," Zone provided. "Maybe a grandee. Say, somebody dicking around with ordnance from the *Edge* or one of the downed aircraft. Uh huh, that'd do it, Wix. There's only one downside for you as a consequence."

Uniday held Zone's gaze but said nothing.

"The consequence is, we don't need you anymore."

Zone struck. That Uniday hadn't been looking for him to lash out so early in their alliance was precisely the reason he did so.

He had had a bet going with himself on how good a fighter Uniday really was. To that end, he had been giving Uniday the subtlest of leading signs—split-second glances to the sternum and knees, nearly imperceptible preparatory moves. Sure enough, Uniday's evasion and blocks were instantaneous, and they would have been in proper position *if* Zone had been going for the leading-signs targets. Uniday's eyes began to widen when he realized how badly he'd underestimated his opponent. Zone had instead aimed a sledgehammer hand strike at his temple.

For a Periapt, Uniday's speed and strength were better than good; they might even have done lesser Exts credit. Zone, though, was dead into his ruthless, abyssal Flowstate. The strength and coordination he summoned were irresistible. Even forewarned, the PolSec man couldn't have stopped him. He drove the blow home with a sanguinary emptiness that was better than any joyous exaltation.

With the horrendous impact of the bottom of Zone's side-on fist to Uniday's temple, the fight as such was over. Even so, Zone hit him again in the same deadly spot while Uniday was still being jarred back from the first blow, then went on to punch the soft tissue of his throat as well as throw a punchpress shot to Uniday's solar plexus.

The place where Uniday had been standing was opportune—the encounter couldn't be seen from the bridge, and lookouts and such had been drawn away by the Nixie attack. Zone held Uniday's limp body upright and bit out terse orders to Roust and Wetbar. Quickly, they relieved Uniday of the Mark VI headset and then draped the carrying strap of the heavy flash lamp signal unit over the LAW's head and right arm and snugged it down hard.

Picking Uniday clear of the deck, Zone flung him out into the dark water, to disappear into the depths where the Nixies still massed.

It was one thing to have seen his son metamorphose from robed, saintly Human Enlightenment *rishi* to bawdy, tattooed barrow-coolie, but now Purifyre was walking

Shattertail's deck looking like a battle god, and Mason knew instinctively that it wasn't simply another disguise but a revelation. The idea of his only child warring, slaying, risking wounds, or perhaps finding his death made Mason want to howl and rend his own flesh.

Instead, he simply allowed Purifyre to snatch the dune-feather sunhat he had fashioned. "If you want it to be in keeping with Trans-Bourne *and* make sure it will stay put on your head, you must do it *so*." The boy showed him by biting off the stem brim so that it wouldn't catch the wind and peeling a fibrous string from the midrib to use as a chin tie.

Purifyre stood squareshouldered and formidable now in armor that made him look like a baroque insect samurai. The hardened segments were shaped from black, scaly cerebit hide and were faced with contoured black-enameled plates of skrim-shawed ivory and bone. Skillfully articulated, the sections were joined by cords of braided boreworm silk. It was a beautiful, strong, and lightweight suit that had the look of a uniform.

In the crook of his left arm Purifyre held a casque helmet that sported a long-quilled crest—a horsetail of varicolored streamers, and curving serrated cheekpieces like saw-toothed mandibles. Heavy, fingerless gauntlets protected him from knuckles to elbow. At his left hip hung a hook-sword with a crescent-sideblade handguard, and tucked through his silver-worked arming belt was a ropedart.

On his right side rode an Aquam parrying spike and, hanging in a pouch below it, the detonator-cap gun he had used to kill a Manipulant at Wall Water. A handsome sling-gun of blond lionwood with black iron fittings, inlaid with pearlescent shell, hung muzzle-down from his shoulder.

Purifyre's barrowman's queue was now twisted up and contained by a headband of plaited human skin, under which were tucked his jug-handle ears. The greasepaint was gone, but his eye sockets were kholed, making them that much more penetrating. The cosmetic appliances he was wearing made his face fuller and harder.

Mason was repulsed.

"Why d'you stare?" The boy's tone was neither friendly nor unfriendly as he handed back the frond sunhat.

"I'm wondering who you are now."

"In this persona, I am Hammerstone. Call me by that in the interim."

Purifyre's attention swung to people emerging from below-decks. Several of them were suited up in war gear similar to Purifyre's, but with distinctive touches. One wore Human Enlightenment robes and somewhat resembled Purifyre, while another had on Mason's own LAW semiformalwear.

"When we stop at Wiseacres, you'll be putting these decoys over the side," Mason surmised.

Essa-Ballyhoot blew her cheeks out in contempt for his stating the obvious. "Genius runs in the family."

Mason hunkered down among the deck freight, hanging on to his sunhat. "What happens if your pursuers aren't thrown off by the ruse?"

Purifyre tossed his forelock in an Aquam shrug. "They're overdrugging their pullers to make that speed."

"Then why not overdrug *our* pullers?"

"It's likely that they are using Manna's Analeptic Fix," Turn-swain said brittlely, "which I refuse to have aboard. Far too hard on muscle and machine alike."

Seeing the warning look on his son's face, Mason refrained from pointing out that the trade-off might be worth it that day. Deep down Turnswain was no more rational about his ship than any other skipper was.

Purifyre made an opening gesture of one gauntleted hand, flinging out his fingers, to convey acquiescence to fate mixed with determination to struggle. "Perhaps their flexors will grow exhausted and we'll outrun them yet. If we have to fight, we'll try for the Panhard, where there's room to maneuver."

Mason knew the place: a dry lakebed only minutes south of Ea in a VTOL but a journey of several hours by muscle car. "I can help—if you return my gun."

Purifyre's face was unreadable again. "I've always done well enough without your help." He pulled on his casque and turned away, cutting off any reply.

The car hill-and-daled across the Scorpian countryside while the decoy team get ready and Turnswain trained his antique spyglass aft. Every so often they caught sight of the pursuing carloads of praetorians, who had closed the lead somewhat. At Wiseacres, a town famous for its breweries, several secondary routes converged. The eight-wheeler barely slowed as the ersatz *rishi*, barrow-coolies, and LAW administrator went over the side.

From high ground five kilometers along Turnswain kept watch with his Optimant lens. Premature elation greeted the sight of the three commandeered cars stopping in Wiseacres, but in minutes the praetorians had reembarked and taken up the pursuit again.

"The rock-eels follow your scent better than they could any Aquam's," Purifyre told Mason. 'That's how the troops connected your disappearance to me and tracked us to the Jitterland Heights and *Shattertail*. We didn't foresee it."

"Put me over the side, then. I can draw them away from you." Mason made an effort to keep his voice from quaking. It wasn't courage or self-sacrifice so much as his ego stake in his son.

"No," Purifyre-Go-lightly-Hammerstone said. "It wouldn't work, and we need you alive, in any case. It's the Panhard if need be—provided we can stay ahead of them for that long." He turned and signaled to Ballyhoot, who hurried to his side.

Essa, too, was caparisoned for war, in a variation of the Hammerstone outfit. Her helm's brow sprouted barbed horns of fine metalwork and tiny rivets and a crest of Catherine-wheel spikes. It sported an open area between the cheekpieces that would let her enemies see her filed teeth as well as allow her to use them in close combat. Her gauntlets' knuckles were fitted with metal fishhook claws; her elbow and knee guards and the toes and heels of her boots were mounted with iron prongs.

She was armed with a quoitlike sunwheelknife, a meteor hammer, a kris sword, and a parrying spike like Purifyre's. From her baldric hung trophies of human hair rather than scalps, tresses of varying color and body, all clean and fine-brushed.

She took a moment to glare at Mason in a way that suddenly penetrated. She was jealous of his natural bond with her leader and guru. Mason had watched the two and was sure there was no sexual relationship, but a comrade in arms and surrogate mother could be even more resentful than a lover.

Ballyhoot unwillingly handed several objects to Purifyre, who in turn presented them to Mason. The LAW flechette pistol was still in its cummerbund clip-on holster; the spare ammo cassette and propellent gas cartridge were in their respective pouches. Accepting them, the notoriously gun-shy Mason said, as if it were an oath, "Your fight is my fight."

CHAPTER NINETEEN

"There's no point loitering here growing icicles," Old Spume told Ghost and Zinsser. "Whatever lies beyond that portal, I say we're better off not knowing."

He was referring to the formidable three-batten wooden door to the *Dream Castle*'s first class staterooms. The door through which Testamentor had disappeared, it was now being guarded by one of the Laputa's saffron-wearing crewmen.

Spume rubbed at the splotch of purple paint on his shoulder, smearing it. "Again, I say, let us seek warmth and what comfort we may."

Ghost made the Aquam head tic of agreement. Her micro-pore dress uniform had dried, as had Zinsser's semi-formalwear. She was hardened to fatigue and hunger orders of magnitude worse, but it would have been nice to lay up and somehow or other promote a little breakfast. Her feet, protected only by the wooden klamps, were aching from the chill and the barefoot walking she had done earlier. She wanted to see to them without further delay; taking care of sore treads was an infantry priority.

In the human livestock pens that were the steve spaces, common passengers had spread clothes or bedding to buffer themselves from the cold, drafty deck. A few sat on their sacks and crates of tradegoods. Ghost eyed them,

169

confirming that they'd been disarmed of sling-guns, long-blades, and polearms, though that still left nearly everybody with belt knives, cooking utensils, tools, and whatnot.

The trio passed another hatch. Like the first, it didn't look to have been opened since the Cyberplagues. Faded Beforetimer icons and stencils indicated a utility access, but the vandalized control touchpad was unlit and the systemry interface was an Optimant connector—nothing a latter-day Aquam could access. No manual backups were evident. Yet still there was no sign of the outerworks being reliably made fast to the Laputa itself.

"Would you expect the Insiders, who disdain and fear all the rest of the world, to suffer holes to be chopped though their hull?" Spume remarked. "Outerworks are held in place by their own circular construction, along with bracings topside and on the base dome. Howsomever, they aren't fastened to the Flying Pavilion as such."

Ghost's discontent factor rose several notches. The outer-works' existence as well as her own depended on the sufferance of the unseen and insular Insiders. Even the hatches offered no useful projections or hull features to which one might cling in the event of an outerworks structural failure.

They passed the ladderwell again, and in time they found a less crowded stretch of deckspace. Settling his huge collar, sacque cloak, and vestments about him, Spume lowered himself in a way and with sound effects that suggested he was planning to remain planted for a while.

Zinsser grunted, massaging his right hand. "Rock climbing, high dives, late-night orienting ... quite an evening." He shifted the rubbing to his left elbow.

Tendonitis, tears, and contusions inflicted by the pitiless rock at Wall Water, Ghost told herself. She was feeling them, too, but disempowered them. Just then, flanked by two crewmen, the supercargo appeared. He stopped before a man who also had a blotch of purple paint on his shoulder—another victim of the gangway sonics—and demanded payment.

Ghost turned to Spume, indicating the cuffs from which she had pulled four buttons on the landing ground embarkation stage. "Bargain for the best fare you can."

"*I?*" His bushy brows shot up, and he began to pat himself down. "But I no longer have your gold. You didn't take them back when we were laid low? Phfft! Seems there's nothing for it but to press some of your many other baubles into service—"

She put her short knife to his ribs. "What did I see you groping at in your sleeve when you got up in the entry lock? Do I slash all this drapery open to find out? You make me find that gelt myself and I'll have a kilo of your flesh and a liter of your blood for my trouble."

Spume continued to pat himself. "What miracle is this? Why, they were right here all the time. I missed them in my haste to serve you!"

The djellabaed supercargo approached a very pregnant woman and her husband or companion. Indicating her belly, he made some joke that amused his aides. The travelers showed only tension; then the super and his saffrons continued on to Ghost, Zinsser, and Spume, waving his baton at their purple marking.

"I'll have your fares now."

Old Spume was struggling to get up. "Ah, yes, fine sir, why don't we step over to the light where you and I can negotiate?"

Ghost knew the old deev wanted to pocket any change, but the supercargo stepped back. "Impermissible! Fares are preset, as constant as the circuit *Dream Castle* flies. The Insiders have installed an elegantly comprehensible compliance policy: Passage is paid in full, in cash or kind, or we fling you overboard. That will be three gold scudos apiece."

"*Three* gold scudos?" Spume sprayed. This time he sounded sincerely aghast.

"Assuming you're going to Gumption. If you wish to be left behind in Passwater, which I'd regard as suicidal, it's two scudos. It'll cost you another two from there to Gumption later, hypothesizing that you have a later."

Spume's jaw fell. "B-but we're going to Hangwitch!"

"In such a case, the conventional wisdom is to wait and board the *Brigadoon*, which goes there, rather than the *Dream Castle*, which does not. Or perhaps you have some feat of levitation to show us. If you don't care to give a performance at the moment, the cost of remaining aboard will be nine scudos."

Spume was pale, running his fingers through the fuzz of new hair Glorianna Theiss had grown him. "*Brigadoon?* But I could have sworn your next port of call was—"

"Passwater, in the Scourlands," the man said, taking pleasure in interrupting him. "Two days across the great Amnion, with flybys over the Flyaway Islands. From Passwater, another two days to Gumption, then down the archipelago to Dunrovin', Square Deal, Rainbow's End. Across to Nineteenth Green, Caprice, and Asylum. Over long waters again to Forge Town in the Trans-Bourne and so on back up to Wall Water."

He wigwagged his baton at the gold buttons on Ghost's tunic. "All those might get you three as far as Nineteenth Green, but I doubt it. Now, your scudos."

Old Spume was so unnerved that he brought out the four buttons. The supercargo examined and bit them, then pronounced them insufficient.

Ghost wordlessly cut free and surrendered two of the big shanked buttons from her tunic bib, with their Battalion of Exts crests. Developments pointed toward confrontation with the Laputa management in due course, and she didn't want any friction with them until she was positioned and ready.

"A hard bargain," Spume gulped, eyeing her fearfully.

"The Insiders' rules are unswerving," the supercargo said.

He indicated the pregnant woman he had spoken to. "Take that couple, for instance. Decided to essay this trip even though she's due soon. If they make Gumption before the baby jumps down, luck will have favored them. But if there's a birth—if it's no Anathemite and lives, that is—they lack the money for a third fare. The newborn will be taken for sale or ejected from *Dream Castle*—or one of its parents will be, if they're self-sacrificing. Either way, they knew the risk when they came aboard."

Ghost tucked in the loose-hanging triangle of her tunic bib's upper right corner, saying nothing. But Zinsser remarked, "I'm surprised no one's tried to liberalize the Insiders' policies."

The supercargo shot him a warning look. "Talk of piracy can get you flung overboard as well, mudfoot. No Laputa has ever been taken from its Insiders. The disaster of the *Gatsby* proves to what extremes they'll go to keep their Flying Pavilions out of the hands of others."

"How much change do I get?" Ghost interposed, to keep the talk copacetic.

"None. This will just suffice," the supercargo simpered, pocketing the buttons. Ghost figured the gold was worth considerably more than nine scudos.

"Do we at least get better quarters for that much?" Zinsser objected.

The supercargo guffawed, and his crewmen elbowed one another. "First-class accommodations were bought up by the DevOcean clerics. Moreover, if you wish to come even halfway around to Lake Ea again, it'll cost you every pretty button you have just to ride in the steves spaces. Therefore enjoy your luxurious deck planks!" He and his men went away laughing, drawing a fearful look from the pregnant woman.

Zinsser turned to Ghost. "There're some food vendors back that way. I suggest we—wait!" Ghost was up and moving. "Where're you going?"

"To case the rest of the steves spaces." She also needed shoes, and other things.

"You should rest first. Warm up, eat something."

"Eating and sleeping are problems, Doctor, not solutions. Just like time."

No sooner had Ghost set out than Zinsser caught up with her. "You're right. We have a crisis here, and we've got to work together to solve it."

Ghost studied him. He had that note in his voice again. Maybe he hoped that in *Dream Castle*'s confines he could pressure or persuade her into some slurp-'n'-slide. He still hadn't accepted her declaration that that would never happen.

For the time being she ignored him, running an optical on the steves spaces. She hoped for a back door to the forbidden first class section into which Testamentor and the other phoney DevOcean zealots had retreated. The two passed common passengers lounging on duffels containing whatever their livelihood depended on. Some were praying earnestly, waiting to fall from the sky.

The walk didn't take Ghost and Zinsser far. A few meters around the bend was another three-batten door, even more stout than the one near the ladderwell head. There was also another hull utility access hatch.

"There's likely one of these in first class," Ghost told Zinsser behind her hand. "We could have a bash at it without an audience watching."

"I'll bet it's been tried before—and we haven't so much as a soldering laser."

"I was thinking of something with a lot more rads."

"You heard the supercargo—trying to break into a Laputa is suicide. Let's go back and get something to eat. Then we'll see what Spume can tell us."

"Speaking of the old man—he had a memory lapse about the *Dream Castle* going to Hangwitch instead of Passwater. He was drinking at the Grand Attendance, but he wasn't *that* drunk. Nor was he too scared to think clearly."

Zinsser winced, recalling his own overindulgence in single-grain Lava-Land Prang-bang. "Something else is going on," he agreed. "Glorianna Theiss's quick-fix rejuvenation?"

She nodded. "Haven forced her to blitzkrieg the job. Spume's body's rejecting it."

"He could be suffering neuritic atrophy, losing cells in the substantia negra and locus coeruleus—a variety of dire cess. Impaired cognition. Sweet reason, he could start falling apart on us just when we need him most."

"Watch him closely. Say nothing about degeneration."

"if he melts down? He could betray us inadvertently."

"We don't need him *that* badly."

When they found their way back to the Sense-maker, a food vendor was haggling with him. Spume sat cross-legged on the deck. Zinsser wondered if they would ever be able to get him back up again. He was salivating visibly, looking at slender wooden brochettes stuck through dripping strips of hot, popping meat that oozed some spicy marinade.

The vendor was a bony, loose-limbed woman with a forelock strung with Oceanic-fetish beads and feathers, the rest of her head covered by a close-fitting cloche. She was bundled into a heavy skirt and a greatcoat that was open for the time being, indicating that she expected it to get colder.

For Spume, she had an exaggerated look of regret. "What you offer wouldn't suffice to cover my costs, Grandfather, and I cannot linger here while my wares grow cold. Later, perhaps, your stomach will feel emptier and your purse fuller."

Old Spume could still move fast at mealtime. He held the peddler's forearm so that she couldn't get out of reach, while his free hand burrowed in his vestment sleeve. He produced an iron scudo, which the meat vendor eyed; then she freed herself, shaking her head in refusal.

Spume sighed, licked his lips, rummaged in his sleeve some more, and brought forth another iron lozenge. The vendor stopped fighting, took the coins, and offered the old councillor his choice of brochettes.

"While you're at it, pay her for ours, too," Ghost said.

Spume flinched, discovering that she had seen it all. "Deep *briny*! For reasons you know, I'm in reduced circumstances."

Ghost hunkered down, picking through the spitted meat, mindful to use only her right hand; the left would defile the whole tray in most Aquam eyes. Zinsser followed Ghost's hand compulsively; her spatulate fingers were grimy, and the nails were clogged with dirt.

She was watching Spume. "Old man, are we in this together or not?"

Spume was taken off guard by her implied solidarity, confused and troubled that she had outmaneuvered him. Hesitantly, he ponied up four more iron scudos. "The mark-up's outrageous."

The vendor shrugged with a forelock toss like the swish of a horse's tail. "A seller's market. All concessionaires work for the Insiders."

Ghost took the skewer she wanted and motioned Zinsser to do the same. The vendor was antsy, wanting to sell the rest of her stock before it got cold. Other concessionaires—men and women, old and young—were moving among the common passengers. All wore charms and fetishes to protect them from the Oceanic. They hawked alcohol, drugs, mandseng and other antimutagens, smokables, warm clothing, and water.

Water. Most of the passengers had brought their own in skins and canteens. That expense, too, would pluck at Ghost's buttons.

Zinsser, licking his lips, had picked a brochette. The vendor hoisted her tray, clinking the money. "Yes, a pretty scudo, but you get good value from me."

She indicated the meat strips. "This young rogue was a highwayman in the Trans-Bourne, fierce and virile. Proper wild game to give you strength for a long, cold flight. Bought his body off the executioner's dock myself. Broke my own fast with a bite today, so I did." She went off crying her wares.

Spume was already feasting. Ghost sat and dug in before noting that Zinsser had gone whey-white.

"You ... bought *human* flesh?" he asked dully.

"I bought what there was," Spume replied, licking his fingers, then wiping them on his sleeve. "If you don't want it, give it here."

When Zinsser turned to Ghost, she shot him a warning glance. "No scenes." She bit off a hunk of meat and began to chew.

"I forgot. This is nothing new to you—"

"The prisoner camps make this seem like a holiday buffet at the Abraxas Ritz, Doctor. I once gave three guards everything they wanted for a whole evening just so they'd let me eat leftovers out of their mess hall garbage—two minutes to wolf down whatever I could. But my stomach was so shrunken that when I got outside, I began upchucking. So I knelt on the ground and caught the puke in my hands, reswallowed it until it stayed down, licked my arms and clothes and the dirt. I woke up that night to find Discards lapping me."

Scientific luminary, academic celebrity, Zinsser wasn't used to listening to other people's stories. "I know you went through hell, and I wish you could put it behind you. But that isn't the situation here."

"But we may need to do that kind of thing and worse before this is over. So it'd reassure me about your survival instincts if you'd eat your breakfast."

"A 'highwayman'! What makes you think it's not that cadaver whose shoes you're wearing?" He gave one of her wooden klamps a nudge. "Or maybe the orphans you gave that first button to!"

"Unlikely but possible." She tore off another strip of meat with her teeth. "What would that change?"

Zinsser lowered the brochette, glancing around. "There must be other vendors—fruit, fish, bread—"

Old Spume laughed gustily. "You eat what they bring out, Zins-zsah! This isn't some fine banquet aboard the..." He stopped chuckling and chewing, his brow knotting. "Your Visitant boat, the big one? Why can't I remember its name?"

He turned as suspicious as a cornered viper. "What's happening to me? I forget things I should know! It's Glorianna's Anathasian cures, isn't it? Those youth medicaments."

Ghost debated the merits of choking him unconscious, silencing him with her blade, or blaming it on altitude and airsickness. He would be yelling at the top of his lungs about Visitants in another moment.

Zinsser leaned close to the Sense-maker like an old confidant. "Your body's renewing itself, that's all. Additional brain cells! You recognize the *GammaLAW*'s name, don't you? Well there you go; you haven't forgotten it! You're getting younger and more vital, so of course your thoughts stray."

He showed the old man his plugphone. "As soon as we contact the ship, we'll be rescued and Glorianna Theiss will finish your course of rejuv. Think of it; you'll be slim, strong, priapic as a satyr, while all your rivals will be *old*. You'll dance on their graves."

Potency was a strong selling point, Ghost saw. The part about outliving enemies was a stroke of genius.

Spume was making the head-canting gesture of agreement. "How delectable that would be. But—you wouldn't lie to an old man, would you?"

Zinsser smiled heartily and patted his shoulder. "I'd never lie to you. We'll look out for you; and you, us. Once back aboard ship, you'll be a new man."

Spume was gazing into the light of the nearest window, lost in the image Zinsser had conjured and perhaps a mental fog as well. Zinsser took the opportunity to shoot Ghost a defiant look and then nibble at the strip of marinated flesh he still held.

"Well, have I reassured you?"

CHAPTER TWENTY

With the Nixies in an electrical frenzy, the sonar gear was down, and there was no return signal on the object hitting the water. In fact, the object itself might have gone unnoticed if Quant hadn't happened to be peering that way via the main hull bow cam.

Given the dawn shadows and the furious swirling and billowing of the Nixies, it was impossible at first to tell what it was. Then, by the glare of a light that seemed to be attached to the sinking object, Quant made out a human form. Without taking his eyes from the body, he had "man overboard" sounded.

Disregarding the likelihood of its being shock-roasted, Quant had ordered the bow cam on line because he couldn't fight the lakebottom dwellers blind. Even so, the body falling limp through the water was difficult to make out, and it became more and more obscure as Nixies flocked to envelop it. Then Quant realized that the bottom dwellers were drawn not so much to the body as to the light source that was dragging it down. Quant finally recognized the light source as a flash-signal unit into which the Nixies seemed intent on burrowing.

Body, light unit, and clinging Nixies were quickly lost in the murk and the swarming of nearer creatures, but not before the tableau had given Quant a desperate idea.

Supposing it would even work, he still needed some way of keeping the Nixies at a distance. The Ext grenades hadn't availed much in that he couldn't afford to have them exploding too close to the ship, and none of the weapons LOGCOM had released to him would serve. Setting the lake afire with aviation fuel or other flammables might do greater damage to the drifting *GammaLAW* than to her assailants.

Thinking things through, Quant realized that while he didn't have a single air asset left, he did have some of the concomitants. The stratagem began to flesh out in his mind even as he was pulling Lieutenant Gairaszhek aside. Germaine Bohdi, his catapult officer, and other flight deck personnel were also going to have to carry the ball. If, however, Quant had misread the Nixies—as was all too conceivable—his ship could be in for her worst savaging yet.

Goaded from their seasonal sleep by the vibrations of the Aquam syrinxes, the Nixies threw themselves with wild resentment at the alien shape and its infuriating electrical fields. The stored-up biovoltage of most of their number was depleted, but—heavy with electrolytics from their interrupted rest—they recharged quickly. Their follow-up assaults were weaker than the initial attack, but their resolve hadn't abated any; the syrinxes' notes had tricked them into the worst sort of territorial fury.

A pounding splash came from the loathed alien shape that was the big trimaran. A mass that toppled from the shape had a strong electrical field that invited attack. Many left off their clinging to the ship to throng after it as the electrical source drove down toward the mud that was their breeding ground and resting place.

The object from the hostile dry reaches above the lakewater was strange to them, but then, most things from the upper world were. Intent on eliminating it as a threat, they didn't know it for a cargo pallet strapped with portable power packs and certain other weights. It so happened that a good many of them were clustered around the object, engulfing it, when the jerry-rigged servo activated and the fuel drum fastened to the pallet was cracked open to drain.

Cold invaded their territory, cold so deep and destructive that even the Nixies understood the danger and the destruction being done to them as waves of supercooled ruination swept out, embrittled them, deadened them, and caused the nearest ones to snap like glass before they could flee. Worse, the slush hydrogen aerospace fuel was lighter than water so that it rose as if chasing those who had sped surfaceward in silent panic.

Stored in refrigerated tanks, slush hydrogen was usually treated with great respect aboard the ship. Nevertheless, Quant had elected to deliver his counterattack in a small drop tank normally used to extend aircraft range. The stuff was already above its own freezing temperature of 4.2 K and was losing all solidity as it passed its liquefying mark of 20.4 K. The first clouds released were already beginning to boil.

The water around the drop tank still answered to its primeval benchmark of zero degrees Celsius, but as the supercooled hydrogen rose, it turned gaseous, altering discrete pockets of lake-water into ice—something with which the Nixies had no experience. The dark depths under the *GammaLAW*'s bows became a roiling, ice-flecked nightmare broth dotted with broken scraps of Nixie. There would have been detonations and underwater fire triggered by the fluttering electrocytes if not for the paucity of oxygen. The Nixies, sensing the nearness of a lake surface they instinctively avoided in any event, began sliding away to all sides, fleeing the submerged fountain of infernally cold H_2 that began breaking the face of Ea with a violent bubbling and an instantaneous smokescreen of chilled air.

On deck, bullhorns and PA speakers were ordering everyone without breathing gear to stay well back from the churning eruption. The ship had drifted clear of it—just far enough that Quant, peering down from the starboard wing of the bridge, felt sure the stuff would not embrittle his hulls—but it still posed a threat. While not poisonous, the cloud of released hydrogen could smother an unprotected person.

H_2 was naturally colorless and odorless, but scent additives were mixed into all the stuff the navy used to alert personnel to leaks and spills. The air was tinged with warning odor now. Quant had the bows manned with all the firefighting gear he had been able to shift forward in the minutes available. Unconfined H_2 wasn't explosive and the night breezes were dissipating it, but it would burn like merry hell if it found an ignition source before it was sufficiently scattered.

The bubbles and domed lakewater seethed, dead fish and debris roiled, but no fire squall flared up. The *GammaLAW* continued her stern-on starboard-to drift toward Wall Water.

Word came that the person who had fallen from the Science Side was Wix Uniday and that Zone and his several-almates were believed to be somehow involved in his death. Quant didn't doubt there would be a lot to investigate or that the facts wouldn't be established soon, if ever. Events since the moment of *Terrible Swift Sword*'s detonation would keep boards of inquiry busy for years.

Quant watched the bows retreat from the hydrogen up-welling. With the ship meandering backwards, he had had a fleeting impulse to shift his conn elsewhere—aft of the signal bridge, say—for a better view of what lay ahead. But no other location offered him the centrality and immediacy to communications and other systems, damaged as they might be.

The departure of the Nixies and the receding of the H_2 didn't dampen his apprehensions much. Word had come that he wouldn't have power back to the actuator disc propellers for an hour more, and something else that had been eating at him now came to the fore.

He was just instructing his junior officer of the watch to furnish him with another IR reading of the thermal buildup at Wall Water when a powerful *thwack* sounded from the main hull stern. With hardwire circuits still out, Quant received the update by way of a bullhorn in the hands of someone back near the wreckage of the CIWS.

"We are under fire! Hard projectile impact aft, just above the starboard actuator disc skeg. Damage appears to be—"

The voice was interrupted by a giant splash, this time amidships and ten meters off the starboard rail. As water was raining back down, Quant heard a sound he had heard distantly when the hydrofoil *Edge* had been holed—Rhodes's steam cannon.

The sky was lightening as *Racknuts* rattled and bounced down off Jitterland Heights, but it was impossible to make out details of the broad countryside.

The route Manna had violated all custom to use as an exit was PostPlague but in reasonable repair and safe enough at low speed. She had taken up a small megaphone of painted leather, verbally abusing foot traffic that didn't move aside fast enough or simply offended her prickly sensibilities. The treadles thumped. The Big Sere air was a hot wind to the moving car, but at least it carried some sweat away.

Acting as lookout, Burning gazed at people caught for an instant in the lamplight. Traders, beggars, palanquin bearers, peasants, urchins—Aquam faces were sliding by him like flickering holo stills. With the *Sword* gone, however, the very future of the GammaLAW mission was in jeopardy. There was a lot more to Dextra Haven's mission than getting the Oceanic to chat with her.

"Snuff them lights, you great prodigal titlap!" Manna called when it had grown light enough. "Or d'you want to make it easier for the grandees' headsmen to sight us?"

Burning complied but ignored her, which she hated worse than backtalk. Souljourner had relashed the outrigger and stood beside him, gazing south pensively, lightly clenching the leather bag at her throat. Earlier, and in few words, she had complained of headaches, residual pain from the Oceanic's reaction to the *Sword* as well as something ominously novel building in the depths of the Amnion, something with which even the Descrier had little familiarity.

The leaden sky showed mostly open country, cultivated fields and paddies bordered by hedge and scrub, set with orchards and copses of woodland. Farther from the roads the land was forested. The landscape was dotted with tiny villages showing the small glows of hearths and a few rushlights; people were already out in the fields, starting the day's labor.

Racknuts treadled-whumped onto the RambleRove, the latter-day Aquam name for the stretch of Optimant autobahn that led south toward the Trans-Bourne. Built for the wheeled and surface-effect vehicles the Optimants' robot freight system and servant class had used, it was sufficiently wide if meandering, owing to the Optimants' fondness for leisurely travel. Time and inconvenience for the cloned exoterics had mattered little to the fugitive techno-aristocrats from Old Earth.

Those afoot stayed out of the RambleRove's fairway or moved to the shoulders as the muscle car approached. Souljourner had explained that right-of-way issues had been settled over the years by sheer physics. An itinerant shoemaker might fling a dried turd at *Racknuts* for coming too close or families of stoop laborers might spit slackwort juice or call curses, but none cared to contest the unwritten rules of the road.

While shanties called shebangs lined the shoulder, no houses or other structures that would have otherwise provided solid foundation stood on the surface course itself.

"Once upon a time they did," Souljourner said, "but not since the muscle cars came. If a shebang encroaches, the treadle wains sideswipe or flatten it."

"People don't complain to the grandees?"

"The cars make the grandees good money in trade and tariffs. Shebangs and the peons who reside within them are replaceable."

By the time the first rays of Eyewash broke over the horizon, *Racknuts* had topped a few rises. Far behind them the parking mounds were only a sprinkling of forge and cooking fire lights on the Jitterland Heights. Burning had expected Manna to speed up, but instead she slowed to a crawl.

"Does she *want* to be caught?" he asked Boner uneasily.

Manna's husband made a diminutive bug-swatting motion, a regional gesture bidding Burning to calm down, wait and see. "She's decided we must go shunpiking."

Burning vaguely recalled the word from his studies and data diving back at Bastion Orman on Concordance forever ago. It was an ancient term for avoiding the main roads to dodge tolls and other entanglements.

They left another village behind, crested a hill, and started down into a little glen where faint dew shone even in the Big Sere. Manna rasped an order astern. Missy and Pelta disengaged the driveshaft and stopped the treadles. Boner freewheeled *Racknuts* to the right shoulder of the RambleRove and eased it onto a cart track, sliding between trees. Yake and Spin leaned into the grabs levers and braked to a halt in a clearing.

Under the trees was a daub and wattle cottage shaped like a two-story mushroom, a thin tail of cooking fire smoke emerging from a centrally placed chimney. Spin and Yake set the grabs and drag staves, hopped down, and sprinted back full-throttle for the road. Boner called, "And mind that you cover all tracks!"

A woman in a sarong appeared at the cottage door, nursing a baby old enough to read. A man in a fundoshi and sampan hat, a wooden mattock over his shoulder, came out of the undergrowth to approach the car. "Throw me the chocks, Manna?"

She gave a slow, rolling nod of the head. "Won't be staying that long." She limped over to the gunwale, ivory peg leg thumping the planks, to sit precariously on the rail. She spit a slackwort gobbet over the side and offered the man a chaw from the little hemp stash bag she carried.

"Just want to rest our flexors a smidge. Let the traffic die down."

The crofter had pushed his sampan back so that it hung from his neck by a cord. He gave the forelock toss that equated to a shrug even though his hair was bound in cornrows and he lacked a forelock. "My holding always receives you, generous Manna." The crofter held his palm out, a universal signal.

Manna spit more slackwort, then crossed his palm with hers. Instead of pocketing what she had paid, the crofter held it up—two brass scudos—and eyed Burning meaningfully. With little room to maneuver, Manna silently handed over a silver lozenge coin. The peon grunted thanks and retreated to the cottage, where he passed the hush money to his wife. Burning heard Souljourner make an irked sound and move to the forward end of the car.

Manna turned and held her palm out to Burning. "Your fare increases to cover the bribe markup you cost me, Redtails."

The gold didn't matter, and it was no time to antagonize her. With any luck, he and Souljourner would be through with her in a few hours. But as he reached for his cuff, Souljourner told Manna sharply, "That will cover your silver scudo and thirty scudos of change returned to us." She returned to Burning's side and began rubbing the buttons of his uniform with blackened fingers.

"Ten," Manna countered. "Or you go afoot from here."

Burning's tunic was already in rough shape, but Souljourner was deliberating making things worse by coating his buttons with a mixture of fish oil from the smashed lantern and soot from the burnt splint broom.

"It's this or you'll end up holding your clothes on with meat skewers," she muttered to him. To Manna she countered, "Twenty-five—and we should charge you for our aid, without which the grandees would have the secret of your Analeptic Fix by now."

"Fifteen," Manna growled, slitting her eyes, "or I commence to question whether that affray back at the mounds was really about my *elixir vitae* at all."

"Too late for second guesses, since you've already crushed assorted Killmongers and Unconquerables. Twenty silver scudos in hand before we give you the button."

"You're slippery as a rock-eel in a gutbag of snot. Are we perchance related?"

They were just making the transaction when the rattle and drumroll of several muscle cars on the RambleRove made everyone freeze. Burning kept his hand near the 'baller and eyed the odd spike-and-tuft Aquam crop fields, picking out the best path for an escape on foot.

The rumbling passed. Spin and Yake came jogging back to report that a convoy of cars crammed with Ean men at arms had sped south—everything from a speedy courier tricycle to a twelve-wheel galleon, one of the newest wagons on the road. The grandeean soldiers hadn't even bothered to inquire about *Racknuts*.

"Then they want *Shattertail*, for whatever reason and wherever it's bound," Boner concluded.

"We're still bound for the Styx, as well, but not by this pike," Manna said. "Not with grandee companies ahead and likely more following behind. We'll veer over to the Staggerwise Turnpike down at the junction."

Hearing the pronouncement, Burning saw his options melt away. If the praetorians caught up to *Shattertail*, Ghost could be hurt in the fighting or taken by Rhodes's men. But if he abandoned her trail now, she might be dead before he could take up the search again.

He had sworn an oath to lead the Exts, but that didn't change the fact that he and his sister, orphaned and taken into Bastion Orman by wealthy clansmen, had watched out for each other for most of their lives. Perhaps the day would yet see the COMSATs back on-line. An aircav assault force from the SWATHship could reach him in minutes and rescue Ghost from an entire Aquam army if necessary—assuming he managed to locate her.

In any case, going deeper into dangerous country was preferable to sitting back aboard the *GammaLAW* agonizing over what might be happening to her. Haven, Daddy D, and the rest would cope with what they had to aboard ship. He would simply do the same on the Optimant high roads.

"We'll see what freight and fares we can lay on," Manna was saying, "to make up for what we abandoned on the Heights."

Burning gave Manna a head roll: negative. "No stopping to drum up business, no side trips, no slowing us down with people and cargo." He yanked free the uppermost right-hand button on his bib—three times the size of the ones at his cuffs—and tossed it to her. "Deal?"

Souljourner, blackening the unit crests on his epaulets, *tched* softly but held her peace. Manna rubbed the sooty grease from the heavy gold and smiled at him with her mouth if not her eyes. "You take the sweetness out of victory, but I won't complain."

"Just catch *Shattertail.*"

"You're lucky, because I'm the only woman in the world who knows how to get one last good run out of overworked flexors. Albeit, if I kill off my pullers in the doing, that'll cost you aplenty extra."

"If we overtake *Shattertail,* and what I want is still aboard, you get the whole tunic—insignia and all."

Souljourner clapped a hand over her eyes, rolling her head in aggravation.

CHAPTER TWENTY-ONE

A s Eyewash cleared the horizon and *Shattertail* fled from the muscle cars commandeered by grandeean troops, the hot breath of early morning rustled up. Turnswain ordered the eight-wheeler's small lateen sails set to take advantage, but *Rut-Rider*, *Rattlebones*, and *Bunbanger* negated the advantage by showing sail as well.

Presumably close to burning out their pullers with over-doses of Analeptic Fix, the chase cars continued to close the distance. Turnswain had his engineer double-dose *Shattertail*'s pullers with Big Styx Invigorant Ambrosia, but it didn't help.

Purifyre instructed the carman to bash through the customs post at the Rumbledowns frontier. *Shattertail* had passed beyond the range of alarms transmitted by Ean semaphore towers, but no command to seal the border could have been sent from Wall Water in any case, since the central semaphore at Rhodes's stronghold had been destroyed by missiles from Starkweather's flying fortress. The Rumbledowns border guards would therefore not be on the lookout for Purifyre and company. On the other hand, there was a danger that they might detain *Shattertail* long enough for the pursuers' warning horn blasts and gongs to be heard, signaling that the crossing be shut down.

The checkpoint was just a counterweighted gate arm between two booths and some wooden partitioning in the middle of the highway. Nothing more substantial was considered necessary because muscle cars could survive only by passing up and down the Optimant autobahns. It would be self-defeating for one to run a barrier and make itself outlaw along an entire stretch of road.

Watching the impact loom, Mason braced himself against the port-side rail. *Shattertail* smashed through the wooden gate arm handily, leaving startled border guards on both sides to fire inaccurate sling-gun bolts in its dust trail.

"Reinforced prow," Turnswain explained matter-of-factly.

Another piece to the puzzle, Mason told himself. Purifyre's organization had *allowed* for this kind of trouble. They were willing to sacrifice an expensive eight-wheeler's regional access—or the car itself—to achieve the aims. Whatever those were.

The chase cars didn't stop, either, and the border guards understandably chose not to challenge them. Mason concluded that the grandees' tasking orders to their elites had been couched in with-your-shield-or-on-it terms. Sending an armed force into a neighboring bailiwick was a grave business, but the combined power of the Ean monocrats would likely make any offended parties sit still for it, provided that no great harm was done and a bit of compensation was offered after the fact.

Over the frontier, the Rumbledowns landscape became rolling and rocky, hot and open, like a rumpled ground cloth. The autobahn wound, rose, and dipped in its descent toward the Panhard. No shebangs crowded the shoulders, only modest hovels built well back off the surface course.

"Will we get to the Panhard before they get to us?" Purifyre asked Turnswain, but the pilot couldn't say.

Purifyre uncased his hooksword with a deft twist and began parting the lines that held down the deck freight. From what Mason could see, every edge of the weapon except its haft was as keen as a lancet, even the crescent sideblade-handguard and the daggerlike pommel. *Whht, whht, whht* came from the hooksword, and fragments of line lay everywhere, with cargo rocking free.

"Jettison the freight!" Purifyre called at last.

Mason jumped to help, glad for the bracing his tightly buckled car rider's stomacher gave his back.

"Dump all that—no, no!" Purifyre barked. "*Aft*, where those behind will have to contend with it."

Mason, who'd been about to throw a leather duffle bag over the starboard rail, lurched aft instead. Ballyhoot had her sunwheel-knife out and was slashing, too. The wavery metal tongues radiating from its quoit blade were as sharp as the hooksword.

Turnswain steered while every available hand began dumping cargo. Most of the containers were there as camouflage in any case, empty or holding only dunnage. Wicker baskets and wooden boxes went tumbling and bursting. Cooking pots clattered, and a small Dutch oven shattered like a piñata.

The Rumbledowns struck Mason as straggly farmed tracts with few people in sight. But Aquam seemed to materialize on the highway when the jetsam began crashing down. Mason hurled a net bag of mudspuds and saw a spindly old woman in sampan hat and waistwrap shamble from behind a rock and nab them on the first bounce, somewhat mashed but still edible.

There was a crash as a large amphora burst, spilling cooking oil in a wide slick. Mason looked to Purifyre, who had flung it. "Is there more? It might make the grandeeans lose control."

Purifyre was taken off guard, unused to being found wanting. "We never thought of that. There's never been much battle between or from cars to speak of."

Obviously, concluded Mason, or the greatwagons would have been provided with fighting castles, hub-mounted spoke cutters, rams, and the like. "What about poles to break their spokes?"

"We need something with which to try. It won't be easy, and I've no wish to close with them."

Mason squinted ahead through the first morning heat waves. "Will we hit an incline where we can roll rocks down on them?"

"Not between here and the Panhard," a crewman grunted, heaving a little yussawood stool overboard. "Count us lucky if they don't roll some after us."

"We're not without our hole cards." Purifyre frowned.

Mason found himself, preposterously, wanting to give his feudal-warrior son a pep talk. He looked around the deck for more jetsam and spotted the cases containing the stolen Science Side modules. "How about those?"

Ballyhoot, grunting, raised the car's water keg over her head and lofted it. "Those're part of what we came to Wall Water for. We'd quicker dump *you*, Visitant."

Looking at the field units, Mason remembered something. "What happened to the two bloopguns you took from the Manipulants in Rhodes's chambers?"

"We couldn't get them to fire," his son said. "But you're free to try." He retrieved them from concealment within the field modules—one from the false ark, one from the equally false coffer.

Mason, however, had no more success than Purifyre. Because he had ducked most firearms familiarization firing on the voyage out, he couldn't tell if there was some release or safety he wasn't seeing. Aware of what horrible effect the bolas rounds could have if someone fired one incorrectly, he tucked them back into the chests. His 'chettergun would have to do.

Mason, having been cornered into range practice once or twice, knew it could put out a copious volume of fire so long as ammo cassettes and propellent gas cartridges lasted. Like most LAW Civilian Side weapons, it was a final recourse, designed for bureaucrats' use against unarmored and—ideally—poorly armed indigs. The theory was that any civil servant requiring more firepower should bloody well make it his or her business to get it. How the pistol would perform against panoplied fighters with wooden hulls and other cover, he hadn't any idea. It was short range, was not terribly accurate, and gobbled up ammunition at an alarming rate.

But as determined as he was to help his son, he couldn't picture himself yanking the trigger. It came like a stay of execution when the *Shattertail*'s crew exulted that the Eans were no longer gaining so quickly.

Over the next hours the praetorians shortened the lead, but not without canny, set-jawed resistance from Turnswain and his hands. The unflappable pilot stayed at the helm, giving terse orders to the grabsmen, who were often the only thing between the eight-wheeler and a roll or nosedive into a Rumbledowns ravine. Purifyre detailed one of his men to stand by the release for the drag irons—the last-ditch stopping mechanism and a thin reed to rely upon under such circumstances.

The Big Sere morning turned kiln-dry. Out beyond the Rumbledowns lay the salt-white gleam of the Panhard. The speeds *Shattertail* hit were ludicrous by the standards of Periapt aircraft, surface-effect vehicles, even unibikes.

Sometimes the car slowed so on switchbacks that Mason wondered if the grandeean armsmen wouldn't try to head it off by scrambling straight downhill on foot. He found, though, that a few dozen kilometers an hour was petrifying when there were hundred-meter drops on the far sides of the gunwales. From somewhere he dredged up the courage to hang on an outrigger like Purifyre and the rest, and counterweight the wagon on the insides of turns.

Mason's one try at a harassment burst from the 'chettergun was hopeless. The twisty road made for difficult angles of fire and the violence of the ride on medieval shock absorbers had the weapon wavering like a yardarm in a squall. The pistol had open sights instead of a scope, and the passive-thermal idiot light antipersonnel targeting system was useless at that distance. The wind blew his makeshift dunefeather-frond sun hat away as he pulled, not squeezed, the trigger.

The brief fusillade went wide of the trike, *Bunbanger,* and ate up a substantial number of the cassette's minidarts. The upside was that the praetorians were likewise unable to hit their quarry with quarrel or bolt.

Shattertail drumrolled past sharecroppers' huts, ville markets, and haunted Optimant ruins, taking hairpin turns and stomach-lifting drops, grabs smoking and spokes threatening to snap right off the wheel naves. The air reeked of scorched axle grease and burning brake pad. Mason and others doused friction fires with the last of the drinking water, and then with what gooner, skeezer, wooze, and other potables were aboard. When the portside pads got hot again, a grabsman managed at horrific risk to urinate on them—not much help, but enough.

When the Panhard was only minutes ahead, the *Bunbanger* began closing in, a rider in the bow readying a grapnel and line. The three men in the trike were too few to try a boarding, but if they could damage a wheel or lodge their hook in an axle and pay line back to the heavier wagons, *Shattertail* would never reach the dry salt lake.

By the time Ghost, Old Spume, and Zinsser had gotten to the last of what Zinsser dubbed "homo-*yakitori*"—the flesh brochettes the vendor had sold them—the outerworks was like a walk-in refrigerator, and, more disquieting, the air was markedly thinner.

Many of the common passengers had fired up cigarittos, spliffs, and pipes. Combustibles didn't do the O_2 supply any good, but complaining was hopeless. The steves spaces were one big, indefatigable smoking section. It almost made the draftiness welcome.

A circle of flax speculators raised the quilted cover from the cage of their bronze boo-hoo and set an oil lamp near the creature to keep it awake. Rather than sound its irritating stridulating and whooping, the carapaced flier screeched discordantly. The intimidating speculators ignored the mutterings of fellow travelers and went on with their game of perudo.

Frigid conditions were to be expected aboard a Laputa, Old Spume said—especially on the long flight north to the Scourlands, the huge island that straddled Aquamarine's arctic circle. Boo-hoos and other annoying songbeasts were to be expected everywhere.

Bucked up by Zinsser's sky-pie promise of rejuvenation, the Sense-maker was holding forth on the fine points of Flying Pavilion travel.

"Travail is simply the nature of it. The Optimants built and programmed their celestial pleasure barges with no inkling that unpressurized outerworks would be rough-handedly mated to them in the aftermath of the Cyberplagues.

"The Optimants were only concerned with following itineraries that struck their fancy, leaving the machines and detector suites to make course adjustments, so as to avoid terrain features and other aircraft, eschew inconvenient weather, wind shear, perturbations of the Oceanic, and whatnot. If that meant altitudes and temperatures not conducive to entertaining on balconies and promenades, a pavilion's owner and guests simply moved indoors until more clement conditions prevailed. The grand terrace atop the Laputa could be enclosed in a clear dome, or opened again, on a moment's notice."

But none of the surviving domes had been opened in eight generations. The Insiders had remained sealed away from the rest of Aquamarine, except for the replenishment of provisions and water, transferal of their profits and treasure, and off-pumping of wastes into the burned and blasted landing pits.

When the Laputas dodged a gale or leapt over turbulence, outerworks passengers suffered through it as best they could, or—commonly enough on a hard voyage—died. Provisions for the crew and concessionaires were somewhat better, but they knew their losses, too. High-altitude pulmonary and cerebral edema were the twin horsemen of the outerworks, and the Aquam had no reliable means of predicting who would be most vulnerable. Gender, age, and general health were no sure indicators. Even a history of complication-free trips to high elevation was no guarantee a given individual wouldn't die his or her next time up.

Changes in altitude could be sudden and were never subject to appeal, not only because the Insiders didn't care about outer-works mortalities, but because the Insiders had long since lost the knowledge that would let them override the automatics.

"Almost nothing is known about Insider life," Old Spume continued. "It is thought that only a couple of dozen inhabit any given Laputa. Few venture out, and then only for as brief a time as possible, under the strongest precautions that could be arranged—usually to treat with other Insider clans.

"On very rare occasions, marriages have been arranged between pavilions. No Insider has ever been verified as quitting a pavilion, but there are legends and persistent rumors of lone figures pinwheeling from the upperworks—usually into the Amnion on a dark night, screaming.

"The Insiders were canny enough to see how much more profit they could rake in by opening the hulls' internal spaces to cargo and passengers, but they are innately incapable of letting Aquam commoners inside their ivory towers."

Ghost was sardonically amused by that. "The conundrum must eat at them." Having licked the last of the highwayman's *au jus* off her brochette, she nudged Spume. "Give me scudos."

Still guilt-ridden that he had led them aboard the wrong Laputa, he dropped two iron lozenges into her palm. Ghost signaled Zinsser to stay where he was, rose, and strolled off, her wooden klamps clunking the pit-sawn deck planks. The bronze boo-hoo screamed at her as she went.

She sauntered to a liquor vendor and purchased a sizable mug of gooner for one iron scudo—a better bargain than Spume could have wangled, she suspected. The liquorman was enthralled by her scars and her look. She feigned to wander some more, not standing out too much from those who were pacing from restlessness or to warm up. A few saffron-wearing crewmen were making the rounds to keep the peace and enforce fire regulations, but they ignored her.

The gooner was malty, sweetish and frothy, with an acid undertaste and a kick like a strap-on booster. She drifted back by the inner hull until she came to the access hatch where she and Zinsser had stopped earlier.

The control unit was thoroughly useless, dug and prized at behind the guards' backs by generations of common passengers with endless hours to kill. She had no expectations of getting the controls to work; she was more interested in having a close look at the systems interface jack, which was more or less intact.

Shielding her actions with her body, she opened the pouch LAW had issued, along with the archeo-hacking wrist-whatties, to members of the Wall Water shore party. The pouch held a selection of adapters, one of which fit a connector in the interface, whose fiber line had been hacked away long ago.

When she got back to Zinsser and Spume, the bronze boo-hoo's screeches were more deranged than ever and the flax traders' perudo game was more animated. Zinsser turned up his nose at the gooner, but the Sense-maker took a gulp. Ghost sat down cross-legged by Spume, removing her right shoe and massaging her foot, all the while gazing at the perudo players.

"Spume, are there utility hatches at all four points of the compass?" As she asked, she made a long, limber stretch along the deck, extending her leg to push the mug of gooner against the back of the boo-hoo cage. Zinsser watched with clinical interest. If the flax speculators were engrossed in their game, the boo-hoo wasn't. The squalling pest stuck its head through the bars of its cage on a serpentine neck and began sucking the stuff down, neck disappearing into the cup by degrees.

"Hatches?" Spume was saying. He saw what was going on with the boo-hoo but refrained from commenting. "What does it matter? They're closed fast, and one cannot fit the finest knife edge in the gap."

"Humor me."

He nudged his chin on different vectors. "There, there, there, and there."

"One in first class staterooms?"

He considered it while the boo-hoo made gurgling sounds. "Even so."

"And first class has wooden walls against the hull, like here?"

"To provide bunk and storage space, what of it?"

Ghost fell silent. Bored first class passengers might not have had a chance to vandalize such a hatch over the years. Which meant a hatch with its control unit connector still wired up...

The boo-hoo was suddenly making dry-siphon sounds. As it pulled its head up to catch its breath, Ghost clasped the rim of the mug with her toes and pulled it back to her, all in one move. She had just gotten her foot back into her shoe and hidden the mug behind Old Spume when the noisemaker gave a bilious caw and a prolonged burp.

The perudo game stopped. The dice cups were put down and the flax men surrounded their pet. But no amount of prodding, coaxing, or whistling could keep the boo-hoo from keeling over on its side, or make it serenade them some more. The speculators tossed their forelocks, covered the cage, and went back to their game.

"I said, why do you ask all this?" Spume added.

"As long as we're traveling, I want to meet a better class of people," Ghost told him.

Chapter Twenty-Two

Rhodes's *architronito* was demonstrably a better piece of ordnance than that of da Vinci's pal, Archimedes—the Renaissance namesake, not the legendary original—and better than that of the Perkins mechanism of mid-1800s Old Earth. Rhodes's shot had been sizable and its range, all of a kilometer and a half. Powerful, no question, but accuracy was another matter. Since the second round was a miss, Quant suspected that the first hit had been due to pure luck.

As a result of the Nixies' havoc, the ship was still running on backup systems and was a conspicuous target on the lake. Dawn, like dusk, abetted the targeting of a surface ship. Once more Quant called for power to the actuator disc propellers, only to be told that more time was needed.

Follow-up rounds screamed in while the *GammaLAW* continued its slow drift toward Wall Water. One blew away a surface search radar antenna; another tore a chunk off the cutwater. A third caromed harmlessly off the last of the No-Loads, the wheeled deadweights used to recalibrate the aircraft catapult, but the fourth punched through a Science Side superstructure close to the bow and killed two members of a repair party trying to undo some of the Nixies' damage. That round told Quant what Rhodes was firing: crude five-kilo spheres of cast iron.

Cannonballs, by JoeHova.

Summoned by a runner, Daddy D reported for a confab on the starboard wing of the bridge. The news wasn't good. Based on observations of surviving shore party members who had seen it in action, the steam gun emplacement would be impregnable to Ext boomer fire, especially at such long range, and the Exts' single fireball mortar had been damaged, perhaps beyond repair, during the Nixie attack.

"I'm thinking raiding party with demolitions," the general said, "put ashore in RIBs."

"With Aquam waiting to greet them at the beach," Quant predicted. "Battlesuits are protection against sling-gun quarrels but not against human wave assaults. And if those syrinxes stir up the Nixies again, that would be the end of any amphibious team."

"What other shot've we got? I've been racking my brain. Even pondered a suggestion from Madame Commish."

"Which was?"

"She wanted to know if there wasn't some way we could use the mutha-guns. Fire 'em from the hangar deck, maybe, out the aircraft elevator door."

Even if they were in their barbette—and Quant lacked the shipfitting facilities to get them there—the two huge naval rifles of Turret *Musashi* would have been of dubious value, since only practice ammunition had been delivered planetside. Fired from where they had been secured on the hangar deck for tetherdrop, the twin 240-mm rainmakers would go through the bulkhead behind them and probably smash breechblocks first into the main hull and likely set the hangar deck afire.

"After I explained to her about recoil," Daddy D continued, "she said she'd try to brainstorm a little harder before she opened her chow hole next time."

"Chagrin from Haven," Quant muttered. "Then the age of miracles isn't over. But what about your contraband helo—the Hellhog? How soon could you get it into the air?"

"Midmorning, earliest." Daddy D frowned, looking as if he would have spit for effect if Quant weren't present. "Talk about Murphy's Law. If just one strike fighter had survived the *Jotan* blitz, you could slot it into the catapult, toss it at Wall Water, and that'd be all she wrote—what?"

He had stopped because Quant was suddenly speaking into his headset. "That's what I said: power to the bow thrusters. The mains can wait, but I want those bow pushers now. *Now.*"

Quant chinned his mike off and turned to the watch officer. "Set conditions for catapult testing." To Daddy D he added, "They may have a steam cannon, but we just may have ourselves a rail gun. I'll need that demolitions detail, after all, General."

The preparations were unlike anything *GammaLAW*'s catapult and flight deck personnel had experienced, but Aquamarine had gotten them accustomed to improvising. As for the slush hydrogen drop tank, the tackle they mated to it was essentially a rerun of the one they had used to depth-charge the Nixies. Fitting it to its unorthodox launch vehicle and preparing the jerry-rig to Quant's specifications opened whole new worlds of beat-the-clock kludging.

When Quant finally had full use of his helm and power to his bow thrusters, he began the slow swing into position. *GammaLAW*'s increasing sternway had taken her so near shallows that he didn't dare pivot her to starboard through an easy ninety degrees; he had to take her all the way around to port, an agonizing three-quarter circle, to bring her to bear.

Crew members and Exts had worked fast, but Rhodes's cannoneers hadn't been idle, either. As shipfitters' mates gingerly swarmed the drop tank, Quant again heard the curt whack of an iron ball hitting Lake Ea, just off the Science Side stern quarter, hard enough to send water peaking five meters in the air. Ten seconds later another round barreled into the lake.

Quant marveled at the rate of fire. Rhodes's *architronito* was obviously equipped with a feed and valve mechanism that let the cannoneers drop a ball into the chamber from a rack, rebuild steam quickly from the previous round, and release a blast. It was pointless to rail that the Aquam shouldn't have been capable of such an invention. A third ball struck the upperworks with a clang like a fire gong, shearing away part of the surface search radar array.

"Mr. Bohdi, prepare to shoot," Quant called. The SWATHship's bows were crawling through the last excruciating arc of her long swing.

"Bridge, catapult; awaiting your go," Germaine Bohdi returned.

Quant chinned his headset and eyed Bohdi's status readings. The big, brushless DC linear motor that was her catapult was charged and ready.

Word came from the flight deck sidelines. "Bridge, special ordnance detail." Quant knew the voice; it wasn't an ordie but rather a servomech engineering officer working on the special detail. "We've got what may be a glitch in the refit."

"Ordnance, bridge. How long for a diagnostic?"

"Bridge, ordnance. It's a test-bench procedure, Captain."

Another steam gun hit drew a hollow clunk from the main hull somewhere around the hawsepipe. Wall Water had *GammaLAW*'s range. Fifteen minutes of test-bench time might as well be all day; in fifteen minutes Quant's engines would be back on-line, anyway. If he was going to have to sit and take a pounding until then, he wanted to get his licks in while he was doing it, even if all he threw were brickbats.

Under Zone's command, Ext sharpshooters were standing by in the bows with incendiary rounds chambered, but it was doubtful that even their marksmanship could remedy a technical failure.

"Ordnance, bridge. Belay diagnostics and make ready to launch. Demolitions team, stand by. Catapult, bridge. Mr. Bohdi, launch control released to you."

"Anybody bother checking the *wheels* on this lead sled?" somebody muttered inadvertently over the circuit.

Quant doubted that anybody had, just as he doubted there had been time to check a hundred other factors. After all, once the catapult had been recalibrated after arrival onworld, why would anyone waste time on the wheels of a No-Load that wasn't likely to be used?

Quant's knowledge of naval lore was considerable, and he was ready to bet that there had never been a munitions like it fired in this or any other fashion. The homely No-Load put him in mind of an oblong raviolo of duracrete and steel provided with four small hard-fill tires, a simple nose tow, and a rear-end holdback. The drop tank of slush hydrogen piggybacked to it was an elongated football, vacuum-insulated but giving off a fog of condensed air in the sultry Big Sere morning.

For all of that, the lashup didn't weigh a tenth of what even a single-seater, fixed-wing fighter did. So much the better for range.

Precision shooting was out of the question; the impromptu plan was to lob and hope. With luck, Quant would get Rhodes's attention in singlestick-to-the-head fashion and interrupt the bombardment for a few critical minutes.

"Cat control, bridge. How're you calculating windage?" Dopplering radar and gunnery computers were still down.

Bohdi explained: "It's pretty much a pinch of dust in the air and a whatty computation, Captain. By guess 'n' by God."

Somewhat better than that, Quant knew. Spanker FarYore, his gunnery officer, had had her input, too. The flight deck's variable-incline ski-jump bow ramp had been adjusted accordingly. He switched to a feed from a flight ops cam. "I read your cat as aligned with the target, Gerry."

He forced himself not to duck involuntarily, the only one on the bridge who didn't, as another iron cannonball tolled like a bell, striking the atmospheric package on the Science Side upperworks. His blouse, already wringing wet with sweat, got a little more sodden. He couldn't help wondering if he should look into getting some autoclave artillery of his own once the crisis was past.

"CatCon, bridge. We need suppression fire, if you please, Mr. Bohdi."

Before he had quite finished saying it, there was the crack of the holdback parting and the trundle of the No-Load's wheels squealing down the flight deck. It was a minor vibration compared to the launch of a real aircraft.

Bigger flight-decked marifortresses in the Periapt navy could fling a one-hundred-fifty ton aircraft down the deck at one hundred fifty knots and better. Quant had himself seen one of the *McMurdo Sound*'s cats throw a No-Load more than eight klicks. *GammaLAW*'s catapult was much less powerful, but by the same token, Wall Water lay only a kilometer off her bows.

Quant knew a vast sense of relief when the No-Load and its drop-tank burden arced away into the air; at a minimum, he had been spared a deck fire. He waited for the ignition to come and intuited after less than two seconds that the demolition had somehow failed.

Somebody else had sensed the same thing. There was a steady thundering of semiautomatic fire from the bows. Quant's visor gave him a split image of the No-Load riding out its flat trajectory and an Ext sharpshooter, his battle rifle braced against the rail by means of its bipod to absorb its fearsome recoil, squeezing off rounds one on top of the other. By the size and position of the shooter and somehow by the nature of the act, Quant knew it was Zone.

The third image in his visor showed the boomer's armor-piercing incendiaries drawing fiery lines through the morning sky on flight paths characteristic of nonpowered ordnance. The 20-mm's covered the first quarter of the way almost instantly, then slowed markedly and yet somehow stayed aloft, traveling what looked like an almost level track.

The shot was impossible, but Quant was consoled beforehand by the possibility that if the No-Load only crashed into or near Wall Water it might give Rhodes pause. Then there was a flare and an orange spark where the 20-mm trails intersected the fall of the No-Load. It was said later that the demo team's detonators must have worked belatedly or that if it was a boomer hit, it had been blind-lucky, but Quant wasn't so sure.

The No-Load became a waxing, rippling comet of red-yellow-orange fire mirrored in the lakewater. The flames it trailed streamed straight up as the boiled-off and burning hydrogen sought to rise.

"Raise some rads, Momma!" Quant heard an Ext yell at the top of her lungs.

He raised his visor and followed the shot by eye. His heart leapt at the thought that the shot would serve its purpose now no matter where it fell—into the lake or splashing a fireball on Wall Water's sheer ramparts. But it did neither.

"Impact on the dam face, right of dead center!" Spanker FarYore called, as if *GammaLAW* were at gunnery practice or in a surface action.

The wreckage of the No-Load and the drop tank flew out and down, but the burning hydrogen flew upward only, highlighting the mass movement of people on the dam crest road.

The dam controlled and enabled the aquaculture that fed much of that region of Scorpia; it also held back the many cubic kilometers of water in the Pontos Reservoir. The shot had hit the dam a bare fifty meters from where two vast, crudely patched ancient cracks nearly intersected.

While he knew from the survey reports that the construction was immensely strong—eight city blocks thick at its base—he held his breath, waiting to see the cracks widen, the dam face give way, the Pontos come rampaging down to swamp his ship and deluge the river valley all the way to the sea.

The hydrogen balled and rose, and in moments it dispersed. The air strained in Quant's chest, but the dam held. While no one on the bridge dared raise a commotion, less perceptive crew members and Exts out on deck cheered the hit, not realizing what might have been. Quant took his mind off it by ordering the flight deck secured from launch ops stations.

There were no further rounds from the *architronito*. Twelve minutes later Quant had power to the actuator disc propellers and eased his ship into deeper water and temporary safety.

"Captain, message from the CIC," Gairaszhek announced suddenly.

Quant swung to him. "Let's have it, Eddie."

"Beginning approximately two minutes ago a barrage of directed-energy beams originating on Sangre began taking out our SATs. Communication, navigation, intel, and Science Side vehicles were targeted along with the armed ones. While there's no way of knowing what's happening over the horizon it's presumed that everything in orbit has been or is being obliterated."

Quant stared at him. "Beam weps from Sangre. Then it's not the Oceanic this time."

"Emissions signatures confirm that the beams were from Roke weapons," Gairaszhek said. "Indications are that the aliens are dug in and command the high ground."

Chapter Twenty-Three

With the tricycle *Bunbanger* closing in on *Shattertail*'s stern, Essa-Ballyhoot appeared at the eight-wheeler's taffrail with a U-shaped shooting rest and the biggest sling-gun Mason had ever seen. Fitting the rest into an aperture in the rail where it sat like an oarlock, she laid the long gun into it, positioning the stock's antirecoil stops just forward of the rest's arms.

Shattertail hit a final straightaway before the plunge to the Panhard salt flats. The braids, knots, and scalp locks of human trophy hair hanging from Ballyhoot's baldric swayed with the car's jarring. As she bent to adjust the sling-gun's rear sight, Mason was provided with another shock. The sight was a scale and cursor design, admittedly crude but far better than anything the Periapts had seen on Scorpian weapons. The shaft she loaded had a bulky, glassy head as large as a 40-mm shell.

When she triggered the long gun, it released with enough recoil to ride the stops partway up the U-shaped rest, but the missile flew on what struck Mason as a uselessly high trajectory. The trike helmsman saw it too late to take evasive action, but the shaft fell short in any case. The helmsman may have been thanking his lucky stars in the split second before realizing that the round was incendiary.

Mason gave a startled yell as the glassy warhead vanished in flame and oily black smoke. The trike came through it darkened, not afire but veering crazily. *Bunbanger* nearly went into the ditch on the uphill side of the RambleRove, then swerved on one rear wheel, cut in the opposite direction, and went sailing off the unwalled shoulder.

Armored men air-scrabbled and shrieked. The trike itself smashed to bits on first impact, then the wreckage and the bodies struck again, faring worse, and arced for another fall.

A flammable sling-gun missile of glass on a world where gunpowder was an impossibility, Mason thought. Had Purifyre's Trans-Bourne polymaths discovered a trove of Optimant technical journals?

"Sodium and water?" he asked his son. "In separate compartments? And fish oil for the incendiary charge?" Mason was no Archimedes, but Hippo Nolan used to talk about such devices.

Purifyre studied Mason for a moment through the slitted eye-cups of his insect-samurai helmet. "You'll have your answers, but not here."

The other two greatwagons hadn't paused to see to fallen comrades but were swerving around the pool of fire on the road, sacrificing headway. As they came on again, Turnswain gave a triumphant laugh. "Y'see? Not so fast to regain speed as they were before. Their pullers are succumbing at last!"

"We'll dance them around the flats till their muscles give out," Purifyre told Mason. "Maybe the Panharders will jump in when they see Ean soldiery invading."

Ballyhoot evidently had no remaining incendiary rounds. Instead, she bore down on the weapon's galvani-stone lever and reloaded with a barbed shaft the size of a

212

javelin. *Shattertail*, meanwhile, was picking up momentum on the long downslope.

The salt flats spread before Mason like an inland sea of unpolished white marble or a plain of tamped snow. Eyewash's brightness reflected so harshly, he feared going glare-blind. The radiance, open space, and swelter of the place had him teetering.

He had seen the Panhard before, and it had always made him think of monster Cyberplagued construction machines run amok. The stretch of RambleRove that had once spanned the dry salt lake was gone; now isolated bits lay shifted and shattered. Long expanses had been gouged out of the ground without leaving a clue to what had happened to them; others had been smashed into the salt and the ground beneath it as if by titanic fists. Still more jumbled megaliths of pavement and roadbed were heaped in piles, now weathered away to low hills of salt, soil, and riprap.

A badly pocked latter-day off-ramp led from the Ramble-Rove proper to a deep-rutted detour around the devastated motorway. Turnswain slowed a lot less than Mason thought advisable as he steered *Shattertail* down onto the flats. Mason could see the scattered, fortified compounds of the various digger gangs in the distance.

With Amnion deposits often inaccessible, salt was a valuable commodity. Over PostPlague generations large-scale excavation from the Panhard had become a jealously guarded franchise, and the digs had become rough-hewn fiefdoms. Currently, only six digs remained, whittled down from twenty or so by feud and skirmish, and even those periodically conspired to knock off competitors.

Digger patrols in each territory kept out independents and claim jumpers. Protracted guerrilla war and pitched battles had long ago settled RambleRove travelers' right-of-way across the Panhard, but stopping to gather more than a scoop or two of salt brought on digger vigilantes in abundance.

Mason concluded that *Shattertail* would get a lot more attention than that as it slammed down onto the rutted bypass and went crashing through the rickety symbolic railing that marked the lateral boundaries of the detour route. There were digger vigilante factions standing around, wild-bearded and glaregoggled, dressed in salt-encrusted robes and climate suits. They were armed with weapons of every kind, but especially longrifle sling-guns. The vigilantes dove for safety, firing quarrels as well as throwing hatchets, *shuriken*, and knife-edged boomerangs.

Glancing back as *Shattertail* hissed across the flatlands, Mason saw diggers who were just beginning to raise their heads and shake their fists, taken by surprise a second time as *Rut-Rider* and *Rattlebones* came careening down onto the flats in hot pursuit, rails thronging with battle-fevered grandeean troops. One of the Dominor Paralipsio's Killmongers on *Rattlebones* was blowing on a fanfaronato as his fellows made wild battle cries.

The diggers had some trouble shifting mental gears from predator to potential road kill. One sling-gunner aiming his long-rifle on a linstock rest was mowed down by *Rattlebones*'s mud-cutter wheels and pressed so deeply into the salt that there was nothing of him to be seen afterwards. Eans and vigilantes traded potshots, but the grandeean soldiers' main attention was fixed on *Shattertail*.

The eight-wheeler was skewing over the multiple layers of narrower and shallower barrow tracks that had accumulated since the last Big Drench. Gray-white granular rooster tails flew up from its spinning rims in what felt to Mason like a nightmare joyride through a toaster oven. Blowing alkali winds seared his nostrils, and the world took on a monochromatic yellow-white light.

"Stay left of that digs!" Ballyhoot called to Turnswain. Purifyre seized the elbow of Mason's gun hand in a grip that made him wince. "Here, to the rail! Before they draw even!"

The grandeean soldiers were raising pavises and individual shields, while *Shattertail's* company had little cover left after all their jettisoning. Mason was thankful the wagon was built to ford streams and Big Drench floods. Had it been open-sided or flatbed, its passengers would have been targets in a shooting gallery.

As a consequence of the dying pullers' last spasmodic responses to the ongoing overdoses of Analeptic Fix, the Eans' speed rose in spurts only to decline again. But if the praetorians' pullers were dying, they were delivering a very insistent swan-song. *Rut-Rider*, a lean and responsive vehicle, had pulled into the lead and was coming up on *Shattertail's* port side, while *Rattlebones*, a twelve-wheeled articulated galleon composed of two halves joined by a central torsion hitch, gained slowly but surely on the starboard. Between them the commandeered greatwagons held forty troops or better.

Shattertail swung to port around a dig compound behind a log palisade. Open gates showed premises that were a mixture of mining and processing site, medieval junkyard, and feudal garrison complete with watch towers and siege engines. Up in arms, more diggers charged out to fire at everything that rolled by, then take up the chase on foot and in wide-tired, slave-drawn jinrickshas. Mason knew that the fiercely insular flats dwellers would be out for blood.

Taking advantage of Turnswain's need to circumvent the salt digs, *Rut-Rider* bore in on the left. Ballyhoot fired her outsize pivot gun again, but its javelin missed the other car's wheels. Rather than pause to reload, she unslung her repeating crossbow and rested its muzzle on the rail.

The weapon's unfletched bolts were stacked in a sliding box magazine mounted atop the stock. A double-legged lever was hinged to both magazine and stock, with its crosspiece serving as a grip. Throwing the lever forward over the top of the weapon moved the magazine in that direction and seated the bowstring in a notch at the rear of the cutout slot. Pulling it back automatically cocked the bowstring behind a fresh round.

The weapon lacked the range and penetrating power of a conventional crossbow, but shooters made up for it by coating the sharpened-dowel tips with a tarry poison potent enough to make even armored opponents duck. The buttstock had a horizontal crescent brace that fit into the crook of Ballyhoot's elbow. The crossbow cycled and shot as fast as she could rack the lever forth and back. In fifteen seconds—much like a machine herself—she sent ten bolts volleying at *Rut-Rider*. Mason could see why she'd prefer it to a self-cocking but single-shot sling-gun.

Purifyre threw himself against the distracted Mason as a Killmonger quarrel zipped through the spot where they'd stood and thunked into the opposite gunwale, its barbs glistening with something yellow and viscous. More bolts, stone pumpkin-balls, and needle-nosed darts were whizzing through the air and striking the muscle car. The grabsmen were trying to protect themselves with wicker hamper covers; another crewman was doing his best to shield Turnswain at the helm with a large barrel lid, but it seemed only a matter of time before the Eans would hit one of the *Shattertail*'s riders.

The crossbow's magazine empty, Ballyhoot dropped behind the rail and began crawling aft to her quiver of bolts. Mason unknotted his capelet with his free hand as Purifyre drew him down by the railing. The wind of the car's passage jerked the little cloak back across the Panhard as easily as it had taken the frond sun hat. Mason steadied the flechette pistol as best he could on the rail and tried to make the open sights line up.

Reminding himself to squeeze the trigger this time, he thumbed the selector to five-round bursts. The gun spit simple ten-grain, arrow-shaped projectiles. LAW did not want amateurs haphazardly spraying explosive or high-penetration rounds. The burst was painfully loud, however. The pressurized propellent gas gave the flechettes a muzzle velocity of over one thousand two hundred meters per second—supersonic at that altitude on Aquamarine. Against that there was *Shattertail*'s swaying and bouncing as well as *Rut-Rider*'s, forty meters off and drawing abreast. Mason saw no sign of a hit, not even kicked-up salt, to tell him he had shot low. He might as well have fired straight up into the air.

"Missed," he rasped.

Purifyre contradicted with a head-rolling gesture, his helmet's serrated mandibles tilting. "I saw a strike—up forward by the prow."

The praetorians hadn't even noticed the hole his shot had poked in the wood planking. He flicked the selector switch over to constant fire. "Tell Turnswain to drive as steady as he can!" he yelled to Purifyre.

He hiked himself up so that he could brace his armpits on the rail and his elbows on the wagon's side; then he fired a second-long burst. This time the minidarts chewed a ragged hole near the stern and smashed fragments of wood off some of the bogey's spokes.

He began to slip, but strength like a living vise closed in on him from behind. Purifyre, clinging to the rail and digging his cleated boots into the deck, braced Mason between the rail and his own armored chest and shoulder pauldron. Mason felt the mandible sawteeth slice his neck, but it was as if the pain belonged to someone else.

His son's voice palpated his left eardrum so hard that it itched. "Shoot at their helm!"

No longer flopping around, Mason steadied himself and held the trigger down. The grandeeans' hostage helmsman was protected by two round shields on the arms of Apocalyptics and a kite-shaped one held by a Diehard. The 'chettergun's rate of fire was so high that the flechettes all appeared to hit at the same instant.

Some missed the mark, plucking at the clinker-built hull, the rail, and the outriggers but others punched nearly invisible holes in the soldiers' shields or armor. Stable in flight, the flechettes tumbled on impact and transferred close to two hundred foot-pounds of energy to their target. The men at *Rut-Rider*'s helm became a tableau of punctured metal and rent tissue. Their hostage, dead before he fell, dragged the wheel to port as he went down. The Apocalyptics dropped the daggers they had been holding to the man's back and chest, but in the struggle to maintain balance the helmsman's weight on the wheel veered *Rut-Rider* away from *Shattertail*. The starboard grabsmen's frantic efforts weren't enough to correct the change in direction. Rising off its left wheels, the car vectored directly at a yawning, abandoned digs pit the size of two city blocks.

Someone released the drag shoes, but they failed to catch. Precariously balanced, the greatwagon looked as if it might stop just short of the excavation, but at the last moment the searing wind yanked loose one the car's improperly furled lateen sails. A half dozen lucky troops and crewmen jumped; most, however, were borne along as *Rut-Rider* went freewheeling into space, dropping from view. Some of the diggers footracing after it cut a course for the pit.

Realization that he'd cut down an innocent victim made Mason gasp in high register. He might have cast the damned pistol away if his son hadn't been pounding him on the shoulder with a gauntleted fist. "Well shot! Well shot!"

Mason's attention was torn from the sight of the wreck when *Shattertail* gave a sideways yaw and Purifyre wrenched him away from the rail. "On the right!" Turnswain was shouting. "They've got us on the right!"

The twelve-wheeler *Rattlebones* had closed in while they were occupied with *Rut-Rider*, and someone with one hell of an arm had heaved a grappling hook that had bitten deep into *Shattertail*'s rail. The grapnel had been improvised from loading hooks and carried a heavy line from a block and tackle arrangement.

Mason, Purifyre, Ballyhoot, and the four other available fighters leapt for the cover of the starboard rail as more salvos of fletched missiles flew toward them on the flat trajectories of close fighting. Only the terrain, rougher there, saved everyone from being pincushioned.

Mason glanced at the 'chettergun. The helical-feed magazine was down another fifty rounds after mere seconds of constant fire, and the majority of his shots had missed their mark.

Ballyhoot and another man in insectile-samurai war gear hadn't been able to dislodge the grapnel, so they were hewing at its line, she with the kris sword, and he with a serrated cutlass. A sling-gun quarrel found a gap in the man's armor. Mason thought at first that it was a shallow wound through the hip, but the Human Enlightenment votary clutched at his side, blood trickling through his fingers.

Purifyre got there, hooksword in hand, as Ballyhoot was lowering him to the deck.

Nothing but fear for his son could have made Mason do what he did then. In the face of the salvos of spiked balls, stone pellets, and barbed broadheads, he drew himself up again and, holding on to the rail with one hand, sprayed *Rattlebones* with the other, hosing its port side from stern to prow.

Three seconds of fire silenced the flechette pistol, but in that time the minidarts burst and tumbled through wood, flesh, cloth, *cuir bolli*, and any gap in chain mail or plate they found. Massing to volley and board, the praetorians went convulsing and stumbling back away from *Rattlebones*'s rails, and the grapnel rope ran slack. Purifyre severed it with a last blow of his hooksword.

Turnswain peeled *Shattertail* off to the left while the chase car lost speed in fits and starts before beginning an immense circle to the right. Coursing salt diggers, waving their weapons, changed direction to pursue it, baying their war cries. It was impossible to see whether any of the crew members were alive or if both the praetorians and their hostage carmen would have to confront the wrath of the vigilantes.

Purifyre steadied Mason, who was weaving where he stood. "Well struck! You fought better than—"

"Don't say anything good about *that*," Mason said, shaking. Ballyhoot tossed her head and snarled through filed teeth she plainly wanted to sink into Mason's throat.

Mason was unfazed. "What happened to Human Enlightenment?" he asked. "What about the weal of all Aquam?"

Behind their helmet cups, Purifyre's eyes blinked, and for just a moment he showed confusion and a kind of wonder. Then he found his voice as Hammerstone. "Human Enlightenment has its place. But so, unavoidably, does this." He swept his fingerless gauntlet at the carnage on the Panhard.

"That's something LAW would say." Mason turned his back before additional words made matters worse. He raised the 'chettergun to hurl it after the slowly curving *Rattlebones*, only to stop himself.

Violence was a constant, he told himself. Violence had been visited on *Terrible Swift Sword* the previous night, and it had been visited on many a world by LAW and the Roke. On pitiless Aquamarine it was nearly universal, and just now it was the only sure way to strengthen his newly forged ties to Purifyre.

Instead of flinging the gun, he looked around for the clip-on holster with its spare ammo cassette and gas cartridge. Ballyhoot had them. Mason expected trouble, but she handed them over with an air of bafflement, as if her understanding of the universe had been turned on its head. He wondered how he must have looked to her.

Mason ejected the spent gas cartridge from the 'chettergun's grip and the ammo cassette from atop the receiver; then he reloaded. Knowing that he would have to husband what remained, he tucked the holster carefully into his wide car rider's stomacher, double checking to make sure the thumb break would keep it in place.

To the northwest he saw *Rattlebones* losing speed as it vanished into the heat-wave mirages, the diggers still racing in for the kill. On *Shattertail* the grabsmen were laughing and singing, half-wild with the relief, helping to bring the car about and head south once more for the enigma of the Trans-Bourne.

CHAPTER TWENTY-FOUR

To Burning the Staggerwise Turnpike suggested a village plaza three hundred klicks long.

"It's every bit of that," Souljourner agreed, hopping down from the *Racknuts*. "The communal floor, as well."

She scraped the hardtop with a dancing slipper that her sizable squarish foot was bursting at the seams. It smeared the dust of the Big Sere, hulls from shelled grains, slackwort gob stains, wheel-trodden scat, and the childish scrapings of a water-hopscotch diagram. The water box was called Amnion, and any Aquam child who touched it was automatically out of the game—dead.

Racknuts was stopped at the crest of an elevation called Revelator Ridge. Manna had called a halt to rest the flexors and purge them of fatigue toxins and to give her a chance to mix up a new batch of Analeptic Fix. Then, too, the crude worn out wheel bearings had gotten so hot that the smoke from their grease packing smelled like a funeral pyre.

Burning's demand that they stay on *Shattertail*'s trail rather than divert to the Staggerwise had become untenable when word had reached him that the praetorians racing after Purifyre had sealed the southern border of the Grandee Rhodes's domain. Because he couldn't take the chance of being recognized by Militerrors posted at the border who might have seen him up close at the

Grand Attendance, he had held his peace when Manna had deviated south to circumvent the border checkpoint. South meant away from Lake Ea, the SWATHship, and the Exts, as well as from the RambleRove. He glanced back upcountry along the Staggerwise. It had taught him a lot in a few short hours.

Muscle car dominion over the Optimant high roads had kept peons from homesteading the autobahns, but it hadn't prevented their butchering animals on it, using it as a town square and open-air theater, and threshing crops on it. Some even spread their grain for the cars' wheels to separate, a kind of automation that had Burning wary of all local baked goods.

Along with "praise shrine" wayside chapels too numerous to count, the high roads were dotted with the wreckage of muscle cars that had met disaster and been shoved off the shoulder. The more Burning saw other flex-buggies, the better he felt about paying Manna to refuse passage to potential passengers. The average car was an overloaded prole omnibus or ferry burdened past any sane limit with people, cargo, and livestock. Many had poorer, short-haul fares clinging to the side of the hull for want of room. The best topside seats were the ones from which a rider had a fair chance of leaping for life if a vehicle overturned. While the stern was safer, it was certainly to be avoided by those subject to motion sickness.

Boner had explained that the unstable wagons frequently flipped, collided, got washed away in Big Drench fordings, and suffered attacks by brigands. Most wrecks were quickly stripped, but Manna slowed only for recent ones to see if a car crew needed succor. Crusty and self-serving as she was, she observed the tenet because her own survival was bound to it. Fortunately, no accident sites had required her service thus far, but there were enough graves, cairns, and long-dead funeral pyres to keep Burning contemplative.

As to why there were no flexor-powered millships on Lake Ea instead of the slave-driven teamboats, Boner confided that the shadowy Trans-Bourne artificers who built the muscle cars refused to share their technology so long as the Ean grandees allowed slavery, child buying, and similar traffic to flourish in that region of Scorpia.

Despite it all, the detour onto the Staggerwise had strained to the breaking point Burning's resolve to persevere in the search for Ghost. He might have walked after her if one last possibility hadn't occurred to him. Revelator Ridge was as good a place as any to test the air, but he needed privacy to try out his idea. When he asked Souljourner for help, she beamed and squeezed his hand until the knuckles ground together, taking it for another step in the grandiose romance her lost dice had foretold.

He stretched to ease the kinks and soreness he'd developed from Hussar Plait bangs to boot soles. After four hours of travel he understood why the muscle cars bore the names they did. The Big Sere sun was already hot enough to broil a rider's brains even through the headdress he had improvised, using the removable bib of his blouse and the braided aiguilette from his shoulder. He would have given a lot to strip to his codcup the way Spin, Yake, and Boner had to their wraparound skirts, but that would have invited terminal sunburn as well as questions about his alien pallor.

His first stop on Revelator Ridge was thirty meters down a path behind the shebangs, dooryards, and truck-farming plots. With a scrap of her gown trim for a cat's cradle and a palmful of sweetkernals to entice, Souljourner diverted the gathered ragamuffins, beggars, and other gawkers. She charmed them without being mistaken for a mark, planting her foot in one stripling's gut and sending him sprawling on his ass when his fingers strayed a little too close to her belt wallet. But Burning felt no mirth as he ducked around the back of the shebang and got away clean.

A hayrick-size boulder was perched just outside the shanty-town on the northern face of the ridge. He hiked himself up onto its flat top, sat, and began taking stock of the items he carried: two spare magazines for the hardballer—a total of twenty-eight rounds—including the ten in the mag well, one chambered; his portion of the first-echelon med supplies the shore party had divvied up, including a few analgesics, topical antibiotics, and such; the wrist whatty and the archeo-hacking 'wares that went with it; Ghost's soot-black saw-toothed dagger; and his own worn issue Ka-Bar.

He paused to squint at the northeast sky, where Lake Ea and the *GammaLAW* lay over the horizon. Then, from his breast pocket, he brought out a field signal whistle on a lanyard. On a muffled chain around his neck was his dog tag chip as well as one of a matched pair of hermetically sealed lockets Ghost had stolen from Dextra Haven's villa on Periapt. The locket contained a tar-black lock of Ghost's hair, just as her locket contained a scarlet one of his. From another pouch he drew the Aggregate-made gaffed Optimant dice and remote control he had confiscated from Zone back onboard *Terrible Swift Sword*.

His plugphone wasn't doing him any good in his ear canal; the spectrum was still roaring with overwhelming static and an eerie jamming that didn't sound artificially generated yet wailed up and down the audible range in a way that made the hair on his neck stand up—some god-wraith lamenting and raging in an electromagnetic tempest.

The Oceanic, something told him.

He set the plugphone aside, took up its control touch-card, and began keying prearranged message code groups into its peewee memory. The best part of the day for his plan had already gotten away from him. At dawn a planet's leading edge swung into any meteor swarms it might encounter, while even by midmorning it was swinging away. That made for fewer hits, and he needed those hits if he was to contact the SWATHship by meteor burst commo.

Standard drill—provided the fallback signal system was up and running and fully manned and enabled. The only way to find out was to have a go at it.

The technique of ricocheting transmissions off streaks of ionized air left behind by meteors immolating themselves in the upper atmosphere dated back to Old Earth. Though some billions of micrometeors hit Aquamarine on an average day, only a relative few would be useful as reflectors between any two given ground stations. But this day wasn't average. Given the destruction of the *Sword*, the planet's atmosphere would consume a lot more than the usual batch of dust motes.

The plugphone's tiny antenna was useless for what he had in mind, but the control touchpad's back surface incorporated an auxiliary—an alloy multilatticework under a protective polymer layer. It could achieve a limited phased-array capability not by physical movement or reconfiguration but by focusing its emissions electronically. On a planet the size and with the atmosphere of Aquamarine, meteor burst commo could work over distances of two thousand kilometers and more.

He pulsed the signal per Battalion of Exts doctrine so that the *GammaLAW*'s adaptive retrodirective antenna array would recognize his atmospheric rebound among heavy, ubiquitous jamming up and down the RATEL band.

His plan of action was also one of inertia. He sat with the touchcard braced on the rock, angled upward for an estimated cushion shot to Lake Ea, and waited. The otherwise useless plugphone would tell him if he scored a hit.

He could only hope that the SWATHship's ARAA was sweeping the sky with its constant probe beam eighty degrees wide. The ionized trail of a meteor would provide a reflective field for the two to meet. When and if the ship's probe detected the one his touchpad was sending, both would narrow to twelve degrees. His card might have only hundredths of a second to send a microsquirt and accept an answer in kind.

Watching the sky, he knew he wouldn't see light from an ordinary micrometeor, but he might well see a piece of the *Sword,* inside which two-thirds of the Exts who had looked to him to bring them home someday had died. To block the thought, Burning roamed his glance over his meager possessions, carefully freeing one hand to take up the locket.

To his plodding human perception the toning of the probe beam establishing contact and the one notifying him contact had been broken were one. Only the Skills kept his hands from shaking as he replayed the burst transmission he'd received in exchange for his own; only the need to keep from attracting locals' attention there on Revelator Ridge made him stifle a growl of pleasure as he heard codegroups from the same Ext PAM cypher he had used.

Message authenticated. Approximate location of Ext Six—Burning—received. Request for ASAP airmobile reaction force air search concentrating on his plugphone emissions source routed for immediate action. Possible need for change in and movement of Ext Six's location noted…

There was no information on the SWATHship's status. It might be hours or even days before an aircav helo, a SAT, or an AWAC got a fix on him. Once air assets were on the job, they would find him quickly, on Scorpia or beyond. When they did, he would have to be able to furnish them with some idea of Ghost's whereabouts.

CHAPTER TWENTY-FIVE

Moments after the caged bronze boo-hoo, swocked to the gills on gooner, had passed out, Ghost heard the street-poet voice of the hawker who had made such a point of admiring her scars. The temperature was falling by the minute.

"Where is she? I, Bravuro, shall know her when I see her dainty bogtrotters, my splinterfoot Cinderella with the scar-scary phiz." He was picking his way through the steves spaces, scouting the huddled common passengers. "She's with a Sense-maker whose travel instincts make little sense to Bravuro and some dapper fellow with a delicate constitution, no stomach for robber-kabob!"

Ghost watched Bravuro come. Wearing a side-sling pack but chiefly burdened with religious and occult items, he suggested a slightly older male version of the young woman who had sold the brochettes, by parts gypsy, huckster, midway sharper and con artist. His face was pale and angular with a closely trimmed brown beard. He wore a poncho, scarf, coarse jute leggings, and gaiters, and thick brogans. The pigtail that escaped from the back of a bulk-knit red watch cap was braided with spiritual tokens and holy medals—more wards against the Oceanic.

"I see you're not the one I seek, madam," he told a woman. "Albeit I have rare items to put you in closer touch with your spiritual endowments and shall swing back this way anon."

His clinking breastplate consisted of scores of charms, wishbones, and lucky pieces. There were also crude miniatures in wood, unfired ceramic, or scudo iron of a *Dream Castle* that sported wings—straightforward metaphysical flight insurance.

Finally, his fast-shifting gray eyes zeroed in on Ghost. "At last, my splinterfoot Cinderella! I've no glass slipper for you but something more suited to *this* castle." He pronounced it "Zin'drella." Ghost hadn't even known the Aquam knew the fairy tale, but some things even the Cyberplagues couldn't wipe out.

Bravuro squatted before her, Zinsser, and Spume with the ease most lower caste Aquam showed, so limber his homespun-clad glutes brushed the floorplanks as he arranged his poncho. He kissed one of his bigger religious medallions, a bronze wheel with the eye-in-the-waves *Yahweh* icon.

"May the One Who Watches spare all here."

He wasn't talking about the earthly Jehovah but rather the being who dwelt in the Amnion, which was never far from any Aquam's thoughts—especially Aquam floating over the endless seas in a two hundred-plus-year-old Optimant dustbin.

"It's being bruited that a demigoddess came aboard," Bravuro went on, "in all that unpleasantness at Lake Ea, light of luggage and short on shoes." He faked surprise at the hard-used foot she had been massaging. "Such a glamorous little road-tamper! Just the thing Bravuro can bedeck and bedizen, lo!"

He loosened the drawstrings on his side-sling bag to tease out a thick wad of merchandise, which he unrolled with a few shakes: a pair of winter footgear, cross between mukluks and over-the-knee moccasins. They were of soft-tanned russet wingle hide, beaded in rickrack patterns and lined with sepia platyprime fleece—wonderful craftsman-ship from sturdy soles to double-stitched cross-ties.

Ghost realized that someone—probably the long-pig *yakitori* seller—had mentioned their clothing needs to the bric-a-brac peddler and he had hastily acquired a sideline. When she confronted him about the switch, he stopped being so voluble and leaned in close to stymie eavesdrop-pers, demonstrating good steve space manners.

"I hear three passengers of means have come aboard hastily, lacking goods and services I can provide. I race to demonstrate my helpfulness, promoting items from the supercargo's stores of general merchandise. Unsparing effort is all a fellow like me has in the outerworks, Cinderella. And some coats and footgear."

"Costing how much?" Ghost asked.

Bravuro pointed to her bib buttons. "One of those bonny little auriferous bosses."

"Five times the rightful price!" Old Spume grunted. "If you traffic with this mountebank, count your fingers when you're done—better yet, your nether cheeks."

Bravuro looked at him fondly, but his tone was acid. "O soul of dispassionate wisdom! The supercargo's first rule is that none may interfere with the commerce he controls. Hold, therefore, thy fat tongue, or all my talismans won't save you from a swim with the Oceanic—"

Ghost yanked the moccasin-mukluks from Bravuro's hand. On her other palm was a cuff button. "I'll give you this for the clothes—provided you answer questions for me in the time we would have spent haggling. Otherwise my bunkies and I will go ask some *other* peddler to outfit us—which won't trouble the supercargo's sleep."

Bravuro grew less frolicsome by the moment. "Payment first."

"Negative. Other peddlers have answers, too."

"And what if my answers don't please you?"

She kicked off the filthy wooden klamps and began wiping her feet on the saque outercoat of Old Spume, who was too outraged at her thriftlessness to either notice or care. "You'll miss the chance to get a button or two all for yourself—no overhead—before this flight's over." She fell to cross-tieing the footgear, then turned to Zinsser. "It's cold, Doctor. Try on that capuchin."

Unhappy at being sidelined, Zinsser shot her a glance, but he was shivering too hard to contest the point. Bravuro extended half boots to him, along with a capuchin made of wingle shearling. He set another hooded capuchin by Ghost.

"I, too, commence to feel like cloud frost," Spume grumbled.

"I'll seek a ground-cloth your size," Bravuro simpered.

Ghost's moccasins had had at least one previous owner, but their warmth and dryness felt like infantry heaven. Bravuro wanted to show her how they were fastened, but she had a system of her own, double-lashing the ankles and leaving the boots loose above the shank. "What d'you know about the people in the first class cabin?"

The question set him back. "The DevOceans? Missionaries from Passwater. Zealots of the faith. Six came aboard with diverse boxes and chests."

"You know them?"

She watched him teeter between greed and self-preservation. "They insist on their privacy, and often wear their cowls and ritual vizards—but no, I didn't know this group."

So Testamentor wasn't necessarily a DevOceanite follower in addition to being a Human Enlightenment votary, Ghost thought. That could mean he was trying to infiltrate Passwater, but why? On the heels of Rhodes's actions against Marrowbone and the other demonstrators? And if for Purifyre, how could he have known in advance that the Grand Attendance would come apart as it had? Unless, of course, Mason's son had helped fashion the chaos of the previous evening.

Either way, it still left Testamentor's cabal as the ones with the overview, the foreplanning, the key data, and the resources, whereas all she and Zinsser had were the prospect of a long Laputa circuit and a shrinking inventory of dress uniform buttons.

When she was satisfied with the knee ties, she pulled on the capuchin and raised the hood, just as Zinsser finished tying the oversize brogans *over* his dancing slippers. "Is the first class cabin ever shared?" she asked Bravuro.

He canted his head, making the pigtail swing and rattle. "Occasionally, though not this time. The DevOceanites have made it clear and paid to insure it."

"Can you get us in there without their knowing? Or let us watch and listen to them through the wall or the floor, something like that?"

Bravuro made a shushing sound as he glanced around to make certain the question hadn't been overheard. "That's as much as you've paid for, Cinderella." He held his hand out.

Ghost put the one button in it. "If you keep your eyes open, your mouth shut, and your sweat glands dry, we'll make you the happiest pendant pusher on this flying wedding cake."

Bravuro made the proffered gold button vanish into his sleeve before he wended his way back across the steve spaces. Her new agent and fink, Ghost told herself, assuming he was honest enough to stay bought.

She, Zinsser, and Old Spume settled into more comfortable positions on the deck planks. With the edge off his hunger, Spume began yawning, making sounds like ice breaking up in a river. To recline more comfortably in the thick wingle shearling lining of his new capuchin cloak, Zinsser removed his formal-wear fanny pack and began transferring items from the pack to the capuchin's roomy interior pockets.

"You realize, of course, that Bravuro can sell news to Testamentor that we're curious about them," he said to Ghost. "Or maybe to the supercargo? Or even the Insiders?"

"'Can,'" she said measuredly, "but won't—at least not until he's gotten more of our money."

Old Spume snorted steamily, propping himself against a broad upright beam. "We'll know when the Insiders are about to have us flung overboard, because that slithering bottom feeder will be here two steps ahead to sell us water wings and aqueons."

"Or measuring us for *brochettes*," Zinsser contributed dryly. He was still consolidating jetpen, plugphone touchpad, and specimen case when he caught Ghost's eye. "The last of the Roke tissue in human possession. The rest went superstar with the *Sword*." He sighed. "Sweet reason! If we'd only gotten Starkweather's analysts to hurry their work. We might have found a way to communicate with the Roke."

Spume was suddenly alert again. "Is that the alien essence? Doesn't appear at all threatening."

Zinsser flared. "This is an enemy who devours worlds, and now they're your enemy, too! Your only hope against them is us. And me—*I'm* the only one who can make sense of them and determine why they appear to avoid this place like a plague. So instead of extorting us and trying to kill us, you bogwogs should be down on both knees—"

"You're important, too, Spume," Ghost said, heading off Zinsser. They needed the old man too much to rattle him with Roke War diatribes. "You're living proof that we can return youth to the aged and strength to the infirm."

Zinsser was clearly irked but got hold of his temper and leaned close to Ghost. "From here on out I'm to be consulted on all decisions. I'm senior mission scientist, and I won't be treated as your inferior."

Factoring in Zinsser's admitted importance to the mission, the drawbacks of more knifeplay, and her growing weariness with his childish, bloated ego, Ghost considered various options. Ultimately, she came back to her musings of a few minutes earlier, sparked by talk of Testamentor and of the timing of *Terrible Swift Sword*'s destruction, which connected with something Zinsser had said at Wall Water.

"Fine, let's share information, Doctor. On the promenade at Wall Water, you told me you were going to save my life. You were heated up to tell me something, and a minute later the *Sword* blew up. Did you know that was coming?"

"Are you insane? I had no foreknowledge *whatsoever*! It's bizarre and unjust of you even to suggest it."

She let him see the danger in her eyes. "I frequently *am* bizarre and unjust, Doctor."

"All right," he said after a moment. "If you must know, Wix Uniday informed me that Starkweather and Captain Nerbu had deployed Pitfall—without my consent, you understand. I feared a reaction by the Oceanic, though nothing on the order of what happened."

Ghost nodded. "Then what exactly were you intent on saving me from?"

Zinsser blew out his breath. "Possible bloodshed at Wall Water. It was plain to me that the grandees would erupt on learning that the Oceanic had been provoked. I thought that if you and I could reach Starkweather's *Jotan* before all hell broke loose…"

Ghost snorted a laugh. "Then I suppose I should thank you for *not* saving me, since we'd be scattered all over Lake Ea by now." When he didn't reply, she added, "Look, we're both exhausted. Clock some sleep. I'll keep watch for a while."

He didn't look sleepy, but he withdrew from the face-off, tugging the capuchin's hood low. She saw Zinsser had acquired *some* basic virtues, probably at sea, making the best of uncomfortable circumstances and sleeping where and as he could. Hunkering around the other side of the wooden upright and curling up against it, he pulled his feet up into the long-sleeved cloak as much as possible.

Ghost leaned back for a while with her back against the upright, knees pulled to her chest and head lowered. The snoring bulk of Spume and the curled form of Zinsser gave her cover for what she had in mind. She drew her knees up, draping the cloak over them again, then drew her arms inside. In making sure the bib of her tunic would stay folded out of her way, she touched her dog tag chain and the sealed locket that contained a lock of Burning's hair. It made her wonder if he was alive and whether he would abide by his promise not to mourn should she fail to make it back from this buggered-up sail through the sky.

Explosions of laser-heated air under the dome on which *Dream Castle* rode sent steady vibrations through the deck planks, the upright, and her derriere and back as she rummaged in her belt pouch. With the RATEL spectrum jammed, there would be no way to utilize the plugphone earpiece for multimedia display, so her scan would have to be visual only.

Her pistol scope was the key. If she hadn't dismounted it back at the landing ground, it would have fallen into the blast pit with her 'baller. She had enough R&D adapters to link it to the archeo-hacking brute memory unit. The scope's target-overlay imaging feature wasn't designed for 2D data viewing, but it would serve.

She got the breadboarded rig working and began her search of the data she'd downloaded from the Optimant computer concealed in the bust of Atheo Smicker at Wall Water. If any Aquam *did* see a glint of light under her hood, he probably would suppose that she was carbureting a chunk of pitchlike bash or some other smokable.

The brute memory gadge wasn't exactly made for data retrieval; its primary function was to store whatever Optimant data the shore party encountered. Consequently, the scan would run either as a painful crawl on the three-inch-wide scope or as a flashing kaleidoscope. But she could find no compromise, so what the hell.

Where she was accustomed to seeing in the scope an aimdot, pop-ups, IR targets, and holo bull's-eyes, data now flickered and danced. Most of what she saw made no sense: Optimant crop yields, improvements in the zero-point energy drive, climatic predictions two centuries old, and proposed changes in legislative bylaws didn't detain her. At a certain point, however, her reflexes triggered even before she knew why, and she froze the cyberstream.

FIREGOD, DOOMSDATA, HORRORGASM, APOCA-LYST, PATHOLOGIC LUCIFAGE, HELLRAZOR…

Flowstate made the names stand out like pillars of fire in the wilderness—the demon demigods of the Cyberplagues. Looking for clues to their inclusion among so many seemingly random data, she drifted into another index, where a half dozen proper names were linked to Aquamarine place names; HYPATIA/Alabaster, ENDGAME/New Alexandria, AKASHIC RECORD/Passwater...

She had to go around again because she couldn't figure out how to scroll back. Even then it made no sense to her. The air got colder, and the sounds of other passengers retreated. *Dream Castle* drifted serenely on thirty thousand K explosions of air molecules as the bytes capered for her incomprehensibly.

CHAPTER TWENTY-SIX

The best place to erect the farsight vision device was aft of the ruined CIWS mount. Zone didn't mind deploying the self-steadying tripod mount there, in plain sight, because if he had spotted what he thought he had, he was going to want everyone to know it.

GammaLAW was once more easing away from Wall Water for the sanctuary of deeper water, so he only had minutes to reestablish a fix on the object his eye had been drawn to after the slush hydrogen burst against the dam face had burned itself out. The farsight field unit wasn't as good as the stuff the SWATHship mounted, but with so much systemry inoperative, it was Zone's best bet. Its range and resolution made it superior to Ext gunsights and goggles, in any case.

His fantastic success in igniting the No-Load's H_2 warhead—sharpshooting that was already a minor legend—had brought him little pleasure. The dam's gates had held. Still, the misplaced admiration of fellow Exts would make it that much easier for him to take over when the time came.

He and Roust hadn't bothered getting permission to break out the farsight from the rapid-deployment stores. With the ship still in chaos from the Nixie attack, the steam gun, and unconfirmed reports that the Roke were now dug in on the larger of Aquamarine's moons, it was a little like freebie night at the whorehouse. The turmoil made for room to maneuver, and there was certainly business to take care of now that Burning and/or Ghost were back in the equation.

Strop, holed up in the ARAA sig center, had intercepted a meteor-transmitted message that placed Burning a hundred klicks southwest of Ea, apparently in pursuit of his sister and waiting for aircav to come to their rescue. It scarcely mattered that the ship had lost all air assets, since no one was going to get wind of Burning's message, in any case. It would be just like the Allgrave to find his way back to the lake at just the wrong moment. In terms of gaining control of the ship, Zone was already compiling a mental list of those who stood with him and those who stood against him.

Daddy D could be a tough old bastard, but he was long in the tooth and no worry. Haven put on airs that she was stauncher than she was and was soon to be cut off at the ankles as all her longev-deferred years began to weigh in. Her genblender, Tonii, might require special precautions, but none that would pose a problem, unlike Quant, who had already proved himself capable of demonstrating ruthless behavior in a clinch. The captain was the sort who would seal compartments and drown mutineers like trapped rats without thinking twice.

A shout from Roust interrupted Zone's musing. "There!"

Zone realigned the farsight to follow Roust's pointing finger, then zoomed in on the objective, which was showing combinations of red and white lights in a repeating pattern, different from the other markers and rescue signals that lit the lake during the night.

"Definite WHOAsuit marker buoy," Roust said, readying the hardwire feed.

Zone grunted. The suit had to have been concealed among the aquaculture debris that littered Ea's surface. "Jack me in and we'll show it to Quant and who all."

The last anyone had seen of it, the WHOAsuit had been clamped on the rear of the hydrofoil *Edge*, which lay holed by Rhodes's steam gun at the quayside below Wall Water. It was unlikely that some Aquam had gotten it out of its rack, much less taken it into the lake, which meant that a GammaLAW mission member had done so. Burning or Ghost. Though why he or she had abandoned the suit and struck for the Scorpian interior was anyone's guess.

"If it was the Allgrave who took the suit," Roust asked, "why not let it be instead of raising everyone's hopes that he's alive?"

Roust saw the anger in Zone's eyes and shut up. Normally Zone had no problem with his severalmates knowing what he had in mind, but he was in no mood to field questions. Roust and the rest would know soon enough, in any event, since they were critical to the next move. What mattered was that the flashing WHOAsuit beacon would be Zone's ticket ashore, where there were details to see to. Details that would put paid to Lake Ea.

Quant's sea cabin was barely large enough for the meeting's pared-down roster of attendees. Even with his ship in deeper water, he refused to stray as far from the bridge as his own cabin, to say nothing of the CIC or commissioner's conference room. Being away from the bridge when crisis broke was something that gave any captain the cold sweats. None of the trio assembled for the confab remarked on the signs of deep fatigue. All of them knew it was sometimes the unavoidable burden of leadership. In that moment no one could shoulder Quant's load but Quant.

The Roke still held the high ground, and in truth, there was no safety for the ship anywhere. From orbit the aliens could strike with impunity, and no amount of deep-water jerry-rigging was going to change that. Neither Quant nor anyone else aboard could say whether they were all combatants under some kind of ceasefire, POWs in the eyes of the Roke, or simply defeated and condemned enemies coming to the end of a brief reprieve. Still, it was nearing midday, and there had been no further aggressive moves from Roke or Aquam.

Quant settled into the sea cabin's desk chair with a contented exhalation, rubbing the slackness that had appeared under his eyes. Dextra Haven saw no reason not to perch at the head of the narrow bunk, while Daddy D sprawled at its foot. Tonii ignored the remaining chair at the foot of the bunk, content to lean back against the bulkhead, letting 'ers height make 'erm a conspicuous presence.

Quant had heard about the gynander making the pickup of an injured Kurt Elide at the CIWS explosion and doing other good work during the Nixie attack, but Tonii's heroics couldn't change old reflexes and bone-deep loathing. Some could gaze at Tonii and see a being whose sexual commingling excited desire, but for Quant the gynander only elicited thoughts of his brother Anu and of personal apocalypse. Bioameliorated pseudo-sibling rather than true brother, Anu had been engeneered from Quant's parents' plasm as part of Byron Sarz's Prime Line Project, which had been aimed at seeking the next, artificially induced step in human evolution.

Possessed of a tricameral brain, Anu was an hermaphrodite whose sexuality was more vestigial than that of the gynanders who came later, like Tonii. Anu was the artifact progeny conceived to smash the boundaries of human achievement. Something went awry, and Anu's culminating achievement was to slaughter Quant's parents and his infant sister, along with Anu's biodesigner and, very nearly, the thirteen-year-old Quant himself. Deep down Quant still fought a lingering, juvenile sense of inferiority because Anu had been his superior in virtually any measurable way, and in Tonii he saw a creature that should never have been.

Like nearly the entire ship, the sea cabin lacked air-conditioning as a result of LOGCOM's holding back the necessary refit equipment. Even with the door open and the cabin circulator running full blast, the place felt like a solar oven. Daddy D had the front of his battlesuit unsealed, and Dextra had changed to a lightweight everywear, but like Quant, they had sweated their clothing through.

"Why now?" Haven was asking about the Roke attack. "They avoid this place for hundreds, perhaps thousands of years, then decide to lay into it weeks after we arrive? Why didn't they show themselves when the *Scepter* was here twenty years ago or attack the *Sword* at full strength when we entered this star system." She shook her head in confoundment. "All our theories about them are obviously so much shit."

"The destruction of the *Sword* could be the answer," Daddy D suggested. "Maybe the Roke were waiting to see just what the Oceanic was capable of before they made planetfall."

Quant looked at Haven, whom he now couldn't help but see as a rapidly ripening middle-aged woman. "I'm inclined to agree with General Delecado. Doctor Zinsser said that the tissue samples he examined supports the possibility that the Roke are related to aquatic or marine creatures. With nothing to stand between them and Aquamarine now, perhaps they've decided to take a closer look at the Amnion."

Haven considered it. "Do you suppose they even know about us—about *GammaLAW*?"

Quant ran a hand over his bald forehead. "With RATEL jammed, I suppose it's possible that they've overlooked us."

"And should they come down the well, what can we do to protect the ship?"

"Little or nothing," Quant said flatly. "We'd do better to put everyone ashore and try to blend in with the indigenous populations."

"Here, on Ea, or elsewhere?"

"Assuming for the moment they don't know we're here," Daddy D said, "why would they choose Ea at all?"

Quant nodded. "If, on the other hand, the Roke were monitoring the *Sword* all along..."

"Then they know about Pitfall and *GammaLAW* and the rest of it," Haven completed. She exhaled loudly, then added, "Well, they certainly wouldn't destroy our SATs unless they had something planned. In the meantime, all we can do is carry on. In some ways I wish they would show themselves. At least then we'd have a shot at explaining ourselves, maybe at ending the conflict." She cut her eyes to Quant. "Now, what about this WHOAsuit marker Zone spotted?"

"Science Side confirms it's the beacon off the *Edge*'s unit. It could have gone adrift or been tossed overboard by Aquam monkeying around. There's no sign of the suit itself or proof of anyone's actually wearing it, much less one of our people."

"I disagree," Daddy D said. "I figure it was worn by the same person who zeroed the 'foil's destruct charges. Burning, I'd say."

"Then why would he abandon the suit, General?"

Delecado shrugged. "The Nixies, maybe. I'm not sure. But if he returned to shore, SOP would be for him to lie doggo in the area where he sunk the thing."

Quant, still rubbing his bare pate with one dark, muscular hand, spoke without hesitation. "We can't take the ship back for rescue ops *or* another look. It's more likely than not that the steam gun is operational. I say let's wait and see if the jamming clears. If we have a reliable report of MIAs awaiting extraction, we'll reconsider."

"Burning might be running out of room to maneuver," Haven thought to point out. "We'd all be a lot better off with him back onboard—especially after this incident involving Zone and Wix Uniday."

"That's being looked into," Daddy D told her. "Zone claims that he surprised Uniday during an attempt to make contact with someone at Wall Water via a mate to the headset Commissioner Starkweather gave Rhodes. Uniday pulled a weapon, and Zone was forced to defend himself."

"By attaching a signal light to him and hurling him overboard?" Haven asked. "Come now, General."

Daddy D tightened his lips and shrugged again. "Like I said, the matter's being looked into. Either way, it's my responsibility to determine if Zone has moved his own designs out ahead of *GammaLAW*'s well-being and survival."

"Word's already out that the Allgrave is alive," Haven pressed. "If we don't do something soon, morale on this boat is going to take a nosedive—at least in the Ext berthing spaces. I think that someone should go ashore for a look. Now."

Quant and Daddy D traded looks. "Might be time to break out the Hellhog, General," Quant said after a moment.

Delecado nodded. "Take us a day or so to uncrate and ready the thing, Skipper. But we owe it to Burning to at least try to save his ass."

CHAPTER TWENTY-SEVEN

The fleeting meteor burst contact with *GammaLAW* gave Burning a rebirth of morale. As he went with Souljourner to see what Manna's latest bellyaching was about, his stride was so energetic that the Descrier, big-boned as she was, had to trot to keep up.

Where he had been picturing terminal disaster aboard the SWATHship—perhaps an all-out indig attack—his mind's eye now showed him Quant and Dextra Haven with the situation fully under control and Daddy D with the Exts squared away, helped by Lod and even Zone. Airborne aid would find Burning as soon as was feasible, and he could foray south after Ghost with an untroubled conscience about having shirked other obligations.

He was braced for a set-to with Momma-Mountain Manna, but when he and Souljourner reached the *Racknuts*, they couldn't find her. "Off buying makings for more Analeptic Fix," Missy told them.

With the wheels chocked and the grabs set, she and Pelta were lounging amidships. The car was otherwise untended, but the local shebang dwellers, panhandlers, and gutter-snipes kept their distance. Burning assumed that was due to the sling-gun carbine and pistol the two engine-room sprites held propped on the rail.

With nothing to do but wait, Souljourner settled onto a two-rock seat under a yussa tree. The crude chair was one of countless rest spots along the Optimant high roads and most lesser tracks and paths. By design, a porter could sit or squat for a breather while propping a backpack or pannier on the shelf behind and thus be spared the trouble of shucking and re-donning shoulder straps, tump line, and the rest.

A circle of kneeling men were shooting craps on the road's surface. Seeing their pair of Holy Rollers, Souljourner wistfully thumbed the empty drawstring bag at her throat. Burning drummed his fingers on the pistol belt pouch where he carried the pair brought back from Aquamarine by Claude Mason.

In need of Souljourner's aid and cooperation, his obvious course of action should have been to further ingratiate himself to her by relinquishing the Optimant relics. But her insistence on reading star-crossed romance into tosses of the dice had already made matters awkward, and his renewed determination to find Ghost obliged him to look at Souljourner more impersonally. She was indispensable to his purpose, but emotional entanglement might impede or even derail it, so he decided to delay handing the things over.

Souljourner's expression said she wanted to talk, but having things to sort through, Burning decided to investigate the muscle car a bit more. He was curious about how the twitchmobiles worked and about whether he should be thinking about jumping ship for a faster one. With Manna absent, he could finally get a look *under* the car, as well.

Shagged-out and dilapidated as it was, *Racknuts* showed twenty different types of wood and what had been fine workmanship. He examined maoriwood skip plates mounted to spare the power train the worst impacts with rocks and other road bumps, the crude differential that had the wagon skidding through turns as much as rounding them, the aperture through which a bevel gear shaft transmitted power to the bogey's rear axle, the six "dished" mud-cutter wheels whose spokes angled inward from the rim to compensate for dynamic wheel deformation caused by the axles' leverage.

About the only fail-safes were the drag shoes—wood and iron devices like angular, flat-backed scoops chained to the pole that ran lengthwise to connect the axles. In theory, the drag shoes were dropped under the front bogey wheels for a panic stop. The rims wedged into the angle of the shoes' sides, and the resistance of the shoes' flat undersides on road or ground slowed and/or halted the car. On examining them, however, Burning decided that bailing out would be wiser.

Even so, the car was a prodigious piece of handiwork, all the more so for having been built by a throwback culture that didn't even *have* cars twenty years earlier.

He discovered, too, that he had been right about one thing. Two prepubescent poppets like Missy and Pelta *couldn't* squeeze the galvani-stone handsets rapidly enough to move *Racknuts* at good speed and keep it up for hours of travel. Instead, there was a simple galvani distributor run by a gear wheel. The gearwheel was driven by either a pedal-powered twist screw or, for a quarter-hour at a time, a coil spring mechanism. The machinery was simple but sturdy and made to exacting tolerances even though it incorporated a lot more wood than it did recycled Optimant metals and latter-day ironmongery.

Burning left off his investigation when he felt Souljourner's hand on his shoulder. She put her lips to his ear. "Did the talking stars yield any answer from your vessel?"

"Talking stars" was local Aquam phraseology for the various SATs the *Sword* had placed in orbit, but as far as Burning could determine, they were gone. "Tell me again what you felt before the starship exploded," he said after a moment.

"Just beforehand I felt the One Who Watches stirring the rocks with Its energies, the crackling of great forces in the bones of Aquamarine." She kneaded her temples, brow furrowing. "And I feel it still, mixed with movements I've never had to reckon. The One Who Watches prepares Itself for a novel display of Its displeasure." She looked hard at Burning. "We would do well to avoid the coast at all costs."

At the Grand Attendance she had talked of "faradaic energies" and some overarching work of the Oceanic. Geothermal power or seismic motion converted to electrical discharge? he asked himself. It wasn't anything he had come across in the *Scepter* mission data. He wanted to pursue the point, but she was wincing with pain.

"Nothing I'm not used to," she told him. "A few tremors later this afternoon, feels like. The epicenter's far out in the Amnion, to the west."

Poor kid, he thought. Racking headaches were a profound drawback of the serotonin abnormality that gave Descriers their sensing twinges presumably triggered by heightened electrical field motion caused by quake-related activity. As a mercy, Aquamarine's seismic activity was usually confined to minor, stress-ameliorating temblors rather than high-richter, *tsunami-raising* plate crunchers. Yet the Oceanic had to be peeved, because Souljourner was genuinely hurting, and she wasn't a complainer even when she had good reason to. Lambasting himself for being an inconsiderate codbanger, Burning dug out a general analgesic and anticephalagia agent—twin to the one he'd given her at Wall Water.

"Swallow the whole thing."

She downed it, then forced a smile. "A warlord of the Visitants must find life on the byways squalid."

"I told you before that you don't need to keep making apologies for Aquamarine. It's no worse than what I'm used to."

Among the Exts, being an officer usually made life tougher, not softer. One didn't eat until your troops had. One didn't drag oneself into one's fighting hole and grab some sleep without seeing to it that they were properly deployed and dug in, guard posts manned, special orders understood, commo arrangements tested. The free fighters wouldn't obey any other kind of officer. The whole nearly medieval structure of allegiances that had let the Broken Country poleis fight as one worked because, at least at maneuver unit levels, leadership meant hardship.

"Redtails, there is something else."

He was about to ask, but Souljourner was giving him eye-sign. Following her gaze, he saw Missy and Pelta back at *Racknuts*'s rail, pretending not to eavesdrop. He rose and followed Souljourner some distance to another porter's rest.

"I predict Manna will start charging us for water and other provisions," the Descrier said when they had arrived.

"After what I paid her?"

"She's whining about the fortune she's losing by refusing other fares and freight. She wants the gold you're wearing whether she overtakes *Shattertail* or not. Those pretties will kick off her new business in a big way."

Burning beetled his brow in bewilderment.

"The Analeptic Fix—her flexor *elixir vitae* formula. It's one of the best. If she builds a mixing works, she can wholesale it up one side of Scorpia and down the other. She's amassed almost enough seed money to make a start at the end of this trip in her little hometown on the southern coast—RakeOff Crimp. So she yearns for the missing capital."

"Yearns enough to finger us to the Militerrors? Or to Purifyre's bunch?"

"It may be."

"Then we need some kind of leverage on her. I'd hate to have to kill her whole family."

He met Souljourner's startled eyes straight on so she would know he meant it, know what she was involved with if she stayed with him. "What about this fast Fix? Do you have any idea what the recipe is? She'd mum up if she thought we could give away her secret."

"Unquestionably. But more's the pity, she shares it with no one. When she prepares a batch, she mixes the critical components in solitude, hidden from view in the treadle compartment—even keeps a tarp over it."

Burning turned a glance to where Missy and Pelta were sitting at the bow. Manna appeared just then and began to belabor her passengers. "Get aboard, you pukefaced gargoyles! We're pulling chocks. Isn't it enough you rob me of honest profit with your insanely exclusionary demands?"

She had taken the weight off the carved peg leg by leaning on her whole one and her sling-gun, a beautiful weapon of polished maoriwood inlaid with silver wire and patterned with glass-headed studs. The size of a longboat oar, it had a matching linstock on which it could be braced for accurate firing.

Porters arrived with assorted casks and stoppered carboys. "Make haste, O tightfisted screwmaggot," Manna aimed at Burning.

Once on deck, he sauntered over to the water firkin secured forward and reached for the wooden dipper. As he had anticipated, Manna yelled, "If you're going to slobber and gulp my precious water, there's a surcharge! A silver scudo per day for firkin privileges. If you don't like it, you can walk!"

Later that afternoon, there were three tremors, just as Souljourner had predicted.

With a long, freezing night and morning in the steve spaces ending at last, the *Dream Castle* turned north for the Scourlands. By a whim of Optimant programming, the Laputa bypassed the few land masses east of Scorpia, including the Flyaway Islands, leaving such surviving populations as were down there forever out of touch with the rest of Aquamarine. However, the Laputa came close enough to one for Ghost to see rickety mockups of the *Dream Castle* in one-tenth scale on the flyspeck's higher elevations—cargo cult lures set out by desperate primitives in the forlorn hope that the tower in the sky would bring down legendary miracles.

Afternoon brought her out of her not quite doze to hear Spume snoring, despite his vow to remain on guard. Having expected it, she'd stood backup watch, keeping herself from falling into a sound sleep. During waking cycles she'd gone over and over her situation. At least the Sense-maker had been warm to sleep against.

More scouting around and cautious questioning of the likes of Bravuro had yielded the fact that money, booty, and provisions rendered up to the Insiders were transferred into the hull by way of a cycling mechanism that was like a grandiose cash drawer fitted with its own security devices. Water wasn't transferred manually because the automatics were tripped when levels ran low. When that happened, the Laputa would hover over a fresh water source and articulated suction hoses would refill the internal tanks for Insider use, plus whatever was required for the fusion reactor.

Ghost had expected membership in the crew and concessionaire staff to be a matter of nepotism or at least of favoritism; as unpleasant and hazardous as the jobs were, they were well worth killing for. There, too, the Insiders' preoccupation with self-preservation prevailed. The last thing they wanted was an entrenched service class, so new hires came from groups of candidates paraded under their balconies at locations and times chosen by them. Supercargos were periodically given a bonus and separated, replaced without warning.

In spite of these and other measures—including informers—the Insiders were ever-apprehensive about plots and plotters; the pavilions were, after all, a kingly source of wealth and power. As evidence of that, the Insiders could apparently trigger hidden releases and let the whole scratch-mounted outerworks simply drop away.

That last-ditch measure had been taken at least once, on the pavilion called *Taj Mahal*. Infiltrators—allegedly Shadow-rats of an ambitious monocrat in Square Deal—had tried to penetrate the inner sanctum by way of trusswork supports. The ninjas hadn't been stealthy enough, and so it had been bombs away for the lumber and the people, crew included. *Taj Mahal* paid dearly in lost revenues and for the cost and difficulty of getting a new outerworks built. But no one doubted thereafter that *Taj Mahal* Insiders or any others would yank the pin in an instant rather than lose their havens and wellsprings of power.

En route to the Flyaway Islands the *Dream Castle* had flown high. Ghost saw signs among passengers and saffrons alike of shortness of breath, nausea, headaches, lassitude, and other symptoms of acute altitude sickness. Spume was suffering again, too. All her false advertising about rejuv wouldn't keep him from compromising their identities if his mental state deteriorated much more. She had begun considering ways to fake his death from cerebral edema or stroke, just in case.

Now, however, the Laputa was descending for the passage over the eastern Amnion, and folks were stirring. Ghost decided to stretch and get her circulation going. There was ice on the fur fringe of her capuchin hood where her breath had crystallized.

Accompanied by Zinsser, she moved to one of the unoccupied window slots to gaze down at the immense and incomprehensible doings of the Oceanic. Laputan crews and frequent travelers had their own lexicon for some of the more familiar manifestations—Swhorls, Locobrates, FireGyres, Skystrokers, Farfeelers, Upwells, and Loveknots— human beings imposing names on formations and activities whose true meaning they couldn't begin to guess at.

Ghost had expected the oceanographer to be preoccupied with observation and recording, but while he looked on with great attention, he didn't become rapturous. "I already know what it's doing and why," he yawned. "The only thing to figure out is how to get it to talk to me."

Ghost looked out on a blue and white sea tinged with green and stippled with cobalt-silver icebergs. The southernmost Scourlands filled the northeastern horizon. Larger than Scorpia, it was a land of austere, snowy crags and merciless sweeps of frosty, windblown desert. North winds made the day as clear and bright as a lens; the air had spent its moisture in the east-west arcs of mountains farther toward the pole.

There was good reason to be grateful for the weather. The Laputa was still below the arctic circle, but within the latitudes of the williwaws—howling cyclonic storms of lunatic anger that could appear without warning. *Dream Castle* had been detecting and avoiding them for two hundred years, but Ghost had no desire to see its agility tested too severely; even the best Optimant workmanship was long out of warranty. As it was, the attitude thrusters were busy keeping the Flying Pavilion upright and stable—relative terms; she would have bet her buttons the ride was a lot rougher than in its builders' heyday.

CHAPTER TWENTY-EIGHT

Mason marveled at the suspension bridge that now spanned one hundred fifty meters of the churning Styx Strait. It was plain even from a distance that the elegant, simple design had been executed completely in native materials without Optimant leftovers or the advice of Hippo Nolan or any other member of the *Scepter* survey team—so far as Mason knew. Some ascension of the Aquam spirit had come to pass in the Trans-Bourne. How and what the bridge signified, were the true question marks.

He pulled down the dust mask Turnswain had lent him for the final inland stretch of choking high road. The clear, deep breath he inhaled was as sweet as new love until its tang—thick with the salt of the Amnion—made him go cold with dread. As a boy he had loved the smell, but since the *Scepter* mission sea air had become an evil omen and a harrowing reminder of what had happened at the Styx years earlier.

The two-day road safari through southwestern Scorpia had been suffocating, griddle-hot, and bone-wrenching. His skin was swollen from bug and pest bites. More, he suspected that he had picked up intestinal parasites from the food.

Then there was the emotional pendulum he had been on, its swings depending largely on his interactions with his son. One moment the boy would be receptive to Mason's cravings for connection, only to rebuff him the next. Purifyre would speak at length about the places through which they were passing—landmarks, terrain, crops, people—but refuse to disclose anything about what awaited them in the Trans-Bourne. He would talk about his upbringing at New Alexandria, Wall Water, and elsewhere, but not about what he'd learned on the roads as a Human Enlightenment lay brother. He would say nothing about his transformation from *rishi* holy man to the lewd and lusty barrow-coolie Golightly or from coolie to dauntless warrior Hammerstone.

If Purifyre was playing his father like a fish, he was appallingly good at it. Still, Mason didn't dare press him for fear of breaking off all conversation. Their relationship progressed as Purifyre dictated. Given his upbringing, his wariness was understandable; it was a blessing, in fact, that he was at all open to reconciliation. At the same time, Mason kept counsel of his own, never mentioning or alluding to the cybercaul, the Aquamarine origin of the Cyberplagues, or his harboring of the AI Yatt.

Shattertail had crossed a dozen frontiers since leaving the Panhard behind but had suffered no further delays. The eight-wheeler's pullers were new and strong, flexing the treadles tirelessly. Now, under a shriveling midday sun, the muscle car was in sight of the Amnion. Gapshot, the burg on the northern side of the strait, lay only a few klicks down the coast, a mecca of trade and teknics built on and partially from the flattened ruins of an Optimant community.

Foot, litter, and car traffic along the so-called Zapzag Thruway had been getting heavier in both directions as the eight-wheeler neared the strait. Gapshot's prosperity was not due to its coastal location—for proximity to the Amnion was not necessarily a mark in favor of a town's thriving. Wealth had come as well to Forge Town, Gapshot's sister settlement across the angry tidal waters.

As *Shattertail* treadled along the last of the Zapzag, Mason scanned the Optimant autobahns that converged there—Drunkard's Walk, the Meander, and the WhichWend—all aimed at an earlier bridge that had spanned the strait, felled during the Armageddon brought on by the Plagues.

Mason gave a passing thought to Gapshot's Jut-hoppers—a caste of dexterous, half-suicidal transporters who used to cross the strait afoot at low tide, bearing burdens of cargo and leading those daring enough to attempt the transit on foot. Having had dealings with them, he couldn't picture them yielding to obsolescence and unemployment without cracking at least some skulls.

Busy as the Zapzag was, it was passable. The ruling powers in Gapshot and other local jurisdictions, economically dependent on the high roads, saw to that. No shebangs encroached; peddlers and beggars importuned people warily and kept a watchful eye for patrollers. Dwellings and businesses had spilled outside the city walls and into the surrounding farmland, but the prime real estate—the only safe spot if war broke out—was behind Gapshot's ramparts.

The flat-black walls were high and imposing, if constructed from a hodgepodge of materials. This close to the source of Aquamarine's new dye trade, however, fields of intense color provided flair everywhere else. Clothing, implements, goods, vehicles, and some of the higher rooftops visible over the wall were splashed with screamingly vivid hues. A common motif on banners and pennons was the four-leafed green herb the Aquam called club-clover, Gapshot's civic emblem.

As *Shattertail* drew up to the waiting line at the gate barbican, Purifyre appeared from belowdecks, still turned out in his black-enameled insectile-samurai armor. Ballyhoot followed in her long-horned headgear. Cries of "Hammerstone! Hammerstone!" went up, though not so much from civilians as from Gapshot legionnaires on guard and customs duty. Mason watched silently, avoiding attention as he had been cautioned to do. The legionnaires wore outfits very different from his son's, but an air of comradeship prevailed. The Gapshotters displayed the green club-clover insignia; some even wore a fresh sprig in helmet or harness.

Purifyre produced a blue-tasseled maoriwood and ivory baton of office. Its headpiece was fashioned in the shape of a man in midleap, his back bearing the double wing set characteristic of most of the planet's flying creatures. Turnswain had told Mason it was the symbol of the Styx Strait Bridge Authority. A wave of the baton and lesser traffic was motioned out of the way.

More halloos and greetings came from those on the streets. Mason divided his time between the din, the mingled aromas and stenches, the garishness of the colors, and the sight of his son acknowledging the hails. It was obvious that not everyone in town thought well of Purifyre's most recent persona. Mason spotted resentful looks as well as gestures: thrusting of thumb and pinkie as horns, thumb between index and second fingers of a fist. The hostilities were subdued, but Mason kept his hand close to his 'chettergun just in case.

Seeing the spot where calamity had wrapped both hands around the *Scepter*'s crew, he knew that old twisting in his belly again. Events there had wiped out nearly half the survey team in one fell swoop. Captain Marlon, the original mission commander, and his Aquam would-be Cleopatra had been atomized. Chain-of-command and seniority regs had thrust Claude Mason, administrative evaluations chief, into the top slot.

He fought the horror he had carried from that spot, fought to keep the knee-jerk reaction from becoming a flashback. Purifyre and his group meant to cross those malicious waters; therefore, he must, too.

The sea below the *Dream Castle* was a forbidden city of white gypsum, indigo, emerald, and delft. Even though it was the Big Sere in Scorpia, there were plenty of icebergs adrift—frozen floating cathedrals and megaplexes convoyed by growlers and remnants of pack ice, as turquoise-white as the planet itself.

Inland, two of the Scourland's rift volcanoes seeped plumes of steamy smoke from craters and fumaroles, the gases rent and scattered by racing gusts from the north. From far snowfields, a glacier as broad as a Broken Country county, unafraid of the Oceanic, flexed its muscles against the rock to form a crystalline river to the sea.

After a full day's travel above the frozen wastes, *Dream Castle* crossed the wide shoreline at two kilometers and descended, floating over a mauve and gray glacial plain of gab-broid pebbles and coarse grit with occasional patches of yellow-green lichen and sprinklings of flowers insanely bright against the starkness. Here and there boulders protruded from the windscape like wrecks sunk in a bog, ranging in size from coracle to broken supercarrier.

A cluster of shapes was moving below, nearly shadow-less in the noon sun. Ghost's vision had always been sharp, and the Flowstate had her open to the slightest details. Before anyone else had sighted them, she pointed. "What're those—Ferals?" she asked a nearby vendor.

In blips of movement that would be the gait of bounders, minuscule figures were appearing from the lee of rocks and the glacier, although she could see no shelter or concealment anywhere. And atop the Ferals' two-legged spring-steeds were the storied fiends themselves.

Bounders were the only animals on the planet that could serve as saddle beasts, if that was the term. While they had proved incapable of surviving on any other landmass, they were superbly suited to conditions in the Scourlands, making the Ferals lords of the entire gigantic island with the single exception of the DevOceanite redoubt at Passwater. Converging on the Laputa's course, scores of hopping mites were tearing out across the open wastes, laying down two-legged tracks like trails of colons.

The vendor next to Ghost was the young woman who'd sold her the highwayman brochettes the previous day. She thrust tattooed pinkie and forefinger at the sight of the Ferals and turned her eyes from them, kissing a fetish of human hair, teeth, and ears.

"If you're wise, Scarmask, you won't go ogling them," she said, shuddering. "The Ferals' bad juju can climb the path a person's eyesight makes! The worst of them can see demonic-fine—good enough to get the details of you and make you their special enemy."

More Ferals were emerging all the time. Ghost didn't see how they could harm *Dream Castle*; otherwise, they would have done so long since. Still, their headlong speed gave the impression of purpose. By angling her head almost through the slot of window, she could peer ahead to where a twisting cilium of smoke was rising from the headland. Something was moving there, as well.

Ghost left her spot at the window, but no one stepped into the vacancy. She went to the boarding lock, where two crewmen lounged on watch, keeping the hatch view slits conspicuously shut. With the supercargo elsewhere, neither saffron was averse to picking up an extra brass scudo for sliding back the bolts on the dog door and letting her out onto the sentry pulpit. It was weather-worn and gouged with graffiti and felt rickety enough to blow away at any moment.

The rushing air tearing at her capuchin felt cryogenic-cold. She locked one arm through the handrail, hooked both boot toes under the bottom rail, and brought out her detached pistol scope. Her fingers, like her face, instantly went numb.

By then there were more kangarooing dots on the flats and along the saddle ridgeline as well as on the far side of the headland. On the high ground itself a mound or construction had been built. Standing back from it on all sides were more of the bounders. In such a harsh environment, where the first glance said that even one human being would starve and freeze, aerial recon and SAT imagery had indicated a large and extremely mobile warlike population.

Aquam folktales had been substantiated to the effect that the Ferals were maniacally opposed to any outside encroachment. They had pulled down and obliterated all Optimant structures in their wastelands. Early proposals to locate the GammaLAW mission's central base and staging area there had been scrapped when analysts posited that an alien presence would have united the Feral poleis. There had also been Dextra Haven's conviction that the mission should minimize its impact, go cautiously, since *any* group or environmental factor might hold the secret to the Oceanic's behavior and to the planet's seeming immunity to Roke colonization or attack.

Ghost maxed the scope's magnification. Riders in barbaric war panoply were spurring back and forth on shaggy, braying bounders that brandished tusks and foamed at the mouth. Every Feral wore his or her distinctive trappings; every bounder, its caparison. If the reports were correct, one of five warriors was a woman, but it was difficult to discern gender from the sentry pulpit—even among the semi-naked ones.

Each sported a disguising and disfiguring headdress or helm. Skin was smeared with greasepaint, ash, or clay or was tattooed, scarified, or decoratively burned. Virtually all wore buckled corselets or tightly laced stomachers, which was understandable, given the jounce of the hop-nags.

In defiance, they fired sling-gun bolts up at the *Dream Castle*, shook moon-guard hooklances decked with scalps and shrunken heads, waved knuckle-duster sabers and barb-spiked mauls. The bounders swung tails equipped with toggle-mounted blades or morningstars, and kicked out with feet whose natural spurs had been augmented with wicked cutlery of assorted designs. As the madness built, riders opened cuts in their own bodies, smearing blood on themselves, spitting it at the Laputa, or flinging it at their comrades.

Ghost traversed the scope to the mound and to a sight that made her feel out of body. Ten meters high, the mound was a pile of rigid corpses. The dead were not mere victims; they wore weapons and accouterments, oddments of armor and headgear, all with markings and prevailing colors different from those of the living.

Fallen foes. Atop the pile, astride the biggest bounder there, the victor stood up in his long-fringed stirrups to wave a burning torch at the *Dream Castle* and bellow up at it. Managing to keep the scope steady on him for a few seconds, Ghost realized that even an Anathemite could rise to the top in the Scourlands.

He was nearly as big and as muscular as a Manipulant, naked to the elements except for his harness and long-quilled war bonnet. His skin was a deep burgundy and of a nubby texture, and his face was stone gargoyle and Javanese Vedic idol, with beard and hair varnished into black javelins. He had oblique eyes, narrowed and predatory yet strangely blank; teeth like a white leg trap; cheekbones sharp and outswept as an icebreaker's bow; a bold curve of nose. In his face was fury, voraciousness, dark amusement. His mouth was thrown wide, muscles standing out as he howled his threats to the sky.

Giving it his spurs, he caracoled his bounder and flung the torch up over his head. The creature cleared the mound of cadavers with one leap, its claws half cleaving the bodies it had been standing on, then hit the ground and took another leap. The torch landed among the dead, and orange-red flames sprang up, widening at a run. Oily smoke was torn away by a stiff breeze, and the conflagration spread. Whatever the Ferals had doused the bodies with, it was excitable. The giant sagamore of the Ferals cantered his bounder upwind of the flames while his followers cantered around and around the pyre, exulting.

Leaning forward for a better look, Ghost found herself staring right into eyes that were hooded and nakedly hungry at the same time. An apparition, the sagamore whirled and snapped a heavy chainsword around his head, laughed, and lapped his tongue, tracing lines on his own face with one thick fingernail, lines that mirrored the ones on her cheek, her brow.

As impossible as it seemed, he had seen her.

Her vision was acute, yet it was tough enough for her to see at that distance—even with the scope. There was no mistaking it; the sagamore drew an imaginary scar on his jawline and then pointed directly at her.

The worst of them can see demonic-fine, the vendor had said. *Good enough to get the details of you and make you their special enemy.*

Ghost felt a sudden tugging at her capuchin. Zinsser had crawled up through the dog door. "*Sweet reason,* stop acting like a madwoman!" he scolded her. "Inside, if you don't want to lose some fingers!"

Glimpsing what was going on below, he pried the scope from her numb, quivering hands. "This planet," he muttered. "Isn't there anything in them but murder and insanity?" He focused on the sagamore. "Did you see that purple muckbrain down there?"

She clung to the rail in earnest because her body was failing her. "Yes, I saw him."

"And Haven thinks she can talk peace and progress to an abomination like that."

"Hardly an abomination. He's beautiful, Doctor." She gazed down at the funeral pyre, realizing that she was smiling and that Zinsser was staring at her, appalled. "The purest thing I've seen in a long while. So very beautiful."

"Pure narcissism," Zinsser said in dismissal. "He's nothing more than your mirror image."

Chapter Twenty-Nine

With the upper stories of Gapshot's homes and other buildings cantilevered over the streets to gain precious floorspace, *Shattertail* treadled slowly along in a shady casbah under drying wash and airing bedding. Mason craned his neck to gaze up at household prayer ribbons, clusters of fruit and vegetables, and ingenious wicker cages containing an endless variety of the tweedling, droning, and stridulating critters the Aquam kept as songbirds. The town's club-clover emblem was everywhere to be found.

Only a central canal of sunlight penetrated, so slime and mossy patches survived in cracks and pockets, in seeming disdain for the Big Sere. The labyrinth echoed with greetings, quarrels, and the cries of children, hawkers, mendicants, and evangelists. The vying tunes and lyrics of street musicians were almost lost in it all.

Thoroughfares, alleys, and bypaths were topsoiled with offal and filth. Mason was glad to be traversing it on mudcutter wheels rather than afoot, though muck was nothing new to him by then. The town kept ahead of the worst of it with lowly benjomen carters and work gangs of prisoners and indentured laborers, yet he would have donned his mask against the reek if he hadn't been so sick of wearing it. There were a few small open plazas but no public wells, naturally; municipal water was supplied by cisterns fed by roof catchments, supplemented by an old aqueduct that ran to sources in the hills just to the north.

Shattertail wound through the last and most gentrified district of Gapshot, where prosperous trading houses and self-importantly rococo town government buildings bunched hard by the cornucopian bridge. The barbican that guarded the Gapshot end had been built up on what was left of the footing, the foundation, and part of the north tower of the old Optimant span. It was as austere and solid as a prison tower, with firing loops and apertures for siege warfare. From it, palisades extended to the drop-off on either side, enclosing the bridgehead.

Traffic arriving from the Trans-Bourne was passing into Gapshot unhindered, since those travelers had all paid their tolls and tariffs on the Forge Town side. Those waiting to cross were lined up for assessment and toll collection. Ordinary foot travelers filed through quickly, while collectors took more time, making sure barrows, rickshas, and their ilk paid appropriate fees.

Mason had been told that the Bridge Constabulary officers served as load regulators, spacing the departures of heavier traffic to mediate strain on the span. Gatehouses at the north and south towers coordinated these efforts, as necessary, by semaphore flag.

Most of them drawn from the best of the Trans-Bourne forces, the Bridge Constabulary were a more strac and dashing lot than the Gapshot Legion. They were turned out in variations on the armor worn by Purifyre, Ballyhoot, and their two comrades on *Shattertail*—a constant reminder that Trans-Bourne interests had conceived, financed, and built the span.

The name Hammerstone was chanted again as *Shattertail* was waved ahead. At the southern end semaphore wigwags halted traffic; a muscle car was about to cross, and prudence required a lightening of the structure's other burdens. The eight-wheeler rolled through the barbican and as it emerged, a gate arm swung across, carrying a figure that leapt lightly to the rail. A new chant was taken up by many Gapshotters and Bridge Constables who hadn't taken part in the Hammerstone chorus: "Kinbreed! Kinbreed!"

Mason saw Ballyhoot touch her crossbow, then lower her hand at a subtle signal from Purifyre. The interplay stumped Mason. Kinbreed displayed the trappings of a constabulary officer, too, so why should Purifyre and Ballyhoot worry? He wore a helm shaped like a rakefang's head mounted with barb-tipped vanes and was armed with meteor hammer, hunga-munga throwing blades, and twin fighting sickles. Decorating his right shoulder was the four-leafed green club-clover.

Turnswain, at the helm, muttered dryly to Mason, "Popular with the Gapshotters is Kinbreed, and a Gapshotter himself. Like all who show the clover."

Despite the fact that Trans-Bourne controlled the bridge, whoever ruled in the south had allowed some Gapshotters to take the oath and serve in the Bridge Constabulary as a sop to their civic pride and to keep relations cordial.

Kinbreed jumped agilely to the eight-wheeler's deck. Evidently a senior among the Gapshot constables, he carried a blue-tasseled baton of rank identical to Purifyre's own. He was a head taller than Purifyre, leaner and older, though not by many years. His face was long and somber with dark eyes that were heavily kholed. His black, wavy mustache and beard were trimmed close except at the tip of the chin, where the beard jutted between the cheek shields.

Purifyre reached out, and the two exchanged a crossed-palm handclasp that was forceful but friendly. "Kinbreed!"

"Hammerstone!" The thin mouth barely curved up. "Back from yet another secret errand on behalf of Cozmote and our other overlords of the Trans-Bourne, hmm?"

Cozmote, Mason mused. On their first meeting at Wall Water,' Waretongue Rhodes had mentioned the man in connection with Purifyre, though the grandee had referred to Cozmote as a devious fellow.

More constables appeared on various barbican vantage points, looking on while cradling sling-guns and other weapons. Purifyre didn't shy away from Kinbreed's staring match. "I knew the bridge was in good hands with you guarding it, camarado. Didn't we help build it together?"

Kinbreed blew air up through his mustache. "Yes, Hammerstone. Cozmote has never had a problem with Gapshot labor, eh? Gapshot parity, now, Gapshot control over its side of the strait—that's something else, no?"

An edgy silence fell on all sides as customs men, travelers, and constables alike listened in. Kinbreed's needling had the air of an old recitation.

"Gapshot claiming profits it didn't earn would indeed be something else," Purifyre said. "Trans-Bourne money and Trans-Bourne know-how spanned the strait. Otherwise Gapshot would still be cadging iron scudos off Jut-hoppers at low tide. But, now, excuse me. I've orders to carry out."

"And if I don't, camarado? If Gapshot's grown tired of seeing its sovereignty insulted, of being bilked of rightful gains?"

Mason had the distinct impression that some line was about to be crossed and that Kinbreed had waited to make Purifyre the man with whom he crossed it. Even Ballyhoot took a few sober glances at how things were sizing up. Regardless, Mason thought he could win Purifyre a chance to get clear as long as he himself was willing to stand his ground and take the bolts.

But Purifyre was a cool head. "I'll relay your grievances to Cozmote," he told Kinbreed. "For that you'll need to step aside." He glanced up at the sling-guns all around him. "All constables are sibs in arms; that's the oath we took. If you're going to break it to prove your point, get on with it."

At Purifyre's age Mason had barely graduated from Essentials Form, too young by years to vote. Precompetent, some Periapt wags called that time of life. Yet here was his strong, homely, driven son, defying death and war with nothing more than his wits and words. He got ready to shoot, but Kinbreed broke the tension.

"Never that, Hammerstone; never that, Brother. Yet tell Cozmote something has to be changed, eh?"

"I will." Purifyre met Kinbreed halfway, and they exchanged a quick, jolting embrace.

Purifyre tossed his head, the serrated mandible indicating Gapshot and burghers in the municipal buildings and trading houses who had grown fat off the money sluice that was the Styx Strait Bridge. "In the meanwhile, see if they'll listen to some reason there, too."

"I'll do it right now," Kinbreed replied.

The two spit on their palms and clenched hands again. Guns had eased back, and constables with and without the club-clover had done the same. Kinbreed yelled to those who might have blocked *Shattertail*. "Gang way! Constabulary coming through!"

As he went to the rail, Ballyhoot intercepted him. Mason thought she might try to take his throat out with those pointed teeth, but he struck first, chucking her under the chin. She slapped him on the rump as he vaulted to the rail. The crowd roared, Kinbreed the loudest among them.

Someone had shoved the gate out, and Kinbreed rode it back, clinging to the draw rope. Constables shouldered *Shattertail* to move it out onto the wood and woven fiber suspension bridge. Mason's horror of the salt sea came howling back into him as he saw the strait churning and grasping far below; there was nothing but weathered lumber and cordage between him and the Oceanic. The treadles whammed and thumped to maintain speed for the critical upslope phase of the crossing.

"You were very effective back there," he told Purifyre, largely to distract himself from the horror of the water. "Very wise about trying to find a middle ground. But can you do it?"

Purifyre was still looking back at the gatehouse and Kinbreed, barely cognizant of the crashing and steepling below. "Either that or some of them will leave us no choice but to kill them."

Mason shut his mouth, afraid of loosing his terror of the Oceanic. Clinging to the rail, he watched, paralyzed, as *Shatter-tal*'s weight pressed the suspension bridge to a deeper arc.

Purifyre swung from Gapshot to look at Forge Town. "Like brothers, Kinbreed and I were. Water boys together when we started out and rigging spiders later. Youngest workgangers on the bridge, Kinbreed and Hammerstone—that is, youngest who lived to see it finished." He slapped the rail and turned to Mason, with Ballyhoot looking on. "The bridge, the muscle cars—they're all subordinate to the overriding purpose. Everything bows to the purpose or must be *made* to bow."

"To the taking of Aquamarine for human beings," Mason anticipated. Purifyre had already made that much clear. "But what if an ... impediment like Kinbreed won't bow?"

"Impediments will bow or break." They both knew they weren't talking only about Kinbreed or the bridge

271

anymore. "For the good of all Aquam. For our freedom to live on this planet like human beings and not as a bunch of wretched, frightened tree imps on the highest twig, fearing any moment that the Oceanic will take us or that LAW will enslave us. Anyone or anything standing in the way of that, I'd destroy utterly."

Mason felt trapped between outrage and loyalty, but he was incapable of giving voice to either emotion. A gust had caught the bridge, letting him look straight down into the ripping currents of the Styx as the muscle car tilted. The Oceanic had chosen that moment to make itself manifest. As if mirroring the water, Mason's horror of it rose up to clutch and choke him.

Zinsser drew Ghost back aboard the *Dream Castle*'s outerworks, away from the sentry pulpit and the sight of the Scourland Ferals' flaming pyre of enemies. The saffron crewmen on watch in the boarding lock regarded her with even more dubious expressions than they had worn earlier, since they still had the main hatch view slits shut to avoid the evil eye and spiritual contagion from the barbarians below.

One saffron covered his uneasiness by spitting on the deck, hitching up his belt, and declaring, "Old Asurao up to his Anathemite tricks. Wants the world to know he's high butcher of the Scourlands with veto power over the galvani trade, no matter what rival poleis might try." With a weighing glance toward Ghost and Zinsser he added, "No matter whether Visitants have come to stay or blew themselves up in their celestial car."

Hewed to her Flowstate, Ghost was still poised and erect despite the spasms of chill that took her every few seconds. "Asurao?" she asked.

"Slaughter boss of the Massacre Cirque Polis. Most fiendish nation of a fiendish race."

"Asurao," Zinsser mulled. " 'Asuras'?"

Ghost had caught the connection, too, the similarity between a barbarian sagamore's name and that of an Optimant immortality project named for the Asuras—the antagonists of Vedic and Hindu mythology, less demons in the conventional sense than antigods. She replayed the triumphant hunger in Asurao's eyes and the way he had traced an imitation of her scars on his own face. Perhaps the victorious giant wasn't an Anathemite, after all, but a creation of the Optimants. However, she didn't want Zinsser speculating in front of the Aquam or pressing his revulsion for the Ferals on her. "When do we reach Passwater?"

"By dusk," the crewman told her. "Depends on headwinds."

Ghost considered it. Testamentor and the others had to have some move planned for Passwater, most likely having to do with their masquerade as DevOcean zealots. There wasn't much time remaining to divine the nature of the plan and come up with one of their own.

"Let's find Spume," she told Zinsser. "We have things to talk over."

They made their way back through the steve spaces to constant, jarring explosions of the Laputa's pumped-laser pulsejets. Thirty thousand K explosions of the very air molecules, Ghost thought, controlled, like nearly everything else in her life at the moment, by whatever lay within the sealed hull. But those pulsejets... Now, *there* was a weapon, if they could be directed...

The landscape below was rolling desert tundra broken by ice-clad and snaggletooth mountains that flew snow pennons driven by the winds. Glacial rivers and tarns reflected the turquoise sky of Aquamarine. Ferals appeared in small groups, linking up to follow the *Dream Castle*'s route.

"He's coming," someone brave enough to look aft said.

Ghost went to the window slot with Zinsser trailing. Teeming off the headland where corpse fire and flesh smoke were climbing higher and higher, the Massacre Cinque Polis warriors were riding madly after the Laputa. Out in front rode Asurao.

Zinsser curled his lip. "Reassuringly stupid." He reached down to give his ankle a good scratching and straightened to gaze at the Ferals again. "We'll be to Passwater and gone long before they can possibly get there."

Ghost watched Asurao. "What's the matter, Doctor? He's merely on the make, like you. Don't you approve of the direct approach?"

"Winning your love by tearing an enemy's head off and serving it up on a platter?" He gave the ankle a more thorough scratch. "Please. For me the civilized method of bedding nubile young women is preferred."

"Poetry and flowers?"

Zinsser grinned. "Bumping up their grade-point average."

When they got back to their steve-spaces spot, Old Spume was wincing from an altitude headache, panting for breath, and looking groggy.

"I heard him go into Cheyne-Stokes breathing last night," Zinsser told Ghost before Spume noticed their approach, "and he was nauseous a while ago. Another two days of flight to Gumption ahead of us—he may not make it."

"Don't let on," Ghost warned. "He could blurt out anything and take us down with him. Keep him happy."

"I suppose there's no use in all three of us dying," Zinsser agreed.

As they settled down to either side of him, the ponderous old man coughed distressingly into his kerchief. He eyed them, fighting for breath. "The rejuvenation ministrations of Glorianna Theiss are killing me. Give me gold that I may buy proper Aquam pharmaceuticants from Bravuro and save my poor life, which you Visitants have blighted."

"What, spoil everything with diffodar-toenail potion and rakefang-liver liniment?" Zinsser frowned, scratching higher up on his shin than he had earlier. "Just when your metabolism's about ripe for rejuvenation phase two?"

Spume looked like a drowning man spying a driftwood log. "I-it is? But we're not aboard your ship, nor will we be in time to save this poor old man who only tried to give good service."

"You're wrong," Ghost interjected. "We got a signal through to the *GammaLAW* while we were out in the sentry pulpit." She waggled her plugphone touchpad.

Spume grew excited. "What did they say? What's happened at Wall Water?"

"No voice contact—just a location chirp. So the rescue plane could be here in a couple of hours."

Spume threw his head back and closed his eyes, breathing a little less laboredly. "Ah, mercy, I may make it yet!"

"They might not reach us until we leave Passwater," Ghost pressed. "Madame Haven will want to know what's going on there, and we might find another opportunity to contact *GammaLAW*. So tell me how I get groundside. Is there a visa fee, a permit I can buy, or do I bribe somebody?"

Spume shook his head. "Merchants get to barter for galvani stones and offer their wares at the embarkation stage trading house. But DevOcean denies the Unsaved access to their holy city."

"Testamentor seems to think he's going there," Zinsser pointed out, scratching close to his knee this time.

"Well he may," Spume allowed, "flying false colors as he is."

"Then we have to get to Testamentor," Ghost said. "Whatever it takes."

Zinsser put on a disapproving expression, seemed about to say something, then went back to scratching. This time he was doing both calves and appeared to be trying to find a graceful way to scratch his crotch. Spume gargled a laugh. "Perhaps Bravuro can come up with a vermicidal amulet for you, Doctor—something the Black Livestock can't abide."

Zinsser stopped scratching, scowling suspiciously. "The *which*?"

"Black Livestock," Ghost clarified, putting another arm's length between them. "Skivvy nanites, fleas, or the local variation." She rejected the impulse to pluck one off him and eat it, as she had back in the POW camps, just to see his reaction.

Zinsser radiated a sense of mission. "That's the limit. I don't care what it takes to get off this leper colony. How do we confront Testamentor?"

Distracted, Spume didn't catch the implication that help wouldn't be screaming through the sky toward them at multiple Mach. "You might begin by turning around, for yonder comes one of his fellow votaries."

Ghost was on her feet and facing the man with no obvious haste but no wasted time. The votary was another of the intense young men of Purifyre's circle, wearing neither DevOcean robes nor Human Enlightenment vestments but cold weather clothes similar to those worn by commoners in the steve spaces.

He held up empty hands. "Testamentor sends me to say that events converge and there are issues you should resolve with him. He invites you to first class that he may set your mind at rest."

Ghost was suspicious. Even so, they weren't likely to get a better shot at Testamentor, first class, or possible hull hatch access to the Insiders. She threw back her hood and swiped her jet Hussar Plaits back over her shoulders. "Shall my companions wait here?"

"They're invited to enjoy the comforts of Testamentor's cabin, as well."

"You're very gracious."

She turned, bending and pretending to check to be sure they weren't leaving anything behind, swiping the mol-fiber-woven plaits out of her way again, shielding her movements with her body as she inserted an Ext spit needle into her mouth. Then she swung back to the votary.

"Lead the way."

The promise of warmth, food, and comfort made Spume amicable. They trooped after the votary. Ghost would have preferred to have armed herself with one of the weapons that had been confiscated and locked away on departure, but on that score the crewmen had been unbribable.

The saffron keeping watch by the entrance to first class made no objection as the votary led Ghost and the others through the three-batten door. The small entrance was spotless and almost fragrant compared to the crappy, grotty steve spaces.

The votary banged a door knocker carved in the shape of a fist, and the inner door opened. Riding the Flowstate, Ghost followed him into a small but tranquil compartment of sanded and lacquered paneling. Heavy cornhusk drapes shaded what looked to be a large shuttered window.

A closet-bed that looked grand by outerworks standards occupied one corner; bunks, a scribe's bench and table, wardrobes, and chests occupied others. A tiny stove had the place livably warm, and there was a semi-private jakes. The air was sickly sweet with incense, but there was an underlying hint of something else in the air.

Bravuro stood with his back to the far wall. Testamentor was facing the doorway, with other votaries ranged around the room, armed with sling-guns, whip razors, double-ended fighting sickles, and throwing hatchets. Ghost had expected as much, since they had boarded and gone directly into private quarters without being shaken down. What surprised her as much as anything could in Flowstate was the bloop-gun Testamentor was holding.

The safety was off, and the drum magazine indicator hadn't flipped, meaning there were rounds in it—bolas, likely. The muzzle was as wide as a drainpipe. If he squeezed the trigger, the twirling pinwheel web of weighted monomol filament would hash her, Zinsser, and Old Spume into gory scraps, the Sense-maker's bulk notwithstanding.

"Move away from the door," Testamentor ordered.

So she did.

CHAPTER THIRTY

Mason had been bracing himself for his first close look at the Amnion since the night on the beach at New Alexandria, so many years earlier, but the sight filled him with terror nevertheless.

The manifestation the Oceanic had elected to exhibit for its own impenetrable reasons was what the Aquam called Farfeelers—surging, branching dendritic structures that came coursing and bifurcating on the wild tide. Other manifestations—FireGyres, Skystrokers, and Swhorls—appeared briefly here and there as what seemed to be garnishment. The Far-feelers wended in through the Styx Strait to writhe and grow their way through and among the Juts, the long horseshoe of jumbled monoliths the sea covered for all but a few hours each day.

The Farfeelers passed through the Juts just under the surface like tentacular fractal patterns, growing and propagating their way past a narrow fretwork. Almost faster than his eye could follow, they quested, proliferating in accordance with their own incomprehensible plan into the open waters beyond. In another hour it would be high tide, and the long roundabout loop of the Juts would be submerged, except perhaps for a few of its higher projections.

Prominent features of the tumbled stone causeway had changed utterly since the last time Mason had seen them.

They did that periodically, between flow tide and ebb tide, rearranged by Oceanic's whims or side effects of its activity.

Like so many of the Oceanic's manifestations, Farfeelers could vary drastically—capriciously—in texture, behavior, and apparent composition. The ones Mason regarded in clammy shock were like luminous coral trees, on the move and expanding. As with most matters concerning the Oceanic, the *Scepter*'s survey team had learned nearly zip about their underlying purpose, substance, or biochemistry.

They found out the hard way that the Big O could be dangerous. The pulses in his neck and temples felt like they were drumming the reminder into him. *Oh, we most affirmedly got a working demonstration of that.*

"What's wrong?" Purifyre demanded suddenly. The boy followed Mason's glassy stare. "Oh, yes, I recall. This is a bane place for you."

Mason nodded. A Bane place even more for Captain Marlon and the forty-three others from *Scepter* who had met their end there. For Mason it was a flashback trigger, a spot where he had had it branded into his psyche that the Oceanic was so alien and so powerful that all human ego and folly opposing it were doomed. He could bear the memories but not the thought that he might fall into it alive. He made to bolt, but Purifyre took him by the upper arms, both bearing him up and holding him fast.

"Are you brainfucked? You can't break and run here. Bear down!"

Mason had borne down enough to cross the water to the *Matsya* back on Periapt, enough to return to Aquamarine, enough even to risk execution by firing squad by deserting the GammaLAW mission. The thought of riding the swaying suspension bridge over the Styx Strait raised the sum mental burden past the breaking point.

That was the case despite his son's shaking him and Ballyhoot hissing, "Coward! We live under its threat every second of our lives! You can suffer it for a minute!"

But Mason couldn't stop himself from struggling until a round, hairless panethnic face appeared before his mind's eye.

" 'Pluck lost, all lost,' Mason ?"

"Yatt!" Mason yelled, unable to control himself.

The AI download had already granted that it wouldn't force or take control of Mason's actions. Even so, Yatt's very *uber-presence,* claiming a part of his field of attention, lessened the awfulness of the Oceanic ever so slightly.

"The bridge has held for years," Yatt pointed out. *"There's a high probability it'll hold today."*

Mason relaxed in Purifyre's grip. The Oceanic was still as ghastly to contemplate as it had been, but the sequence of events that might hurl Mason into contact with it seemed less likely and therefore less unhinging. His thoughts, on autopilot, filled in the rest of Yatt's quote from the great safecracker Old Raffles: "Purse lost, little lost; honor lost, much lost; pluck lost..."

"Lose your pluck and lose your son, as well. Flounder now and your loss of escalation may be irreparable. Whatever Purifyre has in mind, we can help you help him accomplish it. Promote our search for Endgame and we can put the powers of the Optimants at your disposal. With those, you will earn your son's gratitude and you will win incalculable power for yourself. But first you must get yourself across this bridge."

"You're right," Mason panted. "I'll hang on."

Purifyre obviously thought that Mason was talking to him and clapped him on the shoulder. "That's showing your mettle, Father!" His tone held an almost grudging warmth.

The wind subsided, and the bridge swung back toward its vertical bow. Mason and Purifyre propped themselves as the wood and fiber span dipped under the muscle car's weight. Resolved to prove his nerve, Mason gazed down again at the scene of long-ago disaster. The strait's chop still peaked and steeplechased, but the Farfeelers were wraithlike now, more diffuse, running deeper. A high flood-tide wave sent foam over most of the long, irregular horseshoe of the Juts.

Judgment Day for Marlon and the rest had come on a sunny day exactly like that one. Mason inhaled the salt air, and all at once the years fell away before his eyes.

For presumptive acolytes of peace, the Human Enlightenment votaries showed great expertise at dealing with prisoners. With Testamentor still holding the bloop-gun, others moved in to secure Ghost, Zinsser, and Old Spume, handling them guardedly but methodically.

As the inner first class cabin door shut behind her, Ghost cast glances around a floor area from which furniture and baggage had been cleared, much of it piled against the outboard bulkhead. An ark and coffer, sacred repositories of the Creed of Human Enlightenment, were stacked one on top of the other and shoved to one side like spare footlockers. Why take those along? she asked herself. Or did they contain something other than what they normally did?

"Turn around, kneel, put your wrists back for binding," Testamentor ordered, moving to keep his own people out of his line of fire. Again, they were practices that didn't square with rough and ready Aquam behaviors. Ghost, debating whether to go down fighting then and there, didn't have time to wonder who had taught him.

The idea of surrender wasn't unendurable. She had the means to attack and—failing that—the means to end it all, denying them her captivity no matter what. Except that there were complications that blurred the stark line she had drawn between Fiona and her new self. Living or dead, she'd sworn an oath to the GammaLAW mission and owed loyalty to her brother, the Discards, and the other Exts. Burning would be left without blood to guard his blood. The Exts' survival might hinge on her letting them know about Human Enlightenment's covert operations. There was the Zinsser factor—his confidence that he could sort out the inner workings of the Oceanic. Without Ghost, the oceanographer would never make it back to the ship; and Zinsser, Haven's mission to end the Roke Conflict was perhaps odds on to fail.

Therefore, she knelt, as Zinsser and Spume already had. With its passage over land, the Laputa was hitting turbulence. When she went off balance for a moment with the lurching of the deck, she began considering ways of using that kind of motion to her advantage.

The captives surrendered capuchins and Spume's wing-chair-collared sacque cloak; footgear went, too. Purifyre's men moved in with standoff weapons to ensure their immobility. Then they began the trussing with Ghost. Elbows, wrists, and thumbs, as well; knees and ankles, with a line from those to a choke loop around her throat. The various techniques she tried to keep the bonds loose didn't work with the harsh humanitarians of enlightenment.

Meanwhile she ran an optical on the wooden inner bulkhead that concealed *Dream Castle*'s hull proper. Grease- and smoke-stained as it was, the wood could well be two hundred years old and was muraled with more of the inevitable graffiti. Even if it was a replacement of the original, the point was that generations of vandals had been denied access to this part of the Laputa's hull. Again she caught a hint of rot and tried to make sense of it in the context of first class.

Zinsser and Spume grunted and hissed as the coarse-fibered ropes were drawn tight. The oceanographer protested, "We're not your enemies; we came here to help you!"

The Sense-maker's pleas sent jets of saliva in the air. "Cease this! I'm a Sense-maker, a man of rational accommodation who was ever a supporter and ally of your *rishi*, Purifyre."

None of it had any effect on the operatives of Human Enlightenment.

"I must get back to my rounds," Bravuro gulped, subdued for once. "Before the supercargo learns of my absence and flays me with the bastinado."

"You leave when I say you leave." Testamentor's tone was like a cuff to the head. "The supercargo will be well mollified by a cut of the scudos we gave you."

The captives were patted down for weapons. When another buffet of turbulence threw Ghost against the man searching her, he simply righted her; score one more for the professionalism of Purifyre's underground. Her knife was confiscated along with the pistol scope, archeo-hacking 'wares, medpack components, plugphone and touchpad, empty magazines for the lost 'baller—everything. Even her dog tags were taken, in addition to the command whistle and the locket she had stolen from Dextra Haven's villa. Zinsser's possessions went as well, including the hermetic specimen case containing the sample of Roke tissue.

Spume's various hidden pockets and pokes were a jackpot: scudos enough of various denominations to take him another leg aboard the *Dream Castle* after Ghost's gold was exhausted; a punch-dagger, a garrote, and one of those odd little Aquam acid squirters—a two-chambered hand pump of heavy glass; sparkwheel, cigarittos, and comb; pen and inkpot, various Aquam keys, and what looked to be a small jimmy and burglary tool, plus a little stash of rock candy.

"I fully intended to reveal these things to you when the moment was appropriate," Spume sputtered to Ghost.

"That would've impressed me."

"Blindfolds?" asked the one who had led them into the trap.

"Not yet, Boskoh," Testamentor answered. "Help them back around." Ghost ignored the pain in her knees and arms; at least the tunic collar protected her from the abrasion of the choke loop. Testamentor was sitting on a stool, weighing them carefully. He had handed off the bloopgun, but Ghost now noticed what looked like another weapon in his sash, a contoured wooden pistol grip fitted to a hunk of advanced technology. Her memory scared up the image of the holed and burned Manipulant she had seen in Rhodes's bedroom.

"It doesn't matter how you blundered onto the *Dream Castle*" he told them. "You're an inconvenience and a peril to our mission. If you cooperate, you won't be harmed— and in due course you'll end up back aboard your ship. Otherwise we'll cut your throats right now."

Ghost made a great show of sizing the place up.

"No eavesdroppers or peep holes," Testamentor assured her. "We checked."

The Laputa did another minor dip and rise. The ark tilted and righted, seeming heavier than a chest with sacred writ in it should have been.

"Then we'll even help you if we can," she said. "But first, are you Human Enlightenment or DevOcean? Are you with Rhodes or one of the other grandees?"

He didn't believe any of it. "You don't need to know for the interim—"

The *Dream Castle* did another bump, baggage and people and furniture shifting. Ghost rolled over, keeping her leg and stomach muscles clenched to avoid throttling herself with the choke noose. With her feet against the coffer she gave a shove, as much as she could without strangling herself.

The coffer moved, and the ark teetered off it before Boskoh could make a save. The ark crashed down on the deck at one corner. The workmanship was lavish but less solid than it might have been. With a splintering of wood and a pinging of snapped metal, the lid swung partway open, and out rolled the contents: a very dead man in DevOcean robes whose slight decomposition the incense hadn't completely masked.

Old Spume made geyser start-up sounds before producing, "Marrowbone!"

Ghost knew the name. Marrowbone was the high apostle of DevOcean who had staged a protest rally across the chasm from Wall Water during the Grand Attendance but had disappeared by the time she and Zinsser had passed that way. His throat had been cut. Cold as her bare feet were turning once again, she reflected that there were advantages to the outerworks' chill; Marrowbone smelled bad, but he would have been a lot riper in the Big Sere weather.

Bravuro gave up a strangled moan and backed against the wooden wall opposite, looking like he wanted to climb it with his shoulder blades. The other Human Enlightenment underlings leapt to secure the ark and body. Boskoh looked from the corpse to Testamentor to the three prisoners; then he drew a whip razor, testing it with a few flicking strokes that made thin whistling sounds.

"Seems we'll have to kill them, after all," he said as he made straight for Ghost.

CHAPTER THIRTY-ONE

Memory reared within Mason as if five somatic years—almost twenty objective—had been wiped away.

Majestica had been the hereditary autarch of Gapshot back then. The town earned most of its profit from tolls and protection fees levied on high roads foot traffic in addition to tariffs on Jut-hoppers. She was shrewd, capable and relentless; as regal as Glorianna Theiss, as beautiful as Ghost, as politically astute as Dextra Haven. Captain Marlon was older than her even in somatic years and should have had the upper hand, but she had played him brilliantly, making herself what Marlon wanted but couldn't have—beyond one or two sample trysts.

Mason always suspected that the genius of her amatory works had owed more to what she said than to what she did, but no matter. *Scepter*'s skipper was a man whose ego and visions of personal glory responded to stroking even more avidly than certain other parts of him did. She was the one thing the lord of the Visitants would be denied unless he met her price, which was a renewed land link between south Scorpia and the Trans-Bourne that would be under the control of Gapshot.

The other jaw of the pliers squeezing Marlon's head and genitals was the fact that he would eventually have to account for all his command's activities, and the powers on high would *not* look kindly on his having enhanced the lot of one local ruler. Leaving behind a big-ticket construction flew in the face of basic tasking orders because it could allow the indigs to chart their own course in LAW's absence, when it was LAW's right to gain political influence from infrastructural improvements.

It was so fundamental a doctrine that even Marlon dared not violate it for fear of retaliation from on high against him and/or those he held dear. Still, calamity might have passed the survey team by had not some kiss-ass in planetological sciences suggested a solution that could be explained away as an experiment: raise the Juts to serve as a permanent causeway, well above any high-tide line.

Mason hadn't even been peripheral to the decision. As he understood it, however, Marlon was convinced that he could, if necessary, absolve himself with LAW by explaining the Juts operation as an overly successful planetomorphing experiment. Majestica's dominion over the crucial land link would be rationalized as that of a well-co-opted indig sovereign, a woman solidly loyal to LAW objectives. There were also indications Marlon had been pondering ways of circumventing cardinal regs by taking Majestica back to Periapt with him.

The plan called for the use of a prototype plasma drilling rig to punch through the littoral and bedrock on the Trans-Bourne side of the strait, penetrating to a magma bleb several thousand meters down. The engineers expressed a high degree of confidence that the upwelling would plug the Styx Strait, creating a seawall, and that any excess magma could simply be diverted into the Amnion by means of judicious lateral enlargements of the original drill hole.

And since the drilling was to be done at low tide, there would be no contact between machinery and sea, so why should the big, standoffish cell mass in the Amnion mind?

Except that the Oceanic had minded; it had minded most violently. The moment the plasma drill face had perforated the superficial rock and pockets of saltwater underlying the Juts, the Oceanic had shown just what it was capable of. With no technical expertise worth mentioning, the administrative adviser Mason had been relegated to a place at the sidelines while Marlon, Majestica, and the command staff rode in a command and control VTOL. Accompanying the VTOL were two linesman helos on the lookout for any Aquam who might be devout or addled enough to try to interfere, plus a half dozen hoverpods to serve as spotters for the operation.

Most prominent of all had been the big lifter. The team's aerostat-rotor-wing flying crane swung the drill rig in, ready to scrap the whole effort if anything glitched. Aquam, watching from shore with Mason and the other LAW ground observers, pointed or howled, cheered or swooned, swore or gnawed at beards, and tore at their own hair. They shook rattles, clashed cymbals, and beat drums; they slugged down gooner, pyro, sot-mead, and twenty other kinds of local throat exfoliant.

Marlon and Majestica had convinced the indigs, as indeed the skipper and the overseeress had convinced each other, that here was at last a human empowerment that could defy the Gaian superorganism that was Aquamarine's dominant life-form. The legendary bard Hardstrum had been a few meters away from Mason on the Gapshot cliffs, whanging the strings of his flex-lyre until his fingers bled, extemporizing a bawdy paean that used the plasma drill and the Juts as a metaphor for a love bout between starship captain and overseeress.

The big lifter had hovered in, and the drilling had begun. One moment the crowds were cheering history in the making; the next the ground beneath Mason's feet was shaking. That alone was enough to start squawks and screams among the Aquam, who had better reason than most to fear quakes. Then came a manifestation of the Oceanic that no team member and few Aquam had ever seen, although rumors and veteran Laputa travelers had supplied its name: a Skyskein.

Living geysers and ramifications of flowing water had defied gravity to reach up, following the line of the drill rig, and enfold the big lifter like a mountainous thalassic fist, pulling it back down into the strait amid countless tons of brine and Oceanic.

The Oceanic revealed a type of hydrodynamics the Periapts had refused to believe when Aquam myth spoke of it. Mason had gotten a disjointed impression of events as he was buffeted by hysterical Aquam and rocked by the convulsing ground. Perhaps millions of cubic meters of seawater had mounded up and simply moved over onto the beach at the Gapshot side of the Juts, covering the LAW tech support field station—vehicles and aircraft, team personnel, and Aquam gawkers.

Displaced by the water, the air had moaned like a prairie wind, kicking up gusts that flapped his clothes and whirled Big Sere grit and fecal dust. The temperature had dropped fifteen degrees. Farther out to sea the surface of the Amnion had dipped in a huge, shallow bowl. The water had risen until it blocked out the sky, an irresistible divine force swallowing up the big lifter and Marlon's C&C VTOL. Smaller spotter craft and linesmen helos, peeling away frantically, had been nailed and reeled in by flycatcher tongues that shot from the central pillars of uplifted brine.

The apparition had loomed close enough to Mason for him to see monstrous turbulence within it: the up-sliding foam, dim moving shadows that might be bits of broken technology or drowning LAWs, the living ire of the water world filling his field of vision and poised to come pounding down on him.

He had dropped to his knees and flung his arms over his head. Waiting for an end that never came, he had wept and wished that he had never left his several back on Periapt, and he had mourned the fact that he would never see the children they would have chosen to birth by then.

When at last he realized that Eyewash was warming him again, he looked up to find the Oceanic gone, along with more than half the survey team. The shoreline had been changed, and while the monoliths of the Juts were still visible, they had been reconfigured by the great scourging. And Mason, senior survivor, was suddenly commander of the *Scepter* survey team.

Eisley Boon, Mason's closest friend among the ship's compliment despite their dissimilarities, had pointed out that fact to the rest of the crew and had somehow made it stick. In fact, only Mason's access and authority were recognized, but knowing that his decisions and actions might be under close scrutiny back on Periapt, he dared not act simply as figurehead. Boon became his confidant and deputy.

Surprising himself as much as anyone, he had found that he had some talents for leadership, conflict resolution, and consensus building, though they were scarcely talents he enjoyed putting to use. Promising himself that he would complete only what was feasible of the mission, he consoled himself with the attentions—and real affection, he came to believe—of Incandessa Rhodes.

She had gravitated to him, as had so many other illustrious Aquam women, after he had become what Boon called Top Nameplate. He was fully convinced that he was serving out a hardship tour, and it wasn't until much later that he realized he had been living the happiest years of his life.

His plan to return triumphant to his several had come to nothing, however. Boon had died in the waves at New Alexandria, and Mason was irrevocably abandoned by his spouses, who had divorced him in absentia, and were even now on the AlphaLAW mission to Illyria. All he had left was Purifyre, his renegade son.

By concentrating on that, he managed to extract himself from memory of the Oceanic's god wrath; clinging to the rail and an outrigger hinge, he realized unsteadily that *Shattertail* was nearly at the Forge Town side of the bridge. More than ever, it was too late to go back.

"Put that away!" Testamentor barked at Boskoh, whose little whip razor was poised to lay open Ghost's carotid. "It means nothing that they've seen Marrowbone's body. Who can they tell? Can they stop the *Dream Castle*? And later it won't matter who they tell."

"But it violates the plan." Boskoh sulked as he slipped the whip razor back into his sleeve. Ghost, seeing its serpentine glitter and the way he handled it, knew how Marrowbone, late high apostle of DevOcean, had met his end.

Testamentor rested the heel of his hand on the grip of the pistol grip tucked into his sash. "It merely changes the plan. Make ready for Passwater."

"But we won't be there until—"

"Make ready, Bosk, I tell you! And get that old charlatan's carrion into the shroud. Jolly, Sterling, lend a hand."

Boskoh and the remaining four Human Enlightenment men began wrapping Marrowbone's carcass in a burial shroud embroidered with occult symbols. Testamentar addressed a stern glare to the prisoners.

"Crying out will do you no good, and you'll suffer for it. I won't gag and blindfold you unless you force me to. Purifyre has said that the time is fast coming when your lot and ours will need each other, so while all of us mark time in Passwater, you can tell me some things and I can tell you some things."

"'Mark time.' Spring another nasty surprise on DevOcean, you mean," Zinsser said, voicing Ghost's own surmise.

Testamentor struck his forehead softly with his fingertips, signifying Zinsser's stupidity. "How can you Visitants be so mighty and yet so rattleheaded? Human Enlightenment wants to unite the Aquam, lift them up and give them the world that should have been theirs two hundred years ago. DevOcean, contrariwise, wants to give the Aquam to the Oceanic—feed us to It whole."

"That's not what we heard," Zinsser told him.

"Naturally not, because DevOcean is built on lies."

"Then tell us the truth," Ghost pounced, "so that we can convey it to Dextra Haven."

Testamentor looked to where Boskoh and the others were attiring themselves in DevOcean robes. "First tell me how you come to be aboard the *Dream Castle.*"

Ghost let Zinsser and Spume carry the tale, since truth would serve as well as any disinformation. Meanwhile, she continued to case the compartment, working out various scenarios in her head. Stray glimmers of afternoon light found their way through the window shutters and drapes. The Flying Pavilion hit more turbulence from time to time, but its attitude thrusters kept it reasonably stable. The scent of the dead high apostle abated now that he was back inside the ark.

Finally, Testamentor took up his side of the exchange as his henchmen squared away the cabin. "DevOcean professes a love for all people, but what truly drives it is a loathing of mankind. They say humans sprang from seawater and back to it must go, in the end, to merge with the Oceanic. Apotheosis, you see."

"Don't they know it's been tried?" Zinsser asked.

"Not by DevOceans. Their theology has it that when the body of their church has achieved purity of faith, the day of reckoning and the test of the rapture will come. When certain foretold signs come to pass, the Chosen will cast their fate to the seas. The worthy will be received into the body of the Oceanic, spiritually reincarnated and made like unto God, while the damned will be cast into torment."

"They mean to mass suicide in the Amnion?" Zinsser gasped.

"The land will be wiped away," Testamentor said. "For nothing on land is worthy, and all non-DevOcean civilization is inherently warped and evil. Only the Chosen have merit."

"And you're helping along those signs of the last days," Zinsser observed with a nod toward Marrowbone's corpse.

"We haven't the power or the inclination for that. Those signs entail great upheaval. But if the false reports we plant disorganize DevOcean, so be it. If the grandees blame them for the raid on Wall Water, so much the better. The Chosen will have served at least one useful purpose under Eyewash."

"Taking the heat off Human Enlightenment so Purifyre can go achieve his real objective," Zinsser drew him on. "Which is what?"

"In due time? Supplant you Periapts, of course. Throw down LAW and make something better."

For several hours Testamentor and his men huddled on the far side of the rickety stateroom, heads together over a map, running over plans. Bravuro the hustler sat brooding but afraid to move from his assigned spot. The conspirators had also reviewed documents and credentials, some of which Ghost took to be forged.

Testamentor had shown a little clemency by moving his three captives onto bunks and ordering more slack in the choke nooses—a good start, but Ghost needed more and bigger concessions if she was going to turn the tables.

"Why not let us help you?" she said to Testamentor. Her plan might have to wait until Gumption or even the Trans-Bourne, but that was no reason to postpone laying the groundwork.

"What, now you're going to tell us how to machinate against DevOcean?" Testamentor scoffed. "We who've been doing it fifteen years and more?"

"No, but consider what you could do if you had a Flying Pavilion at your command."

"Piracy?" Testamentor did a forefinger tap to the temple—*think again.* "The Insiders can drop these outerworks into the Amnion by the mere plucking of a linchpin."

"Yes, but it's the Insiders' bailiwick I can let you take over, the controls of the *Dream Castle* itself."

Boskoh sneered at her. *"You,* who played into our hands so easily, can penetrate Optimant defenses?"

She was ready for that one. "The Insiders aren't Optimants. They're no different from yourselves, or they would have already discovered how to conn this vehicle generations ago. What's more, we accepted your invitation only to propose this bargain."

"You claim the ability to walk through hullskin?" Boskoh taunted.

She lifted her chin to indicate the planks behind her. "I'm betting that there's an unvandalized access hatch behind this bulkhead. If there is one, I can open it."

"She's the one who had the cybercaul at Wall Water," the one called Sterling told Testamentor. "Without the caul she's helpless."

"We have no need of the Laputa," Testamentor said. "It's taking us to the very places we wish to go."

"But if I reprogram it," she returned the serve, *"it won't come back here."* She let it sink in. "DevOcean will be cut off from the rest of Aquamarine—*truly* neutralized—except for—what?—a few missionaries. No converts come in, no proselytizers get out."

"You'd control the world trade in galvani stones," Zinsser added. "And with that you'd control the trades in sling-guns and muscle cars."

Testamentor's eyes swept Ghost's like radar. Then he picked up the little jimmy–burglar tool Old Spume had been carrying and thrust it at Sterling. "That board between the bunks and the wardrobe is loose. Pry it back."

In the end it also took a thick chopper blade and some other improvised pinchbars to get the base of the bulkhead plank loose and levered back, dowels shrieking and splintering. Testamentor himself knelt before it with an oil lamp. "There's a hatch there, right enough," he announced. "And it doesn't look to have been disturbed since the Cyberplagues."

Ghost maintained Skills composure. "You saw how the bust of Altheo Smicker was opened to reveal the computer at Wall Water? I can do the same with that hatch." The fact was that Claude Mason had opened the bust, but she was banking on Testamentor not knowing that.

He gave her an unexpected smile, blew out the lamp, and motioned for his men to resecure the plank. "If so, you can do it in Gumption or somewhere else once our mission in Passwater has been completed. And with plenty of our troops aboard to handle any opposition."

Ghost cursed to herself. With all the impulsive blowhards running around Aquamarine, she had to fall into the hands of a cautious, canny one. There was a sudden banging on the outerworks gong.

"Passwater, coming up," Jolly said.

"Shouldn't you be in vestments?" Ghost asked Testamentor.

He shook his head. "I'm too well known—while *these* lads are vaunted preachers of the DevOceanic worship."

"Can we at least see Passwater?" Zinsser piped up.

Testamentor took his own counsel. "Very well. I'd like to hear your opinion of the defenses."

Boskoh and Sterling were only too happy to manhandle Zinsser and Ghost to the window, slamming them down on stools and nearly throttling them with the choke nooses in the process. The window's heavy drapes were tied back, and the shutters were opened. Cold took the cabin by storm, driving out the warmth of the little stove. The view of Passwater was worth the pain.

They were coming in over a bleak and forbidding black lava desert that stretched between mountains to the north and an Amnion that looked like it was made of hammered blue steel set with azure quartz icebergs. The coal-dark mountains were mottled with snowfields, making Ghost think of chiaroscuro masks formed up in ranks. Two explosion craters with steep rust-colored rims could be seen, filled with green-water lakes from which rose warm fog. On the flats, hot springs bubbled and vents jetted steam.

Here and there were Scourland Ferals, singly and in parties, their bounders hopping at a moderated pace rather than at the full-bore gallop of Asurao and his horde in their pursuit of the *Dream Castle*. The Laputa was approaching from the east for a wide-angle view of the area. Ghost's eyebrows raised a few millimeters with surprise and Zinsser laughed humorlessly.

"This planet!" he exclaimed.

CHAPTER THIRTY-TWO

A s *Shattertail* gathered momentum, descending the bowed suspension span toward Forge Town and the Trans-Bourne, Mason abruptly had the feeling that he had survived a rite of passage. None of the bridge constables at the barbican astride the southern end of the span were wearing the club-clover of Gapshot, and none glowered at Purifyre. Instead he was hailed, and there were halloos, too, for pointed-toothed Ballyhoot and the others.

A crescent island of over six hundred square kilometers, plus a few outlying spits accessible at low tide, the Trans-Bourne was Scorpia's single modest claw. Other islets dotted the Amnion around it, but most of those had been isolated since the Cyberplagues, excluded from the Laputa routes and too distant for kite travel. Mason took stock of changes south of the strait as *Shattertail* treadled down the dusty main road from the narrow headland where the bridge was anchored. The first thing he noticed was that the colors were even more joyously gaudy than they had been in Scorpia.

Forge Town was four times the size it had been when *Scepter* had departed; by Aquam standards it was a full-fledged city. Because it was no longer constrained by defensive walls, it was much less vertical than Gapshot. Turnswain explained proudly that the walls had come down once feuds, wars, and banditry had been suppressed as part of the regional effort to build, develop, and create wealth.

The architecture was sharply different from Gapshot's, as well. Forge Town ran more to adobe polygons with wide, low-pitched roofs of white tile; open work sheds and shops under thatch; taverns and residences built with a Moorish airiness; and manufactories walled with fretwork, gapped planks, or wattle. Most of the increase in size was thanks to new chimneyed metal and glass works, belling anvils and skirling saw pits, and trading houses and overflowing marketplaces.

But *Shattertail* didn't linger; it left the precincts of Forge Town behind, pumping hard along the Trans-Bourne autobahn. Mason saw tilled fields and family vegetable plots surrounding dwellings ranging from huts to manor houses. Hectare upon hectare was devoted to whackweed, the high-priced, addictive smokable herb that had made such inroads in Scorpia. Businesses of all sorts lined the high road's shoulders, from vendors of singing insects under frond parasols to grinding mills and stone quarries. The dyeworks that had laid the groundwork for the peninsular economic boom were especially noxious and active.

Lacking the natural resources and population of Scorpia, the Trans-Bourne had cultivated a genius for making manufacts and teknics the rest of Aquamarine wanted, turning Optimant wreckage into scudos, establishing centers of learning and artisanry, and brewing powerful new intoxicants and pharmaceuticants, as well as improving on old ones. It was the logical place to seize upon muscle cars and similar innovations and turn them into feudal industries.

The theft of the Science Side modules and Purifyre's changes in guise had convinced Mason that there was more to the Trans-Bourne's progress than a spontaneous outbreak of profit-motive zeal. He wondered if other Optimant computational systems like the one within the bust of Atheo Smicker had survived—systems that were operational and accessible to certain Aquam. Clinging to the secured outrigger once more, he thought again about Kinbreed's reference to Cozmote.

"Cozmote is someone you'll meet in due course," Purifyre said when Mason asked. "A man of great influence."

"Does he have influence over Purifyre the *rishi* of Human Enlightenment, or over Go-lightly the barrow-coolie, or over Hammerstone of the Bridge Constabulary?"

"Over all those and infinitely more."

"More aliases, more identities? How many can you have without forgetting who you are?"

Purifyre's eyes never left Mason's. "Cozmote taught me never to forget who I am, Father."

The boy broke off the conversation on the pretext of seeing to the final disembarking arrangements, leaving Mason to bounce and sway at the outrigger. He had taken in another three kilometers of the roadside panorama when Turnwsain blew a small brayophaunt and swung the eight-wheeler off the autobahn. It trundled toward a large compound encircled by a wall of limestone that was dotted with firing slits and crenellations and fronted by a dry moat grown thick with leper-quills, shingle-wort, and other defensive features unusual in the Trans-Bourne. In response to the brayophaunt flourish, gates swung open under a raised portcullis to permit *Shattertail* to enter. Beyond the encircling palisade Mason could see gables, roof peaks, smoke from multiple sources, and several parking mounds, one supporting a chocked six-wheeler.

The place wasn't a muscle car manufactory, however, though there were a number of them around, some in various stages of construction or modification and others simply parked. Mason wondered why the idle cars hadn't been muscled up onto the remaining mounds to get them out of the way and prepared for use, but then the answer occurred to him. Kept at ground level, they couldn't be seen from the road. Outside observers would have a tougher time gauging the number of fleximobiles on-site.

Shattertail also halted on level ground, something it hadn't done before. The courtyard and shop areas and some of the parking mounds lay under the shade of huge old trees that repelled the worst of Eyewash's dry season fire. There were glowing forges and pounding carpenter's mauls; wainwright and wheelwright work was being done. Mason sensed an air of pending deadline. The men and women laboring there—some of whom were obviously Anathemites—paused to meet his gaze squarely. Armed sentries in commoner attire were walking the parapet, but the people working in the yard had no weapons close at hand.

Following Purifyre and Ballyhoot's lead, Mason disembarked when Turnswain's crew had set the grabs and placed chocks. Tossed or kicked aside to wherever they would be out from underfoot lay worn-out mollusk muscles, withered and catabolized, their sheaths dehydrated and cracked open, the tissue itself gone black with slime. Even after days on the Aquam high roads the smell made Mason gag. He mentally saluted the doggedness of whoever was in charge of hauling them away.

Ballyhoot was keeping a close eye on him, though her main concern was for the two hampers containing the Science Side units and the captured bloopguns. Mason had no doubt the bioanalyzer and DNA sequencer modules had come through intact, incorporating, as they did, lessons learned in the first generation of LAW missions regarding abuse and adverse conditions.

Leaving behind the din, Purifyre, Ballyhoot, and Mason veered away from the savory aromas of a kitchen and hearth pit to wend through flax-matted corridors cooled by adobe openwork. The decor was in muted natural tones, distinctive after the slapdash hues of Gapshot and the clownish color riot of Forge Town. Most chambers and side corridors were closed to view by hangings, curtains, or hinged multipanel screens decorated with delicate line drawings. Though neither a palace nor a showplace, the villa was still an abode of wealth, even by Trans-Bourne standards.

The Science Side modules were being paraded toward the far end of the rambling house, but Ballyhoot pulled Mason out of line ungently. "Go with her," Purifyre ordered before following after his prizes.

Ballyhoot led Mason up a flight of stairs hewn from maoriwood trestles, shoved him between two curtains into a room, and disappeared without stating the obvious—that he was to wait.

Ten by twenty meters, the room was bigger than the communal meeting house in a lot of Aquam villages. It was uncluttered, with more flax mats and strand-weave rugs on the hardwood, a few hangings, and a low table and floor pillows, south-of-Styx fashion, at the far end. Beyond the furniture a tall screen was spread, almost touching the ceiling.

The pillows looked like paradise after two long days of being bounced on a muscle car deck. Wiping the dust and sweat from his face with his capelet, Mason went to fling himself down, then stopped. A self-preserving caution born of the events at Wall Water wouldn't let him relax until he had investigated his surroundings completely. With the tightly buckled stomacher loosened, the flechette pistol came out of its clip holster easily.

Rounding the screen, he encountered a life-size statue of a young Aquam woman mounted on a half-meter-high pedestal. He nearly dropped the pistol on recognizing it as a likeness of Incandessa.

She was carved from some serpentinelike mineral, hydrous silicate of magnesia, he thought, the color her eyes had actually been and the color of Purifyre's eyes—the color of Aquamarine itself. She wore festival attire of the New Alexandrian upper crust of twenty years earlier, breasts bared after the fashion of marriageable women. She was in the pose of a tambouriif dancer, merry-eyed and laughing, tousled hair flying like streaming pennons frozen in time; she was lithe and graceful even if better fleshed than the Periapt fashion templates dictated, the graceful little hands in balletic poses and she half on pointe. Mason knew that buoyant energy intimately, knew the hair was russet even though the stone was blue-green, knew that very laugh and how she did that particular step.

The sculptor had caught her absolutely in detail so faithful that Mason would have thought the figure a laser carving except that he could see from tiny flaws that it had been executed arduously and adoringly by hand. The artist had obviously known Incandessa in those days, for Mason even recognized the outfit of gossamer Siams, the nipple ornament, and the ring with his family crest she had had made into the depicted nose ring. The sculptor had, incredibly, even gotten the crest right, the superimposed level and square of Old Earth freemasonry. Perhaps Rhodes the Elder had saved it from her funeral pyre.

Mason's cry from the heart, venting the deepest pain in him, took him by surprise. Another tore its way out of him as he put both hands around the waist of the statue, head against the smooth curve of its belly, as though he might bring her to life in his arms the way he had in his bed.

He hadn't heard anyone enter the room, but the instant the voice reached his ears—even before the words were intelligible—the puzzle of what had happened on Aquamarine was explained. Mason staggered before insight more intense than a stellar prominence.

"Too late for love, Claude. Too late for mourning, too. So don't bother flaunting any redeeming qualities. It only confuses the order of the universe."

Mason whirled with one hand still clutching Incandessa's cold, bangled ankle. It was Boon, Eisley Boon, returned to life after cold absorption in the Oceanic.

A glacier had crushed and pried its way down out of the Scourlands mountains, depositing its terminal moraine in the heights only three kilometers from the Passwater wall. It had also created a shard forest of serac pillars, many of which supported chance slabs of fluvioglacial drift rock like outsize mushrooms.

A river emerged from the glacier, shedding thermal vapor as it went, to join with melt streams on its way into the Amnion, a scant hundred meters from the fenced-off peninsula itself. Farther upriver tongues of heat mist curled from fissures in the blue-mottled ice.

"Reliable water supply and year-round heat source," Zinsser remarked as the Laputa was descending from one thousand meters. "Good place for the Ferals to live—under the glaciers."

Ghost pictured a tempestuous and unsparing Stygian Valhalla. The image held such appeal that she didn't see how Dextra Haven could entice the Ferals to live any other way.

The wall that kept the Ferals at bay on one side and the town safe on the other was bigger than she had expected—a monolithic rampart that had to have been built with surviving Optimant technology. Twenty meters high, it was composed of interlocked blocks of dark basaltic rock and desert grit that had been fused in some fashion. The side facing the wastes had been sandblasted by thousands of windstorms. It swung in a curve from north to south, its ends extending out into the Amnion. Ghost surmised that the blocks had been lowered by derrick or flying crane.

On the plain outside the wall were scattered Feral picket lines, wickiups, bounder-dung fires, and sept banners planted in ranks. A bounder race was in progress over a well-used course that had been laid out with as many hazards and hindrances as possible. Bunched together, the riders were scourging one another bloody with nettle flails, chain cat-o'-nine-tails, barbed wire quirts, and sjamboks. Ghost didn't see any sign of children, elderly, or noncombatants—only warriors.

Passwater's rearing bulwark lacked a gate or door. Only a hoist platform dangled from shear legs midway along it, with a tier treadmill for power—all crafted of timber that must have been imported.

Testamentor pointed to the hoist. "The lift is lowered for trading with the wild men—Alabaster mandseng for galvani stones. Passwaterites don't trust them or their sense of self-interest. Wiping out Passwater would end the mandseng trade, yet the Ferals would do it for the joy of the moment if their blood was up.

"The Passwaterites also descend to make sure sand doesn't build up along the great partition. The prevailing wind is from the north, *along* the bulwark. The matter still requires attention. Given time and carelessness, the Ferals could simply ride their bounders up and over a ramp of drifted sand and grit."

"What about direct assault?" Ghost wondered. Surely even the Ferals could come up with some kind of siege engines and ladders.

Testamentor pointed to emplacements spaced along the wall. "DevOceaners aren't pacifists. There are stone guns and fire chutes all along. Taking the city would be costly and troublesome for the Ferals, whose feuding poleis don't cooperate well, and who dislike protracted, static warfare, in any case.

"And as I say, the wild men value the trade goods they get for their galvani stones—textiles, gimcracks, and tools, but especially mandseng. The Scourlands are too harsh for the Ferals to support many Anathemites among them."

"Then how do you account for Asurao?" Ghost asked.

"Asurao isn't an Anathemite. Asurao's an antigod who has emerged hither and yon on the Scourlands since time out of mind. Or so folktales say."

Thinking back on the demon-warrior who had locked eyes with her, Ghost believed the first part; not an Anathemite, something more. But what?

Zinsser pointed out that the seawall was above the high-tide line. "Good enough for the worst of the conventional storms or the town wouldn't still be there. But come a millennial hurricane or the inevitable *tsunami* and DevOcean would have its rapture within the Oceanic ahead of schedule."

Testamentor nodded. "Passwater lives on borrowed time in many ways."

The town was not only larger than she had envisioned but far stranger-looking, even after having seen intel files and flyby images of its most striking features: the Boneyard, the Ossuary, and the City of the Sundered Skeleton.

Raised among the ruins of Brobdingnagian Optimant project, Passwater was to have been the site of a towering *Homo sapiens* likeness—a visible physiology standing one hundred fifty meters high, staring out to sea with the same defiance the lighthouse at New Alexandria demonstrated by casting its light over an ocean intolerant of ships.

The statue's construction phase had only begun when the Cyberplagues hit. The transparent and opaque organs hadn't been fabricated, and indeed, the gender of the skeleton—a subject of rancorous debate—hadn't been finalized. In the wake of the Plagues, the scattered skeletal modules, built hollow for systemry as well as sightseeing, had been commandeered for shelter and other construction needs.

Among the oldest PostPlague buildings, some cottages could still be seen to have metatarsals for chimneys, femurs and humeri for central columns, rib cage sections roofed over with polymer for greenhouses, and phalanges for pottery-glazing kilns.

Rearing above those and the whole town was the Backbone Keep, the colossal, articulated vertebral pillar whose coccyx had been shored up, stabilized, and strengthened by settling it into a shallow S curve. Its upper reaches guy-wired with Optimant cable, the keep reached forty-five meters into the air, ending somewhat anticlimactically with the cervical vertebrae but flying DevOcean banners nonetheless. The swaybacked pillar had been retrofitted with praying platforms, meditation cells, astrologers' booths, divinational chambers, and lookout posts.

Directly behind the Backbone Keep—lacking a view but far more stable—was the monument's cranium, the Skull Bunker. By the simple happenstance of where the heavy lifters had set it down, it had remained staring eyelessly at its own tailbone. Heavily fortified and provided with an underground redoubt, it was now the repository of some of DevOcean's most holy relics.

The rest of the town rising up under the Laputa was less quirky, running to houses of basalt block and brightly glazed tile. Part of the peninsular wall under the *Dream Castle*'s flight path had been cleared of people, and the flyway beneath it was sparsely built up—mostly roofed-over subsurface structures with the look of storage buildings and workshops. Ghost couldn't blame Passwaterites for not wanting to live under the Flying Pavilion's route. Even though the explosions that kept the Optimant relic in the air were carefully modulated, it was laying down quite a few joules of heat. Also, while the present generation might have forgotten, it had probably occurred to someone early on that the fusion reactor's containment housing would be giving off rads eventually.

The landing site was a different proposition from the one at Wall Water. Ghost had been considering ways of getting off the Laputa—if and when she managed to put Testamentor out of the way—to prowl at large in Passwater. But now that she had gotten a better look at the set-down area and embarkation stage, she realized that she had underestimated DevOcean's insularity and loathing of the Unsaved. All around the heat-darkened pit were revetments, pillboxes, and sentry positions, and out beyond the backblast radius were watchtowers, heavy sling-guns, and siege engines. Durably dressed DevOcean militiamen were mustered behind thermal dikes and partitions of firebrick with weapons held close. They were set to sprint in and take up encircling positions as soon as the heat from the pulsejet engine abated.

Sensibly, Passwater's defenses weren't intended for action against *Dream Castle*, which would only risk provoking its sonics and other protective features. On the other hand, the residents had left a clear killing zone for dispatching anyone or any group who might seek to leave the Laputa and infiltrate the town. Since the outerworks couldn't carry much of an invading army to begin with, the fortifications made DevOcean all but impregnable from attack by Flying Pavilions.

Boskoh, Jolly, and Sterling were winding their turbans, and tucking smokes and sparkwheels, dice, lucky pieces, and whatnot into the folds, fastening them with DevOcean eye-in-the-waves broaches. They had already knotted handles onto the ropes around the slain apostle Marrowbone's shroud.

Touchdown was routine: the trembling,; the lowering of the gangplank, the gong racket to signal those ashore who were going ashore. The bogus DevOceanite votaries left the window unshuttered but moved Ghost and Zinsser's chairs back, then took up the body of Marrowbone. With some nods and eye contact, they moved to the door. Bravuro tried to depart discreetly, but once Testamentor let him see down the barrel of the stolen bloopgun, he returned to his seat. Boskoh, Jolly, and Sterling bore the corpse out.

The Laputa wouldn't lift off until the following morning, and the votaries were expected to be away sowing paranoia and despair until then. Spume's Cheynes-Stokes breathing had stopped now that he was back near sea level. Zinsser was subsumed in thought but watchful. Bravuro had his forehead on his updrawn knees, arms clasped over his head. Testamentor, having shot the bolt of the cabin's inner door, looked at Ghost.

"Come here," she said, "and I'll let you in on something."

But Testamentor didn't move. "There's nothing I want from you."

Zinsser looked up at him. "Stop before you get her sexually aroused," he advised sourly.

CHAPTER THIRTY-THREE

Mason went to embrace Boon until a closer look at his friend's face stopped him. Boon was almost exactly Mason's age chronologically, but he looked old enough to be his father. Also, there was no bonhomie, no joy of reunion to be read from him. Boon was gazing down at him as if he were an unhousebroken dog, and the tone in his voice was neither teasing nor chummy.

Maybe Boon was looking for him to burst into tears or faint from surprise. But after all the head shots the last few days had dealt him, Mason felt a surreal composure. "I guess they're calling you Cozmote these days, Eisley?" he said at last.

The remark didn't throw Boon. Few things ever had, certainly nothing conjured up in Mason's skull. "Just figuring that out? Fine, I'll take that to mean that the LAW data sifters haven't gotten wind of me yet."

"But how—"

"C'mon, Claude, let's grab a bite to eat. You must be starved."

Boon gestured with one hand to trays of food and drink being brought in and set on the low table by two men and a woman who wore work clothes rather than servant's livery and had the air of household members pitching in rather than domestics. Mason didn't pay them much attention because he was noticing the hand Boon had waved.

It was work-broadened, scabbed, and calloused; two nails were black from having been hit or squeezed. That was the Boon Mason knew: brilliant and driven, but a doer as well as a dreamer, welcoming hard work and never quitting a thing until he had seen it through. The evocation of an earlier Boon made this new incarnation less intimidating. Mason let go of the statue's ankle, fighting the impulse to ask the obvious questions, if only because Boon would be anticipating them.

Instead, Mason pointed to Boon's Trans-Bourne style caftan, which was as varicolored as two palette fish locked in combat. "How many innocent fruit cocktails died to make that party dress, Eisley?"

As sometimes happened when he missed the joke, Boon was puzzled and a bit suspicious. Then he smiled lopsidedly, even though there was no sign of mirth in his eyes. His teeth had yellowed and browned, and two lowers were missing.

"Think of it as a show of manufacturer's pride. You'd be surprised what a pretty scudo loud colors have earned me." He stepped back a pace with a pronounced limp of the right leg.

Boon's presence had always been more a matter of intensity and intellect than of appearance, and that was truer now than ever. His skin, baby pink the last time Mason had seen him, was slack and had the yellowish tinge of lingering jaundice. The bulbous head, too big for his body, seemed ever on the verge of overbalancing him, and what little hair he had left was a snarl of silver, gray, and sulphur blond. He gave off Aquam odors. Mason wondered in return whether he smelled alien to Boon—or like a reminder of home. When he bent to retrieve the 'chettergun, Boon watched without comment.

Alone again, they lowered themselves onto pillows around a table set with quoinseed muffins, sugared bushpears in cream sauce, curried pogopod testicles, mud-spud salad, and ciderlilly leaves stuffed with jillmillet and smokenuts. The spread would have given a Periapt food critic ecstasies, but Mason ate mechanically.

He laid the flechette pistol aside; if it had constituted any kind of leverage in Boon's house, Boon would already have confiscated it. Mason harbored no fantasies of taking hostages, shoot-outs, or heroic escapes. Purifyre was under the same roof, and the last thing Mason wanted was to be turned out.

The servers had delivered gooner, sangaree, nepenthe, and fungo. Boon took only water, purified Aquam-style with vinegar and sweetened with rockslug honey to redress the taste. Dearly as he longed for something with more body to it, Mason opted for water, too.

"Where's my son?" he asked.

Boon wasn't so much taken off guard as miffed. "What paternal concern! He'll be here by and by. *Your boy* has a rather full agenda around here after being away from home for so long."

Home. "Eisley, whatever you're blaming me for—"

"Claude, why not yield the floor, eh? You never dreamed we'd be having this conversation, but I've been mulling it over for nearly twenty years."

"What made you think I'd come back?"

"*JeZeus,* you're *thick!*" Boon slammed his wooden mug down, splashing water everywhere. "Anybody who saw the way your severalmates on Periapt treated you at the *Scepter*'s departure ceremonies and the prelaunch fetes knew! Anybody who saw the looks they gave each other behind your back when you were blathering on about your career in LAW knew!

"I took the trouble to make inquiries with some G-Two acquaintances, so I knew your loving spouses were doing pre-enlistment workups for AlphaLAW missions. Where'd they finally decide on—QueStar? Trinity?"

"Illyria."

"Perfect! Instant retirement—just about the only thing those arrested-development cases were good for. They deserted you, and you suddenly discovered you missed your Aquam wife and child with your whole heart and soul. Is that how it went?"

"Fuck you."

Mason had snatched up a two-tined fork of Optimant steel in an overhand stabbing grip. Boon looked for a moment as if he might take up another, then regained his cool control.

"I apologize, Claude. This wasn't how I meant our initial conversation to go. We're way off script."

Mason threw the fork back on the table; it struck a stoneware plate, eliciting a sustained ringing that gradually subsided while they faced each other. Mason noticed in passing that his hands were surprisingly steady. "How was it supposed to go, Eisley?"

"Well, I was going to savor your astonishment, perhaps have you resuscitated from fainting. Then I would tell you what really happened that night on the beach at New Alexandria and afterward."

"Then by all means go back on script," Mason said.

Boon leaned back on his pillow. "Over the years I thought through so many ways to warm up to my story... and now I find none suitable."

Mason stood up, went to the hinged screen at the near end of the room, and shoved it clattering and whamming into the corner, exposing the statue of Incandessa, laughing and holding her dancing pose for them both.

"Suppose you begin here," Mason said.

Boon bristled and perhaps was about to refuse, when the ones who had served the food rushed into the room in answer to the racket, armed with sling-gun, catchpole, and choke noose. Boon ordered them out, then turned back to Mason in a different frame of mind.

"All right, I'll start with Incandessa." His eyes narrowed. "I loved her."

Mason returned to his pillow. "That makes two of us, then."

"Mmm. But back before you even noticed her, I tried to get her to love me." Boon regarded the statue. "In some other universe maybe that jackass Marlon didn't bring disaster down on us. Which means you didn't become commander and Rhodes didn't steer Incandessa straight at you, groomed as she was to make a good political marriage. She might've seen me in a different light."

"What insane *drivel*, Boon! With Marlon and a full ship's complement around, you'd never have managed to fake your own death—however you did it. You would have had to abandon her, too!"

Boon leaned forward a bit. "I was working almost from day one to stay behind when the rest of you left, Claude. We all knew what a full-fledged LAW takeover would do to the Aquam. Okay, so I was full of myself back then. I figured that if I had a generation or two to give these people a leg up, LAW would have to take them on their own terms."

"And most of all, you'd have had Incandessa," Mason said. "Only she died in childbirth."

"Yes." Boon nodded slowly. "Not the only comeuppance I was dealt but certainly the worst. 'Man proposes and God disposes' and all that."

"Then the GammaLAW mission's bad luck could be your reprieve," Mason thought to point out. "Our starship's gone. There'll be no relief expedition for a long time to come, if ever. Commissioner Dextra Haven is going to need all the help she can dredge up, and now there's no higher authority looking over her shoulder. She'd welcome an ally like you."

Boon snorted. "I've no intention of helping a Periapt get her knee on the Aquam neck. My original game plan went awry, but my objectives haven't changed. And I'm well along toward realizing them."

"Just what are your objectives?"

"Neutralize the Oceanic. Set the Aquam on course for a rational society. Keep this planet an Aquam-controlled world. Hell, those would already be accomplished facts if it wasn't for Hippo Nolan and a spot of bad luck that last day."

"What about that last *night*, Boon? How'd you make it look like you went over the edge of Execution Dock? Were you in league with the Conscious Voices? They threw someone else over—a corpse, maybe?"

Boon smiled to himself. "No, Claude. That was me those women pitched into the Amnion. But it spit me back, Claude. Don't ask me how or why, but it did."

Mason's jaw dropped somewhat. "But I saw you atomized. I saw you *turned inside out!*"

Boon nodded. "And I knew death. But the goddamned Oceanic reassembled me and spit me back onto dry land. Not that any present-day Aquam fully believe that for a minute. But the Conscious Voices saw me walk again."

"Good Christ," Mason said.

"Good Christ, indeed." Boon took a breath. "There's a precedent, believe it or not. Holy Saint Avunculus, the founder of the walled city that's now called Alabaster. An Anathemite who threw herself into the Amnion on behalf of fellow mutants. A DevOceanite at one point, if you accept the folktales, who'd lost patience with the sect and was treated to a vision of redemption at Alabaster."

"The Oceanic spit her back?" Mason asked.

"All in a pile of wet robes but still alive. Those who feared what they'd seen fled; a few others tried to emulate Avunculus, but the Amnion wasn't as kind to them. The rest built a holy shrine, a kind of cathedral, though Avunculus wanted none of it. But oddly enough, it was about that time that mandseng started appearing around Alabaster, all over Cape Ataraxia. No one could harvest it except those of, well, let's say a peaceful nature. So that became the Alabasterites' holy mission: to harvest the gift they were certain the Oceanic had sent them and dispatch it to all corners of Aquamarine to minimize the chances of Anathemite births."

"What became of Avunculus?"

"Died at the ripe old age of one hundred and ten—of natural causes."

Mason blew out his breath. "Then why aren't you worshipping the Oceanic instead of trying to 'neutralize' it?"

Boon wet his lips. "Because anything with the power of life and death needs to be humbled, Claude. And because I need to *know* why I was saved. One way of doing that is to bring it down to size."

Mason leaned into the table. "Commissioner Haven is convinced that the Oceanic holds a clue to ending the Roke Conflict."

"That's a bit of a leap, isn't it?"

Mason weighed his words carefully. "Eisley, we recovered Roke tissue from a ship that attacked soon after *Terrible Swift Sword* entered this system. The tissue suggests that the aliens are marine creatures."

Boon's brows beetled, but he didn't reply.

Mason shook his head in astonishment. "Why do you think it resurrected you?"

Boon compressed his lips. "I've been asking myself that for twenty years, and I still don't have an answer. Oh, I've told myself that it's because the Oceanic divined my plans for the Aquam, but I doubt that. I mean, if it divined my noble intentions, it obviously divined the ignoble ones, as well—my hunger to learn how and why the Oceanic acts as it does."

"As I remember, you never had any love for the Oceanic."

"But I didn't hate or fear it, either. I wasn't hating it when it engulfed me. You see, Claude, I think it's looking to be talked to."

Mason's smile held secret knowledge. "An attempt at communication may have been what got the *Sword* destroyed."

Boon shook his head. "From the accounts that reached me, you people weren't trying to communicate so much as dredge up a sample."

They both fell silent for a moment; then Mason waved a hand around the airy room. "So now you have yourself a nice country estate, several thriving businesses, a piece of the Styx Strait bridge, and the apparent allegiance of my son and the rest of Human Enlightenment. Is that your formula for steering the fate of the planet?"

"I had to start from scratch," Boon snarled. "Haven't you figured that out yet? Those equipment caches Hippo Nolan found just before liftoff weren't Aquam pilferage. They contained the stuff I'd amassed to use after *Scepter* left.

"Rations, weapons, a prefab echelon-two field medicine station, telecom and computer equipment, fabricator rigs and energy modules—even the critical components for a surface-effect carrier and a light helo. Hippo found them when a satellite sweep activated prototype emergency transponders he'd cobbled up for his own edification and installed in a number of vehicle guidance suites—without bothering to tell you, by the way."

"I—we—always laid the thefts to an indig takeover conspiracy," Mason admitted.

"Yes, but I was your personal deputy, going wherever I pleased," Boon reminded him. "Issuing orders and requisitions that carried your authority. I siphoned off resources that would've let me whip the whole planet into line."

Mason filled his cup to the rim with nepenthe. He sipped it, gagging on its corrosiveness, then chortled nastily. "Robinson Crusoe Boon, alone among the indigs without so much as a hat to shit in!"

"Not quite naked and helpless," Boon corrected. "I had a few odds and ends stashed in a New Alexandria hidey-hole I'd used. Some detonator units and a supply of caps from the mass driver experiments; some tools, personal med kit, and whatnot. A commo set whose memory filled me in on the bad news about Hippo cleaning out my caches and let me monitor your departure."

"Just in case you changed your mind and wanted to yell for extraction."

Boon wore the pitying look that had sometimes irked and embarrassed Mason. "My die was already cast. I was sick to my soul of being a needs-assessment specialist for LAW. I'd released myself from my loyalty oath, Claude, and appointed myself a *needs-provision* generalist."

Again, Mason gestured around him. "So you started a dye trade and appropriated Hippo's hobby craft to build a regional muscle car industry. You're still a long way from being Aquamarine's Alexander the Great."

Boon wouldn't rise to the bait. "You're leaving a few things out—like an underground whose effectiveness you've seen for yourself. But a lot of my time *was* spent in, ah, unscheduled learning experiences. Once I'd gotten over the shock of being reborn, I reorganized myself, recovered from Incandessa's death, and established a cover identity. Then I set out to turn Scorpia on its ear. Even made a working model of a windmill and showed it to some New Alexandria honchos.

"But that same night some slave dealers, treadwheel-mill owners, and related bullyraggers killed my bodyguards, destroyed my model, and left me for dead in a ditch. I lay recuperating in a sympathizer's hut for two months. During that time I decided to adopt a more gradual approach.

"Without the data troves I'd lost, I had nothing to fall back on but what was in my head. By the time I was ambulatory, I'd picked the thing least likely to gain me the ill will of organized, powerful competitors: anodyne dyes. If you recall, Claude, there wasn't much around but veggie and animal colorings and some Optimant remnants."

Finding himself doing the sideways head tic that indicated agreement among the Aquam, Mason changed his gesture to a nod. "But for all of that you didn't have Incandessa, and so you decided to draw my son into your orbit?"

Boon took on the staring inscrutability that was, in him, more of a danger signal than any tirade. "You idiot. It hasn't penetrated yet what a better man she made of you? *That's* how good a human being she was, Claude! She could imbue even a bogusly handsome, vapid, self-serving swine like you with some sense of matters greater than your own infantile desires. With a sense of *nobility,* you dense, unthinking, compassionless, moral pygmy!

"Besides, *you're* the one who ran out on your child. I wish it had been you growing up orphaned in Wall Water and suffering 'Waretongue's abuse. You instead of Purifyre."

"I wish it had, too, Boon," Mason said quietly.

For once Boon didn't seem to know what to think, so he went on with his story. "Since I'd built up Human Enlightenment as part of my—Cozmote's—covert apparatus, penetrating Wall Water in the cover of a *rishi* and recruiting Purifyre was the obvious way to go."

"And now he's your surrogate son. Your combination Sinbad and Machiavelli. The ultimate act of revenge."

"Wrong. I looked after him because it was what Incandessa would've wanted."

"And because you knew you could poison his mind to me in the event I returned."

"No. Because Incandessa would've disapproved of that—however much she resented you at the end. The fact is, I avoided even talking about you to your son."

Mason didn't rip into the assertion because he longed so desperately for it to be true. "Even so, you obviously haven't gotten far in your scheme to slay the Oceanic."

Boon shook his head in self-amusement. "Claude, I've no intention of *slaying* the Oceanic."

"But I thought—"

"Kill off the entire marine biomass? Don't be absurd. It's the centerpiece of the planetary oxygen/CO_2 cycle and a number of other crucial processes, besides which it'll be a vital resource for food, material sciences, mineral extraction, energy production—"

Mason made a dismissive sound. "Do you think Dextra Haven is going to be sitting around taking commemorative holos of you while you try to tame millions of cubic kilometers of Oceanic? If she doesn't shut you down—"

"You're in no position to demand answers, my friend. You can be dispensed with, and you're certainly not going to be catered to."

Before Mason could reply, he became aware of another presence. Purifyre stood just inside the door, with Ballyhoot hovering in the hall like a shadow. Both had shed armor and weapons, removed the khol from their eyes, and donned caftans as garish as Boon's.

"The field modules are unpacked for your inspection," Purifyre reported to Boon. "But first I want you to see what bonus prizes of war came into our hands." Ballyhoot lifted into sight the two bloopguns. Purifyre, meanwhile, brought his right hand out from behind him and displayed the cybercaul.

Boon gave an incongruously boyish cry of delight and went to examine the booty. Mason observed his son's terse but proud recounting of events at the Grand Attendance. Boon, ever the technophile, figured out the safety mechanisms and magazine releases of the bloopguns straightaway, nodding in admiration as he divined what they could do.

"These'll be of such tremendous use to us. We must treat them carefully."

Boon was visibly startled, however, to hear that the cybercaul had functioned on a concealed Optimant computer. "Inconceivable! We found one when the *Scepter* was here but got nothing out of it when we powered it up."

"It worked because *I* got it working," Mason put in—even if the act owed less to his talent for cybersystems than to the AI's presence in his neurowares.

Boon looked at him and grinned. "You mean *Yatt* got it working, don't you, Claude?"

CHAPTER THIRTY-FOUR

Having spent a galling night lying bound in the Laputa's stateroom, Ghost had thought more than once that the moment to toad-crank Testamentor was close at hand. The counterfeit DevOceanite was as smart as he looked and had been too wary to give her a chance to attack him. Repeatedly he had checks her bonds, each time undoing the small progress Ghost made against them. He gave her water sparingly, but no food. He also reassured himself that there were no outerworks snoops hanging around the door to first class. Bravuro had lapsed into a seeming torpor, but Ghost noticed that his eyes, too, slid to Testamentor and the door every now and again.

Boskoh and the rest who had gone ashore were obviously meeting with success in fomenting chaos. The frenzy had commenced with the stir they generated in waves as they had borne Marrowbone's body down the Flying Pavilion's gangplank and on through the fortifications around the landing pit. Sentinels and customs officials had fallen into animated conversation, and runners had been dispatched to the Skull Bunker to spread the word of Marrowbone's death. Gagaku drums and alpenhorns had sounded, summoning DevOceanite elders to an emergency caucus. Merchants returning from the trading house wore agitated looks, and the supercargo, returning from a confab with embarkation stage officials, had posted extra guards at the boarding lock. The usual freneticism of a Laputa arrival had escalated to alarm, apprehension, and incidents of panic in the streets.

There was no foreseeing exactly how Marrowbone's demise and false reports contrived around the *Terrible Swift Sword*'s arrival and rapid destruction would sit with the Passwaterites except that the news would probably spook them. And by spooking them, Purifyre's field agents hoped to factionalize them and thus weaken DevOcean's influence with the grandees and the general population.

Dawn was breaking, however, and the Human Enlightenment agents still hadn't returned. Muffled hubbub and flickers of light glimpsed over the revetments made it clear the town-folk were abroad in the streets, perturbed as insects in a jostled hive. As Eyewash peaked over the horizon at the start of a long northern hemisphere Big Sere day, Testamentor's unease began to show. When the first warning tone had sounded, signaling that the *Dream Castle* would be taking to the air again in one hour, he had made distracted, minute poppings with his lips, *pih-pih-pihpih,* the Trans-Bourne equivalent of rattling worry beads or gnawing a thumbnail.

Ghost spoke for the first time in hours. "Let me go look for them. My companions are a guarantee I'll come back." In point of fact, Zinsser and Spume didn't constitute a guarantee; losses were to be expected in any expedition, and she was inured to the fortunes of war.

Testamentor didn't go for it, in any case. He resumed surveillance from the shuttered window as passengers began straggling back aboard the Laputa, the tension in his back and hunched shoulders betraying the toll the long wait had taken on him.

At last the final warning tone sounded. Everyone in the cabin could hear the ratcheting of the capstan as it took up slack in the gangplank cable. Testamentor came off his chair with a single move and seemed about to yell out the window, but instead he turned and began moving baggage and bundling Human Enlightenment vestments and other odds and ends off the cabin's bed.

Surmising that there had been unexpected trouble, Ghost asked, "How many are hurt?"

Testamentor didn't answer her.

Moments later, the ground party stumbled into the cabin, their sea-green DevOcean robes soiled and torn and showing blood. All had wounds. Four were on their feet, but Boskoh was being carried, the lower half of his robe sodden and dark.

Sterling sat down exhausted on a stool, examining his cuts and scrapes. "It emerges that there's a certain hostility in Pass-water that wasn't here when we planned this essay."

Jolly elaborated while he helped Testamentor cut away Boskoh's robes to get at the wounds. "The writings and preachings of Marrowbone have come into prominence because he and his acolytes espouse a severe brand of DevOcean, holding that the test of the rapture is imminent. Extremists say that with his death the last days have begun, that DevOcean must now begin consigning itself to the Oceanic. Word of the destruction of the Visitant's celestial car added fuel. Then there is Asurao."

Testamentor started. "The Feral slaughter boss is here? But that cannot be. We saw him at the funeral pyre, and the distance is too great."

Jolly shrugged. "Perhaps he rode a dozen remounts into the ground getting here, or a hundred. What would it matter to *that* one? Anyroad, he's camped outside the wall. What he's here for, no sane man can know. But Marrowbone's partisans put the worst face on it."

Honesty rather than ego gave Ghost a sudden conviction she knew why he'd come to Passwater. But what did he want from her?

"Why were you attacked?" Testamentor questioned Jolly absently. His examination of Boskoh's wounds drew shuddering cries from the votary as *Dream Castle* made ready to lift off.

Sterling snorted. "Debate at the Skull Bunker became insanity, which spilled out into the street. We were accused of doing Marrowbone in by those who have canonized him and accused by those opposed of trying to make a martyr of him."

"We were denounced as being grandeean spies, Human Enlightenment agents, and Visitant doppelgangers," one of the others put in.

"Some wanted to exile us from Passwater, and others wanted to chuck us off the battlements to the Scourland Ferals," Sterling interjected. "Boskoh was stabbed by Marrowbone's senior wife."

"Calls for the elders to proclaim these the final days facilitated our escape," Jolly said. "The elders are being urged to torch the town, destroy everything, and begin entering the Amnion. We came to kick up a stingers' nest and instead set off a volcano."

"No loss," Testamentor said brusquely. "The DevOceans, Passwater—let the Ferals have them, let the Oceanic." He had finished his quick examination of Boskoh. "It's bad; his stomach's hard with blood."

Bravuro was suddenly animated. "Give me your scudos. One of my loyal camarados has shamanic poultices and secret balms made from the kiss of life itself. I'll go fetch—"

Testamentor spun on him, drawing the peculiar hand weapon from his sash. "Stay put, informer, or I'll burn you in half. Only charlatans and quacks tarry among your bunch. Boskoh must endure on his own strength beyond what little we can do for him."

"What the hell," Ghost said, sighing. "I'll treat his wounds." In the silence that followed she added, "The med-pack instrument you took from me uses intersecting microwaves to cauterize deep lacerations."

She was nodding to the archeo-hacking brute memory unit. She wasn't actually interested in helping Boskoh, but any chance to get out of her bonds was worth a shot. She could see Testamentor wanted to believe her, his sense of obligation to his subordinates working on him again.

"Look, ask the Sense-maker," she prodded him. "They used one on him in the *GammaLAW*'s clinic."

It was a crapshoot. Quiet most of the day, drifting into delirium once or twice, Spume could well betray her or start raving, but even that wouldn't constitute much of a setback under the circumstances.

Testamentor agonized, then said, "Instruct me and I'll do it."

Ghost shook her head. "Takes practice, and you couldn't even read the machine. You could boil his stomach or blow him apart like a roasted poi-pea."

Sterling knelt by Old Spume, laying the beveled edge of his knife along the Sense-maker's throat. "How now, jelly belly? Is she telling the truth?"

Ghost and Zinsser had both hunkered around to gaze down from the separate bunks on which they lay bound. Spume's eyes cleared under Sterling's prodding, but his laugh sounded addled. "They can perform miracles! The question with Visitants is always, *Will* they? And for what price?"

Not exactly a resounding endorsement, Ghost was telling herself, when Boskoh gurgled in pain. The weight of command showed on Testamentor's face as he indicated Ghost with his chin.

"Sit her on the bed. Loosen only her hands. Wrists and ankles and all stay tied. Sterling, take hold of her choke noose." He began to lay out the various items he had confiscated from her.

Not only did Sterling wind the choke loop around his hand, he took up the bloopgun as well. Ghost figured he couldn't know much about it if he was thinking of firing it in close quarters; more likely, he was wielding it to intimidate her. Flexing her freed-up thumbs and fingers, she fumbled at the memory unit and her detached pistol scope, deliberately dropping them.

"I need my wrists and elbows. These two teknics have to be connected, then held on opposite sides of the damage."

Testamentor was feeling more confident now that he had precautions in place. He slipped the knots himself. "If you play false, I'll burn your head from your body."

He set the ropes down and drew the hand weapon from his sash. She saw its compact bulk and tiny aperture but still couldn't dope out what it was or where Human Enlightenment had gotten it. Jolly and one of the others moved to Zinsser and Spume with knives out, just in case.

Marrowbone's senior wife had done a thorough job on Boskoh. Ghost doubted that anything short of Glorianna Theiss's surgery could save him. "A couple of you hold lamps so I can see what I'm doing."

The Laputa gave one of its characteristic little lurches, buffeted by winds over the Amnion as it gained altitude. "Someone has to keep Boskoh absolutely still, understand?

And close the shutters and curtains; it's like a polar storm in here."

She sorted through the adapters, leaving the scope and memory unit on the bed. Then she flexed her jaw, making ready. Flowstate was as deep and steady as a river in her. She would free herself or die—either outcome was a victory.

Testamentor ordered Bravuro to close the shutters. The rest left Zinsser and Spume unattended to look for lamps or take gingerly grips on Boskoh's shoulders and legs. Their attention was divided because they unconsciously assumed that the hazard phase would come when Ghost hooked up her diabolical Visitant apparatus. Only Testamentor and Sterling were vigilant.

She took Testamentor's free hand. "When I tell you to, I want you to push in on his side." She leaned close enough to smell his breath. "And whatever you do—"

While he was still looking confused, she rolled the primed spit-needle around from the side of her jaw to hold it lightly in her front teeth. Her preparatory bite a moment before had primed it, arming the injector and freeing its tiny whisk tail to deploy on release. It would discharge its toxin upon penetration of her target.

Everything around her stopped. She could count the pores in Testamentor's face, the individual hairs of his eyelashes, the irregularities of his strong teeth. She shot with one short, unforced puff. Her time sense was so accelerated that she saw the tiny dart fly true, straight into Testamentor's tongue.

Ghost clutched Testamentor to her as the spit-needle worked its lethal magic; then she threw their combined weight backward across the dying body of the stabbed Boskoh. The first class cabin of the *Dream Castle* became bedlam, but her Flowstate provided a clear course of action.

The onset of the spit-needle's neurotoxin was so rapid that Testamentor's attempt to batter Ghost away lacked strength and coordination. It was the single capsule Burning had given her on the night of the Grand Attendance, a weapon so small even the Human Enlightenment operatives' search had missed it. Even so, the opportunity it afforded would last only seconds.

As Testamentor's weight came with her, she levered him into Sterling's line of fire. Sterling had yet to understand just what had happened, but he was already starting to yank on Ghost's choke noose. Her chief concerns, however, were the bloopgun and Sterling's ignorance of it. Jolly and the other agents provocateurs were still seconds away from comprehending and reacting to her offensive. Bravuro the peddler was flattened against the bulkhead, trying to avoid any involvement.

Boskoh screamed as Ghost and Testamentor landed on him; blood from his belly wound wet her back. She wrestled Testamentor's strange gun from his grip and fired it at Sterling's head, if only because a lower shot might have endangered Zinsser.

Light in the cabin changed to illumination-round-bright as a narrow cone of plasmic fire caught Sterling square in the face. Venturis in the gun blared, dampening the back blast, and a searing wash of heat scorched the overhead planks. Sterling had no time to cry out, yank the choke noose, or fire the bloopgun. As his skull ruptured explosively and his skin melted away, he teetered backward. Old Spume shrieked, and Zinsser yelled in surprise.

To the bellowing and snarling of the other operatives, Ghost kicked Testamentor's body out of the way and propelled herself off the side of the bed toward Sterling's remains. The oddity gun's stellar flare had made the air hot to breathe, and the stench of Sterling's immolated flesh evoked the worst of the battlefield. Wrenching the bloopgun from his hands, she swung her bound knees out of her own line of fire and hastily squeezed off a round at the operative who was about to pierce her with a sling-gun quarrel. The bloopgun made its popping belch, and the Enlightenment man did a real life derezz, flying apart in segments.

Instinctively, Ghost had shrunk away from the hit. The impact performance of the monomol bolas rounds could be unpredictable, and even a stray part of the spinning web was capable of taking off a hand or leg as easily as it had finished the Aquam.

"On your right!" Zinsser hollered at her.

Armed with a whip razor, another agent had circled around and was scrambling across Testamentor's convulsing body and Boskoh's thrashing one to pounce at her. Ghost couldn't bring the gun to bear in time, so instead she angled her head away, swinging her hair and presenting her arched neck. The Aquam naturally aimed for it, thinking to partially decapitate her with a cutting edge almost as keen as carbon-vapor deposition.

The whip razor cleaved neatly through the outer layers of her pitch-black hair but was turned by the bundles of monomol fibers woven into her underlying Hussar Plaits. Hampered as he already was by Boskoh's hemorrhaging body, the man was drawn off balance by the blow, giving Ghost just enough time to clutch the bloopgun to her. Absurdly outsized as it was for a pistol, it was maneuverable at close quarters. She swung it at the razor man and shot the top half of him away, his bottom half adding to the mess on the bed.

That left only the sixth Enlightenment operative, Jolly. Who had flinched back and dropped his double-ended

fighting sickle. He was covered with the blood of his comrades, just as the cabin's walls and ceiling were, his face
running with a visor of red gore through which he blinked
dazedly. Ghost aimed the muzzle at him and Bravuro, who
was still cowering against the bulkhead.

The move threw the peddler into a panic. Snatching
up a sling-gun by the barrel, he swung the stock hard into
the back of Jolly's head, and Jolly fell—probably concussed,
Ghost judged. She kept the muzzle trained on Bravuro,
nevertheless, even after he had dropped the sling-gun to
the floor.

"Would you slay one who fought for you?" he babbled. "I
never wronged you! They threatened my life, as well!"

"Lay that fishhook remover over here," she said, meaning the fighting sickle *"gently*. Then get a blanket and put
out those flames."

The single shot from the plasma gun had set some of
the woodwork flickering. In the relative silence, Boskoh's
death rattle was clearly audible. Bravuro eased the sickle
within Ghost's reach, then slid toward the door.

"I'll alert the fire detail!"

Ghost nestled the back of the bloopgun's receiver
against her shoulder to steady it and squinted at him over
the barrel. "Not without legs, you won't."

Reversing direction, Bravuro yanked a blanket off a
bunk and climbed up to slap at the small flames. With one
hand on the Manipulant cannon, Ghost sawed through
the ropes on her legs and knees. Her circulation had been
restricted for so long, she wasn't sure she could stand, and
so she hiked herself across the deck on her behind to free
Zinsser's hands. The sickle blades being somewhat clumsy at
that angle, she used one of the crescent moon handguards'
cutting edges.

"Finish yourself and Spume, Doctor," she told him. "Then take up a sling-gun, please."

He accepted the fighting sickle brusquely. " 'Thank you for the warning, Raoul' would be asking too much of you, I take it?"

She brushed aside some of the hair that had been chopped through by the whip razor and now lay draped on her right epaulet. "I had him spotted, Doctor. But if it's that important to you, thanks for your good intentions."

He had no time for a rejoinder; someone was suddenly swinging a splitting maul against the outer door. Despite her legs feeling like they had had anesthetic spikes driven through them, Ghost got to her feet, leaned against the bulkhead, and slid back the bolt of the inner door. Cracking it, she cocked an ear in the tiny entranceway.

"This is the supercargo! What's afoot in there? Open up or we'll break down the door!"

Ghost checked the bloopgun's drum magazine. Four rounds remaining—but how many crewmen? It was time to convince the supercargo that Visitants didn't need a Laputa to fly.

CHAPTER THIRTY-FIVE

After Boon, Purifyre, and Ballyhoot left, Mason returned to the table where he and Boon had eaten. Boon hadn't explained how he knew about Yatt, and the AI itself was ominously silent within him despite Mason's attempts to communicate. He intended only to sleep off his suspicion, confusion, and anger on the pillows, but indifferent sampling of the dining board led to famished eating, after which he slept like the dead for the entire night.

He was bathed in his sweat when Ballyhoot woke him in the morning, prodding him to consciousness with the butt of the grip of a fighting flail. "Lay off," he told her. "I'm awake."

"Arise, then," she said with the slight slur her filed teeth made unavoidable.

She had changed clothes yet again, to a unisex traveling outfit of wafty culottes and featherweight blouson. She was unarmed except for the fighting flail, but the flail was daunting enough—a half meter of ironbound maoriwood handle and a swingle nearly as long, joined by a thick three-link chain. The swingle was girded at the tip and midsection with iron collars studded with long pyramidal spikes.

Ballyhoot's hair was unbound and combed out as it had been at Wall Water, a striking fall of pearl-gray and flint-black that flared over broad shoulders, reaching halfway down her back. Mason blinked at the sudden insight that her wild mane would make a nice addition to someone else's trophy topknot collection, which was, of course, the point.

"Cozmote and Purifyre have things to show you," she said. "Beginning downstairs."

Mason took it as a good sign. Boon couldn't help himself from showing off. Soon he was bound to press for details about Yatt's use of the cybercaul, which meant that Mason could press in return for details about Boon's plans for the Oceanic. Ballyhoot gave him a final rap on the thigh, but he refused to give her the satisfaction of wincing.

Instead, he sat and stretched, seeing from the shadows that it was shortly after dawn. He ran his hands through his sweat-soaked hair and foraged for food on the uncleared table. When Ballyhoot shot him a last contemptuous glance, he rose quickly to his feet.

Immediately, she fell into in a half crouch, her thick physique bunching under the lightweight peasant getup. Her forefinger moved just a hair on the flail to slide the little hook on the swingle out of the ring on the handle. The business end of the weapon swung loose and ready by its three links of chain.

"Something to say, Visitant?"

"Only that you've nothing to fear from me."

"That I *know*, berry-balls."

Brows flaring, aquiline nose creasing, she showed her teeth. To Mason she looked like something requiring an exorcist. "Ballyhoot, I care as much about Purifyre's well-being as you do, but I've no intention of trying to edge you out of his affections. We owe it to him to be tolerant of one another."

She spit a gob that hit his bare stomach. "Visitant pule talk!" She straightened from her fighting crouch, giving the flail a deft spin that rebooked the swingle to the haft. "You bare your throat to me and think *that* will make us compatriots? It's beyond my understanding how that boy could spring from any blood of yours."

"Credit Incandessa," Mason muttered.

She shook her head and sneered. "Don't keep Cozmote waiting."

Mason used a hand cloth dipped into a petal-scented finger bowl of water to wipe off the spittle, as well as some of his sweat. Then he fastened the stomacher around him, setting the clip holster into it, and found his rope sandals; none of it was done in any hurry. If goodwill was the wrong approach south of the Styx, he would try another.

Descending the stairs, he was pointed toward the center of the house by an Anathemite domestic. Mason ignored the directions and hunted up a *necessarium* at the rear of the layout, a common arrangement. After relieving and laving himself, he strolled back the way he had been bidden.

He followed the sound of voices through the fragrant afternoon simmer to a small pleasure garden very different from the formal showplaces at Wall Water. His ear singled out Purifyre's voice.

"—I'm sure Kinbreed and his partisans have no inkling of our intentions up north. Yet, if those constables who wear the clover hamper our free access to the bridge, especially if other Gapshotters take up arms in sympathy, it could mean ruin for us."

Boon's tone was derisive. "The clover faction's no better than Gapshot itself. They lack energy and a vision of their own and grow greedy and treacherous watching wealth come hard-earned to the Trans-Bourne."

"Kinbreed's neither greedy nor treacherous," Purifyre remarked stubbornly.

"Then his Gapshot chauvinism has let him be swayed by those who are," Boon replied.

"But how will you answer the clover faction's manifesto?" Turnswain asked. "To yield control of the northern end of the bridge is to yield all."

"We don't need long-term solutions," Boon told him. "Soon our entire strategic situation in the Trans-Bourne will be remade. *Aquamarine* will be remade. For now we'll make concessionary gestures. Bribe, threaten, whatever circumstances dictate—but most of all, delay."

Boon said it with relish, making Mason speculate what would happen if and when Boon and Dextra Haven squared off in the muck-wrestling pit of interplanetary diplomacy.

"I proposed joint negotiations with the Gapshotters," Boon continued, "with the bridge authority paying handsome compensation to delegates from their side as well as ours. By sundown every greedy string puller, mooch, and parasite in greater Gapshot will be climbing over each other's head for a billet, demanding Kinbreed give compromise a chance."

"And should Kinbreed choose not to?" Turnswain asked.

Instead of answering, Boon raised his voice to a half shout. "Claude, you city boy, you're not tromping on my kraken seedlings are you? Get on out here. There's a tour bus leaving and your son and I expect you to be on it."

Mason surrendered to the inevitable and pressed through the screen of foliage as Boon was responding to Turnswain's question.

"If the club-clovers try to dislodge us from the bridge by force of arms, we execute the Horatio option. That's why I built it into the bridge." Boon turned to Mason. "Stop to smell the viperwort, did you?"

Mason had emerged onto a pleasant patio in the center of the atrium's hothouse lushness. Cushioned chaises and tables with light refreshments had been set out.

Along with Boon, Purifyre, and Turnswain were three Aquam men and a woman—Anathemites all—dressed in the apparel of Trans-Bourners of consequence. Ballyhoot stood stiffly to one side, the fighting flail gripped behind her like a swagger stick. On the flagstones sat the two Science Side modules forced into a pair of beat-up, leather-padded freight chests. Two men were lashing them closed.

"Just wrapping up some loose ends," Boon said, "and waiting for you."

"I'm off excess baggage status?"

"You never were excess anything. You count as family here. And I want to see what you think of the *insider*'s Trans-Bourne."

The last thing Mason wanted after almost three days of muscle car travel was to be dragged on a Trans-Bourne sightseeing tour. But so be it, if it was the only way for him to get to the heart of Boon's plans.

Boon and Purifyre led the way, with other Aquam lugging the Science Side modules and Ballyhoot bringing up the rear, fighting flail in hand. Mason trooped with them to a part of the compound he hadn't visited. A muscle car waited on a low parking mound; other wagons were undergoing refit nearby. Some had saw-toothed iron hub blades long enough to shatter another car's spokes as well as shielded firing spots at the rails. A few featured push-off poles and grapnels and linstock rests for big pivot guns like the one Ballyhoot had used to launch the sodium and water incendiary round on the Panhard.

Purifyre had said that economic realities, the requirements of commerce, and the nature of the high roads made war cars and autobahn battle impractical. But Boon appeared to hold a dissenting opinion. The car he showed Mason was a far cry from the fighting wagons or *Shattertail,* however. A ramshackle six-wheeler with leprous scarlet paint almost hidden under grime, it looked as though it had been cobbled together by some gigantic child.

Nevertheless, Boon indicated it with a flourish. "Good old *Arse-Grinder,* my first commercially viable car."

"The name doesn't say much for your marketing instincts, Eisley," Mason commented.

"Your wrong, Claude. Irreverent names were a major factor in public acceptance of these brawn buggies."

Boon's beloved prototype was piled with boxes of metal-reinforced gears and galvani distributor boxes. The freight chests and science field units were nested into spaces among the boxes of parts, then concealed with still more cargo.

Purifyre's confederates took the grabs; Turnswain, the helm. More of the Anathemite household members pulled chocks for the launch, and the outramp gave *Arse-Grinder* a gentle downhill out to the roadway. The exit gate opened, and Mason was headed south once more, buckling his stomacher tight and coughing a bit in the powdery yellow dust.

Missy and Pelta were prancing around out on the *Racknuts*'s deck, giggling and striking poses in the ribbon bonnets Burning had bought them as a diversionary tactic. Down in the treadle compartment he could still hear muffled voices and noises from the parking mounds on Hunchborrow Hill. So much the better for his little caper, he told himself. Eyewash was climbing into clear skies, and the cooking odors were strong. Outlandish as Aquam cuisine was, the smells made him ravenous. He held the tiny wick light out the trapdoor for a last look around before beginning.

The space was cramped, especially forward of the treadles, where the car's foul-weather canopy and similar unneeded tackle were stored. He groaned, stretching his lower back muscles. The previous day's travel had taught him why Boner and the boys kept their sashes knotted tight and why Missy and Pelta, and especially Manna, usually wore cincture kidney wraps. He had found it preferable to stand, but in any posture the ride was like being a buoy bell in a squall.

Arching the kinks in his back, he considered the distributor and Optimant-salvage electrical wiring he had glimpsed on his earlier recon of the car. *Racknuts* also had self-greasing wheel hubs to preserve the axle spindles—simple but clever. It was these Trans-Bourne carwrights that the GammaLAW mission should have been engaging them from the outset, Burning thought.

Step clomping came from overhead—Manna's bare foot and *repoussé*-carved ivory peg leg on the deck.

"What're you about there, you crooked-snouted, rust-haired limpwick?" She scowled down through the hatch at him, hefting a big sloshing carboy of some Analeptic Fix ingredient.

"Just admiring your—"

"Out of my way and make yourself scarce, ya lesion-lipped cloud of anal gas!"

He moved fast despite his aches. Once he had made way, Manna began lowering the makings for the crucial part of her Analeptic Fix.

The parking mounds on Hunchburrow Hill didn't have nearly the bite-mite and blood midge population of Lake Ea, but the air was vile with assorted insect-repellent unguents and the dung-fire smoke that was an inadequate antibug defense. Burning himself smelled gamey, which let him blend in with everybody and everything else in the mounds.

He found Souljourner at a small cooking fire, clasping thumbs with a dry-goods huckster to seal a deal. She forced a smile for his sake, showing him what she had spent the last hour dickering over: two broad waistcinchers of stiff, four-ply pogopod leather, looking like weight-lifting belts or bikers' kidney protectors. He wasn't surprised to see she had bought ones with laces and eyelets rather than metal buckles; metal and crafting were expensive on Aquamarine.

He accepted the cincher gratefully, figuring to wear it under his pistol belt. Ahead loomed another full day of getting jounced and slammed around on *Racknuts,* but with luck, sunset would find them in Gapshot. Souljourner had also bought some cheap coverlets, two singles rather than a double, he was relieved to see.

While he was lacing up the kidney belt to check for size, she showed him other purchases: a three-liter skin of clear water and a crude funnel strainer, tooth pumice and a bristle brush they could share, a wafer of gritty soap, a wooden cup they could use to avoid communal dippers and drinking bowls, a tweezer made from freshwater shell for plucking mites and vermin, and a folded-frond package of dried fruit, pickled vegetable chunks, and fried insect larvae.

"Momma-Mountain Manna's brewing up her medicine," Burning said.

That got her attention. "Do you think she suspects what you've done?"

He weighed the pistol belt in one hand; short a couple of items, it was a bit lighter. "No, or she'd have put a slinggun quarrel through the back of my head and hacked you up for the people-cutlet vendors."

But what Manna wouldn't do was pull chocks and run. She had been eyeing his gold buttons more and more obsessively as the journey wore on. To keep her cooperative, Burning had left them in place, soot- and grease-covered, rather than cutting them off and pocketing them for safekeeping.

Souljourner was screwing up her nerve. He had a pretty good idea what was coming from the way she was thumbing the pouch at her neck. "I was wondering if you'd consider—"

She broke off when a man appeared in the spot the huckster had vacated. This one was well fed, with beautifully oiled and arranged hair, wearing a costly harlequin blouse and knee breeches. He carried a ringmaster's whip, its butt bulging like a blackjack, probably weighted with iron or lead. Sets of crude manacles clanked on his hip, hanging on his baldric.

He was leading four dazed, sunken-eyed children who were collared and linked at the neck by a rope, their hands bound behind them. The slaver wore no vizard because, like most hawkers and hucksters, he supposedly wanted to show the honesty in his face.

"Good wishes to you!" He gazed down fondly at Souljourner and Burning as if he'd run into old friends. "You're a young couple who, I can tell by your looks, prosper and are in need of body servants befitting your status. Here I bring you the finest merchandise at prices forced on me by an overstock."

"Go away," Burning told him.

But like a lot of other salespeople, the child seller believed in persistence. "Buy one and get the second at half price! They're in perfect health, eager to please. Ideal body servants, toothsome love toys when they get a bit more flesh on them. Speaking of flesh, if you're bound east or south,

the meat sellers are paying top scudo for choice tender livestock like this—"

"Flood damn you!"

Souljourner had jumped to her feet with her pot-metal
knife out, held upside down so she could swing the beveled edge up in a gutting stroke. "Go away or die here, you
monster!"

Burning leapt to hold her back—no light work. The slaver stumbled away, calling back curses at them both and
dragging the children after him. If his pistol's 'wailer still
worked, Burning might have headcheesed the man, though
it wouldn't have done much good. The children were probably legally owned. He had seen enough of the high roads
to know that even if he set them free, the kids would odds
on become someone else's property in a day or two. And in
the doing he stood to get himself spitted or found out and
taken prisoner.

Souljourner sank back down of her own accord, putting
away her knife and ramming her fingers up into her hair.
Someone else might have wept, but he knew by now that
crying was something she simply didn't do.

"The wide world's not the way I envisioned it in Pyx," she
moaned, half to herself. "Not the way all the brave, romantic sagas would have it. Redtails, I wanted so much for you
to love ... Aquamarine."

She took out her bibelot, the little book Aquam consulted to interpret the prophesies of the Holy Rollers.
Running her forefinger along it, she did the forelock toss
that corresponded to a shrug. "Nothing's as I dream it would
be. I don't know what to think." She glanced up at him with
such entreaty that it hurt. "I've a favor to beg: money to buy
new Holy Rollers. If I cast the cleromancies with borrowed
dice, it lacks affinity."

And tossing those galloping dominoes in the state you're in might lead to anything, he suspected, from further depression to the expectation that he surrender to romantic destiny between her legs in some Hunchburrow Hill bedroll. Either way it could set her up to loathe him, something he couldn't afford to do.

"I have to think it over," he said after a moment. "We might need every scudo and more to find my sister."

Her forced smile and head tic of acceptance made him feel like more of a shitheel than he would have felt like if she *had* wept. Then she got up, eyes averted to her big hands, digging at one forefinger nail with the other.

"I thought I'd get some ointment for your nose. Can we afford that?"

The Big Sere sun had done a job on his pale, broken snoot. He grinned and thanked her. "Meet me back at *Racknuts* after Manna's done making her Fix additive. We'll see if we can't retromod her attitude a little."

Burning finally rose. He roamed the parking mounds until he located a fortune teller who employed Holy Rollers and a bibelot of the same sort Souljourner used. Business was slow, and for a few brass scudos the man agreed to take him into a tent to explain the significance of each number-color combination, the chapter and verse of the cleromancies.

CHAPTER THIRTY-SIX

At 0900 local, as per Daddy D's order, Zone had mustered the other seven members of his shore party on the flight deck. Even without the heat of engine blast and jet wash, the fierce Big Sere sun made the deck feel like a solar griddle. Still, Zone felt a ventilating breeze pass through him as he contemplated his next move in the game of taking control of the ship.

Daddy D hadn't said why he wanted the shore party mustered, though Zone was certain it had something to do with the discovery of the WHOAsuit marker beacon. Quant and Haven probably had themselves convinced that Burning was hiding on shore, when in fact Zone and his several knew him to be far from Lake Ea in pursuit of his sister. Lacking air assets, Daddy D had to be thinking of lowering the shore party in a hoist to board some sort of improvised amphib craft. But why in full daylight, when an actual landing would be affected under cover of darkness? A practice drill? Whatever games the old man had in mind, Zone supposed that he should string him along for a while. Endgame was downriver, and it was eventually going to be his, one way or another.

Wetbar, Roust, Strop, and the rest were lounging around the pile of equipment they had put together for the mission, casual but alert, as he had warned them they had better be. Drill or not, the materials they were carrying made it an all-or-nothing run. Zone was staking everything on their ableness and daring.

Wetbar eased over to him. "You want us to take Hole Card back belowdecks until we know what's coming down?" Hole Card was code for the item around which the plan revolved.

"No," Zone told him. "I don't trust leaving it behind. If anyone tries to snoop, you give them the straight eye and tell them to go piss up a rope—"

He stopped to listen to a sound that seemed strange on the silent flight deck. The aircraft elevator at the waist was in motion. It had been below, at hangar deck level, but now it was rising with a slow, powerful hum that traveled through the deck and nonskid to their boot soles. People rose or turned from where they had been killing time as the elevator rose into sight with the machine it was carrying.

Every one of them recognized the old Hellhog helicopter the moment they saw it. It was Daddy D's personal ship, antiquated and outmoded but carried for decades on his reserve outfit's TO&E and therefore kept serviceable. The last time anyone had seen it was on Concordance—on Anvil Tor, where it had crash-landed. Zone, like most Exts, had assumed that that was where it had been left.

Suddenly all the crates of supposed community action–related equipment Haven had finessed through LOGCOM added up, likewise the flurry of activity over on the hangar deck the previous night. The Hellhog had been thoroughly rebuilt but still had the air of a bad job of technological taxidermy.

An old crony of Delecado's, Senior Captain Feelie Shumakova, sat in the copilot's seat. Daddy D leaned out the pilot's side window, gesturing to Zone.

"Pile aboard, Colonel. We'll take a spin and see what the locals're doing. I could use the blade time." He touched the control panel in front of him, and the engine came to life with surprising zeal and smoothness. "Don't want to lose my flight qualification," he finished in an amiable yell.

No one but Delecado and Feelie Shumakova could fly the damn helo. Among other things, the reanimated bird carcass had a tail rotor instead of a NOTAR thruster system. Some of Zone's detail could handle VTOLs and modern helos but not Daddy D's museum piece. Delecado had stolen a double march: producing an aircraft instead of letting Zone steal ashore on his own and, at that, an aircraft that his opponent couldn't wrest from him once they had set out. But Zone betrayed none of this.

"Yeah, let's take us a ride, General," he called, motioning to his team at the same time. "Mount up."

Daddy D was first on the scoreboard with a two-pointer, Zone told himself. That was all-around okay; worthy opponents were the ones most worth destroying utterly.

"Travelin' a little fat, ain't ya, Colonel?" Delecado had to yell to be heard over the sound of the chopper's engine and idling blades as Zone and his team piled their equipment aboard. "*Two* RIBs?" he commented, eyeing the rigid inflatable boat transport modules. Various smaller items were clamped and strapped to the modules. "You planning to set up a ferry service?"

One case was for the fifteen-person RIB, the largest one aboard. The other was for a six-occupant boat, and two such would have made more sense given the size of the shore party.

Zone gave the issue an easy dismissal. "Can't tell what we'll need to get into on the lake or the reservoir. I'm just anticipating the unexpected."

You're a lying young turd, as well, the general reflected, gazing back to his controls. But step out of line today, and your ass is mine.

Given the RIB boxes, things were somewhat cramped in the payload space, but the team managed to squeeze aboard. Zone's severalmates grunted disapproval at the stench of death that lingered below the aromas of solvents, fuel, and metal. Despite the Hellhog's having been disassembled, reassembled, and refurbished, the muddy fecal reek of a stalled ground war had followed it all the way from Concordance.

"Anvil Tor!" Roust shouted, barely audible.

Delecado nodded. "A whiff of memory lane." Maybe it would make them realize that things could be worse, he told himself.

Quant's airboss had concurred that the safest procedure would be to lift off directly from the elevator. Shumakova had the cockpit displays well behaved and liftoff-ready. Like Delecado, the senior captain was fond of the old hog with its big cyclical and collective controls. Commo was jammed and the visionics were acting a little glitchy, but the day was clear and the general wasn't about to abort.

Delecado had decided against a test flight under the assumption that it would merely provide an unnecessary opportunity for things to go wrong. His takeoff was a little jouncy, but his old touch returned with each passing second. He went thwopping past the island bridge and swept up the deck and away over the end of the flight deck's ski-jump bow.

Like Zone's doubles, Wetbar and the lanky woman, Strop, slid into the door gunners' seats, hooking up to the harnesses and manning the ancient monobarrel 50s. The general said nothing when he noticed—in the rearview—that the two were trading conspiratorial smirks with Zone. Instead, he jacked the troop stick leader's headset line into his helmet.

The morning light was more white than yellow, the lake-water like a pitted mirror. Like most chopper pilots, Delecado and Shumakova were primarily visual fliers. The ability to maneuver in three dimensions made them wary of relying on instruments. Both were keeping their focus in the air before them nearly one hundred percent of the time, exploiting full corner-of-the-eye lateral awareness.

While he deemed it highly unlikely Rhodes could elevate his steam gun for antiaircraft fire, Delecado veered well clear of its possible field of fire. From five hundred meters, as they swept in toward Wall Water, the magnitude of the damage to aquaculture farming on the lake was apparent. Seeing the swath the *GammaLAW* had cut through the seine kraals, the pontoon walkways, and the harvesting rafts, Delecado marveled that the ship had managed to survive intact He dismissed the notion of trying to give Quant a cam feed of the sight by maserphone. He had other priorities, such as considering and discarding possibilities as to just what Zone was up to.

Taking his time in a long, circular approach, he made his first pass over the dam and the dam crest road. The scorch marks of the No-Load's slush hydrogen fireball were visible, but the immense Optimant structure didn't look noticeably the worse for it except for knocked-loose scraps of latter-day patching.

A few Aquam lingered on the crest road leading from Wall Water south to the muscle car parking grounds and elsewhere. Peons and hoi polloi mostly, the general figured, caught between the conflicts among local grandees and between grandee and Visitant. He made no overtly menacing moves, but the people below cringed and cowered anyway or broke and ran madly. Assuming that some of the munitions Starkweather's *Jotan* had misdelivered had landed among the locals, he didn't blame them one iota for their terror.

He felt bad about adding to their misery, but it couldn't be helped. He began descending slowly, all lights flashing and Feelie Shumakova hollering over the PA for the locals to clear the area. Delecado circled for a landing, hoping they would get the hint and simply make themselves scarce. A few brave souls fired sling-gun rounds or slung stones, and some ballsy type even chucked a harpoon at the chopper. The missiles lofted up lazily, no threat to an armored flying machine.

Some formidable marksman—or lucky shot—sent a quarrel from a large arquebus rattling off the whirlybird's side. Delecado caught the whirr of the servos as Strop swung her door gun around to lay down some scorch.

"Tell your fucknuts mates to hold fire!" Delecado barked to Zone. "Our people might be down there someplace." He had nearly hit the overrides to lock down the door guns but restrained himself.

Zone passed the order woodenly. Strop complied but kept a trigger-happy gleam in her eye. A few more shots came, then the road began to clear as the small crowd melted away. The general made more passes, each one slower and lower, eyeballing the terrain. There were no signs of heliograph signals or of Ext or Periapt MIAs.

The prop wash kicked up a lot of dust. Delecado saw at once that maserphone contact with the SWATHship would be impossible because of shoreline features that obscured *GammaLAW* from his line of sight. As the copter settled, stragglers on the dam crest road pressed back toward the north end.

Delecado hunched around in his armored seat to motion to Zone. "De-ass and establish area security. Then have a look around, see if anybody left us some pasigraphs or trail sign." Ext field symbols could be unobtrusive but would tell rescuers exactly where and how to make rendezvous.

Zone began ticking off people by shoulder touch, giving them their instructions by hand signal with the plain intention of sitting tight in the hog.

"You go with 'em," Delecado ordered. "Make sure nobody gets cantankerous." A quick, glowering calculation flitted behind Zone's eyes. Delecado got the distinct impression that he was mulling a move then and there and that he was not quite ready for it. "Go lead your team, Colonel. Your door gunners'll guard the hog."

The idea of Strop and Wetbar on the 50s must have reassured Zone. He passed the headset jack to Wetbar, piled out, and oversaw the deplaning and deployment of his team.

The area around the helo was trampled flat, empty except for the broken sandals, dropped staffs or packs, ripped clothing, and other debris the Aquam had lost in their hysteria to get away.

Zone had emerged with his rifle in a shoulder-sling carry on his strong side. Confident that his team could handle security and that he himself would spot any danger worth noting, he was concentrating on his troop disposition rather than the Aquam. Delecado watched him trot beyond the rotor's arc in a crouch, retrieving the boomer by cupping the stock and spinning it butt forward clockwise. He caught the fore end of the boomer as it came full turn and held the weapon ready but with no hint of tension.

In answer, Delecado brought the helo's chin turret chaingun on-line. Slaved to his visor, he elevated and traversed the weapon so that it was pointed at the ground between Zone's feet. Still, the colonel showed no surprise or disquietude.

"See you 'n' raise you," Delecado muttered, more to himself. "Let's find out just what kind of game we're playing here."

"Stand down, Daddy," Wetbar rasped from behind him.

Delecado's eyes shifted to the payload bay rearview. Roust and Wetbar couldn't point the 50s onboard due to the pintle interrupter templates, but both had drawn their side-arms. Despite the armored seats, Zone's severalmates had angles of fire for a head shot, and a flight helmet wouldn't be much protection against a 'baller round.

"This hand's over," Wetbar added. "You lose, so fold 'em."

Chapter Thirty-Seven

For an old clunker, *Arse-Grinder* was tight and spry. It wheeled along between fields of royal purple slackwort, hot pink quoinflowers, and cadmium-green summer poi-peas.

Mason was obliged to listen to Boon ramble on about the Lake Thalassa mollusk tissue that powered it: how responsive and durable the sarcomeres were, how resistant to destructive electrogeny, how piezoelectrically potent the organic gems that were Scourland galvani stones … Mason listened with half an ear, watching Purifyre confer in the prow with Ballyhoot and his other intimates. The car rolled past gutted Optimant ruins, thatched manufactories, and adobe manor houses whose gates looked as if they hadn't been closed in years. Field after field was given over to cultivation of whackleaf.

"Another funding source, Eisley?" Mason asked.

Boon gave a tic of confirmation. "Tobacco financed the American revolution, narcotics underwrote Old Earth terrorists, so why not? I hybridized a potent new strain, but the linchpin was to make whackweed a prestige smoke. The snob factor was my best salesman."

"No matter that the Aquam are slowly killing themselves on the stuff."

"They'd smoke anyway, Claude, just as they sell their own children, hack each other up, and think nothing of the wind-carried bacteria from their own shit. So don't imply that I've lowered the wellness factor of the neighborhood. It's the Dark Ages here, you hypocrite."

"*I'm* a hypocrite? You're the one who claims to want to save the place."

"Only from their fears of the Oceanic, friend. Then they're on their own."

The old six-wheeler treadled on through a stretch of parched, eroded unfarmed land, leaving the road at one of the tumbledown PrePlague sites. The place looked like one more lesser Optimant manor half gone to rubble. What was standing had been repaired to livability by some struggling manufacts enterprise. The cottage industry had spilled over into a minimally renovated outbuilding that had obviously been a telecom-SATlink annex two hundred years earlier.

Most of the antenna mounts were bare, their fixtures either scavenged for metal or toppled over by decay and weather, but one ten-meter-diameter marigold dish was still standing, appearing to be made of some composite and therefore not worth the trouble of chopping up as scrap. Frozen in place, it was festooned with creepers and dangle-moss, reminding Mason of the one Yatt had made use of at Wall Water to bring down the *Jotan.*

As the pumpercar jounced closer, Mason saw neatly cleared and tilled land surrounding the derelict manor. Binnies and veejums and other small food animals scrounged in the open or huddled in hutches and pens. He spied thriving tray crops and two aquaculture ponds, enough to sustain a crafts commune or teknics work that was getting by, if not prospering. It was not logically the sort of place to which Boon would bring the science mods.

People looked up, but none registered any surprise or agitation at *Arse-Grinder*'s creaking, clacking passage through their midst. Grabsmen plied their tall levers to halt in what had obviously been a multivehicle garage or freight dock. Now it held agricultural tools, foodstocks in barrels and cribs, odds and ends of lumber and cordage, and small barrows and sledges. There was an assortment of shoulder poles and a mud area for cleaning sandals or feet. Close at hand, both inside and out, were well-used sling-guns, fighting flails, and other farm implements that could be used for defense.

Mason joined everyone in trooping through the corridors and hallways of the manor house, the mods remaining in their leather-padded freight chests. The structure was in far better shape than was apparent on the outside. As much fortified blockhouse complex as agro-artisanry collective, it was as bearable as could be expected in the Big Sere. Mason saw metalsmithing and wiredrawing shops and glassblowing and ceramics workspaces.

Their destination was a onetime grand ballroom where Optimant TechNobles must have staged their spectacles and mounted their experiments in competitive decadence. Now—decor plundered and dead pixel walls a drab null-gray—it was just a place with soaring headroom, clean but frowsy and drab. At the moment it was staffed by only a few of Boon's commoners.

The echoing hall also held equipment whose likes neither Mason nor—he was certain—anyone else in LAW had ever seen. There were banks of handmade thermionic vacuum tubes ranging up to a meter in height; imperfections of the thick, blownglass walls rippled and distorted the images of people and equipment on the other side of them, the electrodes of manually shaped filament and hammered metal wafer now inactive and dark. Leads and power cables of recycled Optimant wire had been painstakingly rewrapped and insulated with plant sap. Routing junctions made of large knife switches stood in multiple rows, representing fortunes in metal in Aquam terms.

The place smelled of graphite, lamp oil, lichen, stone dust, burned insulation, and scorched metal. The device at the center of it all, meticulously but not prettily breadboarded into place on a worktable as if on an altar, nearly drew a laugh from Mason.

It was an inelegant, staunch little backpack telecom station known as an UGLI-44. The device's carry harness and casing had been removed, and its guts had been opened up. Ports, peripherals and power inputs were kludge-rigged to the homemade systemry like some cybernetic patient on Edison-era life support.

"Had it hidden in the dunes the night I died," Boon explained.

"Being marooned with only a few pieces of hardware, you could've done a lot worse than this one," Mason conceded.

One corner of the former ballroom was taken up by racks of wet batteries fed by heavy power lines that led into the chamber from above.

"Primary electrical source is a photovoltaic array I scrounged together from Optimant junk," Boon said. "For backup there's a small generator that'll run off a human-powered treadmill or muscle car drive wheels. For emergencies, a standby bank of galvani stones."

"What, no windmill?" Mason said in obvious sarcasm. "Surely, down here no one's going to engage in restraint of trade with a knife and leave you for dead in a ditch."

Boon was not at all amused by the flip reference to his first, nearly lethal attempt at planetary betterment. "There're windmills on some of the isolated islands, but I don't want anybody in Scorpia or the Trans-Bourne so much as looking at one until I'm ready to disseminate the technology. No more technological revolutions until my organization is in position to control and benefit from them."

Mason offered a begrudging nod. "You always did learn from your mistakes, Eisley. I take it the roof antenna's not a derelict, then?"

"What do you think?"

He led Mason past an improvised condenser the size of a desk, running his hand lovingly along its white ceramic flank. "Even the overgrowth on the dish is phony. But of course we can move it only at night—which usually costs abundant sweat, believe me—and have to have it back in its accustomed position before daylight. But it's yielded dribs and drabs of Periapt traffic these past few years. It told me you were coming, Claude." He held Mason's gaze. "Or rather the Quantum College told me. Yatt, at any rate."

"But how did Yatt determine that you were here?"

"It simply determined that someone downride had been monitoring the *Scepter*'s departure via uplink computers. Yatt then sent a twixt to Aquamarine—which I responded to. After that Yatt made certain to keep me apprised of preparations for the GammaLAW mission."

Mason reeled, expecting the AI to speak up, but his thoughts remained his own. "Then the SATs *didn't* go off-line after the *Scepter* left. You were using them."

Boon grinned. "Hardly any trick to it. After all, I had *your* authority to access the SATs directly. All I did was build in trapdoors, which I opened as soon as *Scepter* launched."

Mason somehow managed to suppress his rage. If not for Boon's takeover, he might have been able to stay in touch with Incandessa's father, might have learned from Rhodes the Elder that the child had survived and that Mason had a son named Purifyre, might even have communicated with the boy as he was growing up, the way Yatt had evidently done with Boon. But Mason only put on a bland face to hide his white-hot musings and shrugged. "What's done is done."

Boon looked at him askance. "I appreciate your saying that—I think."

Mason gestured to the UGLI-44 telecom. "During the raid at Wall Water, I was flabbergasted at how well informed Purifyre was, how prepared. With forewarning, though, I'm surprised you didn't do even better."

"I didn't have as much commo intel as all that," Boon confessed. "After the Quantum College informed me that LAW was dispatching the *Matsya*—the *GammaLAW*—along with one cyberaugmented Claude Mason, the signals deteriorated. Interception of Periapt signals and the *Sword's* in-transit and orbital stuff were spotty, to say the least. Planetary rotation, malfs, weather—not to mention the Oceanic's roiling of the commo spectrum when it gets restless. Then there were just plain quirks of fate." He fell silent briefly, then added, "When do I get to hear from Yatt?"

Mason bristled. "You don't. I'm not Yatt's goddamn mouthpiece. I'll keep you apprised of its deliberations as I see fit."

Boon grinned. "I have to tell you, Claude, it was bitwitted of Haven to have the *GammaLAW* set down in Lake Ea. I'd assumed she'd go with the original plan of splashing down in Thalassa. I've had to alter my plans continuously as her mistakes mount up."

"Blame Commissioner Starkweather for the change in plans," Mason snapped.

"Well, it doesn't matter now. Fortunately, we'd infiltrated Wall Water years back. Rhodes the Younger has a knack for making people dislike him. Fertile ground for recruiting spies."

Mason recalled the beauty from Rhodes's living throne who had passed information to Purifyre on the stronghold terrace.

"And yet some things still went against us," Boon continued, frowning. "Haven's Ext bodyguards were formidable; otherwise we might've nabbed Doctor Zinsser, even Haven herself. And of course I never counted on you people inciting the Oceanic with a tether maneuver."

"Starkweather, again," Mason said. "But suppose the *Sword* hadn't been destroyed. What then?"

Boon shrugged. "We would have waited until it launched for Hierophant. As it was, we did every bit as well as we needed to."

"You have me to thank for the Science Side modules," Mason couldn't help saying. "Me, not Yatt. I was told by Rhodes and Old Spume that Purifyre would be pleased to see examples of Periapt technology, so I talked Haven and Zinsser and the rest into a demo. *I'm* why the units came ashore."

He looked for a reaction from Purifyre, but the boy was already convoying the mods along through a door on the far side of the former ballroom. Apparently, the preposterous Frankenstein's-lab commo center wasn't their final destination.

Mason trailed along through a dark, moldy corridor off the ballroom to find himself in another lofty room not much smaller than the ballroom—a former salon or media chamber, perhaps. There it was all vats, retorts, and other glassware; valves, gauges, pipes, and related plumbing; and the sharp smell of chemical baths mingling with those of metal filings, varnished and caulked wood, and residues of smoke and ash.

"Fish tranquilizer?" Mason asked. When Boon nodded, he couldn't suppress a chortle. "*This* is what you're planning to use on the Oceanic? Eisley, the Oceanic'll neutralize it molecule by molecule! I expected you to have volcanoes hooked up for thermal power, or some sort of blimp air force waiting in the wings."

Boon was more resigned than offended. "I'm *not* brewing tranks, old friend."

Mason touched his mouth in thought. "Then what's all this about? What are you planning?"

"To give the Oceanic a personality crisis. To force it to feel the pangs of rejection."

"The Oceanic is one symbiotic system," Mason countered. "Even LAW was smart enough to figure that out."

"Yes, which is precisely why it abhors creatures like you and me, who have evolved through competition. All that fang and claw nastiness. It wouldn't surprise me if the Oceanic proves unique in our exploration of other worlds, because from its earliest origins natural selection favored cooperation and harmony of all its discrete parts—no predation as we know it. The individual motes that constitute it recognize each other because of a synome—a chemical messenger—basic and common to every one of them."

Mason took another look at the vats and gauges and related plumbing. "You're brewing a ... synome antagonist?"

"A molecular virus," Boon clarified. "And I'm hoping that those science mods will help bring all this to fruition."

Mason's expression mixed revelation and defeat. "I think they just might."

Boon smiled madly. "The virus will need to be introduced in critical mass—in bulk sufficient to overcome the Oceanic's localized resistance. Then it will propagate itself throughout the organism and cause a breakdown of all higher functions." He took a step toward Mason. "After vectoring with the antagonist, the Oceanic will become a broth of altogether healthy but independent and competitive, highly prolific microorganisms, nothing much higher than a string of cells. The Amnion and Aquamarine will belong to human beings."

Mason's jaw dropped a notch. "You concocted a bio-weapon of that order in this, this *soup kitchen?*"

Boon scowled at him. "Use your head! It took years of R&D. Data acquisition, supercomputer modeling, testing..."

When Mason still didn't get it, Boon made an exasperated sound, grabbed the cybercaul from the hands of one of his subordinates, and waved it about. "The Optimants, Claude! Those monstrous egos couldn't bear the fact that Aquamarine's dominant life-form is the Oceanic. It was in their faces constantly."

"They created the antagonist," Mason said in sudden revelation. "Then why in God's name didn't they use it?"

Boon chuckled ruefully. "They were about to—or at least they were in the middle of a planet-wide debate as to whether to use it."

Mason took a moment to puzzle it out. "The Cyberplagues! They began here, on Aquamarine. I—Yatt extracted that much from the Smicker's bust computer."

Boon's sneering grin suggested something on a pirate flag. "You guessed, Claude: the Optimants *created* the Plagues."

CHAPTER THIRTY-EIGHT

The supercargo's fist, thumping the outer portal of the first class cabin, made less of a din than the splitting mauls had, but Ghost knew the mauls hadn't backed off far.

"I plead your mercy, most respected sir, but I cannot open the door," Bravuro called back. "The DevOceanites demand privacy in which to conduct their meditations. They bid me send you these tokens in appreciation of your zeal."

Choking back sobs, the peddler began sliding gold scudos under the door, shoving each one through with Old Spume's pen. Ghost stood behind Bravuro with her fighting knife to his back.

There was momentary peace on the other side, after which the supercargo hit the wood again. "'DevOceanites,' my clanging tallywags! Spies, fugitives, is more like it! I'm told that three furtive characters from the steve spaces are in there. The scarface woman and her man are said to be Visitants in disguise. And what's that smoke I smell?"

"A spilled lamp," Bravuro replied. "But we've seen to it."

That last part was true, at any rate. The flames ignited by the firing of Testamentor's detonator-cap pistol had been extinguished. Ghost prodded Bravuro's back, and he sighed deeply, pushing another gold lozenge under the door.

"There's blood on this one!" the supercargo rumbled. "Unlock or by the flood, when I lay hands on you, I'll cut off your whorepipe and throw it to the Oceanic!"

Two more scudos.

When the supercargo spoke again, he sounded somewhat mollified. "Understand, now, I hate to disturb anybody's religious services, but the Insiders command me by way of the speaking mesh to find out what's about in there."

At Ghost's insistence, Bravuro slid another pair of scudos under the door. "The holy ones ask if you'd reassure the Insiders that all's well. The DevOceanites will make clear their gratitude."

"I shall try, but the Insiders know something's afoot." The supercargo sounded dubious now, but he was retreating. "Placations mean little when they're concerned about the safety of the *Dream Castle*. All who ride the outerworks have good reason for apprehension—including me and thee." The deck planks creaked under him as he went away.

Ghost drew Bravuro up and led him back into the cabin, moving limberly now that the circulation had returned to her legs. He knew the drill sufficiently to go to a bunk and keep quiet. Zinsser had gotten past his nausea at the carnage she had wrought and was completing his search of the bodies with the same clinical detachment she supposed he brought to dissecting marine organisms. Old Spume had been helping, but now he was staring off into space again, looking even waxier than he had when taken prisoner. His veins were dark webworks, and patches of his fuzzy new growth of hair had fallen out.

Ghost helped Zinsser roll Jolly, the only survivor, against the wall. Jolly hadn't regained consciousness from Bravuro's blow to the back of the head, and Ghost didn't expect him to. Even so, she directed Zinsser to tie the man's hands behind him. The oceanographer demonstrably knew his way around ropes and knots.

The possessions they gathered included sling-guns, assorted close-quarters weapons, a fair poke of scudos, some food, changes of clothing, and small personal items. Still, it was insufficient for tackling the Laputa's scores of crew members, concessionaires, and passengers. The bloopgun was a major acquisition, but it contained only four rounds. A dozen charges remained for the detonator-cap blaster.

Gumption, the next groundfall, was the better part of two days away, the Trans-Bourne much farther, and Lake Ea nine full days of flight time from where they were. Ghost doubted they could stall the supercargo for nearly that long. For one thing, a lot of blood had leaked down through the floorboards, and someone was going to notice it sooner or later. For another, the supercargo now had the smell of gold in his nostrils, and his hunger for scudos would be far greater than their means to satiate it. Then there were the Insiders. The outerworks existed only by their sufferance; violent conflict could provoke them to take apocalyptic measures.

Ghost decided that their only option was to try to take refuge in the Laputa's inner hull, the risks notwithstanding. She therefore sorted through the fruits of battle and found Spume's jimmy–burglar tool. Tossing it to Bravuro, she indicated the bulkhead plank Testamentar had prized up earlier for a glimpse of the unvandalized hull hatch.

"Start prying up the bottoms of the wallboards." To Zinsser she added, "If we have to fall back, it might as well be to somewhere warm and pressurized."

Zinsser finished buckling on Testamentar's fine pair of snow boots. "They're picky about who they let in there, remember?" He began shoving his belongings into the pockets of his capuchin cloak—the useless plugphone, the jetpen, and the Roke tissue sample specimen case.

"Don't worry about it," she said. "The panel probably doesn't lead directly onboard. More likely to some utility crawlspace where we can lay up. We'll pull the boards back into place after us, let the supercargo think we went out the window on wings of Visitant magic." She glanced at Bravuro. "Get busy!"

The peddler held the jimmy but rolled his head. "Meddle with the Insiders? I'd rather die."

Ghost grabbed the largest sling-gun, threw the contoured stock to her shoulder, and pointed it at him. Old Spume phased in for a moment, saw dazedly what was going on, and slid away from Bravuro. "Shall I pin you to the wall, or would you prefer to jump out the window?"

Bravuro pirouetted, knelt, and applied himself with the energy of a man on piecework wages, while Ghost and Zinsser heaved the dead and parts thereof out the window. They were spared any agonizing over Jolly, because he had died. Then they turned their attention to the wallboards, shifting the wardrobe over and propping the planks up.

The hull access was coated with soot and grease but otherwise unremarkable. Ghost fetched her scope and her wrist whatty, along with its sundry adapters and archeo-hacking 'wares.

"Even if we manage to hide out until landfall, how do we get groundside without getting sonicked?" Zinsser asked.

Ghost shrugged. "Set the outerworks on fire and lose ourselves in the stampede. Or maybe we try and disable the sonics or the whole works." She found the adapter that had fit the other hatch's control panel and started puzzling over the connections. "Doctor, what d'you know about paravanes, gliders, and ultralights?"

"Not enough to make one."

"We only need the leavings of one—something to convince the supercargo we just *whsshhht!* sailed out the window." She hefted the det-cap shooter. "We can make enough heat, blast, and light to convince them that *something* went rocketing out of here.

"A red herring," Zinsser mused. "Well, for a start I'd say we need some charred scraps of wood, snippets of rope, fabric trimmings. A few boards propped by the window could be made to appear to be a launch ramp." He picked up the double-ended fighting sickle and began digging and prying at a bulkhead plank. "But you're completely insane, you know."

Ghost ignored the remark. As she was turning to her own work, Old Spume reached out to seize her arm. "No rescue's coming, is it?"

Instead of shaking him off, she spoke in a comforting tone of voice. "Rescue's here, Sense-maker, and it's us. Hold on a little longer and you'll be young again, like you were aboard the *GammaLAW.*"

"Oo-ohh, that was *savory,*" he said, spraying a bit. "You Visitants changed my old head with that. Yes, that's worth abiding for—for a little longer, anyway."

When his hand had fallen away, Ghost began tapping into the hatch's control box. Even with what she'd learned from the Smicker's bust data, she had no idea how to probe the Laputa's protocols, but the whatty would see to most of it. Using data from the *Scepter* survey team's findings, the Aggregate had assembled gear that mounted penetration campaigns without user guidance. It was a violation of Post-Cyberplague legislation, to be sure, but Dextra Haven had concealed the gear from both LAW and outside oversight.

Ghost determined that the control box was still taping power and memory from somewhere. As the 'wares wangled their way up the line, moving quickly because she'd tasked them simply with opening the hatch, details of the archeohacking reached a fevered pitch. At the same time, there was renewed pounding at the cabin door.

Leaving the 'wares to continue their cybernetic offensive, Ghost picked up the sling-gun longrifle. "Bravuro, grab the rest of the scudos and precede me."

That he did so willingly told her that he was hoping to find a bolt-hole. At the outer door the peddler knelt to shove another gold scudo under the door. "Most revered overseer, the pious ones are still at their panegyrics and—"

A maul strike set the door trembling on its hinges. "The Insiders will have no more stalling!" the supercargo called. "Open or they'll drop away this part of the outerworks!" With that the frame timbers and between-deck beams began to groan and shift, and the stanchions to squeal. "They'll cast you to the Oceanic, I say! Emerge or die!"

Having had a look at the construction of the outerworks, Ghost didn't buy that the Insiders could be so selective in their jettisoning. Listening closely, she heard the scrape of metal on metal and the ratcheting of the gangplank treadmill. It was clear that crewmen were using prybars and hauling tackle to shift the first class structural members in an attempt to panic the besieged. Bravuro was too terrified to realize that, however, or to consider that the supercargo might now think him a traitor. When he put his hand on the bolt, she warned, "I'll nail you there like an eviction notice if you don't—"

Even Flowstate didn't make her immune to surprise attack, and Bravuro—pumped so full of adrenalin it was practically dribbling out his ears—moved very fast. Holding in one hand the cylinder of Old Spume's acid shooter, he spun, ramming the pump piston with the heel of his other hand and wriggling out of the longrifle's line of tire as the acid spewed at Ghost's eyes.

She ducked away, raising a shoulder and turning so that the thrown-back hood of her capuchin shielded her. Simultaneously, she pulled back the sling-gun so Bravuro couldn't grab its forestock and peeled off an unaimed side-kick to prevent his closing on her. The thick wingle shearling of the hood and shoulder sizzled and shriveled, giving off white-green smoke but protecting her.

It came as no surprise that the side kick missed. Straightening, Ghost saw Bravuro heave the three-batten door open. Two saffron-clad crewmen stood just outside, with the supercargo watching from a safe distance behind. Saffrons with iron pinchbars and long wooden pole levers were at work in the background.

She let Bravuro have the semibroadhead quarrel in the back, high up and to the left of the spine; it was his bad luck to know of their plan to hide in the crawl space. The power of the longrifle drove the quarrel through his chest so that the fletching disappeared into his body and blood pumped from the wound as he collapsed forward.

Ghost had used her one round, however, and had no time to reload. Saffrons with basket-hilted cudgels, having seized hold of the open door, were already reaching for her. Falling back behind the inner entrance door would leave only it between the crew and the first class cabin, with no escape route.

Some of the saffrons had sling-guns, but the ones at the fore were blocking their lines of fire. Ghost parried an oncoming crewman's cudgel with the longrifle while he was still trying to shove Bravuro out of the way. Ramming the muzzle into his eye, she sent him floundering back.

But now a saffron marksman rose out of the press to draw a bead on her with a repeating crossbow. She was at once twisting aside to avoid the bolt and bringing the forestock around to jar his weapon and crease his temple when she heard the slap of a sling-gun behind her. A cork-headed nonlethal round rebounded from the man's furrowed brow, and his eyes rolled up in his head.

Dropping the long gun, she braced both hands on the sides of the entrance and got the sole of one moccasin-mukluk on Bravuro's dying ass. Leg-pressed, the peddler and the crewman went toppling clear, and Ghost slammed the door shut. Zinsser, who had fired over her shoulder, gave her a hand getting the bolt closed. Fists and hammers immediately thudded again on the other side, further loosening it.

"The archeo-hacking 'wares are signaling," Zinsser panted.

Ghost was pleased enough with his timely aid that she didn't fault him for using a knockdown quarrel when he should have taken out his target with a pilehead, a broadhead, or even the bloopgun. Forcing the detonator-charge pistol into his hand, she told him to hold the crewmen at bay. "If they chop a hole in the door, shoot through it."

Back inside the cabin she eased carefully out of the acideaten capuchin cloak and ducked under the pryed-up bulkhead planks. The 'wares were toning and blinking, awaiting her next prompt. If they couldn't arrange an open sesame soon, it would be time to try blowing a hole in the hatch with the det-cap blaster. As she gave the prompt, Zinsser—abandoning his post with civilian unconcern and leaning into the cabin to see what she was doing—shouted, "Not yet! Wait!"

She realized why as long-inert effectuators came to life somewhere. The door unsealed with a kissing pop, and the opening crack blasted a vertical tidal wave of air at her from the dark, forbidden inner precincts of the Laputa. The blast turned to steam and carried long horsetails of dust and thick fuzz planetoids—stuff that hadn't been disturbed in perhaps several lifetimes.

Too late she realized that *Dream Castle*'s inner hull was pressurized while the outerworks were at ambient pressure, many meters up in the Aquam sky. Once more it served to remind her that Flowstate and the Skills didn't convey invulnerability or genius.

Ghost tumbled, aware that Zinsser was fighting his way through the fringes of the air flood and that Old Spume was caterwauling in fear. Warm, damp, and dense under Optimant climate control, the air turned to a snowblower stream as it hit the high, thin atmosphere of first class.

By the time Ghost had taken the fall and rolled clear, however, the storm was already abating; apparently, only a small volume of space in the Laputa proper had been depressurized—perhaps no more than a small room's worth. She came to her feet with ice crystals coating the front of her, stiffening her hair, and sugaring her face and scars.

The poundings at the outer door increased, intensified by the bite of an axe. Zinsser, who had grabbed a lamp, passed it and the bloopgun to Ghost, then edged back to his post. She leaned back into the dark within the Flying Pavilion's skin, only to discover that she had been right: they had broken through to a utility interhull access, with closed hatches a few meters away in either direction. Junction boxes and service units were visible, as well as cable and systemry runs leading every which way. Everything was overlaid with dust and drift like some gray-white, time-bearded tech mausoleum.

Up, down, side to side—Ghost saw no sign of life, security system response, or booby traps. She withdrew and set the lamp aside just as the det-cap blaster gushed a shot.

"What's your status, Doctor?" she yelled over her shoulder.

The banging and chopping at the outer door had stopped, but Zinsser's voice was high with tension. "I doubt I hit anyone, but they've moved back for now. Burned my damn hand."

"Leave the inner door open for now and fall back and help me. There'll be time for another shot if we need it."

A hasty sacking of the Enlightenment agents' weapons, food, water, and other belongings made for a considerable pile, if not enough to sit out a long siege. If things got desperate during the long run back to Wall Water, she and Zinsser might be able to open one or more of the other hatches surreptitiously and forage or burglarize in the steve space.

Ghost shagged ass, transferring weapons, water skins, haversacks of food, and rolls of bedding onboard, laying them on the precious little unoccupied deck space and other horizontal surfaces that came to hand. Her motion stirred storms of swirling motes and wafting rafts of fiber.

She stopped Zinsser as he was about to load up with provisions. "Can you rig up a convincing escape rope and throw it over the side? As if we climbed down to the pulsejet bowl and got away from there?" The odds and ends of purportive glider scraps he had assembled didn't look very convincing, but then, the Aquam probably wouldn't have known a real one if it fell on them.

He glanced at all the rope the Enlightenment agents had left behind. "I can try. But will the supercargo buy it?"

"Probably not, but it'll keep him preoccupied awhile."

Zinsser nodded, considering the longest loop of line in the lot. "I'll singe the end. Maybe he'll think our afterburners—wait." A sudden thought made him glance up. "What if they come at us across the roof?"

She shook her head. "I saw a roof trapdoor in the steve spaces, but there's none in first class. Besides, I doubt that even the fear of the Insiders could make the crew drag themselves across the top of the outerworks while this thing's in flight."

As Zinsser was anchoring the rope to an upright, Ghost sliced three big, irregular bandannas of DevOcean robe and tied one around her lower face as a filter against the angel hair and dust. She threw a second strip of DevOcean cloth on Spume's lap as he sat unmoving, watching her. "Put that on."

He didn't react except to study her unpitying, scar-bordered eyes with his rheumy ones. "I'm dying, aren't I, Lady Frightface?"

"Yes."

"And you lied to me about rescue being on the way."

"I did. But if you stick with us, if you don't quit, you might make it yet. No promises, though."

"I'm very tired. I'd like to sleep, but I don't seem able to."

She stepped back from him, bringing up the shortest sling-gun, which was Y-stocked and decorated with spirals of brass nail heads. It was cocked and held a bodkin-tipped armor piercer.

"I understand, old man, but I can't leave you here to tell them where we've gone. You're not strong enough to hold out once they start racking you around." She leveled the muzzle at his heart. "There's nothing to fear in death, Spume. And once you know that, there's nothing to fear in life. So don't move. I'll make this quick."

On Concordance she had helped many a wounded Ext comrade take the knife. But as her finger was tightening on the trigger, a concussion shook the whole cabin. The crew had rigged a battering ram, and from the sound of it, they didn't fear another short-range tongue of flame from the det caps.

Spume's eyes went wide. Leaning away from the muzzle, he made a hand-opening gesture, flinging his fingertips out from one another—acquiescence to fate mixed with a quixotic need to struggle on.

"Young or old, I want to live. Live until I die."

She put up the quarrel-thrower for the time being. "You'd better. Because the next time you play the poor, pitiful victim, you'll *be* one."

CHAPTER THIRTY-NINE

"**S**hut down your engine, General," Wetbar ordered Daddy D, his 'baller centered on the back of the old man's flight helmet. Sitting behind the copilot's seat, Strop kept Feelie Shumakova covered in the same way.

"We win no matter what," Wetbar added. "Relax; make this all-the-way easy."

"Like I'd come out here without a hole card to play, ya cum-brain?" Delecado said wryly. "That's ripe!"

He didn't even have to move his arm off his seat's armrest to tap the door gun servo overrides he had reprogrammed aboard the *GammaLAW*. The 50s whined on their powered pintles, barrels elevating and mounts retracting into the payload bay, smashing both Strop and Wetbar back against their gunners' seats and pinning them firmly. Strop's 'baller was pointing uselessly at the cabin ceiling, and Wetbar's was directed out the door on his side.

The tactic only gained Delecado and Shumakova a moment's advantage, but they were prepared to exploit it. The senior captain whirled in his seat, Flowstate-sure, 'baller already drawn, set to sonics. With Aquam technology as primitive as it was, Strop and Wetbar had, like most Exts, long since stopped keeping their battlesuits' antiphasing countersonics suites online. At close range and with their helmet breathers open, visors raised, they were easily headcheesed with one good dose apiece.

At the same time Daddy D had returned his attention to Zone, who was standing stock-still to one side of the Hellhog. He had his rifle leveled at the windscreen but was well aware that he was squarely in the crosshairs of the chaingun. Delecado got on the chopper's external PA. "I want you to back off a few steps there, Colonel, while we sort this thing out."

Zone did so, without showing anger or resentment. At his hand signals the rest of his team did the same, fanning out, weapons covering the Hellhog.

"Feelie, get in the back and crack the RIB modules— both of them," Delecado told his old friend. Before deciding how to deal with Zone, he wanted to know just what kind of betrayal Zone had lined up. "You troubled youth out there, just stand fast," he warned over the PA, putting an end to everyone's edging out to improve their cross fire.

Behind Delecado, Shumakova opened the larger RIB module. "Well, God fuck me dead," the copilot muttered.

"What is it, Feelie? I can't look around just now."

"It's the Soosie unit we lifted back on Periapt, General— the superconducting warhead."

"BuddhAllah!" Delecado grated. "Don't screw with it; he might have it rigged."

"Not that I can see. Some antitamper charges, but they're inactive, and so's the Su-C itself."

Delecado didn't waste time wondering how Zone had spirited it out of its high-security strong room aboard the *GammaLAW.* "Zone, you synaptshit bastard," he said over the horn. "First your lucky No-Load detonation, now this. You're planning to blow the dam. By why, for Chrissakes?

Take the knife if life's got you so down. No need to take everyone on the ship with you."

Zone mouthed something impossible to hear; then, in sudden decision, he grounded his helmet, handed off his boomer and 'baller, and opened the front panel of his battlesuit to expose himself to fire. Tentatively he stepped around to the pilot's side to speak directly to Delecado.

Leaving Shumakova to cover the others, Delecado slid back the forward window panel and laid his own pistol across the window frame. "Far enough," he said while Zone was still two meters away. As inhumanly fast as the man was, Delecado was confident that he could put a few sinkers into him before he could close and grapple. With the engine at low idle and the blades barely turning, they would be able to hear each other now. "So your act isn't just a pose to shake up real and imagined competition. You really *are* crazy, son."

"Not about this," Zone countered. "Blowing the dam's lower gates will force Quant to move *GammaLAW* downriver to New Alexandria. What's waiting down there will put the world in our palm. The Exts, I mean—not the Periapts."

Delecado stared at him. "What's the nature of this magic lamp, Colonel?"

"First prove you're with me. Feather the engine; let me back aboard."

Delecado didn't have time for a game of deception and counterconning, not with Zone's team members looking a bit squirmy. "Not likely, son. Now, make like an angel and tell the rest of your people to lay down their arms."

Only when that much was done would Zone be allowed aboard the Hellhog—to be brigged, back on the ship, along with Strop and Wetbar. Then Delecado would return with a flying squad to take the others prisoner. All of them would have enough sense not to take to the boonies of a hostile and aroused Scorpia.

Zone, however, saw things differently. "I've come too far to listen to your crap, old man. No one's laying down arms."

His tone was supposed to be a reminder of just how dangerous he was, how cool under fire, how impervious to the fears that made others falter, fail, lose face. But Delecado was unshaken. "All you've come to is the end, Colonel."

Zone shrugged. "Your end, not mine."

Delecado was looking for him to duck or dodge, perhaps even try to dive under the Hellhog. But instead Zone held something out to him as if it were an offering, and Delecado's moment's indecision in accepting it gave Zone all he opening he needed.

A blast in the cockpit blinded Delecado with white light and burst both his eardrums. Thick smoke filled the hog in an instant, choking pilot and copilot both. Delecado squeezed the trigger regardless, firing blindly until he felt the 'baller wrenched from his hand.

Cocooned in a shockproof bunker of Flowstate that contained the agonies of the explosion and the misery of having been outmaneuvered, he realized what had happened. At least some of the seemingly inactive antitampering charges wired to the Su-C warhead were under the control of a handheld detonator—an ultrasonic, most likely, since it had functioned despite the ambient jamming. All Zone had needed to do was get close enough to use it, and Delecado, unaware, had let him.

The Hellhog shuddered to the firing of the chin turret as Shumakova, too, lashed out blindly. In response came forceful bursts directly in front of Delecado as Zone's teammates used their boomers on the windshield, fragmenting it.

Delecado could feel the concussion of Shumakova's armored seat back being penetrated by the fearsome punch of 20-mm's. Feelie made no sound, but the chin turret went silent and Delecado knew that they'd nailed him. Zone began bellowing for his people to cease firing. If they ignited the chopper's fuel, the Su-C warhead and the module containing the genuine RIB would be destroyed.

Delecado fumbled for his own weapons control side grip, meaning to take the sons of bitches under fire again, but he felt his arm yanked away, his flight helmet torn off, and the muzzle of his own 'baller jammed brutally hard against his temple.

"Endgame, old man," Zone said, passing sentence.

"Yours isn't far off," the general gasped, the smoke residue pumicing his throat.

"I used to think that, Daddy D. But now? Now I'm a man with a future—*the* man."

Delecado spit blindly at the source of the voice and had the impression he scored. "Not a man," he contradicted. "You never quite hacked the qualifications. Just an animal who learned how to pass—"

A world-engulfing force front knocked his head sideways, expanding into his skull with a brutal energy beyond light, sound, and impact. His skull swelled to half again its normal size, and an eruption of tissue, bone, and blood jetted from the round's point of entry. Out of his body entirely, his risen self saw half his brains and skull flung across Shumakova's body and chair armor.

The last of an old guard, dead at his post.

Zone stepped back a pace, still wrapped in a Flowstate as hammeringly chill and prismatic as a cloudless polar day. He signaled his team back to their feet—all but Digger Taraki, who had been hit by Shumakova's blind hosing. Of

Digger there was little left but two bloody leg stumps still in their boots.

Moving around to the open payload bay door on the copilot's side, Zone saw that there had been one other casualty. A stray 20 had caught Strop as she lay, sonicked unconscious, trapped behind the retracted door gun. Her own blood had spattered her face; Zone licked some off for a last taste of her, kissed her once on the forehead, and moved on.

As the others got the RIB and Su-C modules off, Zone began reallocating people to cover all the jobs that needed doing. That now included setting demolition charges on the Hellhog. It had suffered damage, but it couldn't be permitted to fall into Aquam hands; none of his people could fly it, in any case.

Wetbar and Roust had begun prepping the Su-C explosive. Its intended use as a stupendous sapper charge rather than a warhead made it that much easier to set, but Wetbar still looked troubled.

Zone nudged him. "What?"

"I know the modeling says the reservoir'll tamp the explosion against the back of the dam and blow just the floodgates. But now that I see this place up close, I'm not so sure." He indicated the dam's patches and signs of decay. "What if we figured wrong?"

"As long as the water gets from up here to down there." Zone tapped him on the shoulder with Daddy D's 'baller. "You want to worry about something, worry about what we'll miss out on if we don't make this work."

"Due to unforeseen cost overruns I invoke the unwritten laws of fare adjustment," Manna announced. "It'll cost you another button to ride so much as a single wheel rev farther."

Racknuts was finally preparing to unchock and depart Hunchburrow Hill. Keeping well clear of the confrontation, Boner was checking the play in the tall wooden steering wheel, while Spin and Yake occupied themselves raising *Racknuts*'s hinged drag staves and securing them upright. Missy and Pelta remained hidden in the treadle compartment.

"Other cars will gladly bear us for less," Souljourner said.

Manna stamped her sculpted ivory peg leg and leaned conspicuously on her arquebus sling-gun. "You chartered *Racknuts*! Welsh out now and I'll denounce you to the whole camp, let all know the grandees' troops want you! There's plenty who'll have a go at you for reward money."

"Reward?" Burning echoed mildly.

Manna cackled and spit slackwort juice over the rail. "What'll details matter once every roughneck at the mounds anticipates gold scudos from your capture?"

"Maybe we'll save them the trouble and give ourselves up," Burning said with a forelock-tossing shrug. "And while we're at it we can tell them that you make Analeptic Fix with a precipitate of metaflax and a few drops of that decoction of Nixie you keep on hand." To a car's freshwater-mussel muscles, the decoction was analogous to a shot of speed.

Manna almost keeled over on her peg leg. "How, wh—you *witches*! It, it matters not if you know the ingredients. You don't know the measurements or the secrets of preparation."

"In truth we do, fairly well," Souljourner corrected, "just as we know that you don't use the concentrate of pithpod you buy—that pithpod's only a false clue to misdirect any who spy on your preparations."

"And you know as well as we do," Burning added, "that any minor details we get wrong, your competition can work out through trial and error."

"Perhaps we'll set the recipe to music," Souljourner said. "All Scorpia could sing along."

"Now haul your mumu out of our way and pull chocks," Burning said. "We're wasting daylight."

Morose but silent in the bow, the old termagant got them under way. Without Manna's usual bellow and brimstone, it was more like shoving off on a funeral procession. Burning breathed easier once they were thumping west again to rejoin the RambleRove. He and Souljourner rode with their backs to the gunwale just forward of Missy and Pelta's hatch.

"You were right about the Nixie decoction," he told her. "Very, very good."

Earlier that same morning, he had managed to patch his dismounted pistol scope to the whatty auxiliary memory unit and conceal it in the treadle compartment just before Manna had chased him off and settled in to do her alchemy.

"I just give thanks I could make sense from the freakish variegations of your scape pictures."

" 'Scope', not 'scape'. You should be proud. It's not easy making sense of imagery enhancement—even for people who have practiced."

"Fortunate that Manna didn't challenge me on details," Souljourner admitted. "There were particulars the scope didn't pick up." That was due in part to viewpoint angle and in part to the edge of a flap on the folded, unused bow awning in which the jerry-rig had been hidden. "Anyroad, you can thank the former mixmaster at Pyx, who instructed me in the secrets of pharmaceutical brewing and distilling." She smiled brightly despite constant headaches conjured by

Oceanic's foul mood. "Will Manna abide by this enforced truce?"

"If we keep our guard up," Burning answered. He was hoping an aircav rescue would make the question academic. "Between the gold and the Analeptic Fix recipe, it shouldn't be too hard to keep her checkmated." He paused to prize the Holy Rollers out of his pouch. "I got you these to show my appreciation."

"Hoo, Redtails!" She took them eagerly. "They're pristine! They must've cost a fortune! May I read the wyrds again?"

He leaned back, crossing his stretched legs and gesturing to the deck with one hand, the other propped in his blouse front.

She rubbed the cubes lovingly between her palms, eyes closed in bliss at the familiar feeling, then tossed them. They clattered across the deckplanks and bounced off a crate before tumbling to a stop. She didn't have to consult the bibelot. "Red two, white two. Closing the Arc."

He could hear the disappointment in her voice. The cleromancy decreed that mortal matters had to take precedence over lesser preoccupations and personal distractions. By direct implication, the mission to save Ghost came first and the prophesied epic love uniting her and Burning had to be put on hold.

She looked to him. "I'll—explain it later, Redtails. Oh, but, it's... good. A very good augury for the safe rescue of your sister."

She was slow and dispirited in retrieving the dice and stuffing them into the neck pouch. Then she made her way to the rail, looking out at the hot, dusty landscape. Lavender and ocher saw cabbage and tawny burrmillet gave the terrain a primeval look.

Burning let a sustained breath dribble between his lips as he slid the touchpad control into his inner pocket. Holding the touchpad with a hand tucked inside his tunic, he had had to tap out the two-two Holy Roller code by feel. The Aggregate's gaffing system was flawless, and his immediate problems were solved. Souljourner had helped to neutralize Manna, and the loaded dice had helped to neutralize Souljourner.

Hail the conquering hero, Burning thought bitterly. Onward, though; ever forward.

After hearing Boon's plan to introduce a synome antagonist into the Amnion, Mason thought he had been braced for nearly anything—except the fact that the Optimants had created the Cyberplagues.

"But Childress's study proved that the Plagues came from the direction of Old Earth," Mason managed to say, "if not Earth itself."

"I'm not theorizing, Claude. I'm telling you. The Optimants' 'wares when they left Sol were a generation beyond anything they left behind. They used the long voyage to push their computer sciences further, while Earth *lost* ground. They used their centuries here to push further still. Cybernetics was the great pillar of their power."

"Then why create a threat to that?"

"Because they never really trusted one another. Because they feared retribution from Earth and presumed that Earth's might and vulnerability, like theirs, would reside in cybersystems."

Mason looked around him at the once-magnificent Optimant salon, now dank and smelly with Boon's feudal chem warfare lab. It gave an ironic weight to talk of hubris and the crash of civilizations.

Boon was plucking his lower lip. "Rivalries and mistrust among the Optimants ran even stronger than we'd thought. Accidental release or preemptive strike or all-out exchange of cyberviruses—what does the exact scenario matter? The Optimants designed the viruses to propagate, and so they did—on Aquamarine, Periapt, Trinity, Old Earth … " He glanced lovingly at the cybercaul. "Here I thought I was going to need everything Haven brought in the way of archeo-hacking 'wares and data immunology to open up those troves—and you drop the skeleton key into my lap. Was the caul in Rhodes's satin-lined muckpen all along?"

Mason shrugged. "I wasn't the one who discovered it. But yes, Rhodes apparently had it all along."

Boon fingered the caul again. "Now that we've got this, maybe we'll be able to learn the full story of what happened here."

Mason was curious as well but took pleasure in saying, "No, Boon. From what Purifyre told me, there was an explosion in Rhodes's bedchambers shortly after we left. The computer that was inside Smicker's bust has probably been cut into fishooks by now."

Boon dismissed it with a sound that was half laughter and half mockery. "There're at least six surviving, sealed Optimant computer installations spread across Aquamarine. A few I've located; the rest are question marks. They're in places like Alabaster and Passwater—places the worst of the Plagues missed. The most important of them is in the lighthouse at New Alexandria."

"I already know that," Mason told him, straightening Boon's grin. He nodded to the cybercaul. "Thanks to Yatt, Smicker's bust told me a few things before it went haywire."

"Anything you want to share?"

Mason glanced around the room. People were setting the Science Side modules on trestle worktables. He felt certain that the units made use of common raw materials to turn out Boon's synome antagonist in quantity, though filling the vats would take days.

"After you have enough antagonist, then what?" he asked at last. "You run a hose out to the Styx and keeping pumping until the Oceanic is lobotomized?"

This time Boon shook his head to say no. "If you'd bothered to acquaint yourself with the marine bio précis, you'd know better. We can't just *flush* the antagonist into the Amnion. The Oceanic has natural defenses in all littoral and sublittoral zones, to say nothing of intertidal ones.

"In fact, planetwide, the upper epipelagic layer's one big killing ground and molecular remediation barrier down to fifty meters—at least as far as humans and the antagonist are concerned. To be effective I'm going to need to deliver a critical mass *below* the main defenses as simultaneously as a bomb explosion—well out over a volume of the bathyal or even abyssal layer."

"Oh, *that's* all?" Mason said. "Christ, Boon, even an antisub missile couldn't get deep enough, fast enough to keep the Oceanic from stopping and essentially dissolving it. Aside from which there isn't an antisub missile within several lightyears now that the *Sword's* history."

Boon snorted a laugh. "I've got a better solution, a delivery system that'll let us strike at the Oceanic's innards. And I hope that you've retained your well-honed sense of irony, Claude, because it involves paying a call on—"

Ballyhoot's meter-long military strides interrupted him. The old she-wolf touched Purifyre's shoulder, then bent to speak into his ear behind her leathery hand. Mason watched his son's unyielding expression become even more closed.

The unhandsome features that had once been Mason's became even uglier.

Purifyre elected to share the news in Mason's presence. "Kinbreed and the other club-clover wearers of the Bridge Constabulary have staged a mutiny. The Gapshot faction's taken control of the Forge Town barbican."

"Impossible," Boon said, as if someone had misunderstood a homework assignment. "We have covert agents among the watch at the Gapshot side. They've been instructed to utilize the Horatio option—"

"Not covert enough," Ballyhoot contradicted. "Kinbreed has hung the bodies from the Gapshot rampart and sealed the barbican to all traffic arriving from Scorpia."

"He's threatening to destroy the bridge if we don't meet his demands," Purifyre added, stricken. "Set it afire *and* drop it into the Styx Strait."

Ominous as the moment was, Mason reveled in the stunned face on his old shipmate. Looking at him, he said, "The course of true conquest never runs smooth, eh, Eisley?"

CHAPTER FORTY

The decoy escape rope was rigged. Zinsser had put a purchase knot in it every meter or so and made it fast to an upright in the cabin. In keeping with his plan, he had singed the free end with one of the fish oil lamps. Now he opened the window and threw the coils out as winds invaded the cabin, sending debris and masses of Laputa floss on cyclonic rides around and around the place.

Another impact from the crewmens' battering ram evoked a splintering sound from the three-batten door. Zinsser looked to the bloopgun, but Ghost said, "No, I'll deal with them. You finagle that bolt-hole line. It's time to go."

Red resentment flickered across his face, as it did each time she exercised command. For the present he was reining in his ego because his life was in the balance, but Ghost knew that Zinsser still considered her his natural inferior, an unfinished conquest, his rightful sexual vessel. He turned to, nevertheless, grabbing another length of rope from the spoils left by the Human Enlightenment agents and arranging it over the upraised ends of two pried-up bulkhead planks.

Ghost, meanwhile, opened the breech of the Testamentor's handgun and inserted another detonator-cap charge. She was down to ten rounds now, counting the one in the chamber. The ram made the door shiver and give. She leaned into the entranceway, shielding her face.

"Fire in the hole!"

She squeezed the trigger, and a blast-furnace stream shot into the gap that had been bashed open, igniting the surrounding wood. At a minimum, the supercargo would have no doubts that his suspected-Visitant passengers could make otherworldly fire, which in turn might make him more inclined to believe they could soar off into the night the way their aircraft and missiles did.

Ghost threw the inner door and shot its bolt even as backlashed heat was still roiling from the entrance. The inner door was less substantial than the outer; the super-cargo's assault wouldn't be stopped for long.

"Last call! Delta V!" she yelled, reloading once more. Spume had already hammered several of the planks back into place. She caught him before he could nail another down. "You're not *that* wasted away, old man. Get in while you still fit. We'll see to the rest."

Spume squeezed into the breech sideways with an assist from Ghost, who kicked his wing-chair collar through when it got hung up. The supercargo had done some preparing as well. She heard the commotion of fire crews putting out the blaze in the entranceway.

Hammering home two more boards, Ghost edged into the Laputa's utility space. Zinsser brought up the rear, draw-ing down the last two planks behind him. At the same time the cabin's inner door splintered. Ghost figured that the Insiders had threatened to jettison their hirelings unless they broke through. She joined Zinsser on the rope to exert additional force on the final two planks.

Zinsser let go of one end of the line and pulled the other; the free end paid out into the cabin and back into the hiding place by way of two notches he had made by removing knots in the wood. In the cabin sling-gun quarrels struck the walls and ceiling as saffrons fired blindly through the opening.

"Why do you tarry?" Spume whispered, gesticulating. "Close the hatch!"

"As soon as I learn how," Ghost whispered back without looking up.

She had the 'wares connected to the inner control box, but the whatty hadn't ferreted the command protocols necessary to close the hatch. She heard the inner door yield with a splintering of wooden hinges and planks and the sound of saffrons barging into the cabin, yelling and knocking furniture every which way.

The supercargo was screaming at his men to ransack and search even after Zinsser's phony escape rope had apparently been found. Ghost left the archeo-hacking 'wares to their job and drew the det-cap weapon. Zinsser stopped trying to open an interspace connecting panel and came to stand by her with the bloopgun raised. Spume clutched a quarrel thrower, shaking in his robes like a luffing sail but ready to fire just the same.

A heavy boot thudded into the cabin bulkhead, and one of the planks jogged loose at the base. A cry went up. But just when the crewmen began levering at the plank, the 'wares toned and the hatch slid shut. No sooner had it closed than safety illuminors came alive, casting a wan green light through the dusty gloom. There was no challenge by guard or squawk box, no response by containment systems, no reaction from hidden weapons emplacements comparable to the Laputa's external sonics.

Ghost pulled her hair back, swiped as much dust fleece and shaggy detritus as she could off the inner side of the hatch, and set her ear to it. She dimly heard what might be more bulkhead boards being broken away, but she could no longer discern individual voices.

"Do you think they saw?" Spume asked softly behind his cloth breathing mask.

"No," she told him. "And if they did, it didn't incite them enough to violate the sanctity of the Laputa's hull." She brushed cobwebs out of her long black locks and Hussar Plaits. "I doubt they'll try a battering ram here or make much progress even if they do."

"Still, we should move to safer concealment," Zinsser suggested in a tone as soft as a lover's. Coughing, he knotted his bandanna over his nose and mouth. "Who's to say the Insiders can't detect us here—or come looking if the supercargo alerts them?"

Ghost glanced at the space's luxuriant nap of undisturbed dust. She doubted the Insiders could gain entry; otherwise, maintenance activity would have disturbed the floss buildup. Zinsser was right, however: it was better to leave the scene of the crime while they still could.

"You couldn't get that panel open?" she asked Zinsser.

"Not so far. Locked, I think."

She pressed her ear to the inner hull and heard muffled vibrations but nothing identifiable. The hull was warm and she had the impression it was thick and well insulated for sound. It was possible that they were just outside a power plant area.

Ghost checked the archeo-hacking unit where it was still attached to the outer hatch's inner control box. Two strings of alphanumerics were displayed. Borrowing Zinsser's jetpen, she wrote them on the back of her hand, then removed the 'wares modules and returned them to her belt pouches alongside the pistol scope.

This time she was mindful enough to stand to one side as she tried the first string of alphanumerics. The panel slid aside with an in-rushing of warmer, thicker air than the utility space held after having been opened to the outerworks. With only a modest volume to equalize, the influx didn't last long, but it did make their eardrums clamp down. The opening exposed a helical ladderwell just as untraveled and hoary with age as the utility space.

"Mirabile visu," Zinsser observed, yawning and swallowing to equalize the pressure in his ears. "A place where the Insiders don't venture."

"Or can't," Ghost suggested.

She retrieved the carbine-size, sling-gun she had leveled at Spume earlier, plus a quiver of darts, a sparkwheel and lamp just in case the lights failed, and a butterfly sword, which she tucked through her belt. Zinsser took up the matching butterfly and a split-bladed dueling knife to augment the bloopgun.

Old Spume began to finger the double-ended fighting sickle, but Ghost stopped him. "These betweenhull spaces are tight. You'd best keep watch here."

He didn't argue, and Ghost and Zinsser slipped into the ladderwell.

She gazed up into the green gloom overhead, thinking back to the indifferent vizards and masks she had seen on the upper balconies as people milled and fought at landing area.

"Time to get inside the Insiders," she announced, her scars creasing in predatory anticipation.

Oblique sunlight fell on the Styx Strait. The Juts were almost in the shadows cast by Scorpian headlands to the west when *Arse-Grinder* brought Mason, Purifyre, Boon, and

Ballyhoot back to the Forge Town barbican of the bridge. Boon had suffered the ride in silence, fearful that all his carefully laid plans to take over Aquamarine were about to be kicked to the four winds.

Having raised mutiny among his Gapshot faction of the Bridge Constabulary, Kinbreed wasn't ducking a confrontation. As the muscle car ground to a halt near the barbican, he stood forth on the defensive balcony over the barred gate, watching and waiting. Purifyre's boyhood chum, coworker, and constabulary buddy struck Mason as even more the laser-eyed desert prophet than he had earlier.

Loyal constabulary members on that shift had been taken by surprise at sling-gun point and ejected from the barbican. Currently they and the Forge Town civic watch were keeping people back from the open cobblestone circus fronting the place, but the throngs were watching from sidelines, windows, and rooftops.

As he joined the others disembarking, Mason saw that news of the standoff had traveled fast and that human genius for turning quick profits had moved apace. Below the bridge tiny figures were scampering along the irregular horseshoe of the Juts, leaping and scrambling from boulder to slab to projection along the obstacle course causeway, bent under panniers, bundles, and sling-bags.

Jut-hoppers. With the bridge closed and perhaps doomed, the daredevils were in a position to make good if risky money for the first time in almost a decade. What burdens they carried, Mason couldn't guess, but people always had something that had to be somewhere ASAP, hang the cost. Thinking back on the kind of money good Jut-hoppers commanded in the days of *Scepter*'s visit, Mason suspected that many more would appear at the next low tide if the impasse wasn't resolved.

For now the tide had already turned; in a few hours the Juts would be under the Amnion. Mason quieted a shudder at the risk the hoppers were running. A bad fall could plunge them into the resentful waters, and not all could be as fortunate as Eisley Boon—or could they? His usual dread was somewhat lightened by the knowledge that *one* had not only escaped but had been *resurrected*.

Purifyre was suited up in his mandibled helm and gleaming black armor, carrying his baton of rank with its four-winged-man symbol. He went to stand below the balcony, matching Kinbreed stare for stare. Mason was belowdecks with Boon, and the thought of some mutineer skewering his boy was almost enough to compel Mason to show his 'chettergun, but Kinbreed wouldn't know what he was facing, and an intrusion of that sort might only derail Purifyre's parley.

"Has Cozmote sent you to bend a more conciliatory ear?" Kinbreed was saying somberly.

Purifyre used the bluff voice of his Hammerstone persona. "Camarado! You've gotten his attention. I'm told you've come up with a profit-sharing plan that you prefer to the old one."

"Not I, Hammerstone: Gapshot Town. And it's not an issue of preference but justice."

"Justice to kill mutual friends?"

"Justice with regard to a fair share!" For a moment Kinbreed's eyes seemed about to explode outward. "Henceforth all revenues shall be divided as the bridge is: half to the Trans-Bourne, half to Gapshot."

Watching Forge Towners cried out in anger. "The Trans-Bourne built it, and never a scudo's investment from Gapshot!"

"We already *have* a deal, welshers!"

"The Styx Bridge would still be empty air if it was a Gapshot job!"

Rotted vegetables and clots of dung were lofted toward the balcony but fell short.

Purifyre ignored it all, except to brush away a bit of the barrage that had lit on his armored shoulders. "I am empowered to say yes, Kinbreed. Agreed."

The declaration drew even angrier yells from the Forge Town crowd as well as the beginnings of a mass rush at the barbican, until the southern constables cracked longwhips in warning.

Kinbreed was indifferent to it all. "Very accommodating, Hammerstone. And now you seek entrance so that we might thrash out details? Or would you have me come out?"

"Bargains need to be sealed."

"You haven't heard me out. For now Gapshot will hold the gatehouses and the span, while you of the Trans-Bourne keep order on the circuses and approaches."

Purifyre's brittleness told Mason how much it took to say, "Very well."

"Never!" and "Infamy!" came from the crowd. Mason thought the Forge Town constables might have to lash a few or lay them out with flail or sling-gun butt. Even so, Purifyre's acquiescence to the blackmail was proof of Boon's real priorities. Control of and cash flow from the bridge were utterly beside the point compared to having it operational and accessible.

The mob quieted some to hear Kinbreed's reply. "And not that we don't trust you of the south, but we've become aware of certain modifications to some of your muscle cars—changes that would suit them better for battle. Why you would want to fight on the high roads, we can't imagine and little care to. But fighting on and around the bridge we will not abide.

"Hence, your war cars stay in the Trans-Bourne, south of the bridge altogether. To ensure this, inspectors from Gapshot will be free to keep watch at the Forge Town city limits as well as to delve into clandestine doings in Cozmote's assorted manufactories and works."

Purifyre's hesitation brought enlightenment to Mason. Boon was planning to take his war cars across the bridge—*to roll north*—for some purpose next to which even control of the bridge was irrelevant. The timing seemed all wrong for an invasion or coup in the Ean region or even a strike at New Alexandria, whose dormant Optimant systemry Boon considered so important.

Mason thought back to their conversation at the lab. Boon had said that he had found a way to introduce his synome antagonist into the Amnion. There was only one logical target, and it was Yatt who offered whispered affirmation of Mason's surmise.

"Yes, Mason. Boon is going after the GammaLAW, *just as we hoped he would."*

When the sound reached him, more a reverberation than a low-cycle noise or even a thundering, Quant realized that he had been nodding as he sat in his swivel-mounted chair on the starboard side of the bridge.

He had been without sleep for a day and a half, and he suspected that it might be another day or even more before he could permit himself to withdraw to the bunk in his sea cabin. But he had ignored concerned looks from Gairaszhek and the rest, holding to his place on the bridge because it was where he belonged. All the rest of normal life and naval convention would have to wait until he and his ship was out of imminent danger—a status he could scarcely imagine at the moment.

Members of the bridge watch studiously ignored his jerking awake. Gairaszhek, Keeler, Roiyarbeaux, and the others were back after a brutally short rest because Quant was running his two best rosters watch and watch, four hours on and four hours off.

The blunted, elemental quiver seemed to come first through the deck and only after a moment's pause through the air. Work party members paused in their efforts to put the decks in order, looking off to the north, where the sound seemed to have originated. It was far too loud to be Delecado's Hellhog firing—or even exploding.

"Quake," somebody by the empty *Musashi* barbette yelled, but to Quant it hadn't had the undulating feel of a quake.

He was out of the chair, wide awake, pulling his visor back on. "Did anyone mark a visual? A light in the sky?" His thought was that a sizable orbit-decayed chunk of the *Sword* had burst high above the ship.

But no: the vibration had first reached the ship through the ground and the lakewater. Quant asked Gairaszhek if anyone had happened to mark the time differential between the arrival of the ground-conducted and air-conducted sounds but wasn't surprised to hear that no one had. Everyone was too numbed with fatigue, too hard put to keep a clear mind on whatever they had been tasked to do.

Then passive sonar came through with a plot on the huge sound temblor: northeast, directly toward Wall Water. Quant called for another attempt to raise Daddy D's sortie by maser-phone even though there'd been no commo since the Hellhog had flown out of visual contact two hours earlier.

Shore features blocked any sight of Rhodes's stronghold as well as any hope for some sort of cam feed from Daddy

D. Quant chinned his mike to the flight ops circuits and got on-line with the petty officer who constituted one-half of the personnel left in the unmanned and special flight section.

"I need that aerostat aloft *now*," Quant announced.

The humble, homely 'stat was their best hope of finding out what was going on ashore. Each additional few meters of altitude it gained above the ship would increase by kilometers the radius of surrounding lake and countryside its cam could survey.

"We're still having trouble with integrity and hydrogen retention on two of the cells," the CPO in charge reported.

"Will it hold shape and stay airborne with a brisk tow?" Quant pressed. He could practically hear the man writhe.

"Yes sir—short term, anyway."

"Then that's better than nothing." If the aerostat went down, they could always simply recover it. "I'll send you some help. Get that thing up now—and patch the feed through to the bridge as soon as you get the camera on-line."

"Aye aye, sir."

Quant turned the *GammaLAW* into the wind, which had him steaming north on the lake, as furious activity broke out around the aerostat deployment station on the fantail of the Science Side hull. The station had been located there to keep aerostat activity as far as possible from flight deck operations. Between the ship's slow trolling speed and the prevailing wind, the aerostat was unspooled into an effective seven-knot head wind, lifting it smartly.

Quant was waiting impatiently for the visual feed to begin when Row-Row relayed an update from a spotter posted in the signals mast. "Lookout reports a mounding of the lakewater, sir. Bearing three-four-two relative."

"A *what?*" Quant stopped himself from leaping to the rail-mounted optical scope and instead began punching up the partially restored mast cam feed.

"He says the lake's humping up, sir."

The given bearing was just east of where the land cut off the view toward Wall Water. The map indicated farming fiefs and aquaculture villes with names like Fiddlehead and Catchment dotting the intrusions of shore curvature.

But as insane as it had sounded, the lookout was right: it was as if something stupendous had swum out into the water from the direction of the dam, raising up an unimaginable volume of water on its rounded back. Quant's initial thought was that there had been a quake after all, and that it had somehow contrived to throw up a miniature tsunami.

Water did not stay piled *anywhere* for long, however, and now a great swell of it was racing south, straight for his ship. "Helmsman, steer course three-four-two. Lee helm, increase speed to ten knots."

There was no sheltering shore feature close enough to shield the SWATHship from whatever was headed her way, and to be caught side on would probably be fatal, her trihull stability notwithstanding. Quant therefore had the rudder brought amidships and kept his bows pointed to the threat.

"OOD, sound collision."

Not exactly the danger at hand, but the nearest thing his green ship's company was trained for and could respond to without undue time wasted in confusion. Hydrodetectors began picking up a sudden and stiff midlake current as displaced water tried to get out of the way of what was approaching. Quant got on the circuit with engineering personally to inform them that he would need all the turns the mains could give him, and soon.

Engineering's stoic "aye aye" didn't exactly ring with confidence.

The aerostat had climbed high enough to get a bead on Wall Water. Its cam image quality was wretched but clear enough to threaten Quant's hold on his temper.

The dam face had broken open in a deep V notch that followed the ancient cracks that had seamed it. Incredibly, the rest of the Optimant structure had held, strong as a mountain, but the Pontos Reservoir was pouring out through the rift with incredible force, like oil from a punctured tank. Wall Water cowered to one side of the torrent, its lower ramparts already under water.

Quant's immediate, certain thought was that Zone was somehow responsible. He didn't doubt it for a moment.

Panning the 'stat cam didn't tell him much about the hydrodynamic threat, however. The Pontos was emptying into the lake at a spot where it was comparatively shallow and some ten kilometers wide. There was no way to judge how the monstrous influx of water would be redirected by shore and subsurface features, but one thing was clear: the water level was rising as surges raced inland on the strand opposite. Quant hoped the Aquam would have the sense to take to high ground, since there was nothing he could do for them, not so much as flash a signal they would recognize as an alarm.

Nor was there a moment he could spare if he was to save his ship. The murderous upthrust of lakewater was tearing his way at better than sixty klicks, seemingly intent on drowning his ship or knocking her galley-west to smash to bits against some distant highland that was soon to become a lakeside cliff.

The people on the bridge watch had dogged the pilot-house windows and hatches, and were frantically stowing all the loose gear they could spot. Quant found a moment to get on the PA.

"A very large anomaly resembling a rogue wave will be hitting us bows-on in approximately two minutes. Riding it out will demand maximum cooperation from the entire ship's company." He was adjusting his life vest as he spoke. "All hands, get inside the skin of the ship. This includes lookouts and man-overboard watch. I repeat, all hands retire inside the skin of the ship. All personnel not immediately required at stations for under-weigh operations, find your most reliable nearby secure purchase, brace hard, and stand by."

He wasn't quite done saying it when the *GammaLAW* shook as if she had wandered into a rapids. Water darkened with bottom muck and bearing scraps of aquaculture wreckage loomed up before the pilothouse windows, seething and seeming to do a slow boil. Quant grabbed the handrail that ran the width of the pilothouse under its windows; then he spread his feet, warning himself not to strain too hard just yet.

Save your strength, he told himself. Even if she rides this one out, things are only going to get worse.